Fall Silver Artemis

The Old World Saga Book Four

FALL SILVER ARTEMIS

Copyright © 2022 by Joel Preston.

First edition published August 2022.

Book cover art by warrendesign
Manuscript design by Joel Preston

ISBN 978-0-6454676-4-2 (Paperback)
ISBN 978-0-6454676-5-9 (Hardcover)
ISBN 978-0-6454676-6-6 (eBook)

To contact the author email: contact@joelprestonauthor.com
joelprestonauthor.com

FALL SILVER ARTEMIS

THE OLD WORLD SAGA BOOK FOUR

JOEL PRESTON

Other Novels by This Author:

In the Shadow of Monstrous Things

Rise Golden Apollo

In the Shadow of The Old World

Novellas by This Author:

The Wendigo Incident: An Old World Saga Novelette

Earth's Mightiest Warrior: An Old World Saga Novella

This one goes out to Casey and Riley. Whether fighting trolls or falling through black holes, your contributions have helped shape this story.

CHARACTER
AND
FACTIONS
GUIDE

- The Australian Supernatural Taskforce -

The AST is a division of Australia's national law enforcement agency. It has two full time staff, and primarily activates in response to supernatural occurrences, drawing in operatives from other government areas (police and military).

PERMANENT MEMBERS:

- BRETT SAYER -

The officer in charge of the AST known for his laid-back attitude. He is currently the one managing OPERATION THUNDERKING and the one who orchestrated the response to the Australian werewolf incidents in 2019.

First appearance: *In the Shadow of Monstrous Things.*

- LIAM SAGER -

A former national law enforcement officer, Liam was so exceptional in his role that he was moved into the AST to stop him outshining his colleagues. Liam was directly involved in the werewolf incidents of 2019 and captured Joshua Dare. In 2020 he unsuccessfully hunted Jesse Billiau through South East Asia. He is currently leading AST team one.

First appearance: *In the Shadow of Monstrous Things.*

CURRENTLY ON SECONDMENT TO THE AST:
- MELISSA PYTHIA -

An ASIO operative who responded to the werewolf incident in 2019 as part of the AST. She then deployed to Rome and discovered that she was the reincarnation of the Oracle of Delphi, where she pulled the God Apollo from Hell into the mortal world. She is currently leading AST team two in OPERATION THUNDERKING. She has the power to see in the past, present and future. Her vision can also make supernatural creatures susceptible to mortal weapons.
First appearance: *In the Shadow of Monstrous Things.*
Protagonist of: *Rise Golden Apollo.*

- TEVA HENRY -

Intelligence officer for ASIO specialising in technology. He is a Tahitian born Australian spy who was paired with Melissa in her mission to Afghanistan. He is currently assigned to AST team two.
First appearance: *Rise Golden Apollo.*

- MATTHEW PYNE -

An ASIS agent specialising in 'in-the-field' undercover work. Due to the public damage caused during the events in Rome in 2019, he was sent to observe Joshua Dare and manage his affliction in Japan as punishment. He is an expert sniper, with that being his weapon of choice. He is currently assigned to AST team one in Japan.
First appearance: *Rise Golden Apollo*

- DANNI QUINN -

The former girlfriend of the werewolf Joshua Dare, Danni Quinn was offered an opportunity to join the ASIO/ASIS joint training program in 2019, which she completed through 2020. She was instantly drafted into the AST and is working for team two.
First appearance: *In the Shadow of Monstrous Things.*

- MALCOLM SELLECK -

A doctor and professor of history and archaeology with the Australian National University in Canberra, specialising in artefacts. He is the Australian Government's 'go-to-guy' when dealing with unknown objects and first studied Apollo's golden sword when it was recovered in 2017. He is currently working with AST team two.
First mentioned: *Rise Golden Apollo.*

- THE WEREWOLVES -

The werewolf curse was created by the God Zeus in Bronze Age Greece as punishment for King Lycaon. Since then, it has travelled through the ages and mutated. The pure version of the curse acts as a direct link to the power of Zeus. Werewolves will transform into ravenous killing machines on the full moon every month, with silver being their primary weakness.

- JOSHUA DARE -

Joshua Dare was in the wrong place at the wrong time when he was bitten by the pure werewolf Achilles Aetos in 2019. He took the curse back to Australia, where each transformation left a bloody trail. He became hunted by both the Vatican and the AST. The AST captured him and kept him imprisoned, before moving him to Japan. Fate brought Josh before the destroyer wolf Fenrir, who gave him the power to control the werewolf transformation outside the full moon. He also gave Josh a choice, to perform a ritual to assume the empty position of Fenrir instead of Zeus. The God Hephaestus forged Josh a magic bronze hand that holds his Norse sword Vargr Muor inside it.

Protagonist of: *In the Shadow of Monstrous Things.*

- JESSE BILLIAU -

A former police officer who was bitten by the Vatican's werewolf before killing it. Jesse fled into the wilds of South East Asia, where he lasted a year before being captured by the experimental research company Molochtech. He was used as a test subject to see if they could purify his version of the werewolf curse using the God Particle, a magical substances refined from primordial wisps.

First appearance: *In the Shadow of Monstrous Things.*

- HARUKA MASUNAGA -

Haruka was caught up in events in Japan when the Cult of Belial attacked Josh at the Cliffs of Tojinbo in 2021. Haruka is a quiet woman who dreams of a more exciting life. Josh was forced to bite her, so she would transform on the full moon and become a distraction. The plan worked and they escaped Molochtech in Siberia.

First appearance: *In the Shadow of The Old World.*

- United States Supernatural Occurrence Taskforce -

USSOT is branch of the United States military headed by Captain Fiona Shear. Unlike the AST, they have fully-funded positions and a large budget. They have recently created a new tactical operations branch named 'Taskforce A', in response to the revelation that gods and angels are real.

- PATRICK LEESON 'NEANDERTHAL' -

Navy SEAL and head of Taskforce A, Neanderthal first met Josh in 2020 when he recruited him to assist in the wendigo incident. Neanderthal is working with the Australians to achieve the mission as a US representative.

First appearance: *The Wendigo Incident*

- The Old World -

The Old World are a group of supernatural enthusiasts with global hubs. Known more as a hobbyist-group, the Old World's president is the mysterious billionaire Altior Fulgur. They have a wealth of secret information regarding the paranormal.

- ALTIOR FULGUR -

The CEO of iHeal Genetics and the man behind Molochtech, Altior has no known records of birth or family. He is shrouded in mystery and worked with the Vatican to test and refine the God Particle. His motives are unknown.

First appearance: *In the Shadow of The Old World.*

- The Gods -

The new Olympians are a group comprised of the following ancient Greek gods: Apollo, Artemis, Moros, Hecate, Hephaestus, Aion and Hermes. Their goal is to stop the forces of Heaven and Hell claiming the power of Zeus, then attack the angels in revenge for the war of 337 AD and the godly genocide that followed.

- APOLLO -

God of Knowledge and Prophecy, Apollo was wounded in the Battle of the Underworld and sent out of time to heal. When he returned in 2019, he was mortal. After travelling to a secret temple to Prometheus in Afghanistan, his divinity was restored. Now he works with the new Olympians to bring an end to the era of the angels.

First appearance: *Rise Golden Apollo.*

- MOROS -

God of Fate and Doom, Moros has been travelling the globe attempting to unearth all the secret knowledge required to assume the position of Zeus. She spent millennia hiding in plain sight, and over the last century worked as the Vatican's librarian.

First appearance: *Rise Golden Apollo.*

- ARTEMIS -

After visiting Corfu with Melissa in 2019 and finding Hermes, Apollo then set out to look for his sister Artemis. Known as Artemis of the Wildlands, she is a God of Childbirth, the Hunt and Animals. Apollo found her in 2020, yet she was reluctant to join the god's fight against the angels.

First appearance: *Fall Silver Artemis.*

- The Vatican and Hell -

The two other factions working on behalf of supernatural entities to claim the missing position of Zeus. The Vatican is working on behalf of Archangel Michael. A double agent within their ranks is Cardinal Vasilije Markovic, secretly working for the forces of Archangel Lucifer. Michael wishes to claim the power because he fears a slumbering darkness in the heart of the world. Lucifer wishes to claim the power because he believes it will free his physical body from its eternal entrapment in the Underworld.

- THE KNIGHTS OF HELL -

The Knights of Hell are a group of elite angelic warriors who were trapped in the darkness of Tartarus with Lucifer. Five currently reside on Earth, them being: Belial, Leviathan, Asmodee and Oriens and another unknown knight. Because the barrier between Hell and Earth was weakened in 2019, willing human hosts can now be possessed by demons. These demons are known as 'the Cult of Belial' and work for the Knights of Hell on Earth.

First appearance: *Rise Golden Apollo.*

- Earth's Mightiest Warrior -

- SIGURD OF THE VOLSUNG LINE -

A descendant of Odin and the legendary hero Volsung, Sigurd's tale of life, death and betrayal were immortalised in the Saga of the Volsungs. He is most well known for being a wise king and his slaying of the evil dragon Fafnir. Little did historians know, after Sigurd's death he went to Norse Hel, where he subsequently survived the onslaught on the legions of Heaven in 337 AD. For millennia he survived in the Underworld, using an artefact called the Hell Key to escape the Knights of Hell and perform heroic deeds. It is rumoured that to this day he still lingers in Hell, a permanent reminder of the long past age of heroes.

First appearance: *Earth's Mightiest Warrior.*

THE STORY SO FAR...

Author's note: Part one of Fall Silver Artemis *takes place during the events of* In the Shadow of The Old World. *This section will recap events including the end of that novel.*

Our story begins in Bronze Age Greece when Arcadian King Lycaon is cursed by the God-King Zeus and turned into a wolf. He becomes the first werewolf, passing on his curse through history.

Sometime before the year 337 AD, Zeus disappears in mysterious circumstances, leaving behind a pool of power. Faith in Christianity builds in the Roman Empire, and Emperor Constantine converts to the new religion on his death bed. Using their boost in cosmic power, the angels of Heaven attack the Underworld, Olympus and Asgard, finding success in each campaign. Many of the old gods die or go into hiding.

During the Battle for the Underworld, Archangel Lucifer is tricked and becomes permanently trapped.

Apollo is injured in the battle and removed from time to heal. The angels begin a process of reformation, turning the Underworld into Hell, now ruled by the trapped Archangel Lucifer and his Knights of Hell (fallen angels).

From the realm of Heaven, the six remaining archangels, led by Michael, begin a slow conquest of the Earth.

-MODERN DAY-

In 2017, an Australian covert military strike force attack a terrorist cell in Lebanon. Assisting them is ASIO spy Melissa Pythia, who discovers a hidden golden sword. That sword is then stolen from Canberra and disappears.

Two years later, the Soncin crime family (who specialise in dealing artefacts) meet with an old recluse named Achilles Aetos on the Greek island of Corfu. In exchange for a mysterious black book, they give Achilles the last known puppy from the ancient line of King Lycaon. The puppy bites him, giving him the pure werewolf curse. The Soncin's then sell the black book to the Vatican.

-BOOK ONE-

In 2019, Melissa is deployed to a werewolf incident in North Queensland, Australia. A young man, Joshua Dare, has picked up an ancient affliction in Greece that causes him to transform during the full moon. He and his girlfriend, Danni Quinn, are now on the run, being hidden by The Old World (a group of paranormal enthusiasts). After signing a police officer to secrecy (Jesse Billiau), Melissa is pulled off the werewolf case and given a new assignment when her lost golden sword reappears in Rome, now in the hands of the Soncin crime family.

-BOOK TWO-

Melissa and her team (Matt Pyne and Teva Henry) recover the sword. The weapon increases the frequency that Mel has prophetic visions. Mel meets the Goddess of Magic, Hecate, who teaches her that she is the reincarnation of the Oracle of Delphi and is destined to return the lost God Apollo to the mortal realm.

In Hell, Apollo weakens the barrier between Hell and Earth and Melissa pulls him into the modern world. Now mortal, Apollo and Melissa are aided by the God of Doom, Moros, in restoring his divinity.

They travel to Afghanistan, to the hidden temple of

Prometheus, where it is revealed that the forces of Heaven and Hell have discovered a colossal pocket of power up for the taking. The Archangels Michael and Lucifer both have goals for this power, which was left behind by the missing God Zeus.

Sealing Michael away in a black hole, Apollo restores his godhood and sets out to find his sister, Artemis. Before parting ways, Melissa and Apollo go to Corfu, where they find the Messenger God Hermes. When speaking with Hermes, Melissa realises the werewolf curse is a direct link to the power of Zeus. Joshua Dare has just become a very important man.

Melissa returns to Australia, where the Australian Supernatural Taskforce (AST) at last captures Josh and locks him away in a secret facility in the desert.

Jesse Billiau, after being bitten by a werewolf, flees to South East Asia.

Danni Quinn is offered a position on a training program to turn her into an Australian spy, due to her experience with the supernatural. She accepts.

-BETWEEN BOOKS TWO AND THREE-

Due to the events in Afghanistan, Cardinal Vasilije Markovic (a servant of Lucifer) goes to the site of the battle in Afghanistan and discovers the primordial wisps in the ancient temple of Prometheus.

He then takes the wisps to The Old World. The president's secret research company, Molochtech, works on using the wisps to purify the werewolf curse. Molochtech capture Jesse Billiau and use him as a test subject, though his curse is too distant and mutated. They need Joshua Dare.

-BOOK THREE-

Joshua Dare, meanwhile, is moved to Japan in late 2020. At last he has some semblance of freedom. Posing as a government agent there to learn from The Old World and further bolster the group's relationship with the Australian Government, Josh makes friends with Haruka Masunaga.

They go to a popular tourist site together where they are attacked by the Cult of Belial, demons in human husks. Hunted by Belial, Apollo arrives and fights off the fallen angel.

The Australians shelter at The Old World hub in Nagoya, where a meeting is called. Representatives from the Australian Government, United States Government and The Old World discuss Operation Thunderking, the plan to stop Heaven and Hell taking the power of Zeus.

Altior Fulgur arrives, a powerful man that none knew was head of The Old World. He says he will assist the governments in whatever way he can, but states plainly that he thinks the goal itself is waste of time.

For their plan to work, Apollo states that they need to rescue the two captured gods in Heaven: Hecate and Hephaestus. He also states humans are needed for the operation.

Melissa's team is already abroad working on their part of the mission. **This is where Fall Silver Artemis begins.**

-FALL SILVER ARTEMIS PART ONE-

(The following from book three take place during Fall Silver Artemis part one.)
Apollo, Hermes, Liam Sager, Patrick Leeson (US Navy SEAL) and Joshua Dare travel to Israel, the location of the only portal to Heaven. Again, they encounter the Cult of Belial. Haruka is abducted by Belial, who plans to use her as bait to lure in Josh. With the help of Matt Pyne and Ingrid Horjen, they make it into Heaven just in the nick of time.

In a structure called the Citadel, the team separates. Josh unwittingly activates a magical shrub that begins to pull Archangel Michael from his black hole imprisonment. Fleeing, Josh dives deep into the Citadel, where he encounters the chained destroyer Fenrir.

Fenrir offers Josh the ability to control his transformation outside the full moon as a blessing, in exchange for a sacrifice of his hand. The destroyer also states that Josh could assume his missing position in the cosmos instead of Zeus, and fulfill Fenrir's goal of destroying the gods.

Josh accepts Fenrir's blessing. Using his new powers, Josh frees Hecate and the two reunite with the others, who have found Hephaestus. They escape into the Dreamscape (the realm of Morpheus) right as Michael returns.

Michael orders Heaven to begin watching the Earth for divine magic again, meaning all the gods must go into hiding.

In the Dreamscape, Hephaestus builds Josh a new hand made of bronze. Inside of it is held the sword he found in Heaven (also an artefact of Fenrir).

Due to a communication error, Josh is returned to Nagoya instead of Canberra.

He encounters Altior Fulgur, who provides him with the means to get to Siberia and rescue Haruka on his own. Altior says he will alert the AST to Josh's plans, but doesn't.

Josh arrives at the Molochtech research facility and is captured. With no other options, he bites Haruka, passing the werewolf curse onto her.

Molochtech begin experimenting on Josh, hoping to purify his curse.

On the night of the full moon, it is revealed that it worked, and Josh is now a complete link to the power of Zeus. Not expecting there to be a second werewolf, chaos breaks out when Haruka goes on a rampage. The mutated werewolf of Jesse Billiau is then freed and the three brawl as the facility burns down.

Matt Pyne and Patrick Lesson arrive, leading a new team called Taskforce A. They capture all three werewolves and move them to a US military base in Ukraine.

Both Cardinal Markovic and Belial are killed in the battle.

A conference call is organised by the main stakeholders of Operation Thunderking, however when Melissa tunes in, they all see she is under attack somewhere in the ocean. Her screen cuts out.

Now it is time to begin the next adventure in Fall Silver Artemis...

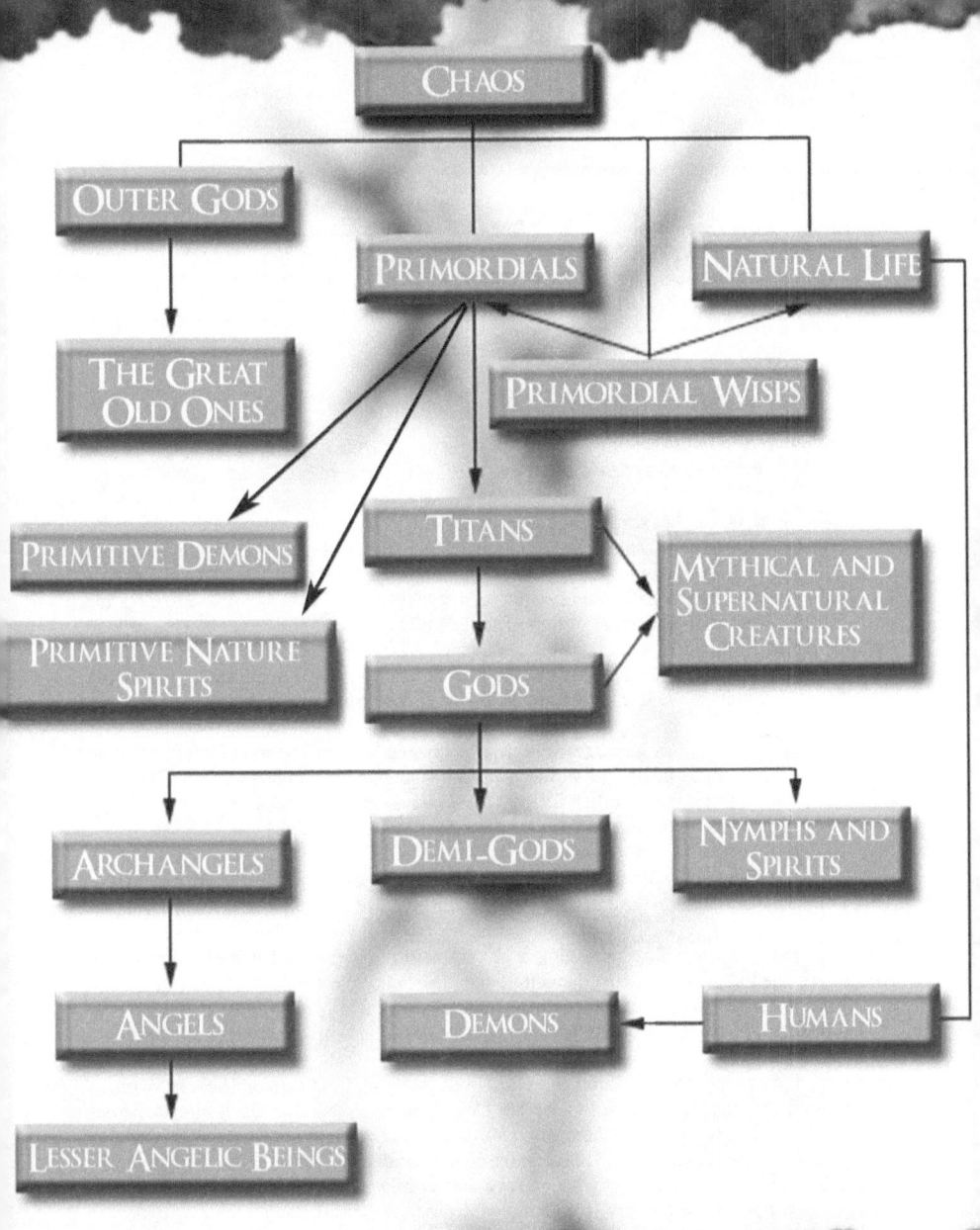

THE SUPERNATURAL ORDER

AST ARCHIVE

The following email has been preserved by the automated Australian Supernatural Taskforce archiving program. Original sender: Brett SAYER. Recipients: Liam SAGER, Melissa PYTHIA. Encryption level: TOP SECRET. Archiving program activated due to the use of the following key words: OPERATION, MISSION, OBJECTIVE. November 23, 2020, 7:28 pm.

- BEGIN TRANSCRIPT -

Liam, Mel,

I am writing (very informally) to cover the main points from the impromptu meeting I've just (unexpectedly) had with Moros, the Goddess of Fate and Doom.

Despite my protests, she has stressed the importance of human involvement in their mission to take the power left behind by Zeus. She stated quite plainly that as the Oracle of Delphi, Melissa in particular, will have to assist. I am currently putting together the order for OPERATION THUNDERKING, though I feel presenting any of this to the Department of Home Affairs or the chiefs of ASIO and ASIS is a waste of time. The reason being that it will never be believed, let alone supported. Fortunately we still have some budget left from the werewolf incidents in 2019. I voiced this concern to Moros, who assured me we will have the gods full assistance in clearing administrative matters when the mission is done (though I doubt it).

Now, as to how I see things going forward. Moros assured me of three ingredients needed to complete the ritual. 1 - A link to the power of Zeus (as already determined - Joshua Dare and the curse he carries). 2 - The blood of Zeus (Moros believes one of his children will fulfill this requirement). 3 - An artefact of Zeus (no current leads).

Moros says she is still unravelling all the pieces of the ritual. Because we are directly responsible for Joshua Dare, I believe the AST needs to be involved. I have agreed to help.

Moros has stated that Apollo is planning a rescue mission. Moros said human assistance is essential, as she has seen it in her 'domain of fate' (her words, not mine). Liam, you will be leading this team. A second team will begin the hunt for an artefact of Zeus, to be led by Melissa. I will be requesting Dr. Malcolm Selleck join team two, due to his expertise in artefacts.

As you are both aware, Joshua Dare has been moved to Japan. I am certain The Old World is behind the information leak that led to the US Government's knowledge about him, however, cannot prove it. Regardless, I fear there will come a time that both the US Government and The Old World will know about the plan to assume the empty position of Zeus. When the right moment presents itself, I plan to inform both groups as to foster an alliance, rather than be working at odds with them. Unfortunately, right now there is too much we don't know...

All of this information is strictly confidential, and on Moros' orders it cannot be shared with anyone. Melissa, I have already secured your release from ASIO. As of this email you are once again working for the AST. I will be in touch with both of you shortly with further information and more specific details. This is just a heads up as to how things are going to go from now.

Regards, Brett.

- END TRANSCRIPT -

"Of all the great evil things in this world, none are so horrific as the dreaded black book. You think you are reading it, but it is reading you. A thousand eyes watch from the infinite cosmic void as you turn each page, driving you closer and closer to madness. But worse is what that book summons... Madness for you, perhaps, and death for the rest of us..."

Ernst Carter, 1993.

A quote from a rare public discussion regarding the attempted theft of a book from the University of Amsterdam. The title of the book has not been confirmed. It is reported to have been destroyed.

PROLOGUE

APOLLO AND ARTEMIS

Under the embrace of a twilight sky, beneath a white rectangular umbrella, sat two unassuming figures. They were indistinguishable from the rest of the crowd, save for the strange aura of the man and the abnormal injuries of the woman. The man was so impossibly perfect that he was difficult to perceive properly. Certainly, many of the female patrons of the bar had taken more than a few fleeting glances his way. Unfortunately, he was so wrapped in deep conversation with the woman who sat across from him that he hadn't noticed.

While the woman was undoubtedly beautiful as well, her appearance raised several questions. She had a large gash along her right cheek, which looked to be recently stitched, and her eyes were shadowed black and blue.

Despite the eccentricities of their appearances, none suspected the pair to be anything out of the ordinary. Most patrons were so taken with the impressive view of Corfu Airport's runway that they didn't notice much of anything else. Had a passerby been able to rip their gaze away from the departing planes and bother themselves by speaking with the odd pair, they would've dismissed the truth anyway. In fact, if any of the merrymakers that evening were told of their true natures, they would have been laughed out of the establishment.

The woman was named Melissa Pythia, and she was an Australian spy. But, more than this, she'd also recently learned of her true nature as a reincarnation of the ancient Oracle of Delphi, blessed with prophetic sight.

The man was the ancient God Apollo, who'd only recently been returned to the world after he'd almost died in the year 337.

Both had come to Greece from Afghanistan after discovering the hidden Temple of Prometheus and the divine fire held inside. As it turned out, an event that scientists had put down to a random genetic mutation was actually the dabbling of the Titan Prometheus. 75 000 years ago, Prometheus, feeling bad for the simple Homo Sapiens wandering East Africa, gave them the spark of inspiration itself. He travelled down from Olympus, disobeying Zeus, bringing the holy flame with him. In Prometheus' honour, a temple Zeus would never find, was built inside a mountain. Apollo and Melissa had found it last month, and a great battle had taken place there.

Melissa was directed to travel to Greece before returning to Australia. She was investigating a case utterly unrelated to that of Prometheus. She was helping the Australian Government hunt a werewolf.

Apollo, desiring to find other missing gods, had joined her. On the island of Corfu they'd discovered Hermes, the Messenger God. Now filled with the hope of finding more survivors, Apollo had set his eyes squarely on uncovering the fate of his twin sister, Artemis.

"How do you know your sister is still alive?" Melissa asked.

"It is a feeling... more than a feeling... we are twins. If any of the Olympians were to have survived, it would be her," Apollo explained.

Melissa looked into Apollo's magnificent blue eyes. Despite his unblemished skin, shining blonde hair, and piercing gaze, Melissa found no comfort in those eyes. They were almost alien.

"Where was she when the angels attacked? Was she on Olympus?" Melissa asked, sipping her coffee.

"I don't know. Artemis never much enjoyed the company of mortals or even other gods. She was a protector of nature and preferred its company. For a long time she dwelt in the overgrown forests of Arcadia."

"Perhaps you can begin your search where Arcadia once was?"

"I will look, but I suspect only a fool would've stayed in Greece when the angels started their purge. She was friends with Bastet, an Egyptian goddess. That is where my search will start in earnest. I have my suspicions as to where it will end..."

"A shame that you can't come back to Australia," Melissa shrugged. "The boss of the AST would love to meet you."

The AST, or Australian Supernatural Taskforce, was a group Melissa was currently attached too. She was an intelligence officer with the Australian Security Intelligence Organisation (ASIO) full-time. The AST was seen as the laughing stock of the Australian Government, but Melissa knew once this month was over, all that would change.

"In time. I will find you soon enough. What is your plan in this mysterious southern land of Australia?" Apollo asked.

"I will go back to Canberra and prepare a lengthy report for ASIO. Then another for the AST where I will have to mention Hermes and what he told us."

Apollo nodded.

"Then I assume I will be sent back up to Cairns. There is a full moon approaching and knowing what we know now, we have to make sure we capture the werewolf."

"Well," Apollo started, taking a swig from his own amber coloured drink, "I hope we are both successful in our endeavours."

Apollo screwed up his face as he swallowed the alcohol, then muttered something about missing ambrosia.

"Tell me about your sister," Melissa said.

"She is the Goddess of Hunting, of Virginity, and of Wild Animals. She is the protector of girls up until the age of marriage and never a goddess to cross. She is also Goddess of the Moon, a role she shared admittedly with Selene and Hecate,"

"More than her titles, Apollo. She is your sister! What is she like? Does she get called Silver Artemis to your Golden Apollo?"

"Artemis of the Wildlands, they called her. Then, in the time of the Romans she was known as Diana. She was very powerful and widely worshipped. Here, give me your hand."

Melissa stretched her arm across the table and placed her palm flat in Apollo's.

"Use the vision of Delphi. You know it lets you see more than just the future. You can see the past, things that were and some things that may be. See my sister and see my past."

Melissa's eyes flashed gold. Corfu was lost in a haze of sparkling clouds as a new vision took shape around her. The clock spun backwards as the Earth turned the wrong way. Melissa travelled across fields of green and through the bluest skies, coming to rest at the borders of an archaic village. Dirty people in simple robes were hollering and shouting at a sobbing woman at the edge of a well.

"Let your vision translate their words," the warm voice of Apollo said in Melissa's mind.

"Get out of here! We don't need no goddesses cursing this place!" a man shouted.

A wild-looking woman chimed in with a screeching cry of, "Whore! Whore of Zeus!"

Melissa drifted through the people like a ghost until she had a clear view of the crowd's victim.

She had to blink several times in quick succession. The woman was unreal, as if the air was bending around her. It was difficult to see her clearly.

"She is a titan," Apollo commented. "My mother, Leto."

"Why can't I see her properly?" Melissa asked, squinting for a better image.

"The titans are a higher level of being than the gods. They are an additional rung removed from you mortals. They are part of a higher order than your monkey brains can comprehend."

Melissa ignored the insult. She had already accepted that Apollo could be a bit of a dick.

The more she looked, the more Melissa's eyes adjusted. Through her glowing radiance, Melissa could see Leto's long blonde hair and sharp blue eyes. Her dress was white and otherworldly, and her skin was unmarred. She looked like an elaborate painting come to life.

"Please," Leto begged, "I must drink from your well."

"Get out of here!" the crowd cried.

The ground shook and Leto looked up in alarm.

Distant trees were bending and cracking under phenomenal pressure. The chorus of destruction was fast approaching.

Leto turned from the well and took off into the forest as fast as the wind.

There was a hiss and a roar, then the screams of the crowd.

"What is the monster?" Melissa asked, somewhat thinking she'd just heard the distant call of a dinosaur.

"Python. He hunted my mother across the world," Apollo answered.

The scene changed.

Now Melissa was in a familiar location, though it was older than she'd seen it last.

"Is this Delphi?" she asked.

"The island of Delphos, yes," Apollo's disembodied voice

replied.

The grand temple to Apollo was absent, as well as the road lined with shrines and treasures. This was the island in its first days.

"Eventually, Zeus took pity on my mother and sent a wind to rush her out to sea. This is where she landed. This is where I would be born."

Melissa looked down at the wailing figure of the heavily pregnant Leto. Beside her was a toddler, pushing at her stomach and speaking reassuring words.

Leto had some how gripped the tip of an olive tree in one hand and a palm tree in the other, bending them both down towards her.

"Who's the kid?" Melissa asked.

"That's Artemis. She was born before me. Nine days later, I am still yet to enter the world," Apollo answered.

"Why is it taking so long?" Melissa asked, not liking the sound of that at all.

"Because Zeus' wife, Hera, has kidnapped Eileithyia, Goddess of Childbirth, to ensure her suffering."

"Artemis seems quite developed for nine days old…"

"This is nothing," Apollo laughed. "My dear brother Hermes, when he was just a newborn, stole an entire flock of my cattle then invented the lyre on his birth night. He was very, very annoying."

A rainbow appeared on the horizon and shot towards them at astonishing speed. Riding on the multi-coloured road were two women. Melissa could tell immediately that they were both goddesses. They had the same strange aura that perpetually floated around Apollo.

"Here is Iris with Eileithyia now," Apollo said.

Eileithyia placed her hand on Leto's temple and her screaming subsided.

The vision jumped forward in time, and now Leto looked down at the infant Apollo in her arms.

Eileithyia knelt down beside the bubbling Artemis and whispered, "People will remember the role you played in helping your mother give birth to your brother. You will be a goddess of childbirth like me." She patted Artemis warmly on the head.

A dizzying rush of air washed over Melissa as she once again moved on the spot, though not far this time. She moved up a hill, into a clearing beside a smattering of trees.

She could see that she hadn't just traversed space; time had also shifted. Apollo and Artemis, now in their early teens, sat on some boulders and laughed amongst each other.

The twins were radiant. While they didn't have the blinding aura of their titaness mother, they both flowed with the golden perfection of the gods.

They both wore white robes, specked with dirt. Artemis had long auburn hair, dropping well below her chest and glistening in the light. Apollo had his signature blonde that contrasted so well with his piercing blue eyes. His hair was longer than Melissa had seen it, streaming casually behind him in the breeze. Both of the teenagers were lean, with barely an ounce of fat on them. They both wore leather sandals, braces and belts. Melissa couldn't help but immediately detect an air of cocky arrogance about the youthful gods.

They were engaged in a heated discussion, the topic of which became quickly evident.

"You were not there for your own birth, brother," Artemis said, picking up a stone and tossing it across the field. "Mother endured days of unending pain."

"For a worthy cause, though," Apollo joked.

"You can jest, but I assure you I will never subject myself to such suffering."

"Time will prove me right and you wrong, dear sister."

"The pleasures of the flesh are a human thing," Artemis responded coolly.

"We are not so different from the humans. Enjoy as they enjoy, I say. After all, you enjoy the thrill of the hunt, do you not? The satisfaction of the kill... as much as any of the hunters of Greece."

"It is different," Artemis shrugged, turning to her brother. "I feel the hunt in my blood. I am certain that is my divine calling. The hunt and the animals."

"Well, the hunt should be all the more satisfying with this." Apollo reached out into nothingness and a spectacular silver bow manifested in his hand. A similarly silver quiver full of arrows appeared on his back.

Artemis smiled and said, "I am also impressed with this gift from Hephaestus."

She summoned her own silver bow out of thin air and admired it. She studied its upper and lower limbs. Across each was carved delicate images of trees and animals. Just by the arrow rest was the depiction of two stags butting antlers. The bowstring was a line of pure silver that was almost ethereal. It looked impossibly light and remarkably accurate.

"Shame he made them a pair. Such a fine object should be singular in its existence," Apollo joked.

"I've always thought that about me and you," Artemis exclaimed sharply. "Why should I have to suffer a twin brother when the world would be all the better with just myself?"

Apollo shot his sister a look of annoyance. Any retort he was formulating disappeared in a sudden shaking of the earth.

A monstrous roar bellowed out from the distant trees.

"Python is awake," Apollo murmured.

Artemis stood up and said, "With these gifts from Hephaestus, perhaps we can at last rid ourselves of the creature?"

"Dear sister, I would not ask you to put yourself in harm's way. It is my destiny to slay Python and claim this island as a site to my future worship."

"Oh, is that so?"

The ground trembled as a huge mass moved towards them. Birds flew from the trees with panicked squawks.

From the woods a gigantic shape came into view. It was the head of a colossal green serpent. It was so huge that Apollo and Artemis looked like insects before it. Its serpentine yellow eyes fixed onto the young Apollo.

"Your hunt ends today, Python," Apollo said.

Artemis shrugged and took to the air to watch the fight from afar.

"Consider your glory a gift from me, Apollo!" she shouted as the young god readied an arrow. "One day, I will ask for similar glory in return!'"

The disembodied voice of present-day Apollo spoke into Melissa's ear, "We can skip the glorious battle between myself and Python. It ended with a dead serpent and a family finally free of entrapment on Delos."

"Nice of Artemis to let you have the win," Melissa smirked.

"I wouldn't say that. Python was destined to be my fight."

Melissa was careful not to push the topic.

Time jumped forward again.

Melissa found herself in a very familiar setting. A crowd of villagers were once again denying Leto and her two teenage children the right to drink. It ended very differently this time. Both Apollo and Artemis shot their mother a side-ways smile. She interpreted their look and with a lazy wave, transformed every person there into frogs. Melissa gasped in horror as she watched the crowd writhe and mutate.

"Seems harsh," Melissa muttered.

"We were young and we were vengeful. Leto had suffered greatly for us and for her love of Zeus. Mortals who insulted us felt our wrath swiftly and brutally."

"What do you mean?" Melissa asked.

"Take Niobe, for example," Apollo said darkly.

The scene changed and Melissa found herself in an elaborate home beside a portly woman. Huge vases and statuettes decorated her living space. She appeared to be quite wealthy. The woman was loudly bragging to her friends about her superiority to, of all beings, Leto.

"I tell you, that Leto thinks she is all that! But how many

children did she have? Only two! I have six sons and six daughters! The brats Apollo and Artemis lack the fortitude and good looks of my progeny," the woman shouted to a roomful of laughter.

Melissa's first thought was that this wouldn't end well for the woman Apollo had called Niobe.

It became night. A large full moon floated above the villa, shining down on Niobe's family in a large back courtyard. The sons mingled and laughed with the daughters. They were a handsome and pleasant bunch. High above, none noticed the floating forms of the twin gods. Both wore scowls on their faces.

"These are the daughters of Niobe," Apollo said, pointing down towards the women.

Artemis summoned her silver bow while Apollo produced a large vial of poison to dip his arrows into.

"Pride is not a desirable trait in humans, is it brother?" Artemis asked Apollo.

"No," Apollo replied, readying an arrow.

He aimed and released. The arrow whizzed through the air and impaled one of the sons through his stomach. It was so quiet barely any of Niobe's children noticed. The poison reacted quickly, causing him to violently throw up his stomach's contents, then blood.

Artemis readied her own arrows and began shooting them towards the young women.

The two gods didn't laugh or joke as they set about slaughtering Niobe's family one by one.

They saw the gods flying above them but could do nothing to escape. Some called out in prayer and begged for their lives, for they had done no wrong by the gods. The fear and pain in their voices carried into the night. Nothing could dissuade Apollo and Artemis from their punishment of Niobe.

It wasn't long before the courtyard was a sea of blood and bodies.

"That was awful," Melissa said, shaking her head. "How is that just?"

"In the eyes of the gods, such retribution is more than just," Apollo answered her.

"It is cruel. You killed them all because their mother boasted?"

"We are not humans," Apollo shrugged. "You would do well to remember that. Do you not swat a fly when it bites you?"

"But you would not treat other gods this way," Melissa protested.

Apollo chuckled at this statement. "Let us see what my dear sister did to my grandson, Actaeon. I hold no grudge over this."

The bloodied courtyard was left behind and in its stead a forest stream appeared. It fed into a deep pool of crystal clear water surrounded by vibrant green ferns. There were several naked women bathing in the water. Beautiful couldn't begin to describe them; because beautiful was a human term, and they were more than that.

On the outer edge of the group, standing in ankle-deep water, was now the very adult Artemis. She was just as radiant as her mother and as impossibly perfect as Apollo.

The bushes rustled beside Melissa and she turned to see a young man step through and freeze in place. When he realised what he had stumbled across, horror became etched on his face.

Artemis saw him and her own look of anger was unmistakable.

"Don't say a word," she breathed, her voice pulsing with venom.

A bellowing raucous of barking was booming behind the young man, who Melissa assumed was Actaeon. It sounded like he had a formidable party of hunting dogs with him.

The dogs' barks were getting louder and more frenzied as Actaeon stood frozen. The nymphs in the pool began to look concerned. Seeing this, Actaeon called out to his dogs, hoping to silence them.

Artemis snapped her fingers, and Actaeon clutched at his throat. New lengths of bone jutted from the side of his skull as his skin sprouted brown fur all over. He cried out, making the sound of a deer in distress.

The distant dogs grew more excited. Their barking was getting closer.

Actaeon, now caught midway between man and deer tried to run but stumbled and fell. Artemis smiled as his hunting dogs caught up with him. Not knowing their transforming master, they set to work ripping him apart. He screamed as the dogs tore the flesh from his bones, all while painfully alive.

Melissa had seen some terrible things, but this was too much for her.

Her eyes flashed gold and she was back at the bar.

"That was awful!" Melissa said, reaching across the table and slapping Apollo on the shoulder.

"You wanted to know my sister. She is like me and I am like her. And we are like all gods, whether you wish to kid yourself about our natures or not."

The man who'd become the deer had been gruesomely punished for being in the wrong place at the wrong time.

Melissa slumped back, trying to soak it all in. Was she on the right side of this, teaming up with Apollo? Were all the old gods actually monsters so indifferent to humanity that suffering meant nothing to them?

"Do not fret, Melissa," Apollo said kindly. "Time and defeat have changed us. The images you saw are from the days when we walked the world. Much changed after the Trojan War. We became absent. When humans insulted us, we did not react with swift vengeance. In the time of the Romans, we would offer blessings, but never be seen."

Melissa, still horrified, struggled to take in Apollo's words.

"And so it will be again when we rid the world of the angels. Do not entertain the thought that they are better than us. Their god has done some awful things in his time," Apollo ended, leaning back.

Melissa sat silent.

"There is a hymn written about my sister," Apollo remarked. "I will sing it for you."

Apollo started quietly singing in the most beautiful voice Melissa had ever heard. His voice was like a choir of angels, perfectly in tune. It was enough to melt the soul.

"In the shadows of mountains and in the wind of mountain-tops
She loves to take her bow.
Her bow made of silver.
And shoot off her shafts of woe.
The peaks of great mountains tremble.
The forest in its darkness screams...
The whole earth starts shaking even the sea, the sea-life...
And when she has hung up this unstrung bow,
When she has put away her arrows,
She puts on over her flesh a beautiful dress
Then she begins the dances..."

PART ONE

Part One takes place during the events of In the Shadow of The Old World.

DATE:
19 JAN 2021 (FLORIDA)
20 JAN 2021 (JAPAN +13 HOURS)

AST TEAM ONE

- Liam Sager
- Matthew Pyne
- Ingrid Horjen
- Joshua Dare
- Haruka Masunaga

Current location: All members in **Nagoya, Japan.**

AST TEAM TWO

- Melissa Pythia
- Teva Henry
- Danni Quinn
- Malcolm Selleck

Current location: All members in **Florida, USA.** With the exception of **Team Leader Melissa Pythia**, who is in **Nagoya, Japan.**

SIT-REP:

The meeting between the Australian Government, United States Government and The Old World has begun in Nagoya. The documentation for OPERATION THUNDERKING is being shared and the Golden God Apollo is presenting his mission. *Team one* will need to infiltrate Jerusalem, find the portal to Heaven and rescue the captured gods Hephaestus and Hecate. Altior Fulgur has offered them his full assistance.

Meanwhile, in Florida, *team two* is on a mission of their own...

1

STRANGE RITUALS IN
THE NIGHT

THE REMOTE SWAMPS OF FLORIDA
- JANUARY 19 2021 -

D anni Quinn grimaced as her boot was fully engulfed by a hidden muddy hole. She felt dirty water soak into her sock.

"Y'all be careful of them sinkholes round here," the man in front of Danni proclaimed. He was a large fellow in a tan shirt that was stretching dangerously around his midriff. Danni didn't enjoy the uncouth noises he blurted out as he moved. His aviator sunglasses dangled from a string around his neck, frequently getting caught on the undergrowth as they pushed through it, meaning she had to frequently pause in the mud.

"How far now, Sheriff?" another American voice whispered

from behind Danni.

"Not far, you can hear 'em," the Sheriff responded, hitching up his police belt.

The entire group paused.

He was right; faint noises were coming from deeper in the swamp. It sounded like dozens of voices whooping and cheering.

The nearby hiss of an alligator lurking in the shallows made them start moving again.

The party crawling through the remote Florida swamp consisted of eight people. First were the Sheriff and two of his officers, nicknamed Lanky Pete and Dead-Eye Jim. Then there was Danni, under the supervision of Teva Henry, a Tahitian-born Australian spy. Next were two United States Supernatural Occurrence Taskforce (or USSOT) members. One was a short, weedy man and the other rather tall and handsome. Danni could've sworn she kept seeing him glancing in her direction. Last was Doctor Malcolm Selleck, a historian and expert in ancient artefacts.

Danni was only brand new to her job. At the end of 2019, she'd been offered a spot on the Australian Intelligence Officer and Operator course. The Australian Government set up an initiative for a one-year course that combined elements of both intelligence training and in-the-field spy work. ASIO and ASIS had collaborated to create the specialist program to create a new kind of versatile operative.

Due to her experience with the supernatural, Danni was asked to complete a further two-week course to become a special operator with the Australian Supernatural Taskforce. Once that was done, she was swept off overseas.

Melissa, her boss, was a confident leader who got the job done quickly and efficiently. This somewhat scared Danni. Melissa was very good at her job, and rumours of how she'd been through the wringer on a recent mission to Rome followed her endlessly.

In all honesty, the entire job scared Danni. A year ago, she'd been a bartender with no prospects for something better in her near future. Then she'd met a man named Joshua Dare, a man who carried a terrible secret.

As it turned out, Josh was a werewolf.

Every full moon he'd turn into a blood-thirsty monster. Danni had been there when he'd discovered his true nature. She'd been there when the Vatican had sent their own werewolf after him. She'd almost died a couple of times, but from that came an incredible job offer.

She often felt during her year of training that it was an unearned job offer. There was nothing special about her; she was just in the right place at the right time. Despite that, she had prevailed against difficult odds and succeeded where many others would've failed. Danni often had to remind herself of that. The 'fish-out-of-water' feeling of doing something new often got the wheel of negativity spinning in her mind, and she had to make a conscious effort to snap herself out of it.

Further complicating things was her romantic past with Josh. She tried not to think about it too much. Sometimes, in quiet moments, she thought about the time they'd spent together. Even though he was a monster, he was still a really nice guy. Probably the best guy she'd dated.

The last time she'd seen him, they'd just finished a hard

day's manual labour at a banana farm in the small town of Tully, North Queensland. She'd gone to take a shower and just like that... Josh was pulled from her life forever. The full moon had risen, the Australian Government had, at last, captured their target monster and she was left with nothing. When Melissa had offered the training, she wasn't in a position to say no.

Now, deep in the darkness of the swamp, Danni was on her first-ever mission. Sure, she'd been a part of a lot of simulated missions during her training. She always did okay. But now that it was real, the butterflies in her stomach were beating their wings so fast Danni was sure a hurricane of vomit was building in there. Yet, she was keeping her cool, for now at least. On the outside, it was only her boots sinking into the mud. Internally she felt her entire being was sinking out of its depth.

"We gonna have to get wet? I ain't swimming with no gator," the shorter of the USSOT agents, named Kip, asked. He was a weaselly man with a pencil-thin moustache.

"No, we aren't going swimmin'," the Sheriff sighed. "It's all dry land; just follow me. I made sure to memorise the path last month when these guys showed up. When they first started appearing in 2020, they set up totally at random. It seems they've settled here."

On and on they crawled, crouched, and shambled through the swamp, moving in single file with no torches. The sounds of the party were growing louder by the minute. It was becoming so all-consuming that even the splashes from the ever-present alligators were being lost in the hubbub.

Danni didn't mind the squelching of mud between her

fingers or the persistent buzzing of mosquitos. Her mind was too occupied with what was coming next.

The glow of an enormous bonfire illuminated the area. Danni started to see the clouds of mosquitos around the covert gang instead of only hearing their annoying whining.

The Sheriff held up his hand in warning, and the group waited as an incredibly long python slid down the trunk of a Water Tupelo tree and moved across the path. Danni assumed it was getting away from the noise of the bonfire.

"Hey boss, when'd you wan' us to bust up this party?" Lanky Pete asked the Sheriff.

"When these USSOT people write their little notes. Remember, we want to arrest as many of these hillbillies as we can."

The two officers exchanged glances.

Danni shot a look at Teva behind her. He'd been furiously scribbling notes on his waterproof pad for the last twenty minutes.

They came to a patch of ground that was wide enough (and dry enough) they could move out of their line.

Crawling towards a thick clump of shrubs, the Sheriff, the USSOT agents and Danni peered through the leaves to observe the raucous party.

It was anarchy made flesh.

Danni had never seen anything like it.

The bonfire wasn't the traditional flaming tower of logs. Instead, a wide ring had been cut into the sand and lit on fire. Through the dancing curtains of flame, Danni could see people moving. They were rotating around a central structure, though she couldn't see that structure clearly. It was definitely tall, dark and thin.

Outside the ring of fire were dozens of people. There were so many in the firelight that their silhouettes formed a shapeless, incongruous mass.

"Well, I'll be," the Sheriff murmured. "At least three dozen by my count."

None of them could have expected the immensity of celebration in the remote swamp.

Danni and her group had spent several hours traversing the swamps via hovercraft, then another couple on foot. How all these people had gotten here was a mystery.

As Danni's eyes adjusted to the orange light, she began to pick up peculiar details. There was no uniformity to these people. Usually cultists (which she assumed they were) lived within rigidly set boundaries. People of different colours, classes and creeds were disavowed. Yet here every kind of person was represented. All ethnic groups writhed and contorted to a disjointed swell of music together. Many of them were older, with wrinkled skin and missing teeth. Some looked like traditional hippies, while others looked to be under the influence of dangerous substances. The waving dreadlocks and dirty bodies swayed and mashed together.

Drums were beating out of tune and individual flutes loudly played singular melodies. Where the musicians were exactly, Danni couldn't determine.

The dancing of the people matched the music in its unnaturalness. It was less a dance and more of a spasming wave. Their eyes were rolled back and their mouths hung open as they screamed into the night. It reminded Danni of how remote tribes were depicted in old films, like it was a voodoo orgy.

Some people jumped triumphantly up and down while others rolled on the ground, splashing mud all over themselves.

Virtually no one had clothes on. Many were as naked as the day they were born, primally flinging their limbs back and forth. It was like they were witnessing a ritual from a time older than recorded civilisation.

Teva approached Danni and whispered, "What are they saying?"

Danni strained her ears to pick up singular words in the mess of noise.

"I don't know… the words I can hear aren't English."

"I'm of the same opinion," Teva murmured.

"They ain't of any language I'm familiar with," Kip, the USSOT agent whispered, joining the conversation.

"Sheriff, do you know what is going on?" Teva asked.

"Haven't the foggiest, I'm afraid," the Sheriff said, still watching the endlessly moving crowd with disgust.

"Last couple of months, fishermen and hunters have reported the aftermath of these little gatherings. We thought it was a joke, way too remote out here. Last month I investigated myself and this is what I found. As you can see, there were too many for me to interrupt the party. I contacted the FBI and they contacted USSOT."

"What are we waiting for?" Dead-Eye Jim asked impatiently. "Let's get out there and start arresting."

"The man in charge," the Sheriff answered. "Let's hope he identifies himself. I imagine a grand speech to the congregation happenin' eventually."

"No intel on who he or she is?" Teva asked.

Both Danni and Teva had been thrown in the deep end here. They'd received no briefing. When their boss, Melissa, had been called away overseas, she'd asked USSOT if there was anything her agents could help with. Now they were here in Florida beside a mass of dirty naked people.

"Nope. The FBI said they had some leads but didn't pass 'em on to me."

Danni sat mesmerised by the orgy of movement before them. The ring of bodies danced with the flickering ring of fire. Every now and then, she caught glimpses of the black structure in the centre of it all. It was definitely an obelisk, probably cut from a gargantuan stone. Every time she saw it, she was filled with an innate sense of dread.

Then, she saw something different. Through a gap in the flames, a fully robed figure was walking.

"There! I saw a guy in the middle!" Danni exclaimed.

"What was different about 'im?" the Sherriff asked.

"He was wearing a long brown robe. Everyone else is naked. He has to be the leader!"

"Right," the Sheriff uttered, moving away from the brush to speak to everyone. "That's good enough for me. We are going in. Treat 'em like sheep and we'll be the dogs. Round 'em up and let's see how many we can grab."

They all murmured agreeance.

"You, girl, go crash tackle the guy in the robes and slap some cuffs on 'im. You saw 'im; it's only fair," the sheriff directed to Danni.

Danni nodded, swallowing her fright and steeling her resolve.

"I'll be with you," Teva said.

"You got much experience arresting someone?" Danni asked nervously.

"No, I'm mostly an IT guy," Teva responded.

"Oh good," Danni replied, standing up.

If it was anarchy before, pure chaos erupted when the Sheriff and his officers ran towards the fire with their batons out. The naked men and women bolted in all directions in a startled panic.

Through the corner of her eyes, Danni saw the USSOT agents methodically corner, tackle and restrain cultists before they could get away.

The police officers were slightly more primitive, yet equally effective. They used brute force to knock people down and place zip-tie handcuffs around their wrists. Dead-Eye Jim even retracted his baton and threw it at a man, hitting him square between the eyes. It was quite the throw.

Danni was small and fast. With Teva close behind, she leapt through the ring of fire, temporarily feeling its intense heat.

The people circling the black obelisk did the same, running in the other direction. Danni didn't quite like imaging how the naked people felt as their exposed areas passed across the licking flames.

She saw the man in the brown robe running. Within a moment, she was on top of him, pure adrenaline allowing her to leap and force him down. His head landed close to the fire pit, and he kicked Danni away violently before scrambling back from the flames.

Despite almost being winded, Danni launched back on top of him, struggling to pin him down. Despite her training, the guy was double her size and difficult to get under her control.

He pushed Danni off again and stood up with a fist menacingly raised. Fortunately, Teva came running in, with his discreet tactical taser drawn. He drive-stunned the man right in the ribs, causing him to convulse and collapse in the electrical punch.

Teva pressed his knee into the man's lower back while Danni forced his wrists together. The pair had restrained the leader.

A torrent of relief washed over Danni the instant she realised she'd completed the one task assigned to her.

She could barely contain her wide toothy smile. This was her first career success. She knew she could do it.

Unfortunately, the scuffle had thrown the man's robes wide open, revealing that he too, was wearing nothing beneath.

Once the stranger had stopped squirming, Danni took a breath and surveyed the inner circle. Much like outside, the soil was damp and laced with sporadic patches of grass. In the dead centre sat the black stone obelisk. It was a monument to dread. Danni could see that its peak was a carven statuette. A very odd statuette.

The Sheriff pushed through the fire clumsily, then spent a minute patting down the flames that erupted across his pants.

"Got 'im?" he asked.

"Yep," Danni said brightly.

"Turn 'im over."

Teva rolled the man onto his back.

The man was wild-eyed and spluttering, spitting dirt from his mouth. He looked to be in his late forties or early fifties, with a perfectly manicured beard and professional haircut. He had a square face with prominent round cheeks and a broad forehead. Danni thought he had the distinct look of a rugby player.

"Name?" the Sheriff asked.

The man didn't answer.

"Don't suppose he has ID?" the Sheriff asked Teva.

"I can tell you there is nothing under this robe," Teva grimaced, trying to look anywhere but the man's lower torso.

"Don't worry, we will find out who you are," the Sheriff said.

"And what is going on here," Teva added.

The man remained stoic in the face of his capture. Danni sensed an air of dignity about him. So many of the naked dancing people had looked… low socio-economic, to put it politely. This guy, not so much.

There was the sound of extinguishing flames as the two police officers kicked dirt into the fire. Once a portion of the ring was no longer a burn hazard, Malcolm Selleck stepped through. The Australian doctor (and professor) had hung back during the raid and was now ready to fulfil his role.

He made a beeline straight for the obelisk.

"Fascinating," he breathed.

Danni quite liked Malcolm. He was 39, relatively young for a professor, and outrageously fit. He exclusively ate from the Mediterranean diet, meaning he basically bathed in olive oil. He believed diet was the key to success in any endeavour, something

Danni agreed with. He was tall with a square jaw and short black hair. While being highly knowledgeable in his field, he wasn't the geeky kind of nerd. Malcolm had spent a good deal of time in the military before he'd embraced history as his true calling. His openness to ideas that were left-field of traditional thinking had landed him with frequent AST call-outs.

"What is it?" Danni asked him as he pondered the tower.

"Basalt, I'm guessing," Malcolm replied. "Drawn with strange hieroglyphs. Unrecognisable hieroglyphs, in fact."

Now that the prisoner was fully restrained, Danni walked towards the pillar. She hadn't even noticed the drawings that lined it up and down. In the firelight they were almost invisible.

"What about that *thing* on top?" Danni asked, pointing towards the shadowy statue at the pinnacle.

"I have never seen any deity, ancient or otherwise, depicted like that. We will pull it down and take it for further study. I hope USSOT has some useful data they can give us."

Malcolm was trying to play it cool, but the tremble in his voice betrayed just how excited he was.

Danni didn't even want to look up at the grotesque figurine; it creeped her out.

The Sheriff's first plan was to kick over the obelisk, but Malcolm, fearing damaging the statuette, talked him down. Then, a heated debate started between the two. When the Sheriff began to loudly brag how he could rope a calf faster than anyone in East Texas, she picked her moment to leave.

Danni walked around the rest of the ritual site. In total, they'd successfully managed to arrest eleven people. It was a significant effort, though none were talking. Many were just gazing off into the abyss.

Lanky Pete and Dead-Eye Jim had moved all of the prisoners to the edge of the clearing and were standing guard.

Before long, Teva walked the robed leader over to join them.

Danni saw the man eyeing her curiously as he passed.

"Got something to say?" Danni asked, trying incredibly hard to sound confident.

"You are too late," he whispered.

"Late for what?"

"In his sunken city, the dead one waits dreaming…"

The robed man smiled a terrifying smile, though his voice was very sing-song.

Danni recoiled slightly. "What do you mean? Who is the dead one?"

The robed man said nothing more. He closed his eyes and started humming.

Before long, Malcolm and the Sheriff emerged, carrying the statuette between them. It was four feet tall and looked exceedingly heavy. How they got it down, Danni had no idea. She wondered if the Sheriff's calf-roping abilities had played a part.

All of the cultists hissed and growled like wild beasts as it passed by.

"I'm calling some choppers in," the Sheriff said, wiping his forehead with his sleeve. "Trying to walk this riff-raff out of here will be too damn hard."

The USSOT agent Kit walked up and studied the statuette

closely. "I've seen this before, only broken."

Malcolm was instantly intrigued. "Where? When?"

"2020, Minnesota. A cabin in the Pine Island State Forest had a statue just like this in it. You AST guys are here to follow up on that, ain't ya? When we get back, I'll give you all the files on it. We couldn't trace its origins."

"You do not want to trace its origins," a voice called from the huddle of prisoners.

The robed-man was speaking again. Only now he looked infuriated.

"Speak up!" the Sheriff commanded.

"You're too late to stop what is happening. In the depths, drums beat and flutes pipe. They signal a coming from the stars."

"From the stars? Of what?" the Sheriff laughed. "Looks like we got a cult of alien-worshippers."

"Not aliens, no. You will see soon. It is all written. Soon, sacred rules will be broken and his eyes will turn upon this Earth again," the robed man smiled.

"Right," the Sheriff said, rolling his eyes. He walked off, not wanting to hear any more.

Malcolm, however, approached and asked for more clarification.

"Tell me what you mean?" he asked enthusiastically.

The robed man looked at Danni and said, "She has a part to play in this."

Danni was shocked. Why was this guy singling her out?

"Don't worry," Malcolm said, placing his hand on Danni's shoulder. "The frenzy of these primitive rituals can really bring out odd things in people. Fire and dancing have physical effects on the mind. We will get clearer answers in the light of a new day."

Danni walked away, no longer wishing to be leered at by the cultists. All of their unblinking eyes were now fixed to her.

She could only hope that when her boss, Melissa Pythia, returned from the meeting in Japan, things would become clearer.

2

DANNI QUINN

The days following the events in the Florida swamp passed uneventfully. All of the cultists were taken to Tallahassee and held at the central police station for questioning. As this was primarily a police matter, Teva and Danni weren't kept up to date on any discoveries.

USSOT, working with the sheriff's department, were hesitant to share anything with the Australians. While an information-sharing agreement between the US and Australian supernatural-focused organisations was in the pipeline, nothing had been formalised yet.

Danni was confused to their entire purpose being there, so wasn't surprised that the Florida Police weren't handing over any revelations they uncovered. Teva assured her that this was normal when working with foreign government agencies.

The team that had travelled to Florida from Australia consisted of Melissa Pythia (their team leader), Danni, Teva and Professor Malcolm Selleck. Melissa had to leave for a sudden meeting in Japan with her superior, leaving Teva, Malcolm and Danni with little to do.

It was Malcolm who offered a few tidbits of information to the Australians. Being an expert in the field, he'd been invited to study the statuette. He'd said everything about it was unique, from concept to the materials used. He was like an excited school kid when he spoke about the oddity, starry-eyed as he rambled on about ancient mysticism and unknown religions.

Danni didn't find herself thinking about work too much. She was chuffed that she was being paid all kinds of allowances to be overseas without any pressing jobs assigned to her.

Plus, an added benefit was that she now had the opportunity to get to know her teammate Teva better.

One gloomy morning they decided to go and find a place that served decent coffee. Their search had been unsuccessful. Danni grimaced as she looked at the steaming mug of tar in front of her. Americans just couldn't do coffee right. The waitress had even offered her cream. Cream in coffee! It was unbelievable.

With great difficulty, Teva swallowed from his mug.

"Just terrible," he mumbled.

Danni laughed and he gave her an appreciative grin.

"So, Danni, how did your training go? I've heard its tough," Teva asked.

Danni tucked her hair behind her ears as she thought about her answer.

"It was… fine, I guess. I mean, I got through it. But I was the odd one out."

"How do you mean?" Teva asked.

"Well, you know how I got in?" Danni said, with a nervous laugh.

"Of course, the werewolves in Cairns. Awesome story, by the way!" Teva laughed.

Danni felt immediately at ease. Teva always carried himself with an easy-going air of enthusiasm.

"Yeah. I was the least educated. Everyone else had university degrees and knew everything about everything! Then, here was me, just an uneducated bartender wandering in."

"I bet you showed them what you were made of though," Teva said.

"Oh, I did. I kicked arse in all the scenarios that involved taking someone down. The ones where you had to talk the person down, I wasn't so crash hot in."

"Can't win them all," Teva said, leaning back and spreading his arms wide.

"My coursemates were good though. They helped me every step of the way. I struggled with the exams at first but by the end of it I was smashing it."

"Ah, good. Having a supportive group is the most important part. And hell, I'm not meant to say this, but you learn everything you need to on the job. In spy work, most of the time you're just making things up and hoping for the best. You have to be reactive and able to think on your feet. You showed in the swamp you could do that."

Danni smiled. She guessed Teva had seen how nervous she was.

Teva continued, "You're on a great team here. Melissa is a good boss. This is her first go of being a team leader, so she might make some mistakes, but we will get each other through it."

"You said you'd worked with her before?" Danni asked, leaning forward and wrapping her hands around her mug.

"I was with Melissa on her first assignment in Afghanistan. I wasn't able to stop her getting captured by a terrorist group. She can be rash and impulsive, but she gets the job done. She's a whizz at paperwork too. Trust me, that is the best quality a team leader can have."

Danni chuckled. She hadn't had the chance to spend much time with her boss one-on-one yet. Formal authority figures scared her slightly. No one in her extended family had a formal bone in them.

"Then, I was with Melissa in Rome when all of this started. I fought side by side with an ancient Greek goddess against supernatural forces beside an ancient temple. That's when things started getting a bit crazy."

"Yeah… when I first read the documentation I was sure none of it could be real. If I hadn't seen werewolves with my own eyes…" Danni admitted.

"I was one of the people that thought the AST was a joke organisation," Teva sighed. "I signed up to do the comical two-week course. After Rome and Afghanistan, I am fully committed to the end of this mission."

"Yep, we are here to save the world!" Danni joked, raising her mug.

Teva clinked his cup against hers and they both took a sip.

The pair exchanged a glance, swallowed uncomfortably, then silently agreed to give up on their drinks.

• • • • •

DANNI SPENT THE FOLLOWING days lazily walking the streets of Tallahassee. Feeling emboldened to take a solo journey, Danni found herself with a backpack on by the sea. She'd decided to visit St. Mark's Lighthouse in the St. Mark's Wildlife Refuge. Danni had spent some time collecting seashells on the sand, and when she'd come across the old white tower, she'd decided to eat her premade lunch. In the warm sun under a blue sky, it was the perfect outing.

The lighthouse was beautiful. Built in the early nineteenth century, it had survived the Civil War. It rose from a dense clump of beach-side trees as a beacon of history where Danni could sit in the shade and unwrap her lunch.

She smiled. Her life was pretty good right now.

As it often did these days, her mind drifted back to the same repeating thought; where she was now compared to where she was a year ago.

It was all just so surreal for her. When she was a bartender, she'd once had a disgruntled patron tell her that she was nothing more than white trash who'd never amount to anything. It had cut her deep, and much in the way that most bullying does, stopped her from trying to pursue anything better for herself.

She'd settled for less, not just in terms of work but in terms of relationships as well. Other than Josh the werewolf, she'd only ever been with losers because that was how she felt about herself.

That was the past, though. Now she was a spy in the USA.

As Danni had told Teva, she'd struggled with the academic side of her training. The weapons handling and fitness elements had gone okay. She hadn't excelled by any means, but she'd got through it. Rivers of tears were shed through the year, and self-doubt had built into a mountain to overcome, but in the end she'd marched out with the rest of her classmates, all deemed competent.

Approaching graduation, each of her peers had been assigned a spot with ASIS or ASIO. Danni hadn't been offered anything. Fear and the ever-present anxiety of failure had risen like the tide inside her.

Danni had no desire to reach out to Melissa, who'd gotten her on the course in the first place. Instead, she desired to appear cool, calm and collected. Her plan had been to hope for the best.

Days before graduation, there had been a knock on Danni's door.

As she bit into her sandwich beneath the Florida lighthouse, her mind took her back to that meeting.

• • • • •

IN EARLY DECEMBER 2020, Danni sat on the floor in front of the mirror. She was hastily applying make-up. She'd just been told someone important was coming to speak to her, and she wanted to look her best.

Three heavy knocks sounded out. She stood up and kicked her make-up box under the bed. It wasn't a work day, but Danni had dressed to impress. She'd put on an immaculately ironed pantsuit. It was dark-grey all over and looked very professional. Underneath, she wore a white blouse. She didn't think pantsuits suited her, but it was what society expected and she was smart enough to play the game.

She took a deep breath and opened the door.

Standing in the hallway was an older man with a round face and glasses. He was wearing a suit, though he looked very uncomfortable in it.

"Danni Quinn," the man beamed. He extended his hand.

Danni grasped it and shook it enthusiastically. "That's me! And you are?"

"Brett Sayer," he answered. "Nice grip. You'll go places with a handshake like that."

"Thank you, sir."

"I wanted to have an informal chat with you, yet every time I'm in Canberra, I am forced to attend meetings and wear a suit."

"I'm not much of a suit person myself," Danni agreed.

"Good to hear. Let's go downstairs. There is a coffee shop in the lobby of this hotel that is perfect for a talk."

"This really is informal," Danni thought.

The majority of Danni's training had taken place in New South Wales. They'd all been shipped to Canberra and provided with hotels for their pending graduation.

The coffee shop had expansive glass windows that allowed in an abundance of light. Decorative pot plants were scattered about, giving the place a tropical vibe. The smell of artisan coffee enveloped every table and flooded Danni's nostrils.

Brett and Danni sat across from one another. Danni made sure to sit upright with her hands folded on her lap, even though Brett couldn't see them.

"Relax," Brett said, noticing her stiff disposition.

A waitress in a bright green apron wandered over and took their order.

Once she'd left, Brett peered at Danni and said, "Down to business."

Danni gulped.

"Congratulations on your achievement. The course is not easy from what I've heard."

"Thank you," Danni replied nervously.

"I don't like to dance around things. In October 2019 you witnessed a police constable shoot a werewolf dead, correct?"

Danni nodded. She'd been there when Jesse Billiau, a friend of her boyfriend, had killed a skinny grotesque werewolf. He'd been bitten then fled the scene.

"So you are aware that the existence of supernatural creatures extends beyond werewolves?" Brett asked.

"I assume so, yeah… but I don't really *know*." Danni looked around nervously to make sure no one was listening in.

Brett laughed. "Don't worry, if this place wasn't secure to talk, we wouldn't be talking here. Future spies and agents are staying here. All of the staff you see, including the waitress who just served us, are undercover federal agents."

Danni glanced again at the waitress in her green apron. She did have a very serious look about her.

Brett continued, "As I'm sure you are aware, the Australian Government has a secret division called the Australian Supernatural Taskforce. It has two permanent members: myself as the OIC and the second in command, Liam Sager, who you will meet soon enough. When we need extra people, we pull them from ASIO, ASIS, the military and the police. They have to do a two-week course and sign a stack of national security papers swearing them to complete secrecy. Then, they continue to sit in a pool of operatives to be called upon when needed."

"You want me to go into this pool?" Danni asked, becoming excited. This sounded cool.

Brett smiled. "Yes, but a step beyond. As soon as you graduate, we will be flying you to complete the introductory course. Then you will be joining us for a mission."

"So that explains why I wasn't offered a spot with ASIO or ASIS yet..."

"I reached out and said we'd be taking you. It helps that the woman who got you in, Melissa Pythia, is currently one of ASIS's star operatives. Getting her reassigned to the AST for the next few months was a real pain in the ass."

Danni chuckled. She didn't expect to hear this high-level government operative speak like that.

"Once you have signed the necessary forms, you will be briefed on Operation Thunderking. Due to the nature of our current objective and a certain secrecy around AST associates, not even ASIO or ASIS are fully aware of our mission. Keep this in mind. Don't discuss with your course members where you are going. We are working with minimal numbers and have a big job to pull off."

Brett looked serious. Danni nodded again.

"Why me?" she asked.

"You undoubtedly remember Joshua Dare. All I can say now is that a lot revolves around him and the curse he has picked up."

"Oh, will I be working with him?" she asked, feeling even more nervous.

"Not at this point. It is an evolving situation, however."

Danni felt both relieved and disappointed at this response.

"Do you have any more questions?" Brett asked, giving a knowing wink as the waitress dropped off their coffees.

"How will I know where to go and what to do?"

"Monitor your emails. Flight details will be sent to you. For now, that is all Miss Quinn. Or should I say, Agent Quinn?"

They both stood up and shook hands again. Brett started walking away but quickly turned back and asked, "Are you familiar with the Greek gods?"

"Ah, not at all," Danni responded quietly.

"Do some reading. You'll want to know all you can." He disappeared from view.

• • • • •

DANNI SNAPPED BACK TO REALITY. The salty sea air

washing over her skin was so relaxing that she couldn't help but reminisce.

Her phone buzzed in her pocket.

"Teva, what's up?"

"Melissa will be touching down soon. She's scheduled a meeting at Tallahassee Police Station at 2 pm," Teva's voice iterated through the earpiece.

"I'll be there," Danni affirmed, clicking the end call button.

It hadn't been long after Danni had completed the two week AST course that she'd had her first official meeting with Melissa. In fact, it had only been a couple of weeks ago.

• • • • •

IN EARLY JANUARY 2021, Danni sat across a brown oak desk from her new boss, Melissa Pythia.

"Well, Danni, I think the last time we spoke in person was that night in 2019," Melissa began casually.

"Yes, ma'am."

"Please don't call me ma'am. Mel is fine."

"Sorry," Danni said, feeling exasperated. "I'm still not sure about all the rules. During the training, you have to be ultra-formal, yet no one actually working in the field cares."

"Yep, just one of the many contradictions of the job," Mel acknowledged.

"Noted," Danni replied.

"How did you find the two-week AST course?" Melissa asked, opening her top drawer to search for something.

"Overall, pretty basic," Danni answered honestly. "It was all kind of vague… except for the werewolf sections. They were quite thorough."

"Only recently updated. Hence why you are here. You are fortunate, you know? To get this job is usually quite the ordeal. Selection is tough, competitive and there are about a dozen testing gateways to pass."

"I know, and thank you so much for getting me here!" Danni exclaimed. She didn't want to seem that she was ungrateful.

"Hey, don't stress. You passed everything of your own accord. I never doubted you."

Danni couldn't suppress her grin. This feeling of pride in herself was taking some getting used to.

"But," Mel continued, "you are here because of your proximity to the werewolf case, which is an ongoing story."

"You caught him, didn't you?"

"Yes, the AST is still monitoring him."

"Monitoring? Isn't he imprisoned somewhere?"

"No, actually. Mr Dare is currently in Japan posing as an English teacher."

Danni frowned. How this had come about, she couldn't even begin to guess.

"Regardless, events continue to escalate around the werewolf curse. Here."

Melissa handed Danni a manila folder with the title OPERATION THUNDERKING stamped on top.

"Operation Thunderking," Danni murmured. She opened it up and began perusing the pages.

"Read it at your leisure. We will discuss the basics now."

Danni promptly closed the folder and rested it on her lap.

"Some of this will come as a shock, but you have no choice but to keep an open mind."

Danni nodded.

Mel seemed unsure of how to phrase the next part.

"Well… let's start with the big picture. Sometime in the distant past, the Greek God Zeus disappeared. I'm not sure how well I understand this myself, but it's like he was torn from the world. When that happened, he left a space in the supernatural hierarchy where he should have been. Like a big pocket of power that is up for the taking by whoever can complete the correct ritual."

Danni was immediately lost, but she didn't let it show.

"Now, for the longest time, no one has sought to claim this power. I don't think anyone was even aware it was up for grabs. That has changed. Two significant supernatural players are going for it. Both are archangels and you will be familiar with at least one of them. Lucifer, or 'the Devil' as he is known in popular culture and his brother Michael. According to our informants, neither of these two parties should claim this power. The very fact that the two are pitted against each other may have world-ending possibilities."

"This sounds a little bigger than werewolves," Danni muttered.

"Right," Melissa said, sounding a little exasperated. "I was there in 2019 when all of this was exposed. Currently, it is only us in Australia and the Vatican that are aware of this. Brett Sayer is working on a plan to share this with the Americans; we will see how that goes."

"Who are these informants?" Danni asked.

"Their names are Apollo, former God of the Sun and Hermes, God of Speed."

"When you say god…"

"I do mean literal god."

"Well, that's something. How do you know?" Danni couldn't help but ask.

Melissa paused as she thought about her answer. "I have a connection to Apollo that verifies it. I won't go into any great detail. As it turns out, almost every god from the old religions are real, and some from the more modern religions. When the Supernatural Taskforce was established, this level of being wasn't factored in. Still, we have to contend with it."

Danni wondered what Melissa's connection to Apollo was. She thought it might be rude to ask outright, though.

"So, our job is to stop the others claiming this power of Zeus. Do we have a huge team on this? Sounds pretty important," Danni asked quietly.

"Actually, no," Melissa frowned. "We have been granted substantial funds because of the werewolf appearances in 2019. That was fully reported up to ASIO, ASIS and the Department of Home Affairs. However, this mission suffers from a believability problem. The heads of each department are willing to accept the existence of some supernatural entities. Still, when it comes to gods and angels, it is a different story. 'Laughed out of the room' was the term Brett used when he discussed how his proposal for more staff went."

"Everything is coming under the anti-werewolf budget?"

"Yes, and now that the Department of Home Affairs considers that issue resolved, they presume we are doing research and prevention, meaning we are on minimal numbers."

"How many do we have?" Danni asked, feeling the unexpected weight of responsibility on her shoulders.

"The AST has two permanent members; Brett Sayer, the boss, and Liam Sager. Liam is leading team one, and I have been brought back on board to lead team two. Other members currently assigned to the AST are Matt Pyne and Ingrid Horjen, from ASIS and the police, respectively. They are with Mr Dare in Japan. I will be calling Teva Henry in from ASIO. He is more of a tech guy, but he was in Rome in 2019, so he is already familiar with the situation. We will also be taking Professor Malcolm Selleck with us; he has been the Australian Government's go-to historical artefacts guy for a long time. And lastly, there is you. That's it."

"So team two is me, you, Teva and Professor Selleck?"

"Yep."

"And what is our job?"

"We need to hunt down an artefact of Zeus. But before that, Brett has a task for us. In 2020, the AST assisted the United States Supernatural Occurrence Taskforce to take down a supernatural threat. They have kept him in the loop with their ongoing investigation, and we will check it out ourselves. I'm not sure how receptive the Americans will be to us showing up, but Brett believes that event is tied to increased cult activity around the world, which in turn could be tied to our mission. It is worth going there to check it out. Plus, if we get the Americans on side, we will get a lot more resources, so a friendly visit never hurts."

"Alright. That's a lot," Danni acknowledged.

"Our first stop is the USA. I recommend packing a bag."

"No problem, ma'am – I mean Melissa!" Danni said, standing up quickly and accidentally kicking the chair.

"Call me Mel," she said again, suppressing a grin.

• • • • •

INITIALLY, THEY'D MET WITH USSOT in Washington. Then, Mel had been called away for an important meeting in Japan. USSOT had invited the AST to join them in the Florida raid. They believed it was connected to the 2020 wendigo incident. They were asked to assist as additional manpower, apparently USSOT was spread thin.

Danni had spent a lot of the travel time reading and re-reading the documentation for Operation Thunderking. She wondered what it would be like to meet a god.

• • • • •

DANNI SNAPPED OUT OF PAST memories and got up. She began the trudge away from the lighthouse.

Before long, the beach was a distant memory as she sat beside Teva in the Tallahassee Police Station conference room. He looked stressed.

It was Teva who'd explained Melissa's connection to Apollo. While on the way from Washington to Florida, he'd told her the history of the Oracle of Delphi and how Melissa was a descendant

48

of that line. Teva said it gave Melissa special powers, though he wasn't specific on the details. Danni was beginning to notice that no one ever was.

A dishevelled and very travel-worn looking Melissa stepped into the room, followed closely by Malcolm Selleck.

"How was Japan?" Teva asked.

"Interesting," Mel said, taking a seat. "It seems both the US Government and The Old World are on board with our mission. Though, I'd hesitate to trust the latter too readily."

"What is the other team up to?"

"They are working at the direct request of Apollo and are headed for Israel as we speak. A group known as the Cult of Belial has revealed itself and is actively working against us."

She turned to Selleck and asked, "Any link to the cult here?"

"No. Whatever USSOT is tracking is far stranger than demon worshippers. I'm not sure what to make of it yet," Malcolm answered.

"Any link to the Greek gods or archangels at all?"

"Not as far as I can see, though it would be foolish to discard that possibility. Are we moving on soon?"

"Yep, team one is on the move, and we should be too," Mel replied.

"I'd like to stay," Malcolm proposed. "I will be happy to rendezvous when you find the location of an artefact. I can't shake the feeling that this cult in the backwoods of Florida is somehow important. The statuette we retrieved is just so... worthy of further study."

Mel allowed Malcolm's request. "Stay here and study the

statuette. While these events don't seem linked yet, like you said, we can't discount it."

"What is our plan?" Teva asked.

"We will fulfil our part of Operation Thunderking and find an artefact of Zeus."

"Do we have a lead yet?" Teva asked, frowning slightly. Danni was well aware that Teva's countless searches and delves into encrypted archives had revealed nothing. Melissa had asked him to keep an optimistic front to the boss of the AST, though, causing a situation where he was forced to outright lie.

Teva had also off-handedly mentioned how Melissa's divine connections were proving useless. The gods, when asked what memories they had of Zeus' possessions, just shrugged their shoulders. Hermes had wandered the world for a long time in disguise and hadn't come across anything. Apollo had said that everything significant to Zeus had been held on Olympus. Hermes assured him beyond a shadow of a doubt that Olympus had been wholly ransacked after Heaven's victory. In the old days, when Hermes could don a disguise and travel to Heaven freely, he'd never come across anything personal enough to count as an 'artefact of Zeus'.

There was hope that the powers of the Oracle of Delphi, possessed by Melissa, could give them somewhere to start. Though Melissa's journey to understanding and controlling her prophetic sight was a slow one. It worked well when prompted by Apollo or in a desperate situation, however, without either of those criteria, it worked completely at random.

"I don't have a lead, but, I do have an idea," Mel announced.

Danni leaned in.

"As you know, our godly allies haven't been very helpful. There is one god that we are aware of that we haven't been able to question. Apollo has a sister, Artemis, the Goddess of the Hunt. Apparently, she is fiercely independent. I say we find her and put forward a case for her to help us out."

Malcolm looked unsure. "Bold plan. Artemis is not a figure to be trifled with. Mythology tells us she is quick to anger and even quicker to vengeance."

"That may be so, but I don't see what choice we have. The other team is preparing to journey right into enemy territory, facing total unknowns. I don't want us to be the group that falls behind."

Danni was still overwhelmed by the unrestricted use of terms like *gods* and *Heaven*. It still didn't seem quite real. She wasn't sure why she found the idea of a man turning into a wolf on the full moon more palatable than an almighty Greek god being real; she just did.

Mel continued, "Brett Sayer and Fiona Shear of USSOT are in discussions right now about a joint approach to Operation Thunderking. So maybe we will get some USSOT support. For now, it is just going to be you, Danni and me."

"We got this," Danni said, speaking up at last and broadcasting her wide toothy smile.

Malcolm laughed.

"Where is Artemis?" Danni asked.

"Apollo said he found her in the United Kingdom. She wove herself into mythology up that way too. So that's where we are going."

"Bags already packed," Danni said.

"Malcolm, when you learn something about this cult, pass it on to me."

Malcolm nodded. He spoke up. "Mel, before you go rushing off, perhaps you could speak to USSOT's key captive?"

"Why?" Mel asked.

"Well," Malcolm started, his mind whirring into action as he spoke, "considering your gifts, you might be able to get something out of him."

Malcolm was clearly referring to Melissa's randomly working prophetic powers.

"I'm not sure it works like that…" Mel uttered.

"Well, in fairness, we have no idea the full extent of the abilities of the Oracle of Delphi. I only ask because the Florida Police are holding these people on the flimsiest of legal reasons, reasons which are due to expire very shortly."

"Will the police let me in to speak with him?"

"I will ask our fellows at USSOT. I'm sure it will be fine."

With that, the wheels were almost in motion; after a quick interview with a backwoods cultist, the hunt for Artemis would begin.

3

AN INTERVIEW WITH A MADMAN

TALLAHASSEE POLICE STATION
- JANUARY 21 -

The central Tallahassee Police Department was a long brown brick building with barred windows framed in white. It was beautiful in its simplicity. In the summer, rows of manicured bushes and bright green trees lined the station's front, giving the place a non-threatening look. In the heart of winter, however, the compound looked sterile and uninviting. The trees were bare, highlighting the dull exposed brick and cracked walls.

Once the Australian crew had passed the extensive waiting room packed with shady characters, they were ushered into a conference room. Both Danni and Malcolm had accompanied Mel. Teva had decided the best use of his time was further research.

The trio was met by the two USSOT members who'd been there for the raid. The thin, gangly USSOT agent, Kip, nervously picked at his moustache while Mel straightened her suit jacket. The other USSOT representative was named Marcus Coleman. He was of Caribbean descent and must've easily stood at six foot four. He was a former college athlete who'd had a stint in the military before moving into USSOT. Unlike with the AST, USSOT had perpetual positions available for those who were willing to pursue them. It was like any other government job, but with a higher degree of secrecy.

Danni found Marcus to be incredibly handsome. He cut quite the striking figure when standing beside his southern partner Kip, who was weedy and short.

"What makes you think she can get anything outta him?" Kip asked in his drawling southern accent.

Malcolm answered on behalf of Mel, "She is an expert in her field. Just trust me. She has a way of learning things that people try to keep concealed."

Danni sat on a chair in the corner of the room. Her eyes darted from poster to poster, reminding officers to turn off their body-worn cameras and when it was okay to use force. She caught Marcus's eyes lingering on her and hastily turned away.

Marcus, taking this awkward action as an invitation, dropped the pile of papers he was holding and sat next to Danni.

"We didn't get a chance to talk during the raid. The name's Marcus."

"Danni," she answered, shaking his hand.

"I like your accent," Marcus said.

"Thanks," Danni said coolly. "I wish I could say the same, but American accents just don't do it for me."

Marcus reeled back, feigning hurt. "Come on now… Actually, I do hear it. You might be right."

"Just kidding," Danni joked. "So, you guys are having no luck with the weirdo cult leader?"

"Straight to business, hey. I like a no-nonsense kind of girl."

Danni rolled her eyes.

Everyone else in the room were too glued to their tablets and mobile phones to pay much attention to Danni and Marcus. Except Kip, the other US agent, who shook his head and sighed.

"Is he your boss?" Danni asked.

"Who, Kip?" Marcus said, looking as if the mere suggestion was utterly ludicrous. "No, he is the more senior member of the two of us, but he's not my boss."

"How does USSOT work?" Danni asked.

"Well, each state has a regional manager. But most teams only have two or three members, usually attached to the FBI in the area. Then we have a national manager. Above him sits Captain Shear; she works out of the Pentagon."

"Wait, attached to FBI? So you guys actually solve crimes?"

"No. We investigate if there is something supernatural about a particular incident. Usually there isn't, but sometimes we get lucky."

"And what exactly does 'get lucky' mean?"

"There are the tell-tale signs of a supernatural entity being involved. We identify, discover a weakness, then enact an appropriate solution."

"Seems easy," Danni said nonchalantly.

"I'm not sure about that... I'm sure we can speak freely with each other here. What kinds of creatures have you encountered?"

Danni glanced towards Mel, unsure of what she was allowed to say. She figured USSOT already knew about werewolves because one had assisted them not so long ago.

"Werewolves," Danni said. "Two, actually."

"Scary creatures, though admittedly easy to kill. Single pop with a silver bullet and it's a goner."

Danni grimaced. She didn't like thinking about Joshua Dare being killed with a silver bullet.

"Well, yeah… but you still don't want one hunting you," she stated, a little defensively.

"I suppose. They are fast and deadly. And if you don't have silver, there is very little you can do. They heal from other injuries too quickly."

"You know your stuff," Danni remarked.

"Well, since werewolves came back onto the radar, thanks to you guys down under, we had to take a course."

"What about you? What got you into USSOT?" Danni wasn't just making small talk now; she was genuinely curious.

"I was in Iraq. Army Ranger. We had choppers going down in cleared areas with no sign of militia or rebels present. We were providing overwatch on a night-time supply drop and we saw what was downing our birds. It was an actual bird, like a huge bird. Al Rukh local legends called it. This thing could fit a baby elephant in one of its claws."

Danni was sceptical, even though Marcus had no reason to

lie.

"How does something that big stay hidden?"

"Al Rukh was no ordinary bird. It was supernatural... or ah, mythological, I should say. These things have a way of remaining undetected of their own accord. However, this one was being protected."

"Do go on," Danni said.

"I won't go into fine detail about how we killed the bird. Once we took out Al Rukh, I was drafted into the USSOT presence in Iraq and we came across another class of being. They were called djinns, and they used a sort of, well... magic. I know it sounds dumb, but I think they were protecting the giant bird with spells... or something." Marcus finished lamely.

"So, you have a lot of experience with the supernatural?" Danni asked, amazed.

"Yeah. Once we encountered the djinn tribes, it opened my eyes to what was out there. You see, they weren't so dissimilar from us. They looked humanish, and one of our guys even killed one in a fistfight. But they had powers they could use to hide or shape-shift into animals and use other magics."

"Did you kill them all?"

"No, not at all. USSOT's role in Iraq was to try and convince those creatures to assist the American war effort."

"Did they?"

"No," Marcus said flatly.

"Probably won't join you if you're gonna fight them."

"It challenged one of the USSOT guys to single-combat. It was a tough situation to navigate. It was a rite of passage in the djinn clan."

"Must have been a good fighter if the djinn is magical."

"That's the thing. Since the djinn is a magical being, their rites of passage weren't magical. They tested themselves and others in an unfamiliar field. The man from our ranks they picked is a Navy SEAL and a hell of a fighter. His name is Neanderthal; you might meet him."

"Not to circle back too much, but how exactly did you kill the magically protected giant bird?"

"That story is one best told over dinner," Marcus said with a wink.

"Oh," Danni mumbled, taken aback. She hadn't expected this guy to so boldly ask her out.

"I don't think you'll have time for any dinners," a voice called from across the room. It was Melissa, who had clearly been eavesdropping. "After this interview, we are wheels-up."

"Rain-check," Danni smiled, thankful for Mel's interjection.

Kip called Marcus over to double-check something on his laptop. He bade Danni a curt farewell before moving off.

The sheriff who'd led the raid on the cult was absent today. Apparently, he hadn't cared if the Australians spoke to the supposed ring-leader. Much like Malcolm had said, they were in a legal grey area holding them this long. Trumped-up environmental damage charges had been thrown at the group, even though the police and USSOT alike knew they wouldn't stick. What they wanted was information, and they were running out of time to get it.

Mel appeared to be getting annoyed at waiting so got up.

Kip yawned as Mel approached him.

"Is there any information in particular you're looking to get out of this person?" Melissa asked.

It was Malcolm who answered over the top of Kip.

"Yes! The name of the deity depicted in the statuette. Or a name of the cult!"

Melissa gave the professor a sharp, disapproving look.

He quieted down, and she turned her gaze to Kip.

"Ask about that black book," Kip said lazily.

"Black book?"

"Yep. When we went back the day after that ritual, we found a book half-buried in the dirt. Large and black with metal fixings. Looks like someone tried to hide it in a hurry. Missing a whole bunch of pages."

"And what do you want to know about it?"

"Lieutenant Commander Leeson recovered a book just like it in 2020, during the wendigo incident. Real funny writing. Bunch of rituals and spells, as far as I can see. This one is very similar, though it looks hand traced and the wording is slightly different. Like it's been translated from a different source." Kip put a toothpick in his mouth as he mulled it over.

"Large black book with metal clasps…" Melissa murmured. "What did the cover look like?"

"Like it had somethin' melted onto it at some point that has fallen off."

"Like a skull with tentacles?" Melissa asked, her eyes going wide.

"What is it?" Malcolm asked, sensing that Mel had just come to a revelation.

"I'll explain later," she answered hastily.

"You'll be interested to know," Kip added, "that the cult leader is also directly connected to that same incident. His son was in contact with a madman in Minnesota, and now resides in an insane asylum."

This had also piqued Danni's interest, though she didn't dare speak up. She'd read in her briefing papers about the incident in 2020. It was a wendigo from Native American folklore. A creature that was, for all intents and purposes, the physical manifestation of insatiable hunger.

Once again, that story involved Danni's former flame Joshua Dare. USSOT had discovered a monster in the Pine Island State Forest in Minnesota. They didn't quite know how to deal with it. Luckily, Australia had a monster of its own that they could borrow. There seemed to be an arbitrary rule that supernatural creatures had a chance of taking out other supernatural creatures due to their sheer natures alone.

During the showdown between the werewolf and the wendigo, it was discovered that the wendigo was enraged by the strange goings-on in a nearby cabin. The way Danni read it, it was akin to witchcraft. That's where the report ended. Now, it seemed that incident had ties to this cult in Florida.

The door to the conference room opened and a square-jawed police officer walked in.

"He's waiting in the interview room, ma'am," he said, nodding his head at Mel.

"Coming, Danni?" Mel asked.

"Oh, you want me to come too?"

"You are still very much in the training phase of your new job; the more experience you get, the better."

"Right," Danni said, standing up. She straightened her own jacket. Much like Mel, she was wearing a black pantsuit with a collared purple shirt beneath. It was the most formal clothing she had. The conversation about djinn and giant birds had really whetted her appetite to find out just what secrets this cult leader had to share.

Mel and Danni followed the police officer out of the room and down a short corridor. There were doors to the left and right marked INTERVIEW ROOM ONE and INTERVIEW ROOM TWO. Unlike in a lot of television shows, there was no room behind a mirror that observers could watch from. Kip, Marcus and Malcolm would be following the conversation via the security camera fixed to the roof.

The room itself was bland. There were only two chairs on either side of a rectangular metal desk.

Danni walked to the far-right corner and leaned against the wall while Melissa sat opposite the man. Danni nervously tucked her hair behind her ears.

The last time Danni had seen this individual, he was wearing a ceremonial robe with nothing underneath.

He looked quite different in his jail-loaned clothes. He was wrapped in grey overalls and his beard looked far less manicured. He had a musky, cigarette smell about him, yet despite his confinement, his eyes sparkled with a curious intensity.

"Last-ditch effort, hey?" he asked, folding his arms and smiling.

"You help me, and perhaps I can help you," Melissa responded.

"Oh, nice accent! Are you Australian? They've really gone left-field now."

"Yes, my name is Agent Pythia. And you are?"

"I'm sure you've already been well informed as to my identity, but hell, let's play the game. Dean Oswald."

"Nice to meet you, Dean," Mel said very formally. "I am led to believe you've been less than helpful in revealing just what you and the others were doing in the swamp."

"Yes, in time, all will be revealed. I'd hate to spoil the surprise," Dean grinned.

He was well-spoken and barely had a trace of an American accent. He looked to be a person who carried himself with quiet dignity. Danni wondered how such a person had become involved in such bizarre events. Most of the others who'd been at the ritual site looked like they had unaddressed hard drug habits. Dean didn't fit the mould.

"Who is the girl hiding in the shadows?" Dean asked, looking at Danni.

"Agent Quinn," Melissa answered.

"Is she the bad cop?"

"Perhaps," Melissa smiled. "Answer my questions clearly and we won't need to find out."

"Ask away," Dean said, stretching back in his chair.

"This cult of yours, any connection to the Cult of Belial?" Melissa asked, pulling a notebook from beneath her jacket and plopping it on the table in front of her.

"Never heard of the Cult of Belial," Dean shrugged.

"Does it have a name?"

"Not one whispered in ordinary circles."

"What about the statuette? What does it show?"

"You're really just going to ask me the same questions?" Dean yawned.

"Alright then, the book. Tell me about the black book."

"Oh, you know, just mad writings. The festival in the swamp attracts people who like to create their own fanciful works."

Mel smiled. "And if I were to tell you I was familiar with the writings of the mad Arab Alhazred, would you tell me the truth?"

Dean looked temporarily stunned but quickly regained his composure.

"If you were familiar with Abdul Alhazred, you would be able to tell me that book's name."

Danni didn't know where Mel had pulled the name Alhazred from, but it seemed to be an effective bluff.

Mel stared at Dean. From her vantage point, Danni couldn't see if Mel's eyes had flashed gold, meaning she was using her powers. However, the following words from the ASIO agent's mouth indicated something unusual had happened.

"Necronomicon," Melissa whispered. Danni felt a chill run through the room.

Dean's cocky attitude was immediately replaced with seriousness. "You are aware of dark things indeed," he murmured.

"Tell me about the Necronomicon," Mel said, pressing her advantage.

"It is the key to understanding future events," Dean uttered, leaning in towards Mel. "It is the only earthly resource we have to understand the *outside*."

"What do you mean by the outside?"

"There are impossible things in the darkness. Things whose gaze we cannot hide from forever. Drums bang and flutes play in the cosmic night. When the time comes, we will welcome what those sounds herald."

Danni found Dean's words adequately spooky but didn't really understand them.

"You worship a dark god? And this Necronomicon is like a bible?" Mel asked.

"No," Dean said quietly, almost fearfully. "This is beyond gods. The Necronomicon is both the door and the key."

"Door to what?"

Danni moved in closer; the two were whispering so quietly that she could barely hear them.

Suddenly, Mel reached out and grasped Dean's hand. Her whole body shuddered.

Danni instinctively placed her own hand on Mel's shoulder as she leaned in to check on her bosses rigid form.

As soon as Danni made contact, Melissa became a conduit. In Danni's mind she was pulled across space to somewhere unknown.

It was dark all around her. It was also cold… and wet. She couldn't breathe, but didn't need to. Distant lights floated high above, but they weren't stars.

Strange structures loomed in the darkness. They were buildings, but not buildings of any human design. The slimy, weedy

Cyclopean masonry of the towers, arches and spheres that stood around her filled Danni with a loathsome terror, one she'd never felt before. The city screamed of supreme horror. It compelled Danni to flee, but some unknown force dragged her through its depths towards a mighty black door.

The only sound was the frantic beating of Danni's heart. Just beyond the gargantuan door before her was a presence. She couldn't see it, but she could feel it. An alien mass was stirring. Some terrible, terrible thing was in there, and it was waking.

A monster of such coldness that its very proximity threatened to steal Danni's soul away.

Distorted voices chanted in the darkness around her.

"Ph'nglui mglw'nafh Cthulhu R'lyeh wgah'nagl fhtagn."

The voices grew into a booming chorus.

The statuette on the obelisk flashed to the forefront of her mind. It glowed a menacing orange, just like she'd seen it in the firelight.

"PN'NGLUI MGLW'NAFH CTHULU R'LYEH WGAH'NAGL FHTAGN!"

Danni screamed. Everything went black.

•••••

THE FIRST THING DANNI WAS AWARE OF was the thumping ache in her head, presumably from collapsing onto the carpeted floor. The next feeling was a tidal wave of shame. She'd actually blacked out during a criminal interview. It couldn't get any more embarrassing than that.

She was no longer in the interview room. She was lying on a small single bed in a room with the door propped open. On its face was a green cross. She'd been taken to a first aid area; the trauma kits stacked neatly on the bench erased any doubt. Sitting on a chair beside her was Marcus.

"Good morning, sunshine," Marcus said, very sarcastically, as Danni pushed herself up.

"Oh god," Danni mumbled.

"Hey, don't go too fast," Marcus stated, putting a hand on Danni's shoulder. "You hit the floor with a solid whack."

"What happened?" Danni asked, cautiously rubbing the lump on her head.

"Not sure; all three of you passed out. It was quite the sight."

"Where is Melissa?"

"She recovered a bit faster than you. She's in a debrief with Kip."

"And Dean Oswald?"

"Still in the interview room, though looking really freaked out. All three of you passing out at once in there just officially made this a USSOT matter, so those cultists won't be getting released anytime soon. We have at least a credible suspicion of supernatural involvement now. Win-win."

"For you maybe, you didn't pass out…"

"Don't worry about it," Marcus voiced kindly.

Melissa knocked on the door, then stepped inside. "How are you?" she asked Danni.

"Fine," Danni answered.

"What did you two see?" Marcus asked.

Mel shot him a look that plainly displayed that information was classified.

"Look, it isn't hard to tell you three experienced a shared vision," Marcus stated, looking annoyed.

"Well, I already gave my impressions to Kip. I'm sure he will tell you."

Marcus was clearly disappointed. Danni's mind flashed back to the visions. The foggy alien city in the dark. She felt like what she'd seen was underwater, but it was hard to tell.

"Danni, we have to get moving," Mel ordered.

"Marcus, right?" she said, turning to the tall, dark American sitting next to Danni. "It was a pleasure meeting you."

Marcus nodded as Danni got up. She said a quiet 'thanks' to him and promptly followed Mel out of the room.

"What was that?" Danni whispered to Mel.

"I'm not sure... but it was powerful."

"What do you mean?" Danni asked.

"I mean, I didn't look inside Dean's mind. Those visions weren't within him. And it certainly wasn't a look into the past or the future. I was used as a conduit to show us that underwater city."

"So it was underwater," Danni thought.

"Well, whatever it was we saw wasn't clear..." Danni muttered.

"I think... I wasn't shown any of that intentionally. It's like we were pulled into a dream we weren't meant to see."

Danni thought about the giant slimy black door and the horrible presence she'd felt behind it.

"Do you think it has something to do with an artefact of Zeus?" Danni asked.

"I don't know," Mel sighed. "I suspect it is connected to our mission in some way. We can ask Artemis when we find her. She may know something about sunken cities and formidable dreamers."

"So we are off to the UK?"

"Yep. The hunt for Artemis begins now."

4

FINDING ARTEMIS

LANCELTON, UNITED KINGDOM
- JANUARY 23 -

Danni impatiently tapped her foot on the sidewalk. Sitting on a blue metal alloy chair beside a small white table, she was doing her best to look like a British lady. She was draped in a textured coal blouse and floppy hat, and was catching the glances of people as they filtered by. She did look good. Her shiny black hair was parted in the middle and straightened, flowing from beneath her hat in a silky waterfall. The steaming mug of coffee in front of her sent its aromatic vapours up into the air. Danni's eyes lingered on a small brown vase with three brightly coloured flowers in the centre of the table. It was all very pretty.

The name of the café, on the other hand, wasn't pretty.

It was called 'Lady of the Brown Lake'. Danni thought it was particularly atrocious, filling the mind with images of the inside of a toilet bowl. Yet, it was quite scenic. A crumbling church on the other side of the street cast its long pointed shadows across the road.

It was a cloudless, sunny day in South England, something that was quite odd for the region. With its handcrafted flowerbeds and perfectly manicured hedges, the idyllic village was no place for the lower socio-economic. Middle-class families fussed over their children, looking for any signs of negative judgement from their peers.

The village was northeast of Glastonbury and had an odd boast; locals claimed it was the actual burial place of Lancelot, the legendary Arthurian knight. Common understanding said Lancelot was buried at Joyous Gard, a mythical place historians associated with Bamburgh castle. The people of Lancelton had their own folklore. They maintained that the Lady of the Lake, another Arthurian figure, was so distraught at the death of her adopted son Lancelot that she took his remains from Joyous Gard to their village.

Danni didn't know much about King Arthur and the Knights of the Round Table. She was having a hard enough time committing Greek mythology to memory, let alone a whole other set of fables. The part of Arthur's story that was important to her was the character of the Lady of the Lake. Even the most dedicated mythographers had difficulty determining where the lady came from and even what she was.

The Australian spies knew better than anyone. The Lady of

the Lake was the Greek Goddess Artemis. Ever proud and defiant, the goddess stayed one step ahead of the onslaught of the angels.

Artemis had continued to play a part in myth right until the end of Arthurian times. The death of King Arthur coincided with the prominence of Christianity in the region and her permanent withdrawal from the human world.

It was the God Apollo who'd managed to track his sister through history and legend to the site of mythical Avalon, which was now Glastonbury. Fortunately for Apollo, the magical protections Artemis had shielded herself with during the Middle Ages meant she'd never left.

Apollo had only offered fragments of the story to Mel, so they were working on educated guesses and predictions on where exactly to find her. Unfortunately, Mel had no direct way of contacting Apollo without putting herself in a perilous situation and hoping her powers activated. Apparently, the Golden God of Knowledge and Prophecy had been less than receptive to the idea of carrying a mobile phone with him.

The flight from Florida to London had been tedious. The subsequent drive west had continued that trend. Teva had elected to stay in London and speak with museum officials, ever on the hunt for an artefact of Zeus. That meant that this mission was just Mel and Danni.

Their objectives were to locate Artemis, then somehow convince her to join their cause.

They hadn't discussed the strange vision they'd seen in the interview room much further. Mel was relying on Malcolm to shed some light on what they'd witnessed.

The professor had been allowed access to the black book USSOT had unearthed in Florida. Malcolm had told Mel that some of the pages of the Necronomicon contained what looked like complex physics formulas.

Mel tasked him with finding a mathematician who could study them. They needed someone connected to the AST who would maintain the utmost secrecy. It was a challenging request, but Malcolm seemed optimistic. The man was positively giddy about studying the ominous black book. Danni felt like she'd been thrown into the middle of a really complicated story and didn't quite have a grasp on all the moving pieces yet.

The Lady of the Brown Lake's owner came out with a steaming pot and offered to refill Danni's mug.

"I'm okay, thank you!" Danni said, way too loudly in a terrible impersonation of a British accent.

"Where you from?" the owner asked. He leered at Danni through the half-moon spectacles on his nose.

"Obviously not from here," Danni answered, in her normal voice, dropping all pretence.

"Australian, hey," the owner stated as he poured the steaming liquid into her cup. "Bad time to visit Lancelton. Dark things about."

This caught Danni's interest.

"It seems lovely," she commented, taken aback.

"Tis normally, but we are cursed at the moment. The black shuck haunts us."

"The black shuck?" Danni asked.

"Omen of misfortune," the owner sighed. "See them about

sometimes, a bit of a local legend. Now they are appearing too much. Dark things for dark times…"

"What exactly is *the black shuck*?"

"Real mangy looking dog. Big too. Black as Satan's pit with eyes the devil's red. Seen 'em about at night."

"Probably just strays," Danni shrugged.

"Nope, they also have the devil's fire in their bellies. I just know they're searching for something. Can feel it in my bones. Some poor lost soul has the hounds of Hell after him. You'll know they are around when an unnatural mist sweeps over the place."

Danni didn't quite know about lost souls, but she could think of one being that hellhounds might be looking for.

"Where have these dogs been appearing?" Danni asked.

"Out on the moors. Don't be going out that way at night."

The owner nodded curtly and walked off. Danni thought the whole interaction had been strange, yet it might have yielded the clue they needed. She pulled a phone from her handbag and placed it to her ear.

"Danni," the voice of Melissa answered. "Any leads?"

"Yeah, apparently big black dogs have been seen congregating on the moor. The café owner seems to think they are a bad omen; possibly supernatural."

"Yep, I have heard the same. It is safe to assume that if we have a lead on Artemis, other forces might as well."

"The café owner called them hellhounds, so I'm guessing that's Lucifer's side," Danni vocalized slowly, feeling her conclusion could be brushed off as silly.

"It makes sense. They need the blood of Zeus to complete

the ritual. As a daughter of Zeus, we need to find Artemis before they do. If these dogs really are hellhounds, then they may have a master nearby. Find the dogs, but be discreet."

"Copy," Danni said simply.

She hung up the phone. In her pre-assignment reading, Danni had come across the Knights of Hell, a group of powerful monsters Melissa first encountered in 2019. According to Melissa's report, there were five knights on Earth, while the rest remained in Hell. One was a known adversary named Belial, who worked with a nefarious Vatican cardinal. Two of the other known knights had been turned to stone and were now presumed to be somewhere in the Saudi Arabian desert. That meant that there were still two out there undiscovered. If the master of the hellhounds was looking for Artemis, Danni was willing to bet it was a Knight of Hell.

• • • • •

DUSK APPROACHED. The air had a bracing chill as it rolled in from the vast expanse of grassland around the village. Both Danni and Melissa were rugged up in thick layers of warm clothing. Each had a belt with a covert holster and pistol around their waists.

The day's attempt at intelligence gathering had proved unsuccessful. People spoke in hushed whispers about the black shuck while others told tales of shadowy figures walking the moors. Danni hadn't seen any demonic black dogs or Knights of Hell around the village.

In the late afternoon, Mel had decided a reactive approach would be best. They'd find a nice lookout and hope to see the hellhounds.

The moors around Lancelton looked threatening in the twilight. The shadows of the sparse trees stretched wide, contorting into grotesque shapes that reached over the grass and bogs. Their gnarled hands gripped at unseen things in the rolling hills.

"Big black dogs on the moors, it's all very Sherlock Holmes, isn't it?" Mel joked.

Danni didn't know how it was very Sherlock Holmes, but nodded as if she did.

"From all reports you did well in the Florida mission," Mel commented. She turned towards Danni.

Both women had jet black hair, though Mel's was longer and wavier, falling past her shoulders.

Danni looked into Melissa's stern face. She didn't look old, though she was almost a decade older than Danni.

"I didn't do much to be honest," Danni mumbled.

"Don't ever diminish your contribution, that's not allowed on my team," Mel commanded, half-joking and half-sincere.

"Sorry boss," Danni smiled.

"I know it is only early days, but how have you found it so far?" Mel asked.

"Good. Other than feeling like I'm always in over my head…"

"That feeling never goes away, Danni. You know, when I joined ASIS I wasn't brave or confident. I was a fish out of water just like you. But I knew what my job was and I knew what was right."

"But-"

"But what?"

"Well, I don't want to be rude and I really don't mean to be, but you're some sort of mythical figure with a destiny. Not just a nobody."

Danni held her breath, worried Mel might shout at her. To her amazement, she just laughed.

"I only found out I was the Oracle of Delphi in 2019. I'd had 28 years of being an ordinary person before that. Look, Danni, if I can impart one lesson to you it is this; it isn't your past or future that matters. It is the actions you take right now in this moment. Do the right thing and believe in yourself, and everything will fall into place."

Danni did find that notion comforting.

"I had an unfulfilling job in Sydney. All of my friends were shallow and toxic. My grandfather saw that my life was lacking something and warned me before he died. I took a chance, just like you have, and ended up here, looking for a goddess of all things!"

"It is pretty wild," Danni admitted.

"I did the background checks on you, Danni, and I know you've come from a pretty rough background. Don't lose sight of the here and now and you will accomplish great things," Mel said kindly.

Danni didn't feel so reassured. Unpleasant images began playing like a slideshow through her mind.

She saw an empty liquor bottle flying over her head and exploding against the wall as her parents raged at each other. She saw herself fleeing home at seventeen, abandoning school and accepting a crummy job to gain a desperate sliver of independence.

She saw one of her ex-boyfriends in his triple XL clothing standing over her while she cowered in a corner.

Danni shook those images from her mind. She hastily wiped a tear away.

"Who are you now?" Mel asked quietly.

"Just Danni…" Danni sniffed.

"Agent Quinn of the Australian Government. Part of the team that will find an artefact of Zeus and stop the forces of Heaven and Hell."

"Agent Quinn," Danni murmured. Mel was right. Her past didn't define her and her future was brighter than anyone in her family's had ever been. She was going to prove herself.

"Just wanted to be sure you were aware of your own power before we confront one of the most powerful women who has ever lived," Mel remarked happily, pulling up a pair of binoculars from around her neck and scanning the horizon.

Mel had decided their best option was to climb a hill by the main road and, from that high vantage point, observe the surrounding grasslands to see if anything satanic spawned.

"If nothing happens tonight, would it be worth just getting a car and driving around the moors? Maybe we will bump into Artemis?" Danni asked after an hour, sounding deflated.

"Apollo said the angels never found her out here because she'd protected herself magically. I suspect that a person searching for Artemis could never find her," Mel frowned.

Danni scanned the horizon with her own binoculars again. It was almost time to switch to the thermal function.

The grip magic hour had on the countryside was lessening

as night slowly crept in.

"Do you know much about the Lady of the Lake?" Mel asked Danni.

"No," Danni answered truthfully. "Do you?"

"The stories of King Arthur never really interested me. A lot of it is an amalgamation of different people and stories that ye-olde writers put together. How exactly Artemis factors in, I'm not sure."

"I have heard of Arthur and Merlin," Danni shrugged.

"It's funny, go back a couple of years and I would've said there wasn't a historical basis for Merlin. He was a fictional character through and through. Nowadays, who knows? He probably was real," Mel said.

"The way that USSOT guy, Marcus, spoke about giant birds and magic people in the desert of Iraq, it kinda seems like everything is real…"

"We are lucky in a sense," Mel noted. "Here we are, working on the very forefront of knowledge. We are writing the pages of a secret history. Perhaps like Merlin did centuries ago. People see him as a story; maybe we will be stories too? Fanciful tales to hide secret truths."

"It isn't so secret, though, is it?" Danni added.

"What do you mean?"

Danni chose her words carefully, "Look at Apollo. For a very long-time, people believed him to be real. Then collectively, for whatever reason, people decided he wasn't. The history we are writing isn't secret at all. It has been told for a long time. People have just been ignoring certain parts of it. They have chosen to believe some parts are real and some aren't. It actually makes a lot of sense to me that basically everything is real."

"You have a point," Mel replied. "Again, maybe one day, like with Merlin, people will assume Danni Quinn and Melissa Pythia, the agents who fought against the apocalypse, were fictional too."

"I hope the author of our story does a decent job of it. Anyway, what do you know about Merlin?" Danni laughed.

"Oh, right. Merlin was an advisor to kings, namely Uther Pendragon and his son Arthur. It was on his advice that the fellowship of the Knights of the Round Table be established. It was he who stated that Uther's heir would reveal himself by pulling the mighty sword Excalibur from the stone."

"I've heard all of these stories in passing," Danni said brightly.

"I only learned this while wandering around Lancelton today. What I find interesting about Merlin, despite his origins in Celtic mythology, is how he was interwoven with elements of Christianity. During King Arthur's time, Merlin was a prophet of the Holy Grail. His magic seems to have been a bridge across two worlds."

"What happened to him?" Danni asked.

"Some versions of his story say he fell madly in love with the Lady of the Lake who sealed him away in a magical forest forever. It certainly sounds like something Artemis would do."

"Speaking of Artemis! Look!" Danni exclaimed.

Something had caught her eye.

Several black shapes were moving at high speed through the grass in the distance. They had the general outline of dogs.

"Let's move," Mel ordered.

Both Mel and Danni could cross vast distances quickly, jumping across puddles and skirting around trees. The moor was a hazardous landscape to navigate in the growing gloom. Sinkholes and hidden bogs slowed their pursuit considerably. They'd seen the dogs from too far away, and after twenty frantic minutes of running, had completely lost them. Fortunately, the dogs had left an unmistakable foul odour in the air. It was the putrid smell of rotten meat, only magnified a thousand times.

Resolute, the two women kept quiet and followed the smell further into the tangled darkness of the moor. The shrill hoots of owls kept them company in the dimming twilight. Occasionally, they heard a distant rumbling bark.

Danni privately hoped they hadn't followed a pack of stray dogs into the wilderness. The pair pushed through a clump of trees and were met with a spectacular sight. Just up ahead was a small hill, and from behind that hill, silver beams of light were igniting the blackening sky. It was a beacon. Was it a beacon for them?

"Is that Artemis? Is she calling the dogs to her?" Danni whispered.

"Come on," Mel mumbled, once again picking up the pace.

They scrambled up the hill. When they neared the top, as a precaution they began slowly crawling through the grass. They could see another grassy mound ahead, with the silver light springing from the gap in between the two hills.

Then, they saw her.

Standing in the natural dip in the landscape was the shining figure of a goddess.

Melissa raised her binoculars.

"What do you see?" Danni asked through chattering teeth. The wind was cold, and now that they were still Danni felt its icy touch.

"Silver Artemis," Melissa breathed. She passed the binoculars to Danni.

She peered through them. What she saw was nothing short of amazing. She saw a god.

Her auburn hair danced in the wind. Artemis wore a tiara of intertwined twigs and vines of the most vibrant green. Several small flowers sprung from it and flashed an array of colours; blues, pinks and yellows. Her unworldly piercing blue eyes radiated divine authority.

Danni ogled at the sleek strapless dress falling like mist around her. The dress was of the purest silver, unblemished by impurities. Not a line or wrinkle crossed it. From her upper thighs down, it became increasingly opaque until it vanished into nothing. Danni could see it was from the dress that the blinding beams of light were originating and in that light, several creatures moving.

Beside the goddess were a doe and her fawn. The fawn pranced playfully through the tall grass while the mother bent her head into Artemis, nuzzling her. A large owl was circling low, close to the goddess's head. Danni could see hedgehogs and squirrels scampering around her bare feet.

Melissa muttered very quietly to Danni, "The animals are a bit of overkill, don't you think?"

"What do we do now?" Danni asked as she handed the binoculars back to Mel. "Should we shout out so that she knows we're here?"

"Oh, she is well aware of our presence," Mel muttered.

Danni peered down into the field and could clearly see that Artemis was staring at them.

"Should we go down to her?"

"I don't know," Mel said slowly. "I feel that there is something else... a reason to stay up here."

All Danni could feel was the cold wind.

Artemis waved her hand, and her animal companions scattered away through the grass.

The moor was eerily silent, and nothing moved for several long seconds.

Then they came.

Cresting the hill behind Artemis and leaving streams of fire in their wake, the beasts moved as a pack.

They were swift and nimble. The dogs had fur so matted it looked like bubbling pockets of skin that had formed into hardened black lumps. Their jaws stretched open abnormally wide in a serpentine fashion. Their heads were too large for their bodies, giving them a crocodilian look.

The creatures were black, save for their orange underbellies and gleaming red eyes. A similar deathly orange glow sprang from the clamping jaws each time they yapped. Danni noticed the trail of small flames that followed their paws quickly died in the wind. These dogs were fire omens.

The black shucks were heralded by a carpet of mist sweeping over the moor. It came like a freight train barreling down the slope towards Artemis.

The pack was four strong. They nipped at each other excitedly as they approached the goddess.

Danni turned her binoculars to Artemis. The goddess summoned a gleaming silver bow from seemingly nowhere. She readied an arrow from the newly emerged quiver on her back and loosed it.

The silver shaft zoomed through the night towards the closest dog. Her accuracy was impeccable.

With a spray of blood and fire, the lead dog went tumbling into the mist.

Artemis looked pleased with herself as she readied another arrow.

The mist rushed forward in advance of the dogs, completely obscuring the view below.

"What do we do?" Danni asked Mel. The swirling mist was so dense all hope of seeing the attack was lost.

Mel shook her head. Danni watched her eyes flash gold.

"What are you trying to do?" she asked. Danni was feeling somewhat panicked.

"I can do this thing…" Mel said, sounding frustrated. "I can look at a supernatural creature and it becomes susceptible to human weapons. We can shoot the dogs with normal bullets, but it is hard to control."

"We shouldn't need to help, though, surely… she is a goddess."

"When I spoke to Brett Sayer, the boss, today, he passed on word from Liam Sager and the other team. Their mission was a success, with one exception. Apparently, the angels are about to start watching the world again for godly powers, if they aren't already. If Artemis got the message too, it means she can't fight these things with any of her divine power, or she will summon a horde of vastly more powerful monsters here."

"But she just summoned a bow from thin air?" Danni questioned. "Isn't that divine power?"

"The rules take a while to wrap your head around," Mel said quickly. "The gods have things bound to them they can call upon; it's the same as you pulling a knife from your pocket. Similarly, their enhanced strength and speed are just part of their nature; they aren't using any power to do that. If she starts shooting fireballs, then we are in trouble. The angels would know it and come."

"So, we need to try and help her?" Danni asked, somewhat understanding.

"Try being the operative word."

Mel stood up. So did Danni.

Below them, the thick blanket of demon-spawned fog was beginning to light up with flashes of orange and silver.

Resolute, both women began sliding down the hill into the mist below.

Danni quickly lost sight of Mel.

The fog was too thick to navigate. She carefully stepped forward, unable to see her feet below her. A well-placed stone saw Danni fall head over heels and begin tumbling down the hillside. With a face full of dirt, she pushed herself out of the muck.

"Goddammit," she muttered.

Something whooshed passed her and thudded into the mist behind. A large creature had just been thrown with considerable force in Danni's direction.

Danni quickly turned. A corridor of air had opened up in the cloud. At the end of that corridor, a huge black dog was getting to its feet.

Its red eyes locked onto Danni.

"Black shuck!" Danni squeaked. She lifted up her sweater and drew her pistol from the covert holster on her belt. She pointed the front sight at the head of the dog and moved her finger to the trigger.

Seeing the monster up close brought a terror into Danni she hadn't felt since the night at the junkyard in 2019. Two werewolves had come for her that night. Now, she was even more frightened. The werewolves had a human element to them, but the black shuck was alien in its physical horror. There was no detail in its glowing eyes. They were saucers of red death leering at her. Its long thin tail, covered with wet drooping hairs, twitched. The black shuck's crocodilian snarl carried with it a primal dread. Not the dread that came from facing an animal, but the fear of a child convinced a monster lingered under their bed. This was a beast born in the tortured grasp of Hell, and now it was facing Danni.

The dog growled. The rumbling from its fiery throat reverberated through the small valley. The muscles beneath its matted fur and bubbled skin tensed. Then the dog exploded forwards. It was on top of Danni before she had time to react. She frantically fired her gun but the shot went wide.

The dog collided with her, knocking her backwards and sending the gun careening away into the endless fog.

Danni's back cracked as she felt the weight of the dog's two front paws on her chest. Its long jaws opened wide around her face. The rows of yellow teeth and revolting stench were nauseating as she stared helplessly down its gullet.

Danni twisted to the side, dislodging the beast's tenuous grasp of her and narrowly avoiding its clamping jaws as they buried themselves into the earth.

The black shuck had attacked with ravenous force. Spitting dirt, it turned and leapt for Danni again, but she was already on her feet and running blindly into the fog.

There was no silver light or orange glow anymore. Just the all-consuming grey mist offering no path to salvation.

Gunshots rang out. It had to be Mel firing nearby.

Danni spun on the spot, only to have the wind knocked out of her by the pouncing dog. She felt its teeth slide into her torso. Then, she felt its crushing bite.

Time slowed.

Danni's eyes went wide as she spat up blood. The black shuck had got her. She felt her ribs break and the bones puncture her lungs as the beast clamped down and thrust her into the ground.

Like a ragdoll, Danni was tossed back and forth with ease. In the chaos, she thought about how foolish she'd been to come here. Why had she thought she could be part of events greater than herself? There wasn't even any pain, just despair as the jaws ripped her open. The dog released, its teeth dragging chunks of Danni's flesh away.

The black shuck's focus shifted. A silver arrow flew from the mist and landed right between its eyes. The dog collapsed.

"Foolish girl," a cold voice said. "I cannot heal you here,

or they will come. If you desire to live, you will hold on as we descend through fire and flame. You have walked into a trap set for a goddess."

Danni spat up more blood. Her body was broken, and the last embers of life within her were dying. "Artemis?" she breathed.

The cold voice didn't reply. Yet through the corner of her eyes, Danni could see glowing beams of silver light.

Danni felt arms hoist her up. Melissa was here. She was doing her best to lift her injured comrade out of the dirt.

There was a chorus of barks. The dogs were now circling the women. Their growls weren't random, instead seeming in tune and melodic. Danni was growing more and more delirious.

Even with her fading vision, Danni saw the ground below her start splintering with glowing red lines. Fire was carving a shape beneath them. A five-pointed star.

"Hold on, Danni," Mel said.

"What's…happening?" Danni choked, her voice hoarse and feeble.

Mel didn't have time to answer as the ground opened up. They began falling through glowing rock into impossible heat.

Danni never hit the ground.

5

CONVERSATIONS WITH DEMONS

HELL
- JANUARY 23 -

Floating in the void between living and death, clinging to the smallest tether of the golden thread of life, hovered Danni.

The pain of the bone-crushing bites slowly began to feel dull and distant. As the pain ebbed her consciousness returned and she was surprisingly clear of mind.

Danni no longer felt the supporting arms of Melissa or the cold presence of Artemis. She was alone, floating in a sea of tranquility.

"Open your eyes, girl," an unusual voice commanded. It was strained and unsettling to hear.

Still, Danni did as it asked.

An alarming scene confronted her. She was floating above her own body, which was lying atop an airborne pillar of rock surrounded by red floating islands. Everything was suspended in a sea of grey mist; the same mist that had haunted the moor and aided the hellhounds.

A nearby floating slab of stone was slowly rotating. As it turned, it revealed a black iron throne on its flatter side. The armrests ended in pronated claws piercing the air around them. A ghoulish face was carved into the headrest.

While the demonic chair was an odd sight, its occupant was far more startling.

Sitting cross-legged, wearing the bottom half of a Roman tunic, was a pot-bellied man. Well, some of him was a man, at least. His bare chest was unnaturally black, like he was made of gleaming stone. His head was also black but alarming for a different reason. Sitting on his human neck was the head of a midnight stallion. The horse head was wearing a bizarre high crown that consisted of a silver stick with three purple feathers attached. Sprouting from his rear end, bunched uncomfortably behind him, was the magnificent plume of an oversized peacock.

The stone stopped turning, and the devilish horse-man eyed Danni's floating spirit.

"A mortal caught in the fading echoes of life, fascinating," the creature exclaimed.

Danni noticed that he wasn't talking to her mangled body below but looking directly at her spectral form.

"Danni," she said simply.

"I appreciate the courtesy," the throne-bound monster said,

slightly bowing his enormous head. "My name is Adramelech."

"I have a lot of questions," Danni grimaced, unsure how to continue.

"Yes, I'm sure you do. It is a thing that has always annoyed me about mortals. Yet it has been such a long time since I have encountered one of you."

"Am I dead?" Danni asked.

Adramelech pondered the question. "No. Looking at you, you are most certainly on the verge of death. But that has been postponed for administrative purposes."

"Huh?"

"Danni, my dear, you seem to have fallen through a gateway between dimensions. I rather suspect one of the earthbound angels put a great deal of time and effort into creating such a trap. It certainly wasn't for you."

"Oh, so where am I?"

"This is a waiting area of sorts. For mortals, I mean. Hasn't really been used since the 14th century. I haven't had much to do."

"Okay… so, who are you?" Danni felt obliged to ask.

"I am Hell's administrator. Back when mortals visited the domain of Lord Lucifer through the proper channels, I used to take their details and admit them. Hades had a gate and a guard dog; we implemented a more civilised approach."

"So, I'm not dead, but I am in Hell. Great."

"Yes, it says here that the portal you were falling through was set to enter Hell's Seventh Circle… ah, third ring."

"What does that mean?"

"Well, that whole region is the playground of Astaroth. He

is quite the person to know down here."

"That is two A sounding names in quick succession," Danni mumbled nervously. "I will forget them both."

"I will send him word that a dying mortal is coming down. Perhaps he will have pity on you. These Knights of Hell often harken back to the days when they were angels."

Danni gulped. So, the Knight of Hell on Earth, who commanded the black shucks, had intended to send Artemis to one of his brethren in Hell. She and Mel had just been caught up in it. Why had Artemis just gone with it? It was like she'd called the hellhounds to her...

Adramelech frowned. He looked off into the shimmering mist.

"There are two others in line behind you. One seems incredibly resistant to remaining in a timeless stasis while we chat."

"Oh yeah, good luck with that," Danni said quietly.

"These could be your last moments of life, Danni," Adramelech stated, rising from his throne. His plume of peacock feathers spread out in a glittering fan behind him. "Though I hope not, for your sake. There is no worse place for a soul to be stuck."

The strange man-horse-peacock hybrid stamped his foot on the ground. The spectral version of Danni zoomed back into her body, and she continued falling.

As Adramelech faded from view, he shouted, "If you do survive and meet that mad Viking down there, tell him to give me back my key!"

The wind rushed past Danni's ears, then there was nothing. The pain of a broken body began overloading Danni's senses upon her second awakening in Hell. She was no longer a spectral vision floating above herself. She was very much within her own shattered torso again.

Danni tried to breathe through the choking hot air. She coughed up blood from her punctured lungs instead. She felt the sizzling dirt below burning her skin.

"You have about one minute," another unfamiliar voice stated. "So, I will be fast. Adramelech told me of your current predicament. Accept this deal and I will save your life."

Danni felt a cool metal object appear in her left palm.

"This item can be used to bring me into the mortal world if you follow the steps correctly. Agree right now and I will save you," the voice offered.

Danni coughed up blood.

"Disagree and you will die here. Then your soul will remain in most unpleasant company. What say you, human?"

Danni's vision was growing dim. The instinct for self-preservation took control. Like a rogue captain commandeering a ship, her will to live made her gurgle a simple, "Yes."

A serene warmth flowed over her. Danni felt it begin in her feet and travel upwards. It was a river of healing that washed her injuries away. Within a moment, she felt fine. Better than fine, in fact. Even the dirt and the air stopped burning.

Danni Quinn was still alive.

She rolled over.

Standing beside her was a muscular, naked man. Only, he wasn't really a man. From his back spread two black bat wings. His face was abnormally long and strikingly ugly. Wriggling around in his right hand was a hissing viper. He wore a gold crown on his head. Beneath it, a curly thicket of brown hair ran down past his ears. His lengthy drooping nose and bulging fish-like eyes made him appear comical. He was like a caricature brought to life.

The naked man held out a hand and Danni grasped it. With no effort whatsoever, he whipped Danni onto her feet.

"Astaroth," he said, crossing an arm across his body and bowing low. As he bent forward, Danni saw dozens of tiny black claws lining his wings.

"Danni," Danni replied again. It was like she was completely refreshed. She felt alert and aware. She began soaking in the scenery around her.

She was standing on a scorched plain under a red cloudy sky. High above, glowing embers were falling from the clouds and floating towards the ground. The entire area was flat as far as the eye could see, save for some rocky mounds periodically rising above the dirt. In the far distance, she could see a ruined city cresting the horizon.

"Bloody hell," Danni murmured to herself.

Danni and the demonic Astaroth weren't the only beings present. Lines of chained creatures were hauling large stones on their backs. They looked human, except their skin was a sickly grey and they appeared devastatingly malnourished.

There were large cages all around with some featuring ghoulish looking people inside, frantically banging against the bars. Their hands were bloodied and broken, with protruding pieces of bone clashing against the metal. Yet they continued ceaselessly banging away, a hopeless madness filling their vacant eyes.

Wailing moans carried through the air. From not too far away, the pings of pickaxes hitting hard stone could be heard. Danni turned back to the grotesque thing that had saved her.

"You are a Knight of Hell?" Danni asked.

"Yes," Astaroth replied, sounding surprised. "You know us?"

"I know *of* you. I guess I should say thank you for saving me."

"No thanks needed. Keep your end of our bargain and that will be thanks enough."

Danni jumped back in fright as a large black dog came running towards Astaroth. It was a black shuck. It looked at Danni with contempt, then playfully began licking the demon.

"Hellhounds," Astaroth explained, petting the dog. "Been a long time since these things walked in your world. The splinters from the incident in 2019 continue to magnify. Creatures like this can slip through to the mortal world again, just like in the good old days."

"They don't sound like good old days to me. One of those almost killed me," Danni said scornfully.

"Oh, not for you mortals. Back in your medieval ages, we used to send hellhounds to drag humans here who hadn't made good on their oaths and promises. They can walk the world completely invisible if they choose to."

While Astaroth played with the dog (with his one free hand - the viper he held in the other was writhing furiously), Danni looked at the object that had appeared in her palm. It was a wide circular medallion made chiefly of bronze. Different precious metals seemed to be randomly interspersed through its shining surface. On its face was the image of an angel dressed in armour wearing a helmet fashioned in the form of a snake's head. The angel was upside down, and all around it were the carved depictions of monstrous things reaching out for him.

"That is an angelic seal. Walk with me," Astaroth commanded.

Danni, seeing no other option in this hellscape, began following Astaroth. They moved in the opposite direction of the procession of chained grey rock-haulers.

It was only now that the enormity of what had just happened hit her. She'd almost died. On her second assignment with the AST, a supernatural dog had brought her within seconds of death. And now, she was in Hell. By the looks of it, she was all alone too...

Danni laughed, and Astaroth gave her a quizzical look.

Danni felt a wave of elation wash over her. No matter what happened now, she couldn't screw up worse than this. If anything, this is exactly what she needed to happen. It could only go uphill from here. Danni was emboldened by a surreal new confidence as she absorbed the absurdity of it all.

One of the chained grey creatures fell, and Astaroth promptly summoned a whip of fire and brought it down upon the struggling thing.

"Hey! What are you doing?" Danni blurted out, running toward the hurt being.

Before she could take more than two steps, she felt invisible ropes bind her in place.

"Do not feel so inclined to protect these poor misshapen

things. They are here as punishment."

Danni looked around in horror. Were all these enslaved creatures people?

"How can you do this?" she asked.

Astaroth released the magical hold he'd placed on Danni and continued strolling forward. "They are sinners. Sinners whose crimes were large enough that they were noticed. Do not pity the damned. Pity the living who will make all the wrong choices and end up here."

Danni frowned. In her renewed state, she wanted to challenge the demon's statement. Trudging through the burning hellscape, she felt completely at the mercy of otherworldly forces, so why not speak her mind?

"Are their sins, like, biblical sins? Because what religion defines as evil isn't always right."

Astaroth cocked his head toward Danni and said, "Religion doesn't factor into Hell as much as you might think. It is all very complicated and I fear I don't have time to explain it in a satisfactory way."

"Try me," Danni said.

Astaroth sighed. "Well, you are right, of course. Evil and good are subjective. But Lucifer doesn't care for the decrees of the Bible or any other holy book. In the early days of our imprisonment down here, Lucifer looked at the punishments divined by the Greek gods in Tartarus. Sisyphus eternally pushing that boulder up the hill, Tantalus unable to quench his thirst or sate his hunger. Famous names for famous punishments."

Danni nodded. She had actually heard the story of the man

who was punished by having to push a boulder up a hill. It would always roll back down when he got it to the top.

"Not many people know this, but Lucifer actually doesn't care that much about humans. He never did. He was young, cocky and arrogant when we seized the Underworld. It was only during his long imprisonment in the dark that he started watching you humans up there. He saw you craft narratives about him. You named him as the one who punished the damned. In his boredom and his anger, he made good on it. When re-shaping the Underworld, he created different lands where souls guilty of certain crimes would come by default. He set the bar high too. Lucifer is not so blind that he cannot see that all beings make mistakes. He and Michael are alike in that regard; they are both big on redemption."

"What crimes bring people here?" Danni asked.

"Violence. Here, specifically, the people are guilty of blasphemy."

Danni paused. "Hold on, blasphemy? Really?"

"Don't think of it as a person is living in a Christian country saying 'God isn't real'. That is no crime. These souls committed a blasphemy that offends Lucifer. They pledged themselves to ideals, enforcing them through horrible violence and in doing so, breaking the truth of the ideal itself."

Danni struggled to put that together in her head. "Right, so like a person who is committed to peace who then starts killing people to obtain that peace."

"Yes, very good!" Astaroth beamed, his eyes gleaming. "If you were to enter this circle of Hell by normal means, you'd first come across a river of boiling blood. In it, you would see the preserved souls of murderers, war-makers and tyrants who are forever boiling. Truly evil people."

"But surely Lucifer didn't do all this because he was bored? What does he care if some dictator somewhere committed genocide?"

"Time and boredom are some of the greatest motivators any being can have. Remember, it was the humans who decided that he was already doing this. He just made those statements true."

"So, it was time, boredom and contempt for people making up rumours about him?" Danni interpreted, still sceptical.

"More or less," Astaroth smiled. "Grand things happen all the time for the smallest of reasons. Speaking of grand things…"

Danni hadn't even realised they'd approached the edge of a cliff. Below her stretched an enormous quarry full of hundreds of tortured souls. They lined its many layers of chipped rock, working in unison to collect huge stones and transport them up a long ramp onto the plane. It looked like a gruelling and challenging task.

At the very base of the quarry were some unusual sights. One of them was as shocking as it was impressive.

Bound in enormous chains fastened to the rock floor was a red dragon.

"Oh my god," Danni gasped. She was looking at a real dragon.

Standing on the edge of that precipice, Danni felt the weight of fear and uncertainty fall over her again. The brief boost of confidence she'd received from her near-death experience faded as she stared at the scaly beast far below.

Was this a dream or a waking nightmare? How had she been

in an English town one minute, then found herself talking to horse-headed demons and dragons the next? Things were moving too fast for her to properly comprehend the enormity of it all.

She took a deep breath and calmed herself. This was just like her spy training. She'd felt out of place there too, but she'd resolved herself to get through it. That's what she'd do now. She was sick of feeling existential dread every time a new situation confronted her, no matter how farfetched it was.

Not far from where the dragon was chained was a square elevated platform. It was dark grey all over with glowing blue runes carved across it. It looked like a demonic boxing ring. Right in the middle, the largest rune glowed ominously; resembling the letter T inside a crescent moon.

"Take my hand, little human," Astaroth said, stretching his thin fingers towards her. Danni deposited the angelic seal in her pocket.

That simple action made her realise the ludicrous amount of clothes she was wearing. She'd been dressed for warmth in England and quickly discarded her layers of sweaters before taking the offered hand in her own.

Astaroth leapt forward, dragging Danni with him. Held up by unknown magic, the two of them floated down the cliff-face to the bottom of the quarry.

When Danni's feet touched the ground, she quickly turned towards the chained dragon. It was even more magnificent up close.

As the entire scorched plain seemed to have been designed using only shades of red, the blood-red scales of the dragon matched its surroundings perfectly. A long horn sprouted from the front of its upper jaw and pointed forward. It had large yellow eyes and two prominent ears at the back of its elongated skull. An iron muzzle was locked around its jaw, causing smoke to billow from the dragon's nostrils. Beneath its cheeks sat a plume of red fur that lined the underside of its throat.

Danni could see the creature's two wide membranous wings folded across its back, held fast by the chains that looped it. The dragon had two front limbs, clasped with heavy shackles and two hind limbs. The only part of the dragon that the chains didn't hold in place was its forked tail, which flicked back and forth furiously. The scale of the beast was hard to imagine while it was so neatly pinned to the ground.

"The dragon is a child of Herensuge, a rather nasty dragon that Archangel Michael killed a long time ago," Astaroth commented, noting Danni's interest.

"None of that means anything to me," Danni replied brightly. Her self-doubt had now been replaced by wonder as she stared at the mythological marvel.

The dragon looked back at her, almost knowingly.

"Why is it in Hell?" Danni asked.

"Before the border to Hell was sealed, all the European dragons were rounded up and sent here. Dragons are intelligent in their own right, and their presence became an annoyance to the angels sending prophets to convert the masses. This one is chained here because he kept swooping down and eating my quarry workers."

"Dragons eat souls?"

"In the physical world, they eat physical things. In the supernatural world, they eat supernatural things. Dragons are inherently magical in nature."

"Why not just kill all the dragons?"

"That is the odd thing about dragons. Of all magical creatures, they are strangely immune to the power of prayer. An angel, or archangel for that matter, will always fight a dragon at its level, no matter how strengthened that angel is. You can see how the legions of Heaven would find this problematic."

"Fair enough," Danni shrugged. It sounded like the best way to defeat the overpowered archangels in Heaven could be as easy as unleashing a dragon on them. Danni took a mental note of this.

The look of longing in the dragon's eyes was unmistakable. Danni wondered how she could break the chains fixing it to the ground. An angry dragon could provide a useful distraction.

"What is this boxing ring thing?" Danni asked.

The dark grey slab had pointed pillars in every corner with holes that looked specially designed for thick wire.

"My brother on Earth is sending me a gift, shouldn't be long now."

"Artemis!" Danni thought. This was a cage for her.

Danni flipped the medallion around in her pocket.

"Ah, about the deal we made-" she started.

"Yes!" Astaroth exclaimed, cutting her off. "This is how you fulfil your part. That angelic seal I gave you will allow me to leave Hell and enter the mortal world. It is simple, really. Find a sinner in a holy place and press that medallion into their chest. I will be able to pull myself out of here."

"That's all? Will it hurt the person?"

Astaroth shrugged. "I assume so. Back when we, the Knights of Hell, were known as the Gladius Vaticanus, Lucifer had these crafted for us."

"Wait... Gladius Vaticanus? There was a mercenary group in Rome called that."

"Yes, yes. Belial stole our original name. We were elite warriors under the personal command of Lucifer. We got trapped with him in Hell when Tartarus, the primordial, rose from the ground and swallowed us. Look at how it warped us. Once we were shining angels, now we stand deformed by fire and darkness."

"Why the medallions?" Danni asked, preferring not to look at Astaroth's drooping face.

"In case, by some trickery, the Olympians trapped us in a realm from which there was no escape. These medallions were made with our very essences, so they will always drag us through to the place where they are activated."

Danni made sure to mentally note all of this too. "What happens if I decide not to use it?"

"The deal is broken, and you die a quick and painful death," Astaroth answered.

"Okay, cool," Danni muttered. At some point, she'd have to summon Astaroth into the real world. This was going to be essential to tell Melissa.

A column of fire spun down from the red sky and onto the runic grey slab. The flames died quickly, revealing the very dazed looking form of Melissa Pythia. She was crouched over on the slab with her hands pressed against it.

"Mel!" Danni shouted, delighted to see a friendly face.

Mel shook her head and focused her eyes on Danni. "Oh, you're alive, thank god," she breathed, sounding incredibly relieved.

"Not the god to thank down here," Astaroth mused.

Mel pointed her gun at Astaroth. Her eyes flashed gold.

"Calm down, Prophet of Delphi. No matter what powers you possess, I assure you that you cannot win down here."

Mel considered the demon's words, then re-holstered her pistol. She walked towards the edge of the grey slab and jumped down.

"Want to catch me up?" she asked Danni.

"Ah, okay, this is Asta... something. He is a Knight of Hell. I guess you met that peacock horse man? That is about all I know."

"Astaroth," the demon replied, bowing again.

"I'm guessing this is a trap for Artemis?" Mel asked Astaroth directly.

"Yes. One that should've activated a while ago now. The problem with having Adramelech admitting people is that he gets lonely up there. Likes to chat."

"Surely he can just leave those floating rocks and come down here?"

"He can't. A long time ago, Hell's administrator made a foolish wager and lost quite the artefact. It was a key he used to move freely between all the different levels of Hell. One of a kind. He's been stuck on those floating rocks for about 700 years. Lucifer finds his punishment fitting."

"He seemed alright," Danni said quietly. She felt bad for the lonely creature up there.

"Don't feel too bad for Adramelech. Back when he was a Sumerian god, he demanded children be sacrificed to him," Astaroth added casually.

All of Danni's sympathy disappeared instantly.

Astaroth paused. He looked up at the sky.

"At last, a goddess approaches," he breathed.

He snapped his fingers, and both Danni and Mel went rigid, locked upright where they stood.

Astaroth threw the viper in his right hand at Mel, and the serpent wrapped itself around her eyes. Astaroth was clearly aware that Mel's vision had powers. Danni hoped her boss had something else up her sleeve.

"Don't want any unnecessary interference now. We will use you as bait to trap Apollo down here too."

The column of fire burst forth from the clouds again and plummeted towards the grey slab.

The flames dissipated, revealing shining Artemis in all her glory. In her right hand was a silver sword; in her left was a black horse's head.

She looked at Astaroth and grinned.

6

THE RED DRAGON

Astaroth looked at the dripping horsehead with disdain.

"Probably should have told Adramelech that Artemis of the Wildlands was coming down," he winced. "Nevertheless, welcome Artemis. Huntress. Olympian. Goddess of Moon and Childbirth."

Artemis surveyed the grey stone on which she now stood. The red rocks of the quarry and the stormy sky spitting its endless rain of fire only made the contrast with her silver glow more extreme and more spectacular. She was a bright singular beacon of hope in the hellscape.

"Name yourself, demon," Artemis commanded.

"Astaroth," the Knight of Hell replied, sounding annoyed at her insolence. "I would think you'd speak more respectfully to your captor. But then I suppose the hunter often doesn't know how to behave when they become the hunted."

"A runic prison designed just for me," Artemis mused, surveying her surroundings. She was right in the centre of the demonic boxing ring.

Astaroth nodded.

"I suspect all of these runes cancel any godly powers."

"Correct."

"And, of course, I have no power to influence any of the runes physically."

"Of course not."

"But in your planning, I'm guessing a couple of mortals weren't factored in?"

Astaroth looked alarmed. He leapt into the air, just high enough that he was looking down on Artemis. He gasped.

All Danni could see was the huge grin stretched across Mel's face.

"What did you do?" Danni whispered.

"When I landed, I scratched out part of the central rune. As soon as I saw that big rune, I guessed that all of the symbols were connected. If there is one broken link, the chain doesn't work."

Danni then turned back to the standoff between Astaroth and Artemis, privately admiring how quickly Mel had reacted after coming through the portal.

Artemis threw the head of Adramelech away. "You realise I *let* your comrade up there capture me, right?" she asked casually.

Astaroth braced and spread his black wings wide. His skin became wreathed in flame; the fire becoming a suit of armour.

"As soon as I got word from Morpheus that Archangel Michael was back, I knew that wonderful reprieve from their hunt was over. It is surprising how I could tolerate centuries of suppression, yet, in this last year, I was unrestricted. My divinity could flow freely again. It had been easy to evade that fool and his dogs. Now, I don't really want to go back into hiding. The angels aren't watching Hell for the divine. Down here, I can do whatever I want."

"Why not run away again, like you've done for centuries?" Astaroth sneered.

"I'm done with running. Facing a true angel is a frightening thought, but you who hunt me… you fallen angels… you were handicapped by Tartarus so long ago that I thought it would be fun to teach you a lesson for bothering a goddess."

"You dare to insult me in my realm. I command forty legions!"

The change in Astaroth had been quick and intense. In his armour of fire, the knight had a commanding presence.

"Your legions will bow before me. What is a demon to a god?" Artemis smirked.

"And what is a god to a devil," Astaroth retorted coldly.

At supersonic speed, both Astaroth and Artemis launched themselves at each other. A powerful shockwave threw pebbles away and knocked the rocks off the tortured souls in the quarry.

The dragon growled in its bindings.

Danni and Mel were released from Astaroth's hold. He was

obviously putting all his focus into combatting the silver goddess.

Mel quickly reached up and pulled the snake from her head, tossing it away before it could bite her.

"What do we do?" Danni asked.

Mel was thinking quickly. "Artemis can handle a Knight of Hell easily on her own. The problem is more of them showing up. Who knows what monsters are down here?"

"So we need to end this fight quickly?"

Mel nodded. Danni grabbed her by the shoulder and turned her towards the red dragon. Smoke was puffing from its nostrils.

"Let's free him," Danni said.

"Say what?"

"Look at his eyes," Danni exclaimed.

The dragon's eyes were filled with unmistakable disgust and locked onto Astaroth.

A second shockwave knocked the two women onto their backsides.

"I think he will be on our side."

"That is a huge presumption to make. I don't think it's a good idea."

There was a scream from above. Then, all around Danni and Mel, the hundreds of grey-skinned workers began changing. Their arms morphed into pikes and swords as they grew in size and stature. A nearby worker looked at Danni with his vacant eyes and smiled, revealing rows of pointed teeth.

All of the workers in the quarry were now sprouting weapons and turning toward Artemis. All of them except those nearest to the Australian spies.

"I think all of these tortured souls might also be soldiers of Astaroth," Danni squeaked. The quarry was jam-packed with the malnourished, mutating things. They were outnumbered a hundred to one.

Mel had an expression on her face that Danni hadn't seen before. She didn't know what to do.

"We free the dragon!" Danni commanded.

"Danni, I-"

"You brought me onto this team for a reason! Trust my judgement!" Danni argued fiercely.

"Alright," Mel relented. "Today is a gambling day. We need to free the dragon."

The two women bolted towards the chained beast as a horde of the mutated souls charged after them.

High above the quarry, Artemis was joyously striking and parrying with Astaroth. The look of wild, unhinged ecstasy etched on her face was unnerving. Her silver sword gleamed as it sliced through the air with deadly precision. It was all Astaroth could do to defend the blows with his own sword of fire and soar backwards. He couldn't match her speed, intensity or ferocity. The fallen angel was no match for the goddess.

"Aid me!" Astaroth screamed.

A single magnified clink echoed through the quarry. The chains that attached the souls carrying rocks unclasped. The tortured humanoid things arched their backs, and grey wings spawned. Astaroth's army was free of its bonds and capable of flight.

The horde took to the air.

Artemis was so enraptured in her toying with Astaroth that

she didn't see the army ascend towards her. It was a swarm of such magnitude it blackened the ground below.

From Danni's vantage point, the newly airborne army was so dense it blotted out the sky behind. They rose like a funnel towards the goddess; an infinite column of demonic ants.

A deadly pointed pike from one of the tortured beings thrust towards Artemis. She glimpsed it out of the corner of her eye and dodged. As she turned, the immensity of the challenge before her became apparent.

Artemis rocketed up, away from Astaroth, who laughed as the cloud overtook him. She summoned her silver bow, but instead of gripping it, she allowed it to float in front of her. She readied an arrow, then, using her divine power, multiplied it. A sphere of arrows surrounded her as she flew ever higher, growing denser by the second.

Artemis grabbed the bow.

She nocked her arrow.

She released.

The sphere of arrows around her flew outwards. It was like a grenade blasting its deadly shrapnel across a battlefield. They zoomed through target after target, plummeting towards the ground.

The wailing cries of Astaroth's army filled the air as they collapsed en masse, punctured and impaled.

"Danni! Watch out!" Mel cried.

She'd seen the shining cloud of arrows begin their descent. She crash-tackled Danni, knocking her into an excavated groove in the ground. Just in the nick of time, as seconds later the pings of showering arrows on stone surrounded them.

They crawled out of the groove, only to be confronted by the grey-skinned workers who'd survived the deadly hail.

A sword arm came down on Danni. She fell backwards and rolled out of the way, only to narrowly miss being impaled by a different pointed arm.

Mel's eyes flashed gold. She dodged a strike and drew her gun. The gnashing teeth of one of the workers bit into her left arm. Mel pointed the gun into the quarry worker's face and fired. The monsters head exploded into a sloppy mass of grey goo.

Mel kicked the body off her and into one of the other workers, who promptly collapsed over it. Mel fired at that one too, killing it.

Danni, who had no powers to help her, threw elbows and knees as best she could. She reacted quickly, dodging blows from attackers on all sides, but she was getting tired and knew she couldn't keep this up forever.

She sidestepped, and a grey blade planted itself between her arm and her torso. The attacker from behind received a bullet to the face from Mel.

"Run!" Mel shouted, shooting down the three closest workers to Danni.

Danni didn't need to be told twice. She sprinted towards the dragon.

Up above, Artemis was wholly enveloped by the swarm.

"Enough!" the goddess yelled, generating a wave of pure energy that knocked all the monsters away from her.

More emerged to replace their fallen comrades, pinning

Artemis's arms back. She began spinning so fast she generated a silver tornado, with winds so vicious it began ripping the workers apart. The gusting gale of the tornado was so intense it threatened to rip Danni backwards. In her struggle, she turned and saw that Mel was surrounded.

Mel pulled the trigger and her pistol clicked. The slide locked back. She was out of ammo.

Mel threw the gun at an approaching foe. A few winged workers soared down towards her, fleeing the tornado and choosing an easier target.

She couldn't run. They were too fast.

Danni made up her mind and bolted back towards Mel, who'd closed her eyes.

Danni heard Mel speak.

"Apollo, I need you!"

Golden energy welled around her. The energy became a protective orb of fire, the fire of the sun god.

"Prophet, I cannot reach you," the thundering voice of Apollo boomed as it filled the landscape. *"But I can give you something. Concentrate your power."*

There was a sound like shattering glass and Mel looked in her right hand. There shined the golden blade of Apollo.

The creatures screamed in agony as they dived into Mel's fire shield. Mel's connection with Apollo on Earth was weak, and the protective orb was already fading. She looked incredibly woozy but steeled her resolve.

The monsters came at her.

Melissa slashed through the air. The sword sent an arced

wave of flame out into the crowd. The workers were incinerated as it spread through the quarry. The creatures lunged, but Mel fought with inhuman speed. Guided by the hand of Apollo in her mind, she fought with the grace and skill of the god. But the connection across dimensions was growing more distant by the second. The walls to Hell were splintered, not broken. At best, Danni figured Mel only had a few minutes.

Thinking fast, Danni turned back towards the dragon.

She reached it quickly and found she was alone. Most of the swarm was still flying at Artemis while a smaller pocket had descended on Mel.

The dragon puffed smoke and eyed her warily. It wasn't so big for a dragon, and its scaly face reminded her of a dinosaur more than anything. Danni estimated it was about as big as a T-Rex and twice as long. It was certainly large enough to swallow a person whole. All Danni could hope was that it wouldn't swallow her.

The shackles on its front legs were robust. The chains wrapped its wings and kept its head down. A large steel muzzle fastened its jaws closed.

"How do I do this?" Danni thought.

She frantically ran the length of the dragon, looking for a keyhole or any way to unlatch the creature. There was nothing. The chains were probably released by magic. If only she knew the spell or phrase that would unbind the beast.

Danni pressed her hand against her side. She was bleeding. She'd been struck and hadn't realised.

The sudden awareness of this new injury caused Danni to stumble. She flung her arms out and grasped the nearest shackle to keep herself upright.

At once, lines of red energy began crisscrossing the binding. There was a hiss of steam and the shackle released.

"What the hell…" Danni murmured. Human blood unlocked divine chains.

She knew what she had to do. With renewed purpose, Danni ran around the dragon, wiping her hand on every chain, shackle and even the muzzle. All of it glowed and unclipped.

With a mighty roar, the dragon stretched out and spread its wings wide. It looked a whole lot bigger now, and Danni jumped in fright when it turned its head towards her. The dragon's eyes showed appreciation in their yellow depths. Then, with a snort, it took to the air.

Just in time too, as Danni could see Artemis was out of options. The horde was endless. They'd managed to grip the goddess by every limb, spreading her like a starfish and holding her in place. Astaroth summoned ropes of fire and coiled them around the goddess.

"You forget Artemis, we were a match for you when we seized the Underworld all those long years ago."

Astaroth squeezed his fingers together, and Artemis' legs and arms snapped backwards.

"Lucifer wants you captured. But I don't think it's worth the risk." Astaroth's eyes sparkled with malevolence as he raised his sword. "So ends your hunt, goddess."

Astaroth didn't hear the beating of giant wings until it was too late. He turned, only to be met by an open maw with rows of razor-sharp teeth engulfing his vision.

The dragon didn't stop moving as it swallowed the Knight of Hell whole. Immediately, Artemis' bonds extinguished.

The dragon manoeuvred around the swarm and sent a jet of fire into its central mass. The workers collapsed to the ground in burning agony. The dragon didn't stop. It circled the fleeing souls and consumed them, one mouthful at a time.

In the dragon-rout chaos, Artemis seized her moment to flee. The goddess was shaken, a victim of her own hubris. Danni imagined the goddess thought herself to be unstoppable, yet Astaroth and his army had almost bested her.

Artemis flew towards Mel and sent a pulse of energy to blast away her attackers. Mel was bruised and battered, on one knee still swinging the golden sword. Artemis gripped the back of her jacket and hoisted her into the air. She then jetted towards Danni, wrapping one arm around her waist.

"Impressive work," Artemis stated. "You both fared better than I in that skirmish."

"Where do we go now?" a weakened and dazed-looking Mel mumbled.

"There is a city; I saw it when I landed. That way!" Danni shouted.

Artemis didn't object. They flew out of the quarry and towards the ruined city on the horizon.

7

THE RUINED CITY

THE RUINS OF SODOM
- JANUARY 23 -

D anni felt deeply uncomfortable wrapped in the arm of Artemis. She was sure her personal space was being violated. However, seeing Mel dangling below like a lamb gripped in the talon of an eagle, she figured it could be worse.

The speed of Artemis' flight only seemed to magnify the heat in the air. The falling embers didn't bother the goddess, but Danni's skin was starting to singe.

The roars and beating wings from the red dragon faded into the background quickly. As they flew over the scorched plain, the throngs of workers disappeared. It was still unclear where they'd been hauling the large stones from the quarry to.

Occasionally, Danni noticed disgusting four-legged creatures scurrying about. They looked like elongated people with missing eyes and long teeth. The way they sniffed the air and dug at the dirt made them seem entirely animal in nature, like they were a more primitive demon. Nonetheless, they were still fearsome and unsettling to behold.

Artemis picked up speed as the city approached. Danni had to close her eyes tight to stop them from burning in the wind. It wasn't long before she slowed and descended. They passed low over the thick outer walls and beside the high towers of the city, very few of which still stood intact. A maze of tightly packed buildings joined by flat rooftops and thin alleys stretched before them. Much of it lay in utter ruin. The city was a relic of a time long forgotten and a reminder of an ancient cataclysm.

They dropped into a back alley, and Artemis released the two women from her grip.

"I'm glad to see you survived," Artemis said, giving Danni a nod of approval.

"Yeah, that Knight of Hell saved me."

"For what price?" Mel asked, shooting Danni a sharp look.

"The price is redundant now. Astaroth was consumed by that dragon. You are clear of whatever debt he placed you in."

Danni felt the medallion still in her pocket. She wondered if it had the power to pull the fallen angel from the stomach of a dragon. She wasn't going to find out, regardless.

"Can a dragon kill a Knight of Hell?" Danni asked. It all seemed too easy.

"Only a fool underestimates a dragon. Some are gods in

their own right. That one certainly seemed greater than a simple beast," Artemis answered.

Danni observed the walls of the alley they'd landed in. Roughly hewn bricks were precariously stacked on top of one another. It was a marvel of ancient engineering that the wall stood at all.

"I wonder what this place is. It doesn't look demonic, just looks like it's been hit by a meteor," Danni observed.

Mel was running her hand along the crudely shaped bricks of the alley wall. She closed her eyes and pressed her temple against the stone.

"Destruction by fire and sulfur… this is the biblical city of Sodom. A city that faced the wrath of God then was pulled from the Earth. It is a symbol of wickedness and divine retribution."

Danni knew of the story of the cities of Sodom and Gomorrah in the vaguest of terms. She was sure someone got turned into a pillar of salt at one point. She felt annoyed at herself; she should know more about these things.

Artemis digested this revelation, then spoke, "Whatever this city was, it is now a home for demons. I suspect a place like this would act as a hub, so there may be a path into the higher and lower realms of Hell here. I saw several temporary structures erected not far in the distance. We will investigate them."

"Quiet!" Mel whispered urgently.

Shrill voices were carrying down the alley. It appeared a group had entered a nearby courtyard. There was copious laughter and the thuds of heavy bags hitting the ground.

Danni clambered up the wall.

"I'll investigate," she said.

"Stay out of sight," Mel warned.

Danni nodded, then began sneaking along the wall. The courtyard was less than fifty metres away, and Danni crouched behind a thick pillar that once held a gate. She peered around and saw who was making all the racket.

Squat, skinny creatures with large pointed ears and long thin tails, were standing in a circle having an in-depth conversation. Their round heads looked too big for their bodies. They all wore loosely fitted breastplates and large cumbersome helmets. One held a short sword while the other two were leaning against tiny comical pitchforks.

"These must be imps," Danni thought, recognising them from her AST learning package. At least she could tell Mel and Artemis something for sure.

One imp was flicking a gold coin into the air while the other two spoke in their high-pitched voices. Danni didn't wait to listen in; she scurried back towards Artemis and Mel.

"I think they are imps. They have weapons but look pretty harmless to me," Danni informed them excitedly.

Mel looked curious, while Artemis was unimpressed.

"So, what is your plan for escaping, Artemis?" Mel asked.

"I didn't plan on getting out," the goddess responded. "I am weary of hiding in the mortal world. I can have some fun here. Hell has nine circles to hunt through and all sorts of prey."

"Until Lucifer comes for you," Mel remarked, barely containing her disapproval of Artemis' response. "You think you can face the Prince of Darkness?"

"Lucifer is not like the other archangels. He is like the fallen angels, the Knights of Hell. When they became trapped in the Underworld, their connection to the power of prayer was severed. They are only as strong as they were in the year 337."

"Apollo said Lucifer and Michael were both stronger than the gods in the battle for the Underworld."

"My brother can discount himself against Lucifer, but he can't discount me."

"Artemis… with all due respect, Lucifer has been the master of Hell for nearly 1700 years. He may not have the raw power boost behind him that the other archangels have, but surely being the Lord of the Underworld has strengthened him in other ways. We need you in the mortal world. The other surviving Olympians need you. Join our cause. Don't surrender yourself to assured fire and death in Hell," Mel stated, sounding a little belittling.

Artemis' immediate annoyance at Mel's insolence was replaced with a look of deep thought. Danni certainly thought Mel was right. They needed her up there. She was wasted down here. The goddess was almost being petty and childish.

"I miss the wilds. The true wilds, not the bogs of Avalon. I will help you find a way back to the mortal world, then make my choice," Artemis announced at last.

"Right," Mel stated happily. "How do we find a way out?"

"We find where the demons spend their time and listen in. Imps being here now is a good sign."

"We will never be able to move through the city unnoticed," Danni added.

"I do not think so either," Artemis frowned.

"An ancient city like this must've had barracks full of weapons and armour," Mel suggested.

"Armour is a good idea for a disguise, but instead of finding it, I say we take it," Danni said.

The chattering from the courtyard at the end of the alley hadn't faltered. The imps in their horned helmets and dull breastplates were still laughing.

Mel nodded at Danni. Artemis summoned her bow and readied one arrow. Noticing that Danni was weaponless, she pulled a knife from a hidden sheath on her inner thigh. It was long and serrated with a mirror finish. It also had an unworldly glow.

"That is a hunting knife crafted by Hephaestus. Once you have slit the throat of that imp, return it to me," Artemis said.

"Slit its throat?" Danni asked, gripping the knife by its leather handle. She didn't want to blatantly murder one of the creatures.

"If these things truly are imps, as Danni says, they aren't necessarily evil creatures. Old European folklore describes them as tricksters. I don't think we need to murder them," Mel expressed to Artemis.

"To develop a conscience in Hell... But alas, I'll admit I am curious to discover why Apollo has allied himself with mortals. Let us do this your way and see how it proceeds," Artemis consented.

"Ideas, Danni?" Mel asked.

Danni pondered for a moment. "If they are tricksters then... let's make a bet. Their armour for... let's say... that golden sword."

Mel gripped Apollo's prized sword a little tighter. Artemis

looked bemused.

Danni continued, "They're pranksters, so they will try to cheat. We just have to outthink them. Or do something so simple they can't outthink us!"

An idea was forming in her mind.

· · · · ·

THE THREE IMPS WERE METICULOUSLY counting the contents of a brown satchel they'd tipped onto the ground. Coins and unrefined jewels were being sorted into piles.

"Angels are moving again," one of the imps said as he studied a giant ruby.

"What do we care?" another said.

"It is interesting. The walls to Hell are weakening. Demons are slipping through and invading human hosts. The hellhounds walk the mortal world again. If the cracks widen further, our kind may be able to return to the Earth."

"That is a fool's hope! No weakened walls will let us through. The door needs to swing open again."

"I prefer to live in hope," the imp said, dropping the ruby and picking up a gargantuan emerald.

"Quite the gems you have there," a female voice interjected. Casually leaning on the rubble of a fountain was Danni. In one hand was the golden sword of Apollo.

The three imps almost jumped out of their skins. They'd been so absorbed sorting their spoils they hadn't heard Danni approach.

"Mortal?" the nearest imp asked, grabbing his pitchfork.

"In the flesh," Danni replied coolly.

"Times have changed," the imp said, turning to his comrades.

"Mighty weapon you have there," the imp with the short sword gasped, positively salivating as he eyed it. "Magical qualities to it. No wonder you have survived to travel this deep."

"Packs quite a punch, this sword" Danni smirked. She tried to lift the sword up to observe it in a disinterested manner, but it was far too heavy. She was exerting a lot of effort, just holding it upright. The imps clearly noticed and exchanged telling glances.

"We could unburden you of such a problematic item. Do you seek gold or jewels?

"I actually wouldn't mind taking your armour off you. But I couldn't bear to give up the sword."

The three little red creatures nodded to each other. "A wager, perhaps?"

"What did you have in mind?" Danni asked.

"Perhaps a riddle? Or a challenge? Something fair to the mortally inclined."

"I'm willing to consider such an idea," Danni mused. "Though I will offer a suggestion first. You understand this sword is magical, yes? It is heavy and difficult to wield. I will bury it into the ground at any spot you choose, and if none of you can pull it out, I win. You will give me your armour. And if you can pull it out, I will hand over the sword."

"We agree," the lead imp answered instantly.

Inspired by their talk of Arthurian myth, Danni had

decided that a sword in the stone approach would be best. Artemis assured her that the imps, being tricksters, would quickly be able to determine what magical protections were on the sword. When they were satisfied it had no mechanisms to become stuck, they would soon agree. What Artemis would do was simple. She would sink beneath the ground wherever the imps planted the sword, then grip the end of the blade beneath, preventing it from being pulled up.

The plan worked like a charm. Each imp, cocky that it could pull the sword from the courtyard easily, had strained and heaved only to be met with an unmoving blade. The imps circled it many times, whispering frantically as they tried to determine what magic held it down. After thirty minutes of trying, the three sorry-looking creatures dumped their helmets and breastplates in a pile in front of Danni.

"I cannot help but feel we have been played. Yet, I dare not cross whatever force aids you."

"Definitely a good idea. Thanks for the armour. Do you guys know a way out of here?" Danni grinned.

The last of the sullen-looking imps turned around while his fellows slinked into the alley. "Try the Hell's Horns Tavern for answers. Not far. All sorts in there."

The malicious sneer that crossed the imp's face made Danni think the sorts in there weren't too friendly to humans. Fortunately, they now had a shabby set of armour each to wear as a disguise. Luckily the imps had such bulbous heads the helmets would definitely fit. Danni was sure all three women could squeeze into the tiny breastplates. It appeared that the denizens of Hell came in all shapes and sizes.

"Killing them would've been much quicker."

Artemis and Mel walked into the courtyard.

"Well done, Danni. I'll put that on your yearly performance review," Mel beamed, slapping her on the back.

"This Hell's Horns Tavern... it can't really be a tavern, can it?" Danni asked.

"I guess we will find out. You two put on your disguises; I will scout from above," Artemis said.

Danni plonked the horned helmet on her head. "Guess we are going to the pub!"

8

THE HELL'S HORNS TAVERN

D anni couldn't believe what she was seeing.

This wooden structure, deep within the torturous fire of Hell, was a tavern. A legitimate tavern.

They'd found it among a plethora of wooden buildings in an area that looked like it'd faced singular, overwhelming destruction near the centre of Sodom. The ruins of human dwellings had been cleared away and a demon shantytown had risen to occupy the space. The Hell's Horns Tavern was sign-posted with a large plaque written in ancient Nordic. They pushed through the door into a wonder.

The tavern didn't look modern. It was a Viking mead hall.

Or at least, a demonic version of one. The elongated shape of the building was unmistakable.

The first thing that drew Danni's eyes were the ogres. Or at least, she assumed they were ogres. Each was at least two metres tall and they sat on wide reinforced stools. Their clawed hands grasped the handles of wide-rimmed wooden mugs. The two monsters looked similar, with minor differences. The ogre on the left was red, and the ogre on the right was sky blue. The red one had a significant potbelly sagging over the black loincloth that wrapped its waist. The blue monster was dressed in a full suit of elaborate battle armour. It looked like a samurai's garb, minus the helmet. Beside them were two substantial black clubs lined with iron spikes.

The two ogres chuckled and bashed their mugs together in cheers.

Danni turned to exchange a glance of sheer befuddlement with Mel, only to notice further monstrous patrons in the tavern. One portion of the wall (which appeared to be made from flesh) was bursting with the twisting silhouettes of dancing shadows; only no visible being was producing them. The living spectres silently laughed and jostled amongst each other.

Once she'd suppressed her immediate horrified reaction to the denizens of the establishment, she fixed her attention to the decor of the building.

Just behind the bar was a blazing orange pit full of slowly bubbling lava. The deep colours of the bottles of liquor were vibrantly ignited in the lava's fiery glow. A drifting candle almost set Danni's hair alight, and she had to quickly duck to get out of its way.

Danni, Melissa and Artemis stood for several long moments

soaking it all in.

The door behind them swung open, and the three of them jumped out of the way as a new throng of monsters entered. There was a thin, gangly, big-nosed ghoul wearing a sack; a bull-headed man carrying a silver axe; and several men and women that looked to be made of black smoke.

They paid no attention to the three strangers in their hodge-podge mixes of armour.

"Everyone seems to be ignoring us," Melissa whispered.

"Let's keep it that way," Artemis stated. She beckoned Danni and Mel towards the nearest table then made for the bar. The red and blue ogres paid the goddess no heed as she ordered three mugs of ale.

The bartender was a sullen creature with a beaked face and sloping neck that sprung up from a dirty green carapace. It looked like a turtle with a wide hole in the top of its head. As the creature bent over, the shallow bowl came dangerously close to letting its watery contents slosh out, but it reared back up just in time.

The group sat in silence as they watched a stunningly attractive woman appear behind the bar and pour their drinks. She carried the three heaving mugs over on a tray, holding it high above her head. It wasn't until she drew closer that Danni noticed the folded leather wings on her back and the small horns pointing from her long black hair.

She gave Danni the most seductive wink she'd ever seen then sauntered off.

"If I'm not mistaken, that was a succubus," Mel muttered, finally breaking the silence. "And those creatures at the bar are oni."

"They were once mortals who were twisted in the Japanese Hell to become those things," Artemis added.

"Japanese Hell? There is more than one Hell?" Danni asked, as she studied the brown contents in her mug. A small part of her really wanted to try this demonic ale, but she noticed neither Mel nor Artemis had touched theirs.

Artemis leaned forward, her armour clanging against the table. "Let me tell you of a time long since past when we, the Greek gods as you call us, ruled the Underworld. In the time before memory, the being Tartarus, a primordial creature spewed from Chaos, gave his body to create a place for mortal souls to rest. This was long before humans walked upright. Long before the angels, gods, and titans ever breathed their first breaths."

"What souls were resting? Dinosaurs?" Danni laughed, only to see Artemis remain stone-faced.

Danni took a sip from her mug. The ale went down rough, burning her throat. It tasted like fire and bee-stings. Yet, the liquid itself was ice cold. Danni wondered how they managed that down here.

"All things that live possess a soul in some shape or form. The divine energy that gives matter true life. When the physical body dies that energy passes into Tartarus to be recycled. The consciousness of Tartarus still resides down here, in a deep slumber. Only someone truly connected to the workings of the Underworld could ever call upon him. I suspect now that would only be Lucifer," Artemis explained, swirling the contents of her drink.

"Tartarus was a central point for every soul to go, right? Then the gods came along and divided it up, creating a whole bunch of different underworlds. Am I right?" Danni said, suddenly brimming with confidence.

The goddess looked impressed. "Yes, you are. Well, I should add that we controlled it. Hades owned all of Tartarus, which he renamed Hades, after himself. When other gods from around the Earth approached him, he gave them space to create their own afterlives to either punish or reward their humans. Countless versions of paradise and punishment existed down here, linked by secret tunnels and hidden portals. Hel, Yomi, Mictlan, Irkalla, Duat and other realms, all pockets in the mastery of Hades. It wasn't until the Battle of the Underworld, when the angels took control, that they removed all barriers and turned the Underworld, into the central region of Hell. As is evidenced by this bar, demons from all religions were brought into the service of the Legion of Heaven. These are much more useful servants than true demons, the monstrous scurrying creatures that dwell in the rocks and the walls down here."

"I've seen that kind. They followed Apollo through the portal in 2019," Mel added darkly.

"Go back a step," Danni said, scanning the room to make sure they weren't being overheard. "What do you mean by true demons?"

"Maybe in the corner of your eye down here you've seen wretched fanged beings; pale, thin and eyeless crawling on all fours with fearsome teeth and long limbs. These are the true demons. Monstrous things that have lived in the dark of the Underworld for ages untold."

"I think I did see them…" Danni said, thinking back to the

terrifying creature she'd seen from above on the scorched plain.

"We have many theories as to their origins. I am a Goddess of Animals, and I feel no affinity with them. I believe they came from Tartarus – the primordial, I mean, not the realm named for him, when his body became this place. I think they were cosmic lice feeding on Tartarus that got trapped in this realm when he surrendered his body to make it. Hades certainly experimented on them, and I am certain other underworld deities would have too, creating their various forms. The demons you have to worry about are the preserved human souls who were twisted into darkness."

"Like the ones in this tavern?" Danni asked.

"Precisely," Artemis answered, once again gesturing towards the troll-like oni at the bar. "They were evil people who were punished, and in their torture became twisted into monsters. Sometimes they retain human intelligence and sometimes not, much as sometimes they retain some empathy or kindness. Mostly they are tools used for malicious purposes."

Hell was incomprehensible. It was far more complex than Danni had ever imagined. An entire society of supernatural beings had developed down here. They had lives and jobs and apparently went to taverns to drink alcohol; when they weren't possessing humans above.

"The demon hunting you, Artemis, who is he?" Mel asked.

"His name is Leviathan. There are five Knights of Hell in the mortal world. They cannot come and go as they please. Asmodee and Oriens currently stand as stone statues deep in the Saudi Arabian desert, thanks to you. Belial is at the whip and call of Cardinal Vasilije Markovic as Lucifer's right-hand man. Leviathan normally haunts the deep places in the form of a terrible serpent. The fifth, I do not know. Apollo's re-emergence caused Lucifer to send Leviathan from his familiar haunts to chase me."

"Why?" Danni asked.

"Apollo told me that for this ritual to work, you need the blood of Zeus. Zeus' blood runs in my veins. Demons must've had their eyes on Apollo when he found me. Lucifer still needs a drop of Zeus' blood," Artemis shrugged.

"Do gods have blood?" Danni asked nervously.

"Not in the human sense. It is called ichor, but blood is an interchangeable term."

Danni was being overloaded with information. Not long ago, she'd been asked to research the Greek gods. Now she was sitting at a table in a tavern in Hell talking to one. Life sure had a funny way of escalating things.

"Leviathan…" Mel murmured. "We will need to add him to our database. After all this time, how did he get you now?"

Artemis frowned. "For the last year, the angels haven't been watching the Earth for the gods. No Knight of Hell alone can match the power of a goddess. But now that Michael has returned, any display of power will draw the attention of the angels of Heaven. Such a foe I cannot face."

"Alone," Mel murmured. "It is time Artemis of the Wildlands rejoined the other Olympians and took the fight back to the angels."

Artemis gave her a knowing look. "Artemis of the Wildlands... that old name. You know, when Apollo found me last year, he said I should adopt the name Silver Artemis to his Golden

Apollo. I quite liked it. Silver Artemis, I will be."

"How come you can use your power down here?" Mel asked.

"The only gods in Hell are the ones who joined Lucifer or have a domain somehow related to dying and death. Some are imprisoned and some joined him willingly. The angels take prisoners of any real value to the Citadel of Heaven in the upper realms. The angels don't watch Hell because of all the gods down here constantly using their power. Plus, this is the domain of Lucifer, not Heaven. Much in the way Zeus rarely interfered with the business of Hades, such is the way with the angels now."

"You really know your stuff. More than Apollo, it seems," Mel said.

"Apollo missed the rise and dominance of the Abrahamic faiths. I lived through all of it. I was there when Arthur lived. His life was defined by a mix of the old magic and the new faiths. I watched in hiding as the angels swept across the world, exterminating the gods. I found solace in the wilds, away from all of it. The angels care about the hearts and minds of humans alone; they care not for the forests and creatures that dwell within."

An argument had broken out at a table in the corner between a bull-headed demon and the ghoul. The body-less, voice-less shadows on the wall began soundlessly cheering as the minotaur threw the table away, sending it tumbling behind the bar. The ghoul shrieked and lunged at the minotaur. The minotaur pulled the ghoul into a tight embrace and squeezed so hard Danni could hear the air escaping its lungs.

The succubus wandered over and watched on, looking

amused.

Danni seized the opportunity to question the beautiful demon. "My drink is cold. Where do you get the ice from?"

The succubus turned and faced their table. "The very bottom of Hell is a frozen wasteland; there is ice in abundance. We have a well in the back room."

"Hmm, interesting," Danni said.

Mel looked alarmed, "Don't draw unnecessary attention, Danni!"

Whether the attention drawn was intended or not didn't soon matter, as the ghoul came crashing down onto their table. Artemis, Mel and Danni all dived out of the way as the charging minotaur exploded the table into fragments of shattered wood.

Both Mel and Danni's poor fitting helmets fell to the floor. The minotaur and ghoul didn't care; they were far too absorbed with their quarrel. The shadows on the wall, however, took instant notice of the mortals.

The black silhouettes began stretching from their two-dimensional home. Like thin strips of paper, they flickered across the room.

Danni shrieked in fright and tried to kick at one. The black coil began wrapping itself around her foot and dragging her towards the wall. She desperately tried to find something to hold onto.

Artemis picked up the sword of Apollo and slashed the black tendrils in half. She then pressed her palm in the direction of the writhing shadows and exploded the tavern's meaty wall.

The entire tavern groaned and shifted on its foundations.

Despite the wall no longer being there, the shadows

remained as thin outlines of humans, barely visible in the open air.

Like a striking snake, they launched toward Artemis at unfathomable speed and began wrapping themselves around her.

Artemis was taken aback by the sudden onslaught and didn't seem to know how to rid herself of the suffocating shades.

The exploding wall, however, caught the attention of every other being there, all of which now turned towards Danni and Mel.

"Run!" Mel commanded, leaping across a table and out into the ruins of Sodom. The minotaur bellowed and charged after her.

The succubus jumped onto the bar top and let out a horrific wailing cry. Her beauty was replaced with a sinister dread. All of her features were distorted. Fangs grew in her mouth and claws sprung from her hands.

She spread her wings and glided across the room, blocking the opening Mel had fled through. The ghoul smiled devilishly, cracking its knuckles as it stalked towards Danni.

Danni felt a hand on her shoulder. Artemis had become almost entirely black. She was drowning in shadow.

As soon as the goddess made contact with Danni, she disappeared. The shadows fell into a puddle on the floor and began sliding towards a new target; towards her.

Danni bolted. With a flying kick, she hit the turtle-like bartender in the head, spilling the water from its bowl. She ran behind the bar and down a short side passage.

She shoulder-charged a closed door and was confronted with a circular stone wall with a wooden platform in the middle. On the platform were pickaxes and buckets. It was connected to a simple lever and pulley system on the side of the room with a substantial length of rope. Danni jumped onto the platform and cut the cord.

The whole thing collapsed. Danni had expected a short drop into a basement, but she kept falling. The air went from warm to freezing, and darkness surrounded her on all sides.

For the second time that day, Danni found herself flying downwards into the fearsome depths of Hell.

9

DANNI'S INFERNO

The platform hit a hard surface with a colossal bang, Somehow, Danni was completely fine, not even feeling the impact. The distance she'd fallen should've turned her into a paste on the ground. She wasn't relieved, however. Danni's mind screamed at her, pleading with her to get away from this place.

There was no light or warmth in the cold depths. In the extreme darkness, hope fell into oblivion while fear became a claustrophobic smoke, blanketing the air. Danni couldn't see and her intuition told her she shouldn't be here.

Danni's skin burned as she felt the walls around her. Her feet slipped on the ground beneath. She was deep in a chasm of ice. She could barely take a step without hitting a rectangular block of the frozen substance or sliding away in the absolute darkness. She breathed the freezing air into her lungs. It flowed through her, turning her veins into rivers of ice.

"Danni," a voice whispered.

"Who's there?" Danni shouted, twisting and falling. Her collision with the ice beneath hurt. She scrambled back to her feet.

"Artemis," the goddess answered.

"Where are you?"

"Inside you. I protected you from the fall. It was the only way I could think to escape those shadow creatures," the voice of the goddess whispered.

"What about Mel?"

"The Oracle of Delphi can handle herself."

"I can't see anything," Danni said. The disembodied voice of the goddess lingered in the air around her. It was so dark the goddess could've been right beside her and she wouldn't have known.

"Hold still," Artemis commanded.

Danni froze in place. There was a feeling like a small electric shock. Danni closed her eyes and grimaced as her stomach tumbled and her heart thumped rapidly.

"What did you do?" she breathed, as goosebumps raced across her.

"Possessed you properly, but do not worry, for I am not taking control," the voice of Artemis said, now inside her brain.

"WHAT?" Danni said, alarmed.

"Not possessed like a demon would; think of it more as

binding myself to you."

"Do gods do that?"

"This god is right now. Wherever we are, it is deep and different to the rest of Hell we have seen. I worry the presence of a goddess may rouse whatever slumbers down here. Now, open your eyes."

Danni did so and was shocked to find that she could see as clearly as if she were standing in daylight. Yet, now she almost wished she couldn't. What confronted her in the cold sterile wasteland was unimaginable horror.

In the blocks of ice around her were frozen bodies. The floor and the walls were lined with them. Each person was utterly submerged and bent in unnatural angles. Directly beside Danni, compressed into an upright cube, was a woman, showing like a jewel encased in glass. Her feet were pushed flat against her face. Danni thought she could hear the woman murmuring in her frozen tomb.

Danni ran forward, letting the temporary fear overwhelm her. She didn't get far until she was confronted with another wall of ice, three metres high containing eight squashed people in its depths. Their backs were broken, and their necks were bent, yet Danni could see their eyes moving back and forth. These people were awake, stuck in a stasis of eternal pain. How long had they been frozen here?

"What is this place?" Danni whispered.

"The Ninth Circle of Hell," Artemis answered in her head. "Hermes came here once, a long time ago…"

"What is being punished here?"

"Treachery. Here in the frozen lake Cocytus lie the traitorous. Apparently, of all the evils of man, the archangels feel the worst crime is betrayal. In the ice these people will remain unmoving for all eternity. Every agonising second of their existence broken in the dark."

The most unsettling thing about the Ninth Circle of Hell was how different it was. It was so still and quiet.

Her wristwatch buzzed. It was midnight, meaning in the mortal world a new day had dawned. This filled Danni with a small amount of hope. There was always hope in dark places.

Danni looked at the columns of ice around her. While she could see tortured souls spread throughout, there wasn't too many. Looking through the eyes of the goddess within her, she could see the beauty of the place. The sharp whites and sparkling blues were like that of another world, the world of perpetual winter one could only see on Earth if they walked through a glacier. If it weren't for the poor trapped souls, Danni would've found it serene.

"Who are they? Do you know them?" Danni asked.

Artemis either ignored the question or chose not to answer.

Looking up, Danni saw that she wasn't in a chasm. It was more like a cave running through the ice. From the frosty roof, enormous pointed icicles leered ominously down.

"These souls were all handpicked by Lucifer," Artemis said as Danni slid down a brief decline.

"Is he a bad guy? Lucifer, I mean," Danni asked, feeling immediately stupid about the question.

"Pray that we do not find out," Artemis answered. "I feel like we are impossibly deep in the realm of Hell, and just by being here, we could draw unwanted attention. I warn you now, Danni Quinn, should the archangel appear, I will disappear inside you so completely that I may not be detected. I will not be able to help you."

Danni found this puzzling. "You're afraid of him? You said earlier how the fallen angels are weak. I thought your plan was to run wild down here?"

"I met Lucifer in days long past. He was arrogant and cocky, but beautiful. The pride of the archangels. I don't know what his imprisonment has twisted him into, but if the legends of humans are to be believed, it isn't good. Twice now, I have almost fallen victim to the creatures of Hell. I am now not so foolish to assume Lucifer is an easy foe. The Oracle of Delphi was right when she said he may have gained some new unknown powers in his long isolation."

Danni was sure that Lucifer would be too busy to be checking up on her walking through the ice cave anyway. At least she hoped so. Surely the Prince of Darkness kept a tight schedule.

After journeying for some time among the glistening spires of ice, Danni had slightly desensitised to the cold, but not the lingering eyes of the twisted people on her. She was desperate to be free of the place, though neither she nor Artemis knew if there was a way out.

Danni slipped as she clambered down a steep embankment, sending tumbling boulders of ice crashing down. They echoed as they rolled into oblivion. The path was treacherous and not even the internal warmth provided by the presence of Artemis could negate all the cold of Hell.

Something different caught her eye. There was light in the distance. She hoped it was a portal.

Following the glow, Danni came to the edge of a tall cliff. Before her was a flat plateau of ice stretching as far as the eye could see.

Some distance across the surface was an aberration in its perfection. There was a wide circle cut into the expanse of ice. Around its circumference, Danni could see colossal demonic letters glowing red. The ring itself was completely black inside, signalling a further dive deeper into Hell.

"What is that?" Danni asked.

"A prison, I think," Artemis replied.

"Not for a person, its gigantic…"

"Let us approach and find out."

"I don't want to go that way!" Danni said abruptly.

There was something about that loathsome circle and its fearsome writing that told Danni she shouldn't approach. It was something more than being scared this time; it was a profound dread. It was a societal dread, a feeling that came from culture. It wasn't like running from a wild animal or being attacked by a criminal; this feeling was like sitting before an exam knowing only failure could come. It was loss and hopelessness and chaos all rolled into one perfectly cut shape.

"There is no other way. I have no power to free us from this place. You must find a way," Artemis urged.

Danni stared at that circle in the ice field. She didn't want to. Looking at it was enough. She wished she were hitching a joy-ride within the goddess, as opposed to how it was now.

Artemis said nothing else. Danni knew the way it had to be.

She scrambled down the icy hill and stepped onto the frozen plateau.

"The lights from those symbols ahead, use them to guide you. I dare not let you see any further with my vision. I sense something approaching. The archangel mustn't know I am with you, or we are both doomed," Artemis stated.

"What do I do?" Danni whispered, panicked.

"Continue forward; there is no other path. Trust in yourself and know your worth. He will try to torment you."

Danni wanted to protest, but knew Artemis was right. The maze of ice behind them was hopelessly tricky to navigate. The vast dark pit ahead was the only thing that looked like a way out.

It wasn't long before Danni reached the edge of the monumental red lettering carved into the snow. It pulsed with its unnatural light.

"I wonder what it says?" Danni quietly asked herself.

She was answered with a nearby rumbling.

Something was stirring in the pit.

From within the darkness, two giant red hands gripped the edge of the circle. Danni stood motionless, painfully exposed on the ice. There was nowhere to hide and nowhere to run.

A giant pulled itself out of the blackness.

Standing waist-deep in the circle, the monster stretched its gargantuan red arms. It had three heads, each with dinner-plate eyes and pointed teeth. Two sharp horns sprang from each temple. The central head leered at Danni.

"A mortal so deep in Hell, how has this come to be?" the

vermillion faced monster laughed.

Danni squeaked in response. She'd hoped Artemis would offer some advice, but the goddess was silent. Artemis wouldn't help now.

The ground cracked. A person was thrown up from a hidden void in the ice below. One of the giant red hands picked up the person with just his pointer finger and thumb. The person, only just getting their senses about them, screamed as they saw the mighty mouth of the right head open. The monster dropped the person into that mouth and clamped down. It slowly chewed as bare legs dangled from its lips.

"I am not a sinner. I am not treacherous and I don't want to be eaten!" Danni babbled, mustering what confidence she could. The dark and the cold seemed to be sapping her inner strength away.

The middle head laughed again, its booming voice shaking icicles free from the roof. They crashed down around Danni, coming threateningly close to impaling her. Chunks of hard ice buffeted her as the falling icicles exploded.

"You are alive. These are dead souls. I chew on the dead, not the living," the monster explained casually.

One of the legs in the right mouth dropped down, vanishing into the blackness of the pit.

"Answer my question," the monster snarled.

"I'm not sure…" Danni mumbled very quickly. "I was pulled into Hell by a hellhound, then fell down all these layers, and now I am here."

"You must've been caught up in the work of one of my

knights. It happens from time to time. Tell me your name?"

"Danni Quinn," Danni answered. She wasn't going to lie to the red three-headed giant.

"Lucifer Morningstar," the giant replied.

Danni gulped. She was talking to Satan. This three-headed red monstrosity was the Devil himself. She attempted to flatten, neaten and brush back her hair with her hands, as if looking more formal would help.

Another person on Lucifer's left came through the ice in a thunderous crack, and this time was plopped into his left mouth to be chewed on.

Danni's hand dived into her pocket, where she felt the cool angelic seal of Astaroth still sitting. She nervously spun it around.

Danni remained quiet, unsure of what to say. She chose to kneel down, as a sign of respect, despite how the cold burned her knees.

"What do we do with you?" Lucifer's central head questioned. "To journey so deep is a feat worthy of poetry. And to dare to speak, not even Dante could muster such courage."

"Do you live down here?" Danni squeaked.

She was trying to make pleasant chit-chat with the Devil. It felt like it was all she could do.

"Hell is my home, one from which I cannot escape. Not yet, anyway."

"It seems nice…" Danni said, again feeling foolish.

Lucifer snorted and the rush of air knocked Danni backwards.

"Nice! I came here a conqueror! A hero to my kind. And I

was tricked! The Greek Goddess Persephone took advantage and cursed me. My true home is in Heaven. You think fire and ice and the tortured screams of the damned are *nice*?"

"Aren't you an angel? Just go back?" Danni suggested way too quickly, trying to undo the damage she'd just done. She'd never been more scared in her life. Even the smell of Lucifer reeked of anger, hatred and all things dark.

"I am stuck down here. For the longest time, I was imprisoned in this very spot. The very bottom of Hell. Only the unfindable prisons of Cronus and Ouranos are below this place."

Danni swallowed her fear. Lucifer seemed chatty, and she was still on a mission. She had the perfect opportunity to press him for answers. She could do this.

"How did you end up stuck down here?" Danni asked. She remembered basic religion class. Lucifer betrayed God and was punished in Hell or something like that. She was sure that wasn't the case here.

"A curious mortal, asking questions to delay your fate, the oldest trick in the book," Lucifer smiled.

"Well… I was thinking, if you tell me the real story, I can go up and tell everyone else, if you let me go, that is…" Danni said, still sounding high-pitched and terrified.

Again, the ice plateau shook under the booming laugh of Lucifer. At least Danni was making him chuckle.

"What a bold assumption to make, that I will let you go. Modern humans know so little of the way things were; trying to explain the story of war and gods would just be wasted breath."

"Try me! After all, I have travelled through Hell and arrived here. I have earned it."

Lucifer's left head spat half a torso from its mouth, and the mutilated corpse went sliding along the ice. Danni was horrified to see the one remaining arm of the man stretch out and attempt to pull what was left of his body away. As if it were living, the ice rose up around him and dragged him back down into the plateau, leaving it clean and flat.

"While I admire your confidence," Lucifer started, running one of his giant fingers over his pointed teeth, "I must say that confidence is a problem among you humans. This thing you've turned me into, 'the Devil', as I am known, is purely a human invention. I had no interest in you, other than some resentment that God designed us off of you. Unwieldy sacks of meat you are."

Danni had never thought of herself as a sack of meat before. Lucifer was surprisingly well-spoken for the Prince of Darkness. She would've thought he'd sound all raspy and evil, but if anything, he sounded very prim and proper. His voice did have a deep gravitas to it, further magnified by the echoing chamber.

Lucifer continued, "From down here, at the very bottom in the very centre of Hell, I can see the world above. I always thought you little people made me the Devil because you needed a devil. A justification for the bad things you did to each other. An explanation for the evil that lingers within. And yet I have watched as you've been given everything. Your society moved away from gods and devils, and you humans declared yourself both. You preach your ideology as if it is divine truth. Your narcissism is boundless. Disasters occur and you take pictures of yourselves at the beach with captions saying how sad you are."

Danni gulped. She knew a few people like that.

"I don't hate the old gods. My brothers and I waged war on them because it was our purpose. But under them, humanity was punished accordingly. The gods of the world kept you in check. The great crimes are easy to punish, but now the world is full of people so entitled they don't see the small evils of their lives. I have grown to despise humanity, and in doing so, have embraced my role as the Devil. Humans are a race of beings who all think they are equal, but everyone is better than everyone else. Simple truths are gone, so beware your confidence little human, lest it be your downfall," Lucifer finished.

Danni never would've guessed that it was social media influencers that made the Prince of Darkness care about his job.

"Yet, how can I judge, for I was narcissistic," Lucifer sighed. "When I assaulted the Castle of Hades and met Persephone, I thought the world was mine for the taking. Now, look at me. Trapped in a ruined land. The humans view me as the monster responsible for their dark thoughts. I will free myself of this place and make things right."

"What do you mean by making things right?" Danni asked, her words trembling.

"The old gods took a step back from humanity. But I have seen that they need the divine for guidance. They are lost and getting more lost every day. I will come to the Earth and in a wave of fire, humble the humans before the divine again."

"Ah, okay..." Danni quietly said.

She had to tell Mel ASAP that Lucifer, under no circumstances, could be the one to claim the empty position of

Zeus. While she figured that was a given, the documentation for Operation Thunderking had Lucifer as a bit of a wildcard.

"It's not like you have chains on you; what's stopping you? Is this pit your prison?" Danni asked.

"This ring in the ice is no prison. It was once. I wanted to kill Persephone for what she did, but in her last moments, she called upon a power I could not fight. The Primordial Tartarus, the being who shaped the Underworld. He appeared and swallowed me. Took me deep into the bowels of Hell. To this spot, where I was bound in the ice for hundreds of years. Eventually, Tartarus let go, and I was free to move about the Underworld. The battle had turned it into a fiery pit, so I reshaped it. I moved the rivers. I created the nine circles and I looked for an escape."

"And you have found one, I'm guessing? You know, because of your whole 'cleansing the Earth in a wave of fire' speech?"

"Yes. My brother Michael was recently alerted to a pocket of power, preserved from a time long ago. I think this power can free me. In fact, I am certain it can…"

"Well, can I go back to the Earth before you cleanse it?" Danni asked, trying her luck.

"Perhaps," Lucifer replied, his eyes narrowing on Danni. "Tell me, wanderer of these frightful depths, tell me about you."

This was the part Danni had been most dreading. A deep and meaningful with the Devil was the last thing Danni wanted. Still, her training had tonnes of interview practice and lessons on how to craft a false narrative. Maybe she could tactfully get through this.

"There isn't much to tell. I'm a bartender-"

The colossal form of Lucifer leaned back in his circular hole and rested his arms against the edge.

"Lie," he said simply. "Lying here is a fruitless endeavour."

"Okay, fine, I used to be a bartender," Danni said, quickly regaining her composure. "Now I work for the Australian Government."

"I'm not asking for a biography. I want to know you. Your hopes, dreams and fears. What do you desire?" Lucifer smirked.

Danni stared at the pointed red horns on Lucifer's bald skull. What did she desire?

"A human lost within the world. Walking an empty path with no destination. A story replicated several billion times over up there," Lucifer's voice rumbled.

"Well, my life has been crazy the last couple of years. Things are falling into place," Danni said, feeling somewhat annoyed at Lucifer's assumptions.

"What I see before me is a loser. Your parents, losers before you, and their parents before them. Menial jobs and pathetic relationships are your ancestry and your destiny."

Danni wasn't a loser anymore. She knew she wasn't. Lucifer wouldn't get to her with such easy jeers.

"I'm doing fine!" she stated defiantly.

"Measure yourself against a low bar and you will always come up higher," Lucifer said lazily. He leaned toward Danni. "Are you the person you should be? The person you could be?"

Danni tried to speak up, but Lucifer cut her off.

"You accept less because you think you deserve less. Each human is born an unlimited ball of potential, but you all throw it away. You are nothing special. Weakness consumes you."

The cold and the terror of Lucifer were consuming her. He spoke with a bitter truth, one that she couldn't deny. It wasn't just his words, it was like the air was sapping Danni of all her strength.

"Why are you saying this?' she asked quietly.

"The fact that you are here should make you exceptional. But looking at you now, all I see is a pathetic little person who has lucked herself into extraordinary circumstances."

The massive hand of Lucifer cast a wide shadow as it approached Danni. She was gently gripped by Lucifer's fingers and raised before his central head.

"What say you?" he boomed, his hot breath washing over her.

Danni didn't speak.

She felt as if she was being compelled to spill her inner doubt and darkness.

"You disgust me," Lucifer spat. "I should entomb you here forever as punishment for your weakness."

Danni closed her eyes. She didn't want to look at that monstrous face. She felt numb.

The squeeze of Lucifer's fingers loosened around her. She felt human hands against her waist. Suddenly, she was rising away from the dark circle below and floating upwards towards the ice ceiling.

Danni looked up to see the human-sized face of an incredibly handsome man before her. Handsome was an understatement. This guy was surreal. Draped in a white robe with six magnificent red wings spreading from his back, she was caught in the embrace of an angel.

"Let me help you," the angel said, offering a charming smile.

He looked different, but his cold red eyes and sinister voice revealed that this was still Lucifer, just in a new form.

"One of the advantages humans have over the divine is that your natures aren't fixed. Duality defines you. Where weakness dwells, strength can be found. From inner darkness springs light. You have shown me your weakness; now I will see your strength."

"Why aren't you always like this?" Danni asked. This Lucifer was far more pleasing to the eye than the three-headed monster in the pit.

"That monster is what my years in Hell have twisted me into. As you see me now is my true form. We angels were modelled on you humans, and in being so, we became better than the gods. We are like you, unbound to rigid natures and capable of being more. I am both the morning star and the monster in the pit, eating the unworthy."

"Why are you telling me any of this?" Danni asked, as the pair continued to twirl upwards.

"I am no fool, Danni Quinn. For you to be here now means you are part of the journey to claim the lost power of Zeus. I feel Markovic and Belial will soon fail me. I am giving you the chance to prove your value. To help me build your species a better world."

"Why would I do that?" Danni mumbled.

"You and I are one in the same. We are the product of circumstance and our own failure. Weakness defines us. I would be free of this place and you would be free of your past. Work with me and I promise the world to you. I know you; I understand you. The gods don't care for the plights of mortals. You are just tools to them. Playthings."

"You said you'd wash the world with fire."

"A holy fire that will only wash away the failures of humanity. Paradise is coming. The fires of Hell do not hurt the unworthy. Demons do not torture the good. Eden across the world."

The roof above them split open and ice tumbled down.

"It doesn't sound right..."

"And what do you think the gods will do with this power?" Lucifer said calmly. "Do you think Apollo will just let faith in Abrahamic religions wain naturally? He is scorned by us. We get our power from humans believing in us. Apollo will spread his own fire across the world, the fire of the sun god of old. The worthy and unworthy will burn alike in his quest for vengeance. Giving him the key to that power is a mistake. Humanity will feel his fire before the angels of Heaven do."

"What do you want me to do, though?" Danni asked quietly.

"Complete your mission. When you have all the pieces with you, call for me and I will collect them."

Lucifer leaned in and planted a soft kiss on Danni's lips. Danni immediately recoiled, wholly bamboozled. But the damage was done.

A blinding light appeared above the pair. Danni could vividly see the blues and whites of the ice walls around her. Lucifer had infected her with his sinister magic; to what end, she didn't know.

"Until next we meet, Danni Quinn. You are now marked by

me. When the time is right, call for me and I will claim my freedom. Three… two… one… the Viking arrives."

Danni saw a ring of fire manifest in the corner of her eye. There was a thunderous boom and a blaze of orange that ignited the air around them.

Danni's stomach flipped upside down as she rapidly descended.

In the blink of an eye, she was once again in the grip of the giant red monster in the pit of ice. The three-headed demonic form of Lucifer was slowly raising her towards his open mouth.

The scene had changed so fast Danni hadn't fully comprehended what was going on.

Her eyes turned upwards.

Sailing through the air, with two axes held above him and wild eyes burning with fury, was what looked to be a Viking ripped straight out of a documentary on television. His blonde braided beard flew majestically backwards as he soared towards Lucifer's outstretched arm.

"LUCIFER! DID YOU DESTROY MY TAVERN?" the Viking screamed.

His axes collided with Lucifer's arm, slicing deep into the fallen archangel's flesh. The Viking heaved and propelled himself up onto Lucifer's muscular forearm. He turned and grunted with exertion as he pulled his axes free.

Lucifer brought his other colossal arm down in a clumsy attempt to grab the warrior. The Viking was too fast, nimbly dodging the attack and running towards Danni.

"TAKE SOMETHING OF MINE AND I WILL TAKE

SOMETHING OF YOURS!"

His eyes were fixed firmly on Danni.

The Viking thrust his dual axes into Lucifer's thumb, quickly hacking away until he severed it. Danni squealed as Lucifer's grip released.

She started sliding from his hand towards the ice below. The thumb crashed down with a thundering boom.

The Viking dived down, catching Danni and collapsing onto the thumb, bouncing off it, then hitting the ice. He attached the axes to a sling on his back and pulled a curious key forward from around his neck. The Viking thrust the key outwards and a portal opened. Inside it was a totally different landscape.

With Danni flung over his broad shoulders, the Viking dived through, narrowly avoiding Lucifer's closed fist slamming down on top of them.

10

EVIL THINGS IN DARK LANDS

NIFLHEIM
- JANUARY 24-

Danni felt a striking change in the temperature the second she crossed the threshold. The Viking released Danni gently, dropping her to the floor. She swayed slightly as she found her balance again. The last few minutes had seen her teleporting all over the place, and she felt a little nauseous.

The thought of beautiful Lucifer's lips on hers also made her feel sick. She rubbed her eyes. Who was the man who'd rescued her from the grip of the Devil, if rescue it had been? Lucifer had strongly indicated that he knew the intruder was coming.

"Thank you," Danni breathed.

The Viking eyed her curiously. "You are alive?"

"Ah, yeah," Danni stated. Now that she could see clearly, she had a hard time not letting her jaw drop.

The Viking was a specimen of a man. He had a barrel chest thick with hair and a stomach lined with impossible rows of abdominal muscles. The braids in his beard matched the braids in his flowing blonde hair. He was tall as well, absurdly tall. The man had to be close to seven feet. He had a youthful face with light scarring across it and his eyes were steely, battle-hardened and unnervingly bright. Danni had never seen eyes like them before.

On his right arm was a detailed tattoo that displayed a dragon in the Nordic style. His left rib also showed a plethora of Nordic runes plastered there. He wore long brown trousers and primitive hide boots.

The Viking removed the sling holding his axes and slipped a crudely hewn tunic over his head, slightly disappointing Danni. Lucifer, in his angel form, had been movie-star handsome. This Viking was a rough outdoorsy lumber-jack handsome that Danni really couldn't get enough of.

"Are you... not alive?" Danni asked, feeling a little lost for words.

"I am long departed from the mortal world," the Viking answered in his thick Nordic accent, placing his two axes on a roughly hewn wooden table.

It was only then that Danni realised she was standing in a simplistic house.

"What is your name?"

"Sigurd."

"Just Sigurd?"

"I suppose you could say Sigurd of the Volsung line."

"Okay, Sigurd it is," Danni said. "Where are we?"

"Somewhere safe from the long reach of Lucifer and his servants. We are outside his infernal rings of torture."

"We aren't in Hell?"

"No, we are still in Hell," Sigurd answered.

He twisted a nozzle on the wall and amber ale began flowing from it. Like an experienced bartender, he filled two enormous mugs and thrust one towards Danni.

Thinking about the demonic alcohol in the Hell's Horns Tavern, Danni didn't take a sip.

"Drink!" Sigurd demanded.

"This demonic beer doesn't agree with me," Danni started.

"That is my ale! I brew it myself for my tavern!"

"Your tavern? Wait, you mean the Hell's Horns?"

"Ah! So, your travels took you there! It was quite nice before someone blew up one of the walls..."

"I have so many questions," Danni said, sitting down on a wooden stool.

"The Hell's Horns is a place to drink and to fight in this accursed land! Though, I will admit some of its building materials are less than desirable."

Danni had to shuffle to dislodge a splinter from her stool. "Where'd you get this furniture from?"

"Built it myself," Sigurd said proudly.

"Of course you did," Danni murmured.

This guy had to be the manliest man who ever lived.

Danni thought about telling Sigurd that it wasn't Lucifer

who blew a chunk out of his precious tavern wall, but she didn't have to. She felt a strange release, then Sigurd was back on his feet with his fists raised. Foam clung to his beard.

Artemis stood beside Danni and eyed Sigurd up and down.

"I no longer sensed the foul presence of the archangel," Artemis scowled. She turned to Sigurd and commanded, "Sit!"

Sigurd collapsed to the floor, not of his own accord.

"You are a god," he marvelled.

"I am Artemis of the Olympians. You, I know, Sigurd. Descendant of Odin and widely touted as the greatest warrior Earth will ever see."

Sigurd looked humbled by such an introduction from the goddess.

Artemis turned to Danni and asked, "How did you escape the clutches of Lucifer?"

"Sigurd saved me. He kind of flew in from the sky and grabbed me, then teleported us out."

"How?" Artemis demanded of Sigurd, who was getting back to his feet.

The Viking pulled the key from around his neck and handed it to Artemis.

"This is the Hell Key. A one-of-a-kind artefact crafted for the being known as the Grim Reaper. No creature can traverse Hell through teleportation; it was a constraint Lucifer put on the place. The Grim Reaper can have a need to be places quickly, however. This key was his exception to Lucifer's ruling."

"How did you come to possess it?"

"A being named Adramelech came into possession of it.

Long ago, I met Adramelech and won the key from him."

"Can this key remove us from the Underworld?"

"No," Sigurd answered simply. He took a hearty swig from his mug.

Artemis threw the Hell Key back to Sigurd, who caught it and returned it to its original position around his neck.

"Where are we? Specifically?" Artemis demanded.

"Outside the First Circle of Hell. There are walls and fortresses not far from here that border Lucifer's realm. All roads lead into the First Circle. These empty wastelands are only home to wandering demons and are never ventured into."

Danni was sure the story of this singular Viking in Hell had to be an interesting one. How had Earth's mightiest warrior come to live like this? A lost soul in Christian Hell…

"Valhalla was wiped clean by the angels. How did you escape?" Artemis asked.

"I never went to Valhalla. Odin's halls were reserved for those who died a noble death. I was betrayed and murdered!" Sigurd slammed his mug down, spilling the remaining contents everywhere. "I went with the rest of the ordinary dead to Hel. When the angels came, I fought with Baldr. A powerful union we made in the face of that onslaught!"

Sigurd's eyes glazed over as he remembered the glorious battle from long ago. "Hel fell, and I found myself a rat in cracks of the Underworld as it was reshaped by Lucifer and his Knights of Hell."

Artemis seemed satisfied. Danni, however, wasn't. The specifics of past events didn't matter now; there was a more pressing question at hand.

"Do you know a way out?" she asked.

"For the living, I might. There is a way in the ruins of Niflheim… a path mortals can walk. There were rumours long ago of a secret road from Midgard into those depths."

"Niflheim still exists?" Artemis asked.

"Yes," Sigurd replied. He didn't seem to be one for overexplaining.

"I thought the angels folded all the old regions of Hell into their nine circles?"

"Niflheim was the land of the evil dead that sat on the very borders of creation. Its mist-ridden hills and icy valleys fall into the void itself. You cannot change a place that is shaped by the void. Niflheim still sits cold and untouched in the deepest places of Hell, outside Lucifer's circles, much as we are now in this wasteland."

"What about Mel?" Danni asked suddenly.

Sigurd raised his eyebrows. "Another mortal?"

Artemis turned to him and said, "In the ruins of Sodom lingers the Oracle of Delphi. Fetch her for us, if she still lives."

"You would command me, foreign goddess?" Sigurd asked.

Storm clouds rose in Artemis's eyes. The room grew dark. Sigurd, sensing he didn't have a choice, gripped the Hell Key and opened another portal. He stepped through and it sealed behind him.

Danni turned to Artemis in a panic.

"Artemis! Lucifer infected me with dark magic! He said that I will summon him when we complete the ritual."

The goddess frowned. "Keep this information to yourself

for now. I will discuss it with my brother. I'd prefer the human element didn't react poorly. A connection to Lucifer could prove advantageous if used properly."

"Well," Danni smiled weakly, "at least it seems like you're committed to helping out."

Artemis said nothing.

• • • • •

TIME PASSED SLOWLY IN SIGURD'S long windowless home. Danni thought she heard wailing yelps and vicious cries in the distance. Artemis told her that was just the sounds of the wild primitive demons out there.

Sigurd was a simple man. He held very few possessions and no artwork whatsoever. Danni assumed he must've kept some of his treasures at the Hell's Horns Tavern.

Danni did discover a thin piece of parchment that had a poem dedicated to something called Gram. It was an object Sigurd clearly missed.

Danni wondered how she could read Sigurd's writing and understand him at all. There should've been a massive language barrier between them. Artemis told Danni that when she'd hitched a ride in her body, she'd given Danni the ability to hear, speak and read all languages. Danni felt both violated and overjoyed. It was an incredible skill to have.

After an hour of sitting around, the room lit up with the glow from a portal. Sigurd was back, and with him came Mel.

Danni jumped up and gave Mel a resounding hug. She

figured the circumstances they'd been through today negated professional decorum.

It was the Viking who now held the golden sword of Apollo at his side. Its arduous weight didn't bother Sigurd at all.

"A mighty weapon," Sigurd mused, admiring it from all angles. He slashed the air three times, all the while smiling more and more enthusiastically.

"That thing was impossible to drag around. I'm glad this fellow showed up." Mel said exasperated.

"Oh, this is Sigurd," Danni said quickly.

"We made introductions," Mel laughed. "When he successfully wrestled both those onis we saw at the bar into submission."

"I could not kill them. They are my friends, though twisted creatures they are," Sigurd said absent-mindedly. Danni thought he sounded a little sad.

"You can understand ancient Norse too?" Danni asked Mel.

"I noticed that when my powers as the Oracle of Delphi awakened, I suddenly got very good at languages," Mel answered.

Artemis spoke up, "Let us travel to Niflheim and find the hidden path. I assume with this key we can skip a lot of the sightseeing."

"If you want to skip the castle of serpents on the corpse shore, we can. Though, I'd say you're missing out," Sigurd laughed.

The joke was totally lost on Danni.

"Do you need to rest?" Danni asked Mel.

Artemis didn't allow her to answer.

"We can rest when we are free of Hell. Portal, now!" the goddess commanded.

Sigurd lowered the golden sword and pushed the key forward. The portal showed a cold desolate place.

The three women, followed by Sigurd, stepped through the portal into the ancient Norse land of the evil dead.

$$\bullet \bullet \bullet \bullet \bullet$$

DANNI HAD AN INSTANT FLASHBACK to the Ninth Circle of Hell. It was cold and dark, though a low light permeated the place from an unknown source. There were no blocks of ice with frozen bodies in them. Instead, they stood at the bottom of a hillside. A path snaked its way up, and along it, rudimentary caverns had been cut into the earth. A vicious wind blew, making Danni wish she hadn't discarded all of her warm clothes on the scorched plain.

Artemis took to the air, heading straight up. Then, her shining silver figure quickly descended.

"Mountains for some distance then nothing but darkness. We face the primordial void," she said.

"How do we find the way out? If there is one?" Danni asked.

"Perhaps there are some demons down here we can ask for directions?" Mel suggested.

Sigurd looked sheepishly at the group. "I am ashamed to admit I have not explored this place fully. The lingering presence of the dragon Fafnir has kept me away, though we are well past him now. The only life we will encounter here is the life that fled here from Helheim and managed to remain hidden these long years."

"Why do you think there is a path here for mortals?" Danni asked Sigurd curiously.

"Rumours and whispers from a long time ago. The dead god Baldr made mention of a secret door in Niflheim. A path cut so that the dead couldn't access it. We thought to regroup there when the angels came, but defeat came too quickly."

"I have a few questions," Danni said hesitantly. "What is Helheim? Who is the goddess Hel? And where exactly are we right now?"

She was sick of biting her tongue while everyone else rattled off mythological terms.

"Helheim was the land of the dead for the ordinary," Sigurd answered.

"Scandanavian regions, specifically," Mel whispered to Danni.

"Helheim was ruled by Hel, a daughter of the trickster Loki. Half of her was an image of divine beauty, the other half a rotting corpse."

"I thought all of the dead from Scandanavia went to Valhalla or something?" Danni asked. She was sure she'd read the Vikings battled for all eternity after death.

"Those who died in battle did," Sigurd said darkly. "It was the greatest honour a person could have in life, a noble death. I was stabbed while sleeping."

"By who?" Danni was so curious. It wasn't often you got to ask the dead how they died.

"Guttorm, on request of my friend and ally Gunnar. It was all to do with a woman scorned."

"A tale as old as time. History can be discussed later. Let's get out of this cold," Mel said.

"We are looking for the deepest, darkest place in this frozen wasteland. It looks like we have to enter the caverns that line the hillside and make our way down," Sigurd said.

"I will advance alone. Follow my footprints in the unchanging snow," Artemis ordered.

She began transforming. Within moments the silver goddess was gone, and a beautiful snow leopard stood in her place. With a snarl, the goddess took off through the snow.

Danni, Mel and Sigurd trudged after her.

The descent into the caverns provided some much-needed warmth. The still air and eerie silence of Niflheim were enough to induce paranoia in even the most hardened soul. Even Mel was beginning to turn and jump at imagined noises.

Sigurd broke the quietness by telling Mel and Danni of his life. He spoke of the treachery of the smith who'd raised him. He told them the grand tale of his slaying of the dragon Fafnir and his ability to understand the birds. His life was war, victory, conquest and love. It was retold with such passion that Danni could almost see herself there. She pitied Sigurd's death but admired the life he had lived.

The caverns weren't natural in their formation, looking like something had long ago pushed its way out of the mountain.

Sigurd loudly speculated that these tunnels were dug by the roots of the world tree, Yggdrasil. However, he couldn't answer how the concept of such a tree binding the universe together fit in with the world as they knew it.

The path had a pleasant downward slope that made for easy walking. The tunnels were illuminated by the silver light springing from the snow leopard ahead. They navigated forks in the path by following Artemis' godly glow.

Before long, the tunnel widened into a mighty underground cavern. Evidently, Artemis had gone the correct way, as before them stretched a narrow bridge that ended against a flat stone pillar suspended in darkness.

The pillar had a circular bronze carving etched into it, which they all immediately assumed to be the portal.

They came to a halt beside Artemis, who hadn't yet stepped onto the bridge.

"What is the delay?" Danni whispered to Mel.

Mel pointed out across the bridge. About halfway down, a large shape was shifting.

"What is that?" Mel asked Sigurd.

Sigurd squinted and said, "Garmr."

Artemis morphed back into her usual form. "What is Garmr?"

"Guard dog and personal attendant of the goddess Hel. While he is no Fenris Wolf, he is a fearsome foe. Even able to tangle with gods. Back in my time, he was called the chief of dogs."

"What is he doing down here?" Mel asked.

"Waiting for reinforcements that never arrived…"

"I will skip the dog and head for the portal gate. Perhaps I can deduce how to open it. Sigurd, as you cannot pass, hold the dog at bay so my human companions can," Artemis instructed.

Sigurd cracked his knuckles, enthusiastic at the challenge. "Mightiest of dogs fights mightiest of men," he grinned.

Artemis now became a silver eagle and took to the air. She soared down the length of the bridge. The black shape of Garmr began to follow the bird until it heard Sigurd running towards it. His heavy footsteps echoed through the vast cavern. Apollo's golden sword was swinging at the Viking's side.

"I will pin Garmr!" he shouted back to Danni and Mel. "You two make for the gate!"

The bounding Garmr leapt at Sigurd, who caught the dog in a bear hug. The Viking almost looked panicked as the dog's gnashing teeth grazed his face. Somehow, he managed to retain hold of Apollo's sword while the dog frantically tried to free itself.

Garmr managed to generate enough upward force to flip Sigurd onto his back. Released from his tight hold, the dog leapt backwards and prepared for another assault. Sigurd threw jabs at the dog's face, which only served to enrage it further.

"Looks like we are running again," Mel sighed.

She and Danni took off, much like they had when they saw the hellhounds near Lancelton. The rolling, tumbling fight between Sigurd and Garmr quickly got in the way. With a well-timed leap and graceful summersault, Danni cleared the fight with Mel not far behind.

Garmr turned for them faster than Sigurd could react. The dog leapt and caught Mel right in the back, slamming her hard into the icy stone.

Danni saw and felt the impact. She turned to help Mel, only

to see Garmr latch his teeth into her left arm. Danni knew the feeling.

Garmr yelped as Sigurd grabbed him by the hind legs and pulled him back. Danni lifted Mel up and said, "Let's go!"

Garmr turned back on Sigurd, who this time managed to flip the writhing animal around and press his entire body weight against the dog.

"Now!" Sigurd shouted.

Sigurd pinned the snarling, snapping Garmr to the ground as Mel and Danni made the final push toward the gate.

Artemis, back in human form, had her eyes closed, trying to figure out the magic that opened it. The ornate circular door wasn't budging.

What a door it was, decorated with metallic bronze struts fashioned in the image of wolves, warriors and dragons. It was five metres tall and at least five wide, stretching well beyond the bridge's width.

Danni looked back. Sigurd was barely containing the madly struggling beast. Any second now, he'd be pushed away, and the ravenous dog would be on top of them.

"This path is designed for Asgardians. It will not open to anyone but them," Artemis murmured.

"Can't you just blow it up?" Mel said, pressing down on her bleeding wound.

"No. We need one of the Norse gods."

"Wait," Mel snapped, "Sigurd is a descendant of Odin, right?"

"The path will not open to the dead."

"You are a goddess!" Mel replied. "Life and death are just quirks of matter to you!"

"Life and death are specific domains to specific gods. I cannot simply will life into a departed soul. I am neither Hades nor Thanatos."

"But you can do something! You are a literal GOD who has dealt so much death! I know you can give life as well!"

"I cannot bring life the way you think. I can perform an act of great evil," Artemis said, bowing her head. "I can take a life to restore a life. It is against the order of things to do so. It was forbidden by my father and his father and his father before him."

Danni gulped. Even if Artemis wanted to do this, whose life would be taken?

Mel collapsed onto her knees. Blood was gushing from beneath her hand, spilling onto the icy bridge. "Now is not the time for ancient superstitions, even if they are divine," Mel pleaded.

Garmr pushed Sigurd away, at last, almost knocking him from the bridge. Sigurd managed to grip onto the edge with one hand, perilously dangling above oblivion.

The beastly dog came bounding forward, jaws open. It was headed right for Danni.

It leapt towards her in a spray of saliva.

"Not again," Danni groaned, bracing for the bite.

Garmr froze in mid-air. He made a strange noise, like a deflating balloon.

Artemis had moved in front of Danni. The goddess was suspending Garmr in mid-air with her power and using considerable effort to do so. Danni could see the strain on her face.

"We will pay for this abuse of divine power," Artemis said, shooting a sharp look at Mel. "Remember this moment, Oracle of Delphi, for not even your gaze sees the horror in the dark that will come if it senses what is about to happen."

Artemis closed her eyes. Garmr twisted in mid-air, then his eyes went white. Sigurd hoisted himself back onto the bridge, just as a strange orb of light left the floating dog's mouth. Artemis directed it towards Sigurd.

The life energy collided with the tall Viking's chest, causing him to convulse and fall to the ground.

With a sharp inhalation of breath, Sigurd got to his feet. Garmr's lifeless corpse fell to the bridge, unmoving.

"You could've done that the whole time!" Mel stated, with venom in her eyes.

"Enough of your insolence! There are reasons why the God of the Hunt does not grant life to humans!" Artemis bellowed, turning on her.

Danni couldn't help but notice that Artemis looked shattered. Her divine radiance was gone, and her face was etched with tiredness. The process of transferring the life of Garmr into Sigurd had taken a significant toll on her.

Sigurd, still looking at his hands in awe, marched forward towards Artemis. He bowed low before her.

"I cannot thank you in any words of any tongue enough for this gift."

"Thank me by opening this door," Artemis demanded.

Sigurd did as asked. The door sensed his divine lineage, and upon his touch blew backwards. All that was left in its place was the swirling black void.

Mel pulled herself up with a groan and jumped through. She vanished into nothingness.

Next went Artemis, looking tired and deeply concerned.

Sigurd looked back at Danni and smiled. "A second chance at life, what a thing to behold."

He too stepped into the eternal blackness.

Danni took a moment to breathe. She was alone in the darkness of Niflheim. The land of the evil dead, where apparently a divinely evil act had just occurred. She looked back at the corpse of the dog Garmr. His life had been stolen for their escape. Danni hoped that it was just godly superstition and that breaking that rule wouldn't end up bringing ruin upon them all.

Resigned to an uncertain future, Danni passed through the gate and back into the mortal world.

11

SACRED LAWS AND ANCIENT CITIES

OSE, SOUTHERN NORWAY
- JANUARY 24 -

Danni inhaled sharply. She'd spent a minute being compressed and twisted as she travelled between dimensions. The second her feet fell into mounds of glistening white snow, she collapsed.

Feeling the chilly powder on her skin, Danni jumped up. Her head was pounding and an intense barrage of tiredness began pummeling her from within.

Dawn had just broken over the world of white. The scenery was unfamiliar and the crashing of a mighty waterfall, still thundering away despite the freezing temperatures, rang out from nearby.

A cry of joy bellowed out from nearby, briefly overpowering the chorus of the waterfall.

"ALIVE! I AM ALIVE! Look at the snow! Look at the trees!"

Sigurd was leaping up and down in a wild display of ecstasy. The ground crunched beneath his hide boots as he punched the air.

"Where are we?" Artemis asked the ecstatic Viking.

"We are in the lands of my forefathers, where I cannot tell. But what a joy it is to be here."

Mel spoke next, though she didn't sound good. The bite of Garmr had done a lot of damage. "According to my phone, we are near the village of Ose in Southern Norway."

Artemis observed her wound and coldly stated, "You should have let me heal it while we were still in Hell."

"I was preoccupied with escape," Mel answered, too exhausted to be angry.

Sigurd removed his shirt and wrapped it around Mel's arm, creating a makeshift tourniquet.

"We need to get out of this cold," Danni chimed in, her teeth chattering.

"Ose is about thirty minutes north of here on foot," Mel informed them.

The giant Sigurd was trying to support Mel as she stood, but he was just too tall.

"You are wounded, I will carry you. Let us move!" Sigurd stated, lifting Mel up.

Mel briefly looked like she was going to object, but was too weak and needed the help.

The morning sun caught the waterfall, shooting a glorious rainbow from it. Danni briefly forgot the cold as she got lost in its beauty, though that was only momentary. The waterfall had to be two hundred metres tall, twisting through trees at the top of a sheer cliff face before falling with tremendous force. Danni deduced that with the sheer amount of water that was moving, there had to be a substantial river nearby.

They pushed through a clump of winter trees, still maintaining their foliage, and came into a clearing beside a road.

As she'd suspected, the road ran along a mighty river that twisted through a valley of high cliffs and rocky precipices. Across the highway was a long building with a black roof that was up to its windows in snow. Danni could see other buildings stretching along the river banks, though all looked abandoned in the depths of winter.

Danni, wanting to test her new language abilities, ran towards an information sign.

"This waterfall is called Reiårsfossen, and we are in Norway!" she called out.

The sign told her the main river was called the Setesdal and was still liquid despite the freezing temperatures. The water closest to the banks had frozen up, yet the cold hadn't penetrated the river proper. A chunk of dry ground shaped like a V stretched out into the middle of the waterway, connected to a thin land bridge by the road.

The swathes of forest that surrounded them assured Danni that this place would have been a beacon of the Earth's natural beauty in the summer. Even in winter, it was wondrous enough to inflame her senses.

Gone was the suffocation of Niflheim and the despair of Hell's Ninth Circle; she was overjoyed to be back in the beautiful winter of the mortal world.

A small blue sedan travelling along the highway stopped when it saw the motley group in the parking area.

A man in a red and black checked beanie with a wiry blonde beard called out from the driver's side, "Do you people need help?"

His accent was thick and his words a little broken.

Danni imagined that to the stranger, seeing the tall shirtless Viking holding the bleeding Melissa in his arms would've been odd enough. Let alone the two additional women, one wearing nothing but a sleek silver dress and the other turning blue from the cold.

"Yes!" Danni said, running up to him. "Please take us to Ose!"

The stranger, bracing the cold, got out and opened his rear passenger doors. He ushered them in, all the while rubbing his hands wrapped in thick gloves.

Being by far the largest member of their troupe, Sigurd squeezed into the front seat. Danni, Mel and Artemis all squished into the back. Artemis did not look impressed by this transport or the seating arrangements. Her ever-present scowl seemed to chill the air more than nature itself did.

The stranger assured them that Ose was very close and would only be a couple of minutes. He carefully eyed Sigurd up and down, seeming bewildered by the man's huge stature and wild look.

At last, it seemed, he had to speak up. "My friend, you are an enormous man. Viking blood in you, most certainly."

"Volsung blood," Sigurd replied.

The driver had to think about Sigurd's words. Then he laughed and said, "Ah yes, we all wish we could claim our ancestors to be Ragnar or mighty Sigurd, slayer of Fafnir. Maybe you can get away with it."

Sigurd had a broad smile on his face. Danni understood why. To have been dead for centuries upon centuries and have some mortal name drop you would be flattering for anyone.

"What is your name, my good man?" Sigurd boomed.

This time, the driver couldn't quite grasp what he'd said.

"That sounds like Old Norse you're speaking. I am familiar with a little. Definitely the word Volsung, but not much more."

"What is your name?" Danni asked quickly. She didn't want the ancient Viking raising any more suspicion than was necessary.

"Andreas. Only a few minutes and we will be in Ose. I will take you to the market. There is no hospital." Andreas gave Mel a concerned look through his rear vision mirror.

"I fell trying to climb the waterfall," Mel improvised.

"Ah yes, very dangerous in winter," Andreas said solemnly.

As they drove into Ose, it became immediately apparent that it was a tiny town. So small, in fact, Danni wondered why the portal had brought them out here. It seemed to be a random stretch of forest with no prominent temples or ancient structures around.

There were little more than a dozen buildings, most of them tall sheds for farms. Andreas pointed out a hotel and a café before pulling into a clearing before the supermarket.

The supermarket was painted a vibrant red and had a triangular black roof. Wooden tables and benches lined its front, though they were so snow-laden they were unusable. A noticeboard with a handful of fliers sat right outside the entrance. However, Danni suspected the cold stopped anyone from perusing them.

Before they scrambled out of his car, Mel asked Andreas, "Is there anything significant to the old Norse religion here?"

Andreas raised his eyebrows and responded, "Yes. Not far from here they unearthed a place where a grand temple to Thor and Odin once stood. It has caused quite the archaeological rush in this area."

"Well, that explains it. This region was a holy one, probably due to the fact there was a secret portal to Niflheim here," Danni thought.

"I wish I could stay, but I really must go. The market has medical supplies and a telephone. Best of luck to you," Andreas said warmly.

"Your kindness has been noted," Artemis informed him, rather formally.

Andreas nodded, looking a little bewildered, then jumped back into his car and sped off.

The goddess watched him go with a curious intensity.

"What did you do?" Mel asked, eyeing her suspiciously.

"I have blessed him with good luck. How it will manifest, I do not know."

Mel looked aghast. "Won't that cause the angels to descend on this place?"

"No. If I were to heal you now, that would be divine magic creating a physical change in the world, and they would find me. A blessing or a curse, if not grand in scale, is unnoticeable."

"The rules are so complex," Mel sighed, shuffling through

the snow towards the door of the supermarket.

"Hecate, the Goddess of Witchcraft, got around it for years. She would use the most advanced magics, yet the angels never found her because she would set the spells into physical markings. Runes, like those that are tattooed on Sigurd here."

Sigurd looked down at the ancient symbols that lined his rib.

"Since the magic activated from the rune, and not from her, the angels could never detect her. Their system for detection is flawed and can be exploited in small ways. Simple magic with no physical consequences is mostly fine."

"Can you do rune magic like Hecate?"

"No. She is a goddess of magic and that is within her domain, not mine. But while we are on the subject of blessings and curses…"

Artemis waved her hand through the air, and Sigurd clutched at his throat. He sucked in a huge breath.

"We cannot have our Viking companion here speaking a long dead language. You are now gifted with the ability to understand all human tongues, as the rest of us are."

Sigurd nodded gratefully.

Danni, now almost entirely blue, pushed through the group and into the warmth of the shop.

An elderly woman pushing a straw broom greeted them.

"Bandages," Danni asked through chattering teeth.

Upon seeing Mel enter, she immediately ran off to fetch medical supplies.

Danni applied the wound dressings to Mel. The dog's teeth

had sunk deep, and the wound would take time to heal. Sigurd assured them the risk of infection was minimal, with Garmr being a divine being and all.

Sigurd, unable to contain his fascination with the buildings of the small town, picked up a jacket from a nearby clothing rack and rushed outside to explore it. Danni paid for the jacket.

The shop-keep brought them out a steaming tray of mugs filled to the brim with the most delightful hot chocolate. The steam danced in the cool air, and even Artemis, though sceptical at first, gave the drink a go.

"Magnificent," the goddess murmured as she swallowed the marshmallow that floated inside.

The shop-keep asked no annoying questions nor bothered them in any way. Once Mel was adequately attended to, Artemis went out to join Sigurd in his wanderings.

Danni made sure no blood was seeping through the bandages. "That'll do until you can get it properly looked at."

Mel thanked Danni, then also graciously thanked the shopkeeper.

The pair watched through the side window as Sigurd began lumbering up a snowy hill out of sight. His wonderment could barely be contained.

"Wait till he sees a city," Danni said to Mel, watching Sigurd's figure disappear.

"I guess he is stuck with us now," Mel replied. "Mind you, there a worse people to pick up for a mission than a legendary Viking hero."

Danni's smile faltered. "I'm worried about what Artemis

said. That it is an act of evil to steal life from one being and give it to another if you aren't a god of death."

"Yes, me too. We will have to face the consequences of that when they arise. We are no good stuck in Hell for all eternity," Mel sighed.

"She said something about drawing the attention of some monster. What was that about?"

"I don't know. It is safe to say there is a lot we don't know about the gods. Perhaps they have their own myths to contend with? Regardless, we have a mission to complete still. I will call Brett Sayer and see if he can get us out of this village. At least we can report that Artemis is here and willing to help," Mel answered.

Just as those words left her mouth, Artemis re-entered the store. She was actually smiling.

"That Sigurd reminds me of the great heroes of old. Memories of Orion the Hunter stir in me."

"Artemis, thank you for getting us out of Hell," Mel said, a little stiffly.

Artemis nodded curtly, the smile vanishing from her face. "Let us hope it went unnoticed. There are sacred rules even among gods."

"Who enforces those rules?" Danni asked.

"There are legends from the primordials about the origins of such laws, though I never put much stock in them. That was until Zeus disappeared."

Danni knew that their mission was to fill the empty position of Zeus. Still, she hadn't actually heard much about what happened to the God-King of Olympus.

Artemis continued, "What happened to my father was… strange. He just vanished out of space, time and all dimensions. We desperately searched, but then we stopped. I always felt like we were being influenced from the outside. Like a fog descended over the Olympians, and we just let it go. Perhaps in the wilds I was less susceptible… but I couldn't help think there was something of the old sacred laws in it."

"So, Zeus just vanished into thin air?"

"He was pulled from our reality, violently, it seems. Otherwise, this pocket of power you now try to claim wouldn't exist. My father was the greatest of us, at the height of his power. If something took him from this universe, it is to be feared."

Danni gulped. She even thought she heard concern in Artemis' voice.

"Well, that comes to why we needed your assistance in the first place," Mel added. "We were hoping you had an idea on where an artefact of Zeus's would still be in the mortal world."

Artemis thought about the question for a long moment.

"Are you humans familiar with the ancient civilisation?"

"Yes," Mel answered.

Danni wasn't. Artemis clearly saw the doubt in her eyes.

"A long time ago, the early gods were impressed with humans. But they were lacking the spark of greatness. Your whole species was confined to North-East Africa, or so the old stories go. This was before I was born. You tried to leave your homelands several times, but the other types of humans pushed you back. Zeus was one of the gods who saw your potential. He ordered his titan ally Prometheus to craft better humans from clay. Then my sister Athena breathed wisdom into them. It was these people who formed the ancient civilisation."

"There was another race of humans created from the gods?" Danni said in surprise.

"Yes. They weren't like your kind, all expansionist and aggressive. They built large, wondrous cities and never left them. They shunned you. As the Oracle of Delphi here knows, Prometheus took pity on the naturally evolved humans. He brought the divine flame down from Olympus and offered you the spark of greatness. From then, your people spread across the world and advanced rapidly. At the same time, the ancient civilisation, in their stagnant halls and unchanging societies, fell to ruination, one after another."

"Are any left?" Danni asked.

"Some interbred with your kind. Their genetic legacy certainly lives on. But their cities and wonders are long extinguished."

"Save the Temple of Prometheus in Afghanistan," Mel interjected. "If that is out there, perhaps more ruins are."

"That is why I raise this point. In my time as an Olympian, rumours prevailed that the island nation of Atlantis wasn't completely obliterated. Legends said its temples and statues still lingered deep under the sea. The people of Atlantis were gifted many things by the original Olympians: Zeus, Poseidon, Hades, Hera, Hestia and Demeter. If those temples do in fact linger in the lightless depths, perhaps so to do artefacts of Zeus," Artemis ended.

"Okay, good. We have a target now. We just need to find the lost city of Atlantis." Mel seemed bolstered by this potential lead.

She pressed her phone to her ear.

"Brett, how are you?"

She paused for a moment as he replied, then said, "Oh, you know, we've been to Hell and back. We need a ride and a rendezvous point in Europe."

· · · · ·

A COUPLE OF HOURS LATER, Danni, Mel, Sigurd and Artemis all stood in ankle-deep snow beside a clearing outside Ose. The shopkeeper had been kind enough to supply all of them with cold weather apparel.

The sun was high in the sky and the day was still. It was incredibly beautiful in the valley, though none could register it. Everyone was so tired it was difficult for them not to collapse where they stood.

After receiving Mel's call, Brett Sayer used the Australian Government's alliance with The Old World, a group of paranormal enthusiasts run in secret by the enigmatic billionaire Altior Fulgur, to get them out of Norway. He'd also called Malcolm Selleck and Teva Henry and ordered them on the first flights out of the United States and the United Kingdom, respectively.

Both Danni and Mel had previous experience with The Old World.

While Danni was busting up the ritual in Florida, Mel had been at a meeting in Japan with the United States Government and The Old World. She'd stated she left feeling quite unsure about The Old World and its global activities. To Mel it seemed like they were hiding secrets.

Danni had first met The Old World in Australia when they'd taken herself and Joshua Dare in after the events of a full moon.

Jan and Petra had been a kindly old couple who wanted to keep the pair off the police's radar, in return for being able to study the werewolf curse. The government had ultimately picked them up and moved the couple to Alice Springs in Central Australia, where Danni assumed they still were.

The roar of a helicopter filled the air as one zoomed over a nearby hill and into the valley. There was a spray of ice and powder as it began its descent about twenty metres from where the group stood.

For a private helicopter, it was exceedingly large and looked luxurious to match.

"What sort of helicopter is this?" Danni shouted over the roar of the spinning blades.

"Augusta Westland AW139," Mel shouted back.

The helicopter landed, and the side door slid open. A man in a bright orange vest jumped out and ushered them in. Ducking low, despite the blades being too high to reach standing upright (except for maybe Sigurd). The group pushed through the snow and stepped into airborne luxury.

Once the door was closed, Danni asked, "How do you know the exact model of this chopper?"

"Because it belongs to Altior Fulgur. I've done an intelligence profile on him before," Mel answered darkly.

Before long, they were flying southwest over the mountains, valleys and fjords of Norway. Their destination was Amsterdam, the location of the European hub of The Old World.

If Sigurd had found the small town of Ose a monument to wonderment, nothing could describe his sheer bewilderment at the concept of the helicopter. His mouth had hung open as it descended. He couldn't remove his eyes from the view of the world below as they climbed ever higher.

"This is the world now? Men fly through the air?" Sigurd whispered.

"You haven't seen anything yet," Mel smiled.

"With this flying vessel, you could conquer any fortress! You could invade the known world in a day!"

"We don't want to conquer the world; we want to save it."

"Right, yes, of course," Sigurd added quickly, unable to tear his eyes from the window.

"You are now a part of big events, Sigurd the Viking. I'm going to need you to adapt quickly," Mel vocalized formally.

Sigurd puffed up his chest. "I was once a leader and ruler of men. But for this second chance of life, I will follow you in your cause. You have my allegiance."

Mel looked a little taken aback and slightly flustered. "Ah, okay, good. Thank you."

It was strange to see the Oracle of Delphi so lost for words.

Almost as soon as they'd begun soaring over the serene valleys of Southern Norway, Danni had closed her eyes. They didn't open again until they descended onto a helipad at a major metropolitan airport.

• • • • •

"WHERE ARE WE?" Danni asked, bleary-eyed.

"Amsterdam," Mel answered. "Schiphol Airport, to be precise."

"Cool," Danni said. She'd always wanted to go to Amsterdam. "Oh! My passport is in my hotel room in Lancelton!"

"Don't worry, when you are flying in Fulgur's helicopter, I don't think the rules apply to you."

Mel was quite right. A limousine pulled up beside the helicopter on the tarmac. A single driver stepped out and bowed graciously, tipping his hat to the group.

"The Old World?" Mel asked him quietly.

"Yes, ma'am."

He opened the door. After the extravagance of the helicopter, even the extremely comfortable limo was a letdown.

Without having to navigate the nightmares of customs and quarantine, they drove out of a side gate, around an industrial area and onto the main road towards the city.

"Where is The Old World hub?" Mel asked the driver. She'd decided to sit right at the front near the open divider.

"On the River Vecht. We are headed to outer Amsterdam, ma'am. Protocol dictates that we drive through the city first to avoid being followed," the driver responded.

Even in Danni's tired haze, she wowed at the concentric canals that spread about the cities' streets. Evening candlelight tours looked so majestic that Danni wished they could stop to jump on board. The colours and the architecture of the town were like nothing she'd seen in Australia.

As they passed side streets, they got glimpses of the

abundance of curious little stores selling all kinds of bizarre wares.

"It has been a warm winter. Normally, the canals are frozen by now. Rare to see cruises operating this time of year, but here we are," the driver said.

The towering churches and ornate buildings were a feast for the senses. The liberal city with its endless boutiques and museums was calling to Danni. Young people walking hand in hand laughing made her wish she was here on holiday.

They drove beneath the Mint Tower, with its multitudes of clock faces and bells and passed the red and white I AMSTERDAM sign, where throngs of tourists were having their pictures taken.

As the last embers of daylight left the city, they drove past the Magere Brug.

"Stop," Mel commanded the driver, startling everyone.

Mel had seen Danni positively salivating over the sights of the city. And of all the views, this might have been the most spectacular.

The Magere Brug, or Skinny Bridge, crossed the River Amstel and was lit up with hundreds of lights.

Lovers held each other in the glow of the place. As the name implied, the bridge was narrow and featured a draw-bridge in the middle to allow boats beneath. Its wooden, white-washed facade and low underpasses gave it a fairy-tale quality. The dazzling display of the lights was reflected by the still water beneath.

Danni, Mel, Sigurd and Artemis stepped onto the bridge. Sigurd, the manliest man to have ever lived, was equally lost in the romance of it all.

"The beauty of this city is phenomenal. It is like a city of the gods!" he said in hushed awe.

Danni leaned on the railing and looked out over the canal.

"Beautiful," she whispered. In that second, she was in another time, in another place.

"This is a bit unorthodox," Mel started, "but I feel like things are about to heat up. So, let's take a moment to be in a beautiful place where we are not under attack."

Danni completely agreed.

Even Artemis nodded her approval. "You are wise to take a moment to enjoy the peace. While the woods show the beauty of this world, there is certainly something to these modern cities."

"Everyone, come in!" Danni urged her team. She reached into her pocket for her phone but felt something else. It was the angelic seal of Astaroth. She'd work out what to do with that later.

Danni grasped her phone and handed it to Sigurd. "Press that big middle button, get all of us."

Sigurd looked incredibly confused but held the phone out high as instructed. He almost dropped it when he saw himself reflected in the front camera.

"Is that me?" he asked.

"Yes, get with the times, man!" Danni laughed, patting him on his meaty bicep.

Mel looked like she was going to protest this group selfie being taken but didn't say anything. Artemis, curious about what Sigurd was doing with the phone, leaned in for a better look.

"Now!" Danni said.

Sigurd pushed his thumb down, almost too hard, but got the snap.

Danni snatched the phone back off of him and opened her gallery. There were the four of them with the canal and lights of the city behind. Mel and Danni were smiling, Artemis, the goddess, looked confused, and Sigurd had only managed to capture two-thirds of his own face. Yet the picture was perfect.

There stood the adventurers of Hell on a bridge in Amsterdam.

"Send me that picture," Mel whispered to Danni. "Don't tell Brett."

Danni laughed. She almost felt normal.

After they'd soaked in the scenery for a while longer, they piled back into the limousine.

Once again, Danni was out like a light, only waking sometime later to be shuffled through the doors of a mansion into a bedroom.

At last, alone in her own room, Danni collapsed onto the bed. She desperately needed a shower but couldn't summon the strength to sit back up.

The strangest smile crossed her face. She'd been to Hell and come back. She'd fought demons, freed a dragon and conversed with powerful supernatural entities. Yet, here she still was. Alive and ready to go again the next day. She actually felt like she'd done a good job too.

Danni didn't know what the new day would bring, but she was starting to feel like she was ready to meet any new challenges head-on.

12

THE OLD WORLD AMSTERDAM

Danni yawned and stretched wide in her double-queen bed. She'd had the most fantastic dreamless sleep.

She wiped the gunk from her eyes and kicked the quilt away. Last night she'd barely registered her surroundings. Now that she was refreshed and could properly soak it in, she was very impressed.

The light was streaming in through a glass door at the side of her room. It led onto a balcony that overlooked hectares of immaculately mowed grass.

Danni was reminded of a time before technology when ladies in elaborate dresses were escorted from carriages that crunched along the gravel, bringing the wealthy and sophisticated to the mansion.

Danni didn't know much about architecture, but she could tell the mansion wasn't modern. At least, the building itself wasn't. The stables and tennis courts that surrounded it certainly were.

Her balcony included a pond view that featured an eighteenth-century stone fountain spitting water into the sky. Lily pads and reeds floated in the water beside trimmed hedges and sculpted bushes.

Danni could see a herd of deer frolicking in the distant trees. It was like the fairy tale from last night had continued into this new day.

She returned to her room and headed for the other door.

It was time, at last, for a shower.

The steaming hot water washed the last few days away. Danni let it run down her body, enjoying the sensation.

That shower was relief and ecstasy all in one. Gone was the red sand of Hell trapped in her hair. Gone was the heat of the scorched plain and the chill of Niflheim.

Once she pulled herself free of the exquisite marble bathroom, she wrapped the towel around herself and went on the hunt for clean clothes. When she'd stayed at The Old World house in Cairns, she'd awoken to find clean clothes outside her door.

She headed for the exit and pulled on the door handle. She was pleasantly surprised to find her suitcase sitting in the hallway. She'd last seen it in Lancelton. How it'd gotten here, she had no idea. But she was grateful for its appearance nonetheless, as she could now slip on her work-approved clothing. Simple jeans, a comfortable shirt and a jacket lined with pockets were all she needed.

For good measure, she slipped her belt with an undercover holster around her waist, then took it off when she remembered she no longer had a gun. She'd thrown it at the black shuck on the moors. Danni would get a serious talking to for that.

When she was ready, having done her hair and makeup, Danni set about exploring the house. She quickly learned it was several stories tall.

The ornamented ceiling and marble columns told her that this place was an oasis of luxury. The designer had made ample use of Italian marble and robust oak. Danni imagined herself sitting in front of the elaborate fireplaces. She gazed at the pictures of old men in suits lining the walls, some dating back to the turn of the last century.

Danni found a gym, a sauna and a swimming pool. Much to her surprise, she only saw a small library and a dusty computer room with severely outdated PCs in it. She thought The Old World would be a bit less rich and a little more mysterious.

On the mansion's ground floor, she bumped into a couple of old-timers drinking coffee and laughing. Both men had to be in their seventies, dressed in cardigans and golf caps.

"Hi," Danni said as she approached.

"Hello," the first man said in a thick Dutch accent, pushing his glasses up his nose to get a better look at her.

"Welcome to The Old World Amsterdam," the other said.

"Who are you guys?" Danni blurted out. She turned red, her mind shouting that it might have been more tactful to formally introduce herself.

"I am Wilhelm, and this is Petteri. We are regulars here."

"Oh, and what do regulars here do? I'm Danni, by the way..." Danni breathed a sigh of relief. The men didn't seem offended.

"Very pleased to meet you, Danni. I have spent my retirement years trying to uncover the truth of the story of the pig-faced woman."

"Okay..." Danni mumbled. "She wasn't just a really ugly woman, was she?"

"No, no, no. Witchcraft was involved. She had the head of a pig and the body of a woman. I am close to finding her bones and proving it is not just local superstition."

"You and your pig-faced woman," Wilhelm blurted out, waving his hand dismissively. "There are bigger things to learn than the pig-faced woman."

Danni giggled.

Wilhelm continued. "We had friends here, a long time ago. Jan and Petra. They went all the way to Australia because Petteri won't shut about the pig-faced women."

"I know Jan and Petra!" Danni exclaimed.

"How are they? I hear not much from them these days."

"They are fine, I think. Why did they go to Australia?" Danni remembered vaguely that they'd moved when a cyclone had emerged near Cairns in 2016.

"Ah, it is a sad story. Their son worked on a fishing boat that disappeared at sea. One survivor told strange stories of men with big lips and bulging eyes coming from the water. That is when they came to The Old World.

"Ever since, anything strange that happened in the ocean they went to it. That cyclone was suspicious. Government snooping around, not just Australian. Many ships with big cages were found. Some were wrecked with their occupants missing. I believe Jan was working on it for years out there," Petteri answered.

Danni thought about the cages her uncle had acquired. She'd locked Josh the werewolf in one during a full moon. Her uncle had said they'd come from a boat that was found destroyed by Cyclone Bolton.

"That is sad. They never mentioned it to me. I felt like they wanted to avoid the subject," Danni said quietly.

"How did you meet them?"

"I grew up in Cairns…" Danni responded slowly. She didn't want to mention the werewolf stuff; it might not be for the casual members of The Old World to know.

"Well, when you see them again, tell them I am on the verge of a breakthrough in the case of the pig-faced woman," Petteri boasted.

"Ah! Enough! She doesn't want to hear it!" Wilhelm shouted.

Danni laughed again. "Hey, where can I get some breakfast?"

The two men directed her down a series of halls, but all she found was the entrance to a terrace that looked out over the river.

As she admired the view of the River Vecht from the expansive outdoor terrace, she finally found one of her companions.

Teva walked up casually to say hello. Danni gave him a big unexpected hug. The Tahitian-Australian spy gave her a pat on the back with a chuckle.

"How are you?" Danni asked, beaming at him. Seeing Teva

after her trip to Hell felt like reconnecting with a long-lost friend.

"Tired. As if speaking to museum curators in London isn't boring enough, I have to rush down to Lancelton to get your bags, then rush back to London and fly here," Teva grumbled.

"Still no luck?"

"No," Teva frowned. "The best I've gathered is that if we were to find anything at all of Zeus', it would be one of his lightning bolts. Where though, I have no idea. According to what I've told Brett, we have promising leads. I really hope you guys found something. I needed to get him off my back."

"We found Artemis," Danni said brightly.

"Yeah, I met the goddess already. She's very similar to Apollo."

"She has some ideas. Where is everyone else?"

"Malcolm is arriving soon. The head of The Old World here has gone to pick him up. When he gets in, Mel wants us all to meet. Apparently, we are cleared to discuss our plans with The Old World, which seems odd to me."

"That big meeting in Japan must've yielded some results," Danni shrugged.

"Maybe. It revealed that Altior Fulgur is the President of The Old World. He is a dodgy guy."

"Why do people keep saying that? I've never even heard of him."

"He is beyond rich," Teva said, somewhat dramatically. "But when you dig into his life, you find nothing. No records of birth, or marriage or family. The wealthy can cover their tracks, but he does so exceedingly well. Then to find out he is in charge of

The Old World; it just feels like we know too little to be trusting his organisation."

"Well, his money is coming in handy," Danni offered as a positive. "Hey, where can we get breakfast around here?"

"Oh, there is a kitchen down the hall and to the left."

"Thanks, Tev," Danni beamed. She was outrageously hungry.

"Meet in the conference room on the first floor in about twenty minutes," Teva said.

"I'll be there," Danni replied as she bolted towards the kitchen.

• • • • •

AFTER A HEARTY MEAL OF OATS with banana and honey, Danni found the conference room. It wasn't the traditional interpretation of a conference room as it had no table and several leather couches arranged in a circle. A roaring fireplace lit the area with a pleasant glow.

Mel was already there, fussing over a notebook. Sigurd and Artemis leaned against the windows on the far wall, both looking bored. Teva walked in just after Danni and took a seat. Soon, they were greeted with the sound of rolling wheels on wood as Malcolm Selleck with his suitcase entered, followed by a stranger.

Mel stood up and formally shook Malcolm's hand. He smiled and gave both Danni and Teva a curt wave. When his eyes met Artemis, a look of amazement crossed his face. It was shortly altered to confusion when he looked at the gigantic Viking, now dressed in a polo shirt and jeans.

The stranger walked to the centre of the room and introduced himself.

"Welcome, Australian Government operatives! My name is Harry Raatikainen, the head of The Old World Europe. Our president, Mr Fulgur has informed me of our new information-sharing arrangements, so consider us at your service."

"Where is Mr Fulgur?" Mel asked sharply.

"He is still in Nagoya attending to things there. Apparently, they had an oni show up at the Cliffs of Tojinbo, and the Japanese Government wants their help. Exciting times."

Harry turned to Danni and clapped his hand. "You are Danni Quinn, yes?"

Danni looked at him, alarmed to have been singled out.

"Don't be shy. I know you from Jan and Petra, who are held against their will in Central Australia. Something we will discuss," Harry glared, looking at Mel.

"We appreciate the helicopter ride," Mel said, ignoring Harry's comment and standing up. "We will also appreciate any information you can provide in our hunt for an artefact of Zeus."

"I will admit that the mere proposition of finding an artefact of Zeus does seem ridiculous to me. Perhaps you should tell me what you have so far," Harry frowned.

It was now that Mel addressed the room.

"First, I want an update from Teva and Malcolm."

Teva sighed and said, "I've got nothing. No leads. No idea."

Mel nodded, expecting this answer.

Malcolm now spoke. "I have some idea. The last few days,

I've done my best to study the Necronomicon. I believe I've found a passage that links to the vision you and Danni shared in Florida."

Malcolm stood to address the circle around him.

"To catch everyone up, Melissa and I had a discussion last night around the location of the lost city of Atlantis. As a historian, the best insight I can offer is that it's in the Mediterranean somewhere. After studying the black book in Florida, I am optimistic that we can lock down a precise location."

"That book has Atlantis in it?" Teva asked.

"Maybe," Malcolm answered quickly. "USSOT didn't let me take any pictures of the book, but I did manage one quick snap of an important page. I think it can give us the coordinates to an underwater city."

He pulled up an image on his phone. From the ceiling, a projector descended and turned on. The wall lit up with Malcolm's mobile display after connecting to the Bluetooth.

"The copy of the Necronomicon from Florida is problematic. It is basically a hand-drawn recreation of a more complete book. I don't believe the imagery or symbology is one hundred percent accurate."

"So, we need to get a better copy?" Mel asked.

"Ideally, yes. As we have previously discussed, I also need a person more mathematically minded than myself that can help me identify this certain passage."

Malcolm zoomed in on the photo displayed on his phone. The images drawn around the border of the page looked oddly familiar to Danni. She thought she'd seen them somewhere before, but before she could confirm it, Malcom had focused the image on on a string of strange symbols in the page's centre.

"These drawings of strange black buildings seem similar to what you described seeing in that vision in Florida," Malcolm continued. "I have a suspicion that the writing might be directions to that place, but I need a physicist or a mathematician to help me decipher it."

That was it! Danni had seen the drawings in the vision of the underwater nightmare city.

"Artemis did state Atlantis could hold an artefact of Zeus. The city in the vision was underwater," Mel noted. She sounded unsure; it was a tenuous thread at best.

"It is a long shot. Next to the code, as you can see, are a pair of small images. At first I couldn't place them, then it hit me! I think they are meant to be two islands, two big islands. I believe they represent the north and south islands of New Zealand. If we can get a better copy and someone to assist me, then we may, at last, have a firm destination."

"The security around this mission makes it almost impossible to bring someone else in," Mel stated in no uncertain terms.

Malcolm smiled. "I believe I have a solution. Your werewolf, Joshua Dare, is currently working with the other team, correct?"

Mel nodded.

"He has a younger brother who is quite the physics prodigy. He is currently studying in Geneva on a lucrative and highly sought-after scholarship. He is already loosely connected to the case. I recommend we bring him in."

Mel frowned and mulled the suggestion over in her mind.

Josh had told Danni a lot about his brothers. He'd described

Randall Dare as an awkward genius gifted in the mathematic arts. He had another brother, Kane, who seemed perpetually lost with life and entirely directionless. Danni didn't know if they'd been briefed on Josh's moon-borne affliction. His parents, Gary and Heidi, certainly had; they'd been there for a werewolf attack.

"And we need a better copy of the book," Mel added, after thinking it over for a minute.

"The Necronomicon is illusive. It is talked of as if it is mythical. I have no idea where we'd even start to look."

"We are in the perfect place to enquire. If anyone has a lead, it is The Old World. I know there is a copy in the Vatican Secret Archive, though that is out of our reach."

Danni was unsure. Something didn't seem right about any this. "If you think those islands are New Zealand, then it isn't Atlantis, is it?"

"Atlantis is a mythological city. Its true location could've been lost before whispers of it reached Greece, and they decided it was in there area somewhere. I believe it is worth investigating regardless. A lead is a lead after all," Malcolm suggested.

Mel stood up. "Right. Danni and Malcolm, go to Geneva and fetch Randall Dare."

Sigurd chimed in with, "I am capable of assisting in your quest as well!"

Danni watched Mel biting her lower lip and knew what she was thinking. The cost of the Australian Government buying an extra return airfare from Amsterdam to Geneva would be something Mel would have to justify at some point. The fact that it was for a legendary Norse hero brought back to life wouldn't matter.

"Fine. Malcolm, take Sigurd too."

"Glorious victory awaits," Sigurd smiled.

"It is just a pick-up, big guy," Danni laughed.

Mel turned to Harry, "This Necronomicon, are you familiar with it?"

"Yes, I am," Harry said proudly. "When you devote enough time to the supernatural, the name Necronomicon shows up eventually."

"Do you know where we can get a copy?"

"A few select universities possess copies under lock and key. It is a banned book, even among communities that know of its existence."

"Is the University of Amsterdam one of them?" Malcolm asked.

"It was. Many years ago, members of an unknown cult got wind that the black book was in the university. They did quite a bit of damage breaking in but couldn't retrieve it. My friend, a professor of philosophy and history, Ernst Carter, declared the book more harm than good and destroyed it, or so he told the world. I know for a fact that the university's copy of Necronomicon is locked in his personal treasury. He would never let anyone see it, though."

"If that is the case, his permission isn't needed. I fear we are running short on time. If a Knight of Hell manages to track us here, we will have a powerful foe to contend with," Mel stated.

"Ernst's home isn't too elaborate. He has some security measures in place to protect his collection of artefacts, but it is nothing substantial," Harry added.

"So, you definitely need the book?" Mel asked Malcolm.

Malcolm nodded.

"Looks like we are breaking into a professor's house then."

Harry chimed in again, "Actually, you do not need to break in. Well, at least not all of the way. You are very fortunate, for tonight he is hosting a party. And I have an invitation."

"How many of us can you bring without arousing unwanted attention?" Mel asked.

His eyes darted towards Danni and Mel. "Two beautiful women will not attract any suspicion at all."

Danni shuddered at the way he said it.

He then looked at Artemis.

The goddess, noticing his gaze, simply stated, "I am not a tool to be used to befuddle mortal men."

"He's got camera systems and tripwires, I assume?" Teva chimed in.

"Cameras, yes."

Mel gave Teva a knowing look, and he nodded.

"You've got the day to get set up."

"Danni," Mel said, turning now to her. "You need to be back before this party commences."

"We're on it," Danni stated.

"We do have an additional problem. Say this works out, we get a copy of the book and can decipher the code; how do we get to an underwater city?" Teva pointed out.

Mel looked to Harry, who shrugged.

"The Old World does not own submarines. Our computers here barely work. This is more of a social club."

"What about the president?" Mel asked.

"I guess… I can ask Mr Fulgur. He is invested in many companies and may have connections."

"Can you ask him right away? Something in New Zealand, ideally," Mel requested, the urgency in her voice unmistakable.

"Ah, okay. I will call The Old World Japan and see if he is available."

Harry wandered off down the hall, presumably to find a landline phone. He didn't appear the type who'd mastered the mobile phone.

Teva spoke up again, "I know iHeal Genetics has invested in deep-sea exploration. There was a company on the South Island of New Zealand they were connected to. I remember reading it in their intel profile a few years ago."

"It does seem that Altior Fulgur has his hand in a lot of jars of honey. I don't trust The Old World," Mel said quietly. "I don't want anyone to say anything to its members unless absolutely necessary."

Malcolm, Teva and Danni nodded.

"By this time tomorrow, I want to be on the move for an artefact of Zeus. Everyone knows what they are doing, so let's get going."

"What are you going to be doing?" Danni asked Mel.

"I'm going to find us some dresses. We are going to have to look good tonight."

13

KANE AND RANDALL DARE

As it turned out, The Old World mansion had a substantial armoury. They allowed Danni to take a pistol and refill her magazines. Mel hadn't been comfortable with the idea of her team travelling to Switzerland unarmed, even if it was for a relatively simple mission.

Apollo's golden sword was left in the armoury for safe keeping. Danni thought about putting the angelic seal of Astaroth in there with it, but decided to keep it in her luggage. She wasn't concerned about pulling the fallen angel into the real world since he'd been eaten by the dragon. Danni viewed the large coin as a souvenir of her journey through Hell.

The three of them didn't even need to pack bags. The flight was only an hour and a half from Amsterdam to Geneva. The plan was to grab Randall and return on the next available flight.

When Danni had dated Joshua Dare, he'd mentioned in passing that Randall was gifted in physics. This seemed to be underselling it. As soon as Randall had graduated high school, he'd been offered a scholarship to study and work for a private research company in Geneva. A private company that was rumoured to be at the forefront of technology. Years ago, they'd even had a hand in assisting the European Organisation for Nuclear Physics in constructing the Large Hadron Collider, and to this day had exclusive access to it.

The company was called Offenes Universum and had an office fifteen minutes out of Geneva's city centre. According to a brief intelligence profile Teva put together, the place had significant internal security, with visitors restricted to the reception foyer.

Fortunately, Offenes Universum had ties with several Australian universities. Mel made a quick call to their office, stating that a delegation from the Australian National University's Research School of Physics would be arriving shortly to meet with Randall.

She even had her ASIO colleagues make up some digital passes for identification. The planning went like clockwork, and within an hour, they were boarding a plane to Switzerland.

Sigurd was initially assigned a seat near the back of the jet. When the flight attendants realised he physically couldn't fit within its small confines, he was upgraded to business class.

Danni and Malcolm weren't so lucky. They got squashed amongst a family with a disproportionate number of loud, snotty children.

Yet, the flight was quick. After they retrieved Danni's firearm (which had to be declared and checked on as oversize baggage), they made for the small rent-a-car they'd been assigned.

It was immaculately clean, though the roof was so low Sigurd had to crane his neck forward.

The drive was also short. The sky's grey matched the sterile grey of the buildings around Geneva's international airport.

Within ten minutes they pulled into an expansive parking area that circled a singular building surrounded by trees.

The Offenes Universum office was six stories tall and featured glass windows on the corners of every level. It was quite easy to see inside and watch people walking about, holding binders or sipping coffee.

The building was rectangular and got progressively wider as the levels climbed. It was a simple but effective architectural design, making the place look like a square spinning top.

As they stepped from the car, Danni stated, "Remember guys, we are ANU employees from the School of Physics."

"I still do not understand what that means," Sigurd joked, stretching out his neck.

"Ah, just let me do the talking," Malcolm proclaimed.

The glass sliding doors to the reception whizzed open, and Malcolm approached the receptionist, a hook-nosed brown-haired girl in her mid-twenties.

Malcolm flashed their fake ID cards on his phone, and the receptionist directed them to the third-floor lecture theatre. She said it was an auditorium they couldn't miss. She gave them a guest pass programmed for the elevator.

After a quick ride up, they arrived on the third floor.

A long white hallway confronted them. The group walked past a lab and found a sign on the wall stating LECTURE THEATRE. Beneath it was an electronic message board with the lettering: LECTURE NOT IN PROGRESS.

"You wait here, Sigurd. We don't want to overwhelm him," Malcolm suggested.

Sigurd nodded and casually lent against the wall.

Danni entered the lecture hall and saw a somewhat familiar face.

Randall Dare was only 19 years old. Yet, he stood at the front of the auditorium pondering some extremely complex math problem. The equations used up almost the entire board. Danni couldn't recognise any of the symbols.

Randall was tall, taller than Josh at least, and much leaner. He had a patchy beard that ran along his jawline and long brown hair. He did look a lot like Josh, as did the room's only other occupant.

Lounging across several chairs in the front row of the hall's amphitheatre-style seating was someone unexpected.

Danni instantly recognised Kane Dare, the third Dare brother. He had a round face and sported a full beard. He was significantly taller than Randall, making Josh the runt of the family. He looked strong, too, with arms packed with muscle, though he had disproportionately skinny legs.

"Randall Dare?" Danni asked from the entry door.

"Yes," he said, turning away from the problem he was studying.

"Danni Quinn," she replied promptly.

"*The* Danni Quinn?" Randall asked.

"Yeah. You know me?"

"Well, yeah… Josh told us about you ages ago. Before he disappeared off the face of the Earth."

"That's kinda why I'm here. I'd like to introduce you to Professor Malcolm Selleck."

Malcolm strode into the room and shook Randall's hand. He then moved over to Kane, who stood up to shake the professor's hand too.

"Pleasure to meet you two. I haven't met Josh yet, but I've heard a lot about him."

"Maybe you could fill us in, then," Kane said, approaching without bothering to introduce himself. "Our parents have been super vague about where he is and what he's doing. I wanted to get in touch with him about coming to Switzerland too, but couldn't reach him at all."

"Why are you in Switzerland?" Danni asked.

"Well, Randall is here on this scholarship, and I recently quit my job. So, I thought I'd come and pay my little brother a visit."

Danni and Malcolm exchanged glances. They hadn't factored in Kane. She guessed he'd have to come with them back to Amsterdam too.

"Forgive me for asking, Danni, but aren't you a bartender? What are you doing in Geneva?" Randall asked.

"I work for the government now. And we are here because we need your help."

"Me? Why?"

"Josh is also employed within a special division of the Australian Government. Because of the classified nature of our work, we need someone who can solve a potential mathematical problem, who is also close to the case. I've heard you are quite a prodigy," Malcolm stated.

Randall blushed slightly and muttered something about 'not being that good'.

Kane snorted indignantly. "He's just a nerd."

"Now is a good time to be a nerd," Malcolm said warmly.

"Guys. Let's sit down. I have a lot to tell you, and you're going to have a hard time believing it," Danni said.

On the flight over, Danni had tried to think of ways to broach the topic of Josh being a werewolf and make it plausible. In the end, she'd figured it was impossible. She'd just have to brief them on the specifics of the mission at hand. After a robust fifteen-minute discussion, Danni paused to let them ask questions.

"So, Josh is a government agent?" Kane quizzed.

Danni nodded.

"And you need Randall's help to figure out if a passage in some book is a formula that reveals a location?"

"That's it."

"And we get a free flight to Amsterdam?"

"Correct."

"Well, Randy, pack your bags; we have a plane to catch!"

"I can't just take off," Randall mumbled nervously. "I have a lot to do here."

"I'm not giving you a choice," Danni commanded. It was a bluff, of course. Still, it seemed to work.

"I guess… let me go talk to the physics professors. I'll see if I can get some leave approved. Just for a few days, right?"

"Maybe just for tonight. We need to crack this right away, so be prepared for an all-nighter," Malcolm yawned.

Danni looked at the faces of Kane and Randall. She felt a strange pang of loss and despair. She did hope one day she'd get to reunite with Josh. She snapped herself out of it. Like Danni always told herself, she'd only known Josh for a few months. She had to get over it.

"Do you have a copy of the equation you need solved?" Randall asked Malcolm.

"I do, but it is a poor copy, and I'm certain it is missing elements. Tonight, we should have a more complete version to study."

There was a sound from somewhere down the hall. It was the shattering of glass.

"We left Sigurd alone beside that lab. I bet he has accidentally broken a beaker or something," Malcolm sighed.

There was a much louder crash, then a thump. It was the sound of a fight. Danni drew her gun from her holster.

"Stay with the guys, Malcolm. I'll check on Sigurd."

Danni moved past the podium towards the door.

She saw him.

At the top of the amphitheatre, quickly descending the stairs, was a man in a brown robe. He was moving swiftly towards her.

"Who are you?" Danni demanded.

The man said nothing. He kept running. Then, he leapt.

He crashed into Danni and pinned her down.

"Hey, what's going on?" Kane shouted.

He ran towards Danni and wrapped his arms beneath the attacker's shoulders. Kane was so tall he could easily lift the man from the ground.

Danni scrambled to her feet and faced her attacker. She pulled the hood of his robe down.

This man had vacant white eyes and a strange shape carved into his temple. It was a five-pointed star slashed with a knife. Mel had described people like this when she'd flown in from Japan. Apparently, Josh's protection detail had to fight off monks in brown robes with the same symbol on them.

They were members of the Cult of Belial. Demons who had possessed worshippers of the fallen angel and now used their bodies as hosts. How they were here in Geneva, Danni had no idea.

"Ah, Danni!" Malcolm yelled. He was pointing to the top of the auditorium. Another four robed figures were descending.

The man held at the mercy of Kane Dare spun his head 180 degrees with a sickening snap of bone and bit into Kane's neck. Kane released and kicked the man away.

"What the hell!" he said, covering the flesh wound.

The cultist's neck righted itself, and he got up.

Suddenly, another brown-robed man was thrown through the main entrance to the auditorium. He crashed into the seats. A wild-eyed and furious Sigurd followed.

"This man is a demon inhabiting a human body!" Sigurd bellowed.

"Wait, what?" Randall babbled, arming himself with a

nearby collection of whiteboard markers.

"How did they get in here?" Malcolm asked. "What is outside the door at the top of the auditorium?"

"Another hall that exits onto the fire escape," Randall answered quickly.

Somewhere outside, the Cult of Belial was scaling the metal stairs and climbing in one by one.

Everything slowed. Danni counted the attackers. Five in the auditorium. Who knows how many still coming. At least one had made it into the hall to meet Sigurd. There could be more.

"Are they alive?" Danni quickly asked Sigurd.

"No," Sigurd spat. "Once these foul things take a host, that person is gone."

"Good," Danni said, raising her pistol and firing two shots into a fast-approaching cultist. He collapsed.

Danni was horrified to see that no sooner than he'd landed, his body convulsed and spat out the bullets.

"Nothing is ever easy," she sighed.

The brawl erupted in earnest.

The cultists descended the stairs and, in a mad fury, attacked.

Sigurd fought as a one-man army, the white Hell Key swinging around his neck as he rained blows on the interlopers. It was clear the Viking was an expert martial artist, throwing kicks, utilising chokes, locks and pain techniques to subdue the attackers. Even weaponless, he took the attention of three of the cultists on his own.

Malcolm raised his fists and threw quick jabs at his attacker. He'd spent time in the army and could fight. Yet, against these supernatural foes, he was outclassed. He took a terrific elbow to the face, which floored him.

The cultist placed his foot on the professor's neck, only to be brought down by a hail of gunfire from Danni.

Kane leapt from the podium and crash tackled a cultist. He wasn't a natural brawler, but he had size and weight on his side. Even so, the demonic strength possessing the skinny cultist could push him off with ease.

Standing behind the lectern, Randall threw whiteboard markers at the cultists in a vain attempt to be helpful.

A cultist lunged at Danni.

Danni turned, pivoted, and with a well-aimed hip thrust, pushed the cultist against the wall.

"We can't win this fight!" Malcolm shouted.

"You cannot!" Sigurd shouted, gripping a cultist around the head and slamming him into the whiteboard.

Sigurd was jumped on by four demon-hosts, who pinned him down.

Like a charging bull, Kane ran in to assist the Viking, pulling two of them off him.

Sigurd rolled back onto his shoulder blades, then launched himself up.

The two largest men stood back-to-back and faced the onslaught together.

Danni was hitting her targets with expert precision, but bullets were no good against these foes.

Randall ran up to her, ducking beneath another cultist thrown by Sigurd.

"There is a gun in the next lab," he said frantically. "A particle beam generator. Come with me!"

Randall bolted out the door, followed by Danni.

Malcolm joined Kane and Sigurd, who had drawn the attention of all of the attackers.

Randall ran past the long steel tables towards a reinforced glass door in the back.

He punched in a code and there was a hiss of releasing gas. Randall pulled the heavy door open and disappeared inside.

He returned moments later, holding a most curious object. It was a long white tube with three metal claws on the front attached to an array of rectangular magnets.

From Danni's vantage point, it looked like a jet engine.

Randall had one hand underneath it and the other on a simple trigger.

He thrust the cannon into Danni's arms and said, "Use the trigger!"

She pointed the cannon at the door, just as a cultist rounded the bend.

Danni fired.

Instantly, the cannon whirred to life, releasing a pulse of energy that shattered every beaker and test tube in the room.

When the cultist was hit by the ring of energy, manifesting as a translucent circle speeding through the room, two-thirds of him disintegrated. The remaining part of his corpse fell to the floor in a cascade of spurting blood.

"Heal from that!" Danni shouted.

"It only has a few shots, so make it count," Randall informed her. He looked horrified at the gory effectiveness of this weapon.

"So, this is what you are working on here? Are you a supervillain?" Danni asked.

"This isn't my work. I solve equations. The tech guys like boasting about this gun," Randall answered lamely.

Danni felt the weight of the particle beam cannon in her hands. It was surprisingly light.

She sprinted out of the room to see the fight had entered the hallway. A cultist was standing there with two broken arms. Behind him, Sigurd had another one pinned against the wall.

"Sigurd! Get out of the way!"

Sigurd recognised the peculiar white tube as a weapon and leapt back into the auditorium.

Danni pulled the trigger again.

The gun fired, destroying every window in the hallway.

The cultist was hit in the centre of his chest, causing the top half of him to explode into red mist. The cultist behind also felt some of the blast, though only his head was vaporised.

"Awesome," Danni grinned. She immediately felt horrified for enjoying this.

She ran into the lecture theatre to see both Malcolm and Kane cowering on the ground beneath two attackers.

Sigurd grasped both the cultists by the backs of their robes and heaved them upwards with a throw of colossal strength.

Danni pointed the cannon towards the roof and fired. In a shower of sparks, the projector exploded along with the cultists.

There was a puff of smoke and distinctive electrical crackling. The experimental weapon died.

There were four blank-eyed cultists left.

A very out-of-breath Sigurd looked at Danni and stated, "Get out of here. I will take care of them."

Danni didn't need to be told twice.

She and Randall helped Kane and Malcolm to their feet, as Sigurd roared and ran at his foes again.

"Where are the stairs?" Danni asked Randall.

"End of the hall," Randall puffed.

The hall went dark as the lights momentarily cut out.

Showers of sparks rained down from the ceiling as the lights began to flicker on and off.

Danni hoped the electrical distortion was a side effect of the particle gun. But, in her gut, she knew why the lights were going haywire. Something new was here.

Her two-week AST intensive course had covered the most common signs of paranormal occurrences. Ghosts, spectres and other undead phenomena often wreaked havoc with electronic paraphernalia. While there wasn't much official research into demons, she suspected it would be the same.

In the dark, Randall tripped over part of a body.

Making sure the dead monk wasn't magically healing, Danni grabbed Randall by the hand and pulled him up.

"Let's go!"

The four of them bolted down the sterile hall. The lights above continued to buzz on and off.

"What is going on?" Kane gasped.

"I fear we are in the presence of something more powerful than those monks," Malcolm said, wiping blood from his face.

"We need to get out of here before it finds us," Danni urged, reaching the door with the words EMERGENCY EXIT plastered across it in English.

She reached for the door handle.

"AH!" Danni breathed, pulling her hand away. The metal was so hot it had burned her.

The lights went off.

At the end of the hallway, the power returned, igniting each LED one by one.

"Who is that?" Kane asked.

The outline of a man was silhouetted in the returning glow.

"Go," a deep voice muttered.

From around the corner, two smaller shapes emerged. On four legs, with an orange glow radiating from their bellies, the hellhounds bounded towards Danni's group.

Randall squeaked in fright as the dogs, with their crocodilian heads, yapped as they ran.

Danni was out of options; she couldn't see a way out.

The two hellhounds stopped just short of them. They snarled menacingly.

Kane, temporarily overtaken with fear, tried the door handle too. He exhaled sharply as he felt the bite of the super-heated metal on his palm.

"What are these things, Danni?" Malcolm whispered.

"Hellhounds," the voice from down the hall answered. The unknown man was now walking towards them, the lights turning on as he approached.

They all stood silently in the long seconds it took for the

man to get closer.

Now that his features were illuminated, Danni shuddered in horror at what she saw.

He looked like a person of about 35, yet his skin was pale and flaky. His eyes were sunken and his hair seemed to float in the air of its own accord, almost as if he were underwater. He was gaunt, barely more than a skeleton with skin stretched tight over his bones. He appeared as a drowned corpse that had somehow regained life.

"Where is the Oracle of Delphi?" the drowned man asked.

"She's not here," Danni said defiantly, stepping in front of the group.

"A pity," he replied, patting his hellhounds on the head. "Without her, the rest of you are nothing more than a feast for the dogs."

"Who are you?" Malcolm demanded.

"Leviathan," he grinned.

This was the Knight of Hell who'd been hunting Artemis in England. The one who usually dwelled in the deep places of the world.

"You don't look like the biblical Leviathan," Malcolm noted.

"This is but a shadow of my true form. Where is the Oracle of Delphi? And the gods, Apollo and Artemis?"

"I don't know," Danni answered.

One of the hellhounds barked, causing both Kane and Randall to jump. Danni stood firm and fierce.

"Dear girl," Leviathan said in no more than a whisper, "do not let this day be your last day."

"She shall not!" a booming voice behind Leviathan decried.

Sigurd had appeared, looking a little battered and bruised, but alive with the thrill of the fight.

He wrapped his arms around Leviathan and gripped him in a reverse bear hug.

"You!" Leviathan spat, turning to see his surprise attacker.

"You are looking awful, as usual, Leviathan. I was so sad to see you and Belial depart Hell those long years past."

With a heaving throw, Sigurd slammed the fallen angel into the ground. The hellhounds turned and leapt, their teeth gnashing at the Viking giant.

Sigurd managed to catch both dogs in each arm and hold them in headlocks.

"I have lived and fought a hundred lifetimes in Hell. Demons in human bodies? A foe so pathetic to best a thousand wouldn't earn me Valhalla's favour!" Sigurd boasted.

Kane, who was only slightly shorter than Sigurd, seized his moment and shoulder-barged the door. With a crack, it swung open into a grey stairwell.

Leviathan, with fire in his eyes, got back to his feet. He held his right arm wide, and a sword of ice manifested in his hand.

"How you escaped Hell, Sigurd, I don't know. But I will be much obliged to put you back!"

"Run!" Danni commanded.

The two Dares, Malcolm and Danni, bolted into the stairwell, leaping several steps at a time to descend.

"What about Sigurd?" Malcolm puffed.

"He can handle himself," Danni said, jumping onto the rail

and sliding down. "Thank god everyone in Hell seems to know and hate him!"

"Did that guy up there look a little bit off to anyone else?" Kane asked, panting as he lumbered clumsily after the rest of them.

Before anyone could answer, they made it to the ground floor.

"How the hell do we escape?" Malcolm asked Danni.

They barreled into the reception area, one after another. The receptionist looked highly concerned as the group sprinted towards the glass sliding doors.

"Tell the professor I'm going on leave!" Randall shouted as he ran past.

"Oh, yes, of course, Mr Dare," she stuttered.

Soon they were across the parking lot and beside the rent-a-car.

"We can't leave Sigurd. He is just a man. He can't match a Knight of Hell," Malcolm said.

"That Hell Key around his neck stops any Hell creatures using their magic on him. Leviathan will have to fight with skill. Sigurd told me so," Danni mumbled, fumbling to unlock the door.

"Ah, guys," Randall said.

Figures in brown robes were fast approaching from all sides of the parking area.

"God damn, the entire Cult of Belial must be here," Danni murmured. She was thinking fast. They couldn't abandon Sigurd, yet none of them had the means to fight the Knight of Hell or his hellhounds.

"Get in the car," Danni ordered.

They piled in. Kane sat in the front while Malcolm and Randall squashed into the back.

"I just bought a Mustang," Kane stated.

"Really not relevant right now," Danni said, flooring it.

The wheels spun as they took off. A cultist leapt towards them, but a sharp turn threw him into the windscreen of a nearby Hummer.

They all held on for dear life as Danni recklessly swerved out of the parking area and onto the road.

Malcolm's gaze was fixed back onto the building.

"Danni, go back and circle the building! I can see Sigurd on the third floor!"

Danni braked hard and turned around, causing another vehicle to slam into a light pole.

"Oops."

Danni swung wide to avoid the cultists still careening in their direction.

"Give me your gun!" Malcolm shouted.

"Just take it!"

Danni felt Malcolm's hand fumbling around her waist until he found the holster. With some difficulty, he drew it. He then cracked his window and pointed towards the third floor.

He fired two shots, splintering the glass and catching Sigurd's attention. Danni could see Sigurd release Leviathan from their grapple, then look at the fast-approaching car below.

It all happened in slow motion.

Sigurd jumped through the splintered glass in a graceful swan dive. A rain of clear pieces fell with him as he hung in mid-air.

Danni didn't adjust her speed; she just kept driving.

With a crash and crunching of metal, a man-sized dent appeared in the roof.

They heard Sigurd cry out in pain.

"That woulda hurt," Kane grimaced.

The tyres screeched as Danni slammed on the brakes.

"Pull him in!"

Moments later, a very dazed and bloody Sigurd was sitting next to (and somewhat on top of) Malcolm and Randall.

Half a dozen cultists were surrounding the car. They had nowhere to go. Leviathan leered down at them from the third floor.

"Break the Hell Key," Sigurd spat through mouthfuls of blood.

Malcolm pulled the key from around his neck. At its thinnest point, he applied pressure. It snapped.

The car rocked as a mighty gust of wind blew up. A look of fear crossed Leviathan's face and he bolted out of view.

The cultists all stopped moving, then curiously began floating.

A fiery circle, no bigger than a dime, opened up where the key had been broken. There was a clap of thunder, and from each of the cultists poured a thin stream of shadow.

Their bodies fell flat to the ground, unmoving. The circle quickly faded away into nothingness.

"Go! Leviathan was not pulled into the fracture. Get us away from here," Sigurd commanded.

"You can explain what happened later," Danni said, once again flooring it out of the parking area and onto the main road.

"Are you okay?" Randall cautiously asked the Viking.

"Broken nose and ribs," Sigurd announced, leaning back. "Ah, it is good to be alive."

"Should we take you to a hospital?" Malcolm asked.

"No, just wipe the blood off my face and I can make it through this aeroplane flight."

"The Old World does have suitable medical facilities," Malcolm said to Danni.

"Yep, we are getting on this plane and back to Amsterdam. If Leviathan found us here, he can find them there. We need to get moving."

Through the rear vision mirror, Danni saw Sigurd smile.

"You are a fighter," he beamed. "Keep fighting till the end."

14

MOROS

I t took a stern word from Malcolm to stop Danni from driving so erratically. He was afraid of catching the attention of the local police.

"I've purchased the tickets," Malcolm said, relief washing over his face as Danni took a deep breath and straightened up the car. "Next flight back to Amsterdam is in forty minutes."

"What happened?" Randall asked from the back seat, totally confused.

The heavily battered Sigurd, holding one hand over his ribs, answered. "Those men who attacked us were cultists dedicated to the scum Belial. Or at least, they once were."

"Okay… several questions: who is Belial? What do you mean by once were? And who exactly are you?"

"I am Sigurd of the Volsung line. Recently returned to life thanks to the Goddess Artemis."

"Ah-huh," Randall said, with no trace of emotion.

Kane spoke up, his voice full of disbelief, "Are we supposed to believe any of this? For all we know, those robed people were Green Peace or something. And you exploded them with a cannon."

"They weren't Green Peace. If I understand correctly, they were husks being controlled by demons. Perhaps you can explain better, Danni?" Malcolm said.

Danni cleared her throat. They were only a few minutes from the international airport.

"Right, so in 2019, there was an incident that caused the walls to Hell to splinter."

Danni was trying to remember everything covered in the Operation Thunderking documentation.

"From this event, demons can now slip through. But they can't stay. Because the barrier is still somewhat there… they can't, like, possess someone like in the movies. If you get me?"

"I assure you, I don't," Kane answered sarcastically.

"It is hard to explain. Back in the dark ages, demons could come to Earth freely and possess people. Hide in their bodies and that. Then, Hell was sealed off. Because that barrier is still there, to come through, a demon has to fully take someone over, killing that person in the process. Because Hell is constantly trying to suck them back in."

Kane just nodded, not looking convinced at all.

"You said Cult of Belial? Who are they?" Randall asked.

"Belial is a widely-worshipped demon in occult circles. A few years ago some atrocious murders were committed in his name. When the walls of Hell were weakened, people that pledged themselves to Belial became free targets for possession," Malcolm said.

"So, Belial is a demon?"

Sigurd answered this time. "Belial is a fallen angel and Lucifer's right-hand man. He and four other fallen angels were given permission to permanently stay on Earth when Hell closed its borders. I had several run-ins with him and Leviathan in the past."

"That drowned looking bloke who called himself Leviathan was a fallen angel?" Kane asked.

"Yes," Danni said simply.

Danni drove into the multi-story parking structure and looked for her designated spot.

"So why was this Leviathan leading the Cult of Belial to attack a research lab?" Kane asked.

"I assume that Belial's cult act as foot soldiers and the fallen angels are their generals. Christian mythology tells of Leviathan as some sort of creature of the deep. A sea-serpent if you would," Malcolm answered.

Danni pulled the car to a stop. "You guys wait here; I'll return the keys."

"As to why they were attacking that lab, I don't know," Malcolm ended simply.

"One would suspect they knew we were coming for this boy here," Sigurd said, pointing at Randall.

"How, though?" Malcolm pondered. "He also asked for the Oracle of Delphi, Apollo and Artemis..."

Danni closed the car door and rushed off to find the key drop-off. Her mind was racing and she was still pumped full of adrenaline.

In her scattered state it took a few minutes for Danni to return.

Both Kane and Randall exchanged several nervous glances when she appeared and Danni understood why. They didn't know who she, Malcolm and Sigurd really were. It wasn't unreasonable for either to assume they'd just been kidnapped.

Danni pulled her small black pelican case from the boot of the car. She drew her gun and released the magazine, catching it in her left hand. She put the gun in the case and threw the magazine, now almost empty, into a separate lockbox inside.

She addressed Kane and Randall's pained expressions. "Don't worry, guys. Once we figure out why the Cult of Belial attacked, we can get you back to your lives."

They checked in without any issues, though the air services agent asked a lot of questions about the limping Sigurd. They all did look like they were fresh from a brawl and their appearances attracted a lot of chatter from the staff. Still, they got through security screening and into the waiting area by the departure gate.

Malcolm and Danni helped Sigurd to a seat.

"Are you sure you can do this?" Danni asked.

"This is a light beating. I will have your medicine man look at me back at that spectacular home," Sigurd groaned.

Malcolm looked at the broken key dangling around the

Viking's neck.

"What happened out there exactly?"

Sigurd shifted his position with a grunt of pain and exertion. He pulled the Hell Key from its chain and looked at it sadly.

"As I told your companions, Hell has no freedom of movement except for he who holds this artefact. It was created with the very essence of Hell itself, the kind of essence that doesn't dim. When the key broke, all of that internal power returned to its point of origin, sucking those hellspawn with it. Demons are soaked in the essence of Hell, as they are formed by it."

"How'd you know that would happen?"

"By spending a long time in Hell learning its rules."

"If Leviathan is an angel, would it have even worked on him?" Danni asked.

"If he was in range, it should have. It was worth a shot."

"If you don't mind, Sigurd, I'd like to have the key to study," Malcolm asked.

"It is powerless now, so by all means, take it. Next time I die, I have no intention of returning to the fiery pit of Lucifer again."

He thrust the key into Malcolm's outstretched palm.

Danni checked her watch. It was 2:15 pm, providing their flight wasn't delayed they should make it back by 4 pm, just in time to get ready for the party.

"That weapon you used to explode those demons. You should have taken it," Sigurd remarked to Danni.

"Ah, I don't think stealing from that institute is a good idea. We will be lucky not to have the police track us here and stop the plane. I'm sure they will be reacting to all the lifeless bodies there now," she replied.

Malcolm scoffed, "I assure you, with weapons technology like that in the building, the police will be delayed until they can hide everything they want to. I bet they have private CCTV that they won't allow the police to access. When we get back, I will ask Mel to get onto ASIO and have them contact Offenes Universum to straighten this all out."

"Not ASIO," Danni interjected. "Brett Sayer has to be our first point of call."

The airport intercom sprang to life, stating that the flight to Amsterdam was now ready for general boarding.

"Now, Sigurd, you're going to have to look like you aren't extremely injured while we scan your ticket," Danni explained.

"A simple task," Sigurd groaned again as he struggled to lift himself from the seat.

Before long, the five of them were seated across the plane en route to Amsterdam. Geneva had presented Danni with new concerns. Previously, the Cult of Belial had gone after Josh and team one. Now, it seemed their focus had shifted.

Though, Danni didn't want to sit there in the unyielding grip of worry. She had an hour and a half to get some precious sleep in. After all, who knew how long the party would go for tonight?

· · · · ·

THE GROUP ARRIVED BACK in Amsterdam far more battered than they'd left.

When Danni reported the events in Geneva to Melissa, it didn't seem to be the only bad news she'd heard that day. Brett Sayer had been in touch, saying Joshua Dare had gone missing.

Apparently, he'd been left in the company of the gods. The AST's second in command, Liam Sager, had departed a realm called the Dreamscape first, leaving Josh behind. Now the AST had no idea where their link to the power of Zeus was.

Danni noticed Mel pacing back and forth, and figured that the stress was building. The mission to steal the Necronomicon tonight had to be a success.

Harry Raatikainen had assured them that The Old World mansion had layers upon layers of supernatural protection built into it and that no demon could ever set foot inside its perimeter. While it was a comforting notion, they had no choice but to take him at his word.

Danni did consider whether she should tell Mel about the kiss of Lucifer. What if the Cult of Belial had tracked them through her?

Though, that was unlikely. The cultists had to have been there before they arrived. They definitely hadn't been on the same flight in.

Then, Artemis's words sounded in Danni's ears, warning her to keep the kiss of Lucifer secret.

Feeling the crushing weight of guilt, Danni went to get cleaned up. Harry had assured them that this Ernst Carter fellow was very susceptible to manipulation through alcohol.

He would almost certainly discuss the Necronomicon but wouldn't show them. They'd need to determine where he had it hidden and how to access it.

When Danni returned to her room, she found a spectacular dress waiting for her.

Laid out on her bed was a royal blue cocktail dress embellished with diamond studs along its top. It fell just above knee-length on Danni and looked far more extravagant than anything she'd ever owned. Beside the dress was a small black jewellery box containing diamond earrings crafted in the shape of a blooming flower and a silver necklace with an enormous sapphire attached to it.

"Wow," Danni breathed, trying it on. She felt like a princess. When she discovered the Louis Vuitton heels left beneath her bed, that just confirmed it.

"Yep, I'm now Cinderella," she thought.

She'd be turning some heads at this party tonight. If Mel had gotten her this, she wondered what her boss had grabbed for herself. Obviously cost hadn't been a factor.

Danni tried the entire ensemble on. Then, after twirling in front of the mirror, hastily pulled it off, not wanting to wrinkle anything.

She pulled her jeans and shirt back on, then headed out looking for something to eat. Having chosen not to eat plane food, Danni was dreadfully hungry.

She stopped by the first aid room, where a shirtless Sigurd was being patched up by a very flustered looking nurse.

Then, she walked down the spiralling stair case to the ground floor entry.

The main door opened and in walked Artemis.

She had gotten changed. No longer draped in the shining

silver dress, the goddess, too, was wearing jeans and a long-sleeved jacket. Her hair was wrapped in a neat ponytail. Gone was the tiara of vines and flowers. She looked incredibly human. Still, her cold, stern gaze chilled Danni when it fell upon her.

"Miss Quinn, fetch the Oracle of Delphi. We have a guest," the goddess ordered.

Another equally fierce-looking woman entered behind Artemis. The stranger made Danni feel instantly uneasy.

Fortunately, Danni didn't have to go searching the mansion for Mel. A door at the other end of the foyer creaked open, and Mel entered.

"Moros?" Mel uttered in surprise.

"Melissa Pythia," the stranger beamed. "It has been too long."

"Danni, I'd like you to meet another god. This is Moros, the Goddess of Fate and Doom," Mel said.

Danni approached Moros and offered a professional handshake. The goddess accepted.

"We must speak. For fate waits for no man, or woman, in this case," Artemis directed at Mel.

"Of course," Mel responded, checking her watch. "Just to the right is a conference room."

"I will not stay long. I feel the ever-deepening pressure of time upon us. Forces move above and below," Moros stated, eyeing Danni curiously.

"Should I come too, or..." Danni asked, hoping Mel would say no. It wasn't that she wasn't interested; she was just hungry.

"Yes, of course," Mel answered.

Danni repressed her disappointment and followed the goddesses into the conference room.

"What are you doing here, Moros?" Mel asked, taking a seat on the comfortable lounge suite.

"Michael's sudden return has made my travel slow. I am still on a quest to uncover answers. A quest that grows more complex the more I learn," Moros sighed.

Moros turned to Danni. "You are Danni Quinn, lover of Joshua Dare?"

Danni cringed at the word lover.

"Ah, yeah, he is my ex-boyfriend, I guess…"

"I met him very recently. I saw the curse upon him and I fear for him now."

"Why?"

"He journeyed across dimensions with Apollo and Hermes. I felt something terrible happen, though I could not see from the mortal world. My intuition tells me that a time is soon to come when that man will make a decision that will affect us all, gods and mortals alike. You have a part to play in that."

"Um, okay," Danni replied lamely.

"Do you know where he is?" Mel asked Moros.

"No, I cannot see him. The infernal cloud that blocks my gaze continues to be a problem."

Artemis nodded. "Something impedes the vision of the gods. Is it the angels?"

"Perhaps. They have been known to craft weapons that inhibit us."

"Well, now that Hephaestus and Hecate have been rescued

from Heaven, surely we can craft such weapons?" Artemis suggested.

"That is why I am here," Moros said, turning to Mel. "We have no hope of completing the ritual to assume the position of Zeus while the angels are watching for divine magic. Even with the skill of Hephaestus, we cannot match the six archangels in Heaven."

"What can we do about that? Perform the ritual without the gods?" Mel asked.

Moros shook her head. "From what I have uncovered, following a bizarre trail through Europe, the magic involved is so phenomenally complex that I believe only Hecate has the ability to do it."

"Well, the ritual needs to be performed on Olympus, right? Can the angels see that old realm of the gods? Artemis said they can't detect divine magic in Hell."

"The angels watch the Earth and some pocket dimensions that they've conquered. This includes the ruins of Olympus and Asgard. Divine magic cannot be used there, lest the angels see it. We have no hope of completing the ritual before the archangels intervene."

"Let them come and see them fall before my arrows," Artemis boasted.

"Right now, you are but a gnat to Michael," Moros retorted.

"Even equipped with the power of the divine flame of Prometheus, Apollo could, at best, match Michael. And that is a power-boost beyond comprehension."

"Apollo told me he used that to fight Michael. How? I thought any exposure to the divine flame was fatal to us? Is that not why it was locked away on Olympus?"

"Apollo was mortal when he touched it. It restored his divinity and gave him a temporary, colossal surplus of power. If he were to attempt that again, the flame would kill him."

Danni knew what they were talking about.

The incident with Apollo and the Flame of Prometheus took place in Afghanistan in 2019. Apollo and Moros had successfully sealed Michael in a black hole, giving them the year of divine freedom that had just expired.

Moros turned to Mel, "We need mortal assistance yet again."

"Well, we have built this alliance for a reason. What do you need us to do?"

"I still have eyes and ears in the Vatican. And through them, I have learned of the Pope's recent movements abroad. Further investigations have revealed how the angels monitor for divine magic. The device they use to detect our magic has been here on Earth all along."

"Where?" Mel asked.

"Africa. Specifically North-East Africa. On the side of a sleeping volcano stands a monastery. The path inside leads to a mighty tower of white and gold standing in the mountain's hollow. The tower is a repurposed structure from the ancient civilisation, bent and corrupted by the angel's will."

"The ancient civilisation strikes again," Danni muttered.

"The only sleeping volcano I know in Africa is Mt Kilimanjaro," Mel stated.

Moros nodded.

"This objective is of extreme importance. The gods need to be unshackled. The tower must be destroyed," Moros affirmed.

"Do we know how to destroy it exactly?" Mel asked.

"The same way you'd destroy any building. Blow it up," Moros answered simply.

Mel looked at her, confused.

"I suspect that the tower is very precise in its design. Height, location, width and all other factors would play a part in allowing whatever mechanism is inside to function. To be safe, I will create an explosion of magical energy that can be utilised along with more mortal means."

Mel didn't speak. Danni knew exactly what she was thinking. They were currently behind on their mission to find an artefact. Now they were being given another dangerous task by the gods. When would it end?

"We do have a problem, however. Since Michael's return a couple of days ago, I have it on good authority that he has tasked the Archangel Gabriel with permanent overwatch of the Kilimanjaro facility. I cannot stress this enough. Gabriel is not a foe that can be defeated. To destroy the detector, you will need sneak and subterfuge."

"Aren't the archangels super impossibly powerful? Can you even sneak around them?" Danni asked.

Moros frowned. "Complete your current task. I will return to you with more details once the artefact is found and secured."

"Is there any more information you have on this white and gold tower? I will need to brief up right away," Mel said, pulling out her notebook.

"It is a skyscraper topped with a golden crescent moon and a carven angel sitting inside it. You will have to topple the entire structure. It was modified with the guidance of Hephaestus during his long imprisonment. Damage it beyond repair, and their ability to track divine magic will be lost."

"Easier said than done," Mel said slowly.

Danni grimaced. This sounded like a mission where a lot could go wrong.

"It needs to be done. When the gods are unshackled, everything will become easier."

"I will take this new objective on board and await further information," Mel concluded.

"How goes the hunt for an artefact of Zeus?" Moros asked.

"We are working on it. Tonight, we should have a location."

"Good. It is better you know now where things are headed. Find the artefact and destroy the detector. Then we make for Olympus."

"You haven't heard whispers of any artefacts of Zeus in your travels this last year, Moros?" Mel asked.

"No, my journey has been singularly focused. To take the missing place of a god, I have never even considered such a possibility. Certainly, the titans and gods had no knowledge of such a ritual. So, where has it come from? I have found clues left by humans, of all things, on how to do it. A tablet in Spain gave me the ingredients needed. In England, a long-buried scroll listed runes and incantations of unimaginable complexity. So complex that even the longest-lived and most advanced human sorcerers could have never conjured them. There is a mystery here that must be unravelled..."

"If you found the scrolls and tablets, how did the Vatican know about the ritual?"

"Another question that needs answering. The angels seem to know the ingredients required, and I suspect it has come from human sources. But I do not know. Hopefully, I will uncover the truth soon."

"It seems obvious to me that this has primordial origin," Artemis interjected.

"I considered that," Moros started, sounding unsure, "but when has a primordial ever consorted with humans? They don't write runes or give instructions. That would be like a human writing out computer code and giving it to a butterfly. The butterfly cannot comprehend the information being shared, and there is no way to pass it on so that it could."

"Perhaps in the sunken city we seek, answers will reveal themselves," Artemis shrugged.

Moros tried to smile, but it came across as more of a grimace. "I do hope so. I must go. Normally I would teleport or fly across great distances, but thanks to the watchful gaze of the angels, I must take a bus. How has life come to this?"

"Where are you going?" Mel asked, standing up.

"Nijmegen, near the German border. Not too far from here. There are answers I seek in these lands."

"It is lucky we are here at the same time."

"It is not luck; it is fate," Moros winked.

When the group found themselves standing at the front door again, Moros embraced Artemis.

"Your brother has declared the new Olympians, and we

stand among them."

"Of course Apollo would do such a thing without his sister there."

"The gods linger in the Dreamscape for now. When the mortals destroy the detector, they will emerge again."

Moros nodded curtly at Mel.

"Melissa Pythia, your vision can see what even mine cannot. There is no other mortal I trust greater to achieve this task."

Mel bowed, and Moros walked away.

Artemis stated, "I will join you tonight, Moros, for I am not needed here."

Moros nodded at her.

Mel looked at the time on the grandfather clock by the stairs.

"5pm!" she gasped. "We need to get ready. Harry will be down for us soon."

Finally, the talking was over and the party was about to begin.

15

THE PARTY

AMSTERDAM
- JANUARY 25 -

Harry had left strict instructions for them to meet at 5:30 pm sharp. The old man had been somewhat helpful, and to Danni at least, embodied what The Old World Europe had turned out to be. It was casual but interesting, light-hearted with important undertones.

The party tonight was an annual event that Ernst Carter hosted in honour of his great-grandfather, a renowned archaeologist and explorer, William Eisenhein Carter. Though Harry was scarce on the details as to what was actually being celebrated about William.

Danni did a quick internet search while she prepared. There was never any harm in having some additional information at the ready. However, the impromptu meeting with the Goddess of Doom had meant a rush job was in order.

As Danni curled the long strands of hair falling in front of her face, she typed the explorer's name into the search engine.

The few black and white photos online showed an elderly man with a tremendous bushy moustache in safari attire. He'd travelled the world, leading and partaking in expeditions across Northern Africa and South America. There were even hints that he'd travelled to Antarctica, but trying to follow that thread of information proved difficult. A few conspiracy websites showed up, but nothing substantial could be gained from them.

What Danni found much more interesting than the mysterious exploits of the grandfather was the subsequent family history. William's son hadn't followed in his father's footsteps. He'd invented a new pair of loafers that sold like crazy across Europe, establishing a shoe empire that expanded throughout the western world. His son had then further expanded their business. Danni thought she might have even owned a pair of their shoes at one point.

It wasn't until Ernst came along that William Carter's passion for history re-emerged in their gene pool.

Ernst was a tenured professor at the University of Amsterdam. While he was a poor shadow compared to his great grandfather, he had a respectable body of work behind him.

He'd specialised in studying the Hispanic Ninth Legion, a Roman military force that disappeared from history. Much in the way his great-grandfather's work provided fuel for the internet conspiracy engine, it seemed Ernst's work did as well.

It was fitting that Ernst Carter would be wrapped up in mysteries, considering his secret fascination with the Necronomicon; enough to steal it and pretend like it was destroyed.

Danni was curious to learn whether Ernst would be the kindly old-grandfather type of professor or the creepier 'favours-for-grades' kind. The cynic in her was leaning towards the latter option. Still, she'd reserve judgement for now.

She was actually kind of excited about this party. Even though it was for work, Danni hadn't really had a chance to unwind for over a year now. Maybe talking to a bunch of gruff old university professors in stuffy suits would be fun.

She didn't have enough time to look as good as she could have, but she'd never been the type to put hours into her appearance anyway.

Once Danni was satisfied, she took a very brief moment to stand on her balcony and soak in the views of the sculpted lawns. Something inside her said this would be the last moment of peace for a long time.

The sun was moving low over the trees. The herd of deer had returned to amble across the lawn. The Old World mansion never failed to impress with its picturesque beauty lingering from centuries ago.

Waiting in the foyer, Danni's jaw dropped slightly when her boss came down the stairs.

Melissa was a vision.

She was elegance and class wrapped in a pearl dress. Her long black hair sat like a shining waterfall, falling down her shoulders. Her makeup was understated, highlighting the divine symmetry of her face, with bright red lipstick to top it off. Her dress ended below her knees and wrapped diagonally across her chest. She wore black heels and dangling diamond earrings.

Her outfit was finished with a short black jacket, which Danni assumed she was only wearing to cover the bandages on her arm.

Teva playfully wolf-whistled.

He'd only just returned himself from setting up his spy van. He'd also been tasked with scanning the streets of Amsterdam for the Cult of Belial, though he didn't find a trace of them. Malcolm was also waiting in the foyer.

Mel smiled. Danni almost thought she saw the hint of a blush.

Mel was always working. She probably enjoyed the chance to get properly dressed up too.

The woman Danni used to be a long time ago would've felt the ugly head of jealousy rear up within her, but she'd grown beyond that now. She'd decided that being envious of someone else's physical appearance was entirely pointless. It was a road that only led to despair.

"You both look wonderful. We will go in my car. I know Ernst will be very interested to meet you," Harry said.

"Let's quickly go over the details. My codename is Maggie Steelehart, and Danni is Sandra Mountainflower," Mel stated.

Everyone grinned at Danni's name. It was the codename The Old World had given her when they hid her in North Queensland. It seemed appropriate now.

"Teva?" Mel asked.

"I have procured a van and as much as equipment as I could find. I only have my laptop and a couple of cheap monitors. Still, I should be able to access his private security system. If one of you finds the wi-fi password, it will make my life a lot easier. I'll be a couple of streets back."

"Right, good. The plan is a go."

"Wait. Is Malcolm not coming?" Danni asked. He was a history professor, Ernst Carter was a history professor, she figured it was a way in.

"No. I will be working with Randall to try and decipher the incomplete copy of the formula we have. Finding matches to the symbology used will be timely and tedious work," Malcolm explained, looking eager to get started.

"Yep, we aren't there to make chit-chat. We will get the book and get out," Mel added.

Danni privately thought it might take a fair bit of sleuthing to learn the book's location.

Fortunately, Harry chimed in, "Please, I know you are rushed, but Ernst is a man of class and sophistication. You will need to charm him before you can even broach the topic of the Necronomicon."

"Will you be able to help?" Mel asked the old man.

"No, my dear," Harry smiled. "I am going to a party. Whatever your business with Altior Fulgur is, it is no concern of mine."

"What about the submarine? Have you spoken to anyone?" Malcolm asked.

"Oh yes! Good thing you mentioned it. Speaking directly to

Altior is difficult. However, I did get the CFO of iHeal Genetics, his big pharmaceutical company. Apparently, they have funnelled significant funds into a New Zealand based deep sea exploration group, The Kiwi Sinkers. Let's just say this company isn't exactly on the books in legal terms. They have a submarine equipped with… a smaller submarine that can go very deep. I spoke to them, and they seemed very enthusiastic."

Mel looked intrigued yet perturbed as Harry kept waffling on.

"So, we can use this sub?" Malcolm asked.

"Yes, yes. They will have it prepared in the next two days, thought the man in charge seemed agitated I couldn't provide him coordinates now."

"That was easy," Danni smiled.

"Because Altior Fulgur is in bed with a lot of secretive companies," Mel murmured so quietly that only Danni could hear her.

"What is in it for them? Why would they just help out like that? It's expensive, and they don't know who we are," Malcolm sounded very sceptical.

Harry looked annoyed at the question. "Oh, I don't know. They are looking for something underwater; you are looking for something underwater… When the stars align, why question it?"

Teva, Malcolm and Melissa all had expressions of doubt and mistrust etched on their faces.

"We will face this undersea adventure when we get to it," Mel concluded.

It appeared no other members of The Old World Europe

were joining them.

Harry, Mel and Danni walked towards a spectacular black car waiting for them. It looked similar to a Rolls Royce, though it featured a strange hood ornament.

Danni peered at it as she walked past, soaking in its immense detail. It was a bronze rectangle with continents carved across its face. In the middle was a circle with what appeared to be an altar and some men performing a ritual. Beneath the rectangle was a smaller box with 'The Old World' spelt out. It was a car fitting the mansion.

Danni had been impressed with the house of The Old World members in Cairns. Had she realised that was just a taste of the grandeur the organisation offered, she would've considered signing up herself.

· · · · ·

UNLIKE THE MANSION BY the River Vecht, Ernst Carter's home was near the city's business hub. Somewhat fittingly, Ernst lived in Apollobuurt, an area of Amsterdam where the streets were named after Greek legends and artists.

Stately apartment blocks, townhouses and villas lined the roads while hedges lined the canals. Danni loved the look of the place, with moss clinging to the red bricks of the buildings and some of the older houses having climbing vines reaching around doors and windows. It was poetic, and the sort of place a history professor should live.

It wasn't long before they pulled up beside a knee-high

brick wall so thick with moss that it was impossible to determine its original colour. Behind the wall was a sparse garden with a singular enormous tree reaching high above the pointed black roof. The home was three stories high and built with the same red brick that defined the area.

"We are here," Harry grinned.

The trio stepped out of the car and were met with a brisk chill in the air. Both Danni and Mel, their dresses offering no warmth whatsoever, immediately made for the front door.

"Women's clothing really is impractical," Mel murmured.

"Hey, it is the price we pay to look better than the men," Danni laughed.

Harry, however, directed them away from the front door, moving instead down a paved path. It led around a corner onto a back patio alive with activity.

Though patio was far from an adequate description of the monstrous open area before them.

Against the rear wall of the house was a large white screen with a projector set up in front of it. Four round tables sat atop a vast expanse of dark grey tiles, before opening into a stately garden.

There were replicas of renaissance statues sitting among circular garden beds, which would contain myriads of blooming flowers in the summer.

There was also a unique and disturbing fountain designed as a pyramid of disjointed fish-heads spewing water from a hundred mouths. Danni saw a pool, a spa, and a meticulously planned pathway that moved amongst it all.

Fortunately, the main patio area was equipped with tall

heaters ablaze with flame and large industrial electric heaters fixed to the roof.

They were quickly met by a man in an elegant blue suit who introduced himself as Ernst Carter. He enthusiastically shook hands with Harry, then turned his gaze towards the two women.

"Harry, my good man! A pleasure as always. And who might these two beauties be? Clearly, retirement is treating you better than expected!"

"Maggie," Mel smiled, offering a hand.

Ernst bowed down and kissed it.

"And Sandra," Danni added, allowing him to do the same.

"They are enthusiasts from The Old World," Harry said brightly.

"Not your usual demographics," Ernst laughed. "Tell me, has Petteri found the pig-faced woman's bones yet?"

"No, his decade long search is still ongoing," Harry replied, giving Ernst a knowing look.

Ernst didn't look at all like Danni had expected. He had a mop of brown hair with greying streaks throughout. Ernst had a bulbous nose and hypnotic light blue eyes. His eyebrows were bushy, and he had wrinkles indicative of someone who spent a lot of time with a furrowed brow. He was tall, solidly built, and carried himself with the casual dignity usually found in the successful.

"Ladies, go and mingle. I will have to perform a speech at some point, which you are more than welcome to avoid if you wish. There is copious food and drink, and several of my students are here if you desire the companionship of people your own ages," Ernst stated.

Danni scanned the crowd. Many younger people were, in fact, standing in circles, talking and laughing. The university crowd was most certainly present, but it also seemed there were a lot of socialites.

One particular man caught Danni's eyes. Standing in a dark corner, talking with a pair of women, was a man draped in the elaborate garb of the Catholic Church.

Danni tapped Mel on the shoulder and directed her attention towards him.

"That is the Archbishop of Utrecht, the highest position of the Catholic Church in the Netherlands," Mel informed her.

"I am amazed you know that."

"I've been to the Vatican and seen how they dress," Mel smiled. "It might be wise for you to eavesdrop on his conversations. They have my face on record."

"What if he speaks to me?"

"Then speak to him back."

"Right. Uhm, who is the Pope again?"

"Pope Leo XIV currently reigns supreme over the Catholic Church, at the whip and call of Archangel Michael."

"And what is this guy's name?"

"He is Archbishop Luuk de Graaf."

"Impressive… again," Danni muttered.

"I used my phone," Mel winked, her screen lighting up with a display of the names of the Netherlands church hierarchy. "Let's mingle until Ernst delivers this speech of his. Hopefully, after some wine and conversation, his tongue is loosened as to where the Necronomicon is hidden."

Danni and Mel split up. Mel wandered off to engage a group of academics in conversation while Danni slinked toward the archbishop.

Fortunately, the table featuring the smorgasbord was in her path. Despite the class of the affair, Danni was pleasantly surprised to see paper plates and cheap napkins in abundance.

She grabbed a plate and began piling the food on. Black caviar, the finest cured meats and the most fragrant exotic cheeses all found their way to Danni's mounting pile. There were raw vegetables with infinite dips and more normal offerings. Barbeque steak (though heavily marbled), hot dogs (of the finest German meat) and seafood all appeared too.

Danni had no idea how hungry she was. Sauce dribbled down her chin as she engulfed a hotdog coated with onion.

Seeing the bemused smirks of a few of the university crowd, Danni wiped her face clean and got back to her task, feeling slightly embarrassed.

With her paper plate in hand, she casually leaned against a concrete pylon, just within earshot of the archbishop.

The archbishop was having a heated discussion with the women, the topic of which was soon revealed to be recipes for a cold tomato soup dish.

Danni shook her head. She would try again later.

Someone tapped her on the shoulder.

A nervous-looking man in his early twenties (judging by his poorly grown beard) had approached her.

He looked down at his drink and nervously mumbled something so quietly and poorly phrased that Danni couldn't make it out.

"Speak up, where's your bloody confidence then," Danni almost-shouted, sounding very Australian.

The young man looked taken aback. "I am sorry, miss, my friends dared me to come up and talk to you… if you could just play along…"

"Play along to what? Talking?" Danni laughed.

The man looked slightly less nervous. "I suppose I didn't think this out properly."

"I'll give your approach a zero out of ten," Danni grinned. "Hey, where'd you get that cocktail from?"

"There is a bar just inside. I will show you if you like."

And just like that, Danni was escorted into the living area, which had been turned into a makeshift bar and dancefloor. She ordered a fruity red mocktail.

"How do you know Ernst Carter?" Danni asked.

"I am his nephew. And you?"

"Friend of a stranger," Danni replied.

The young man didn't quite know how to take Danni's playful answer, so instead, he introduced himself. "I am Arend, by the way."

"Sandra." She'd struck gold. The man who'd approached her would surely know his way around Ernst's house.

"I have not seen you around," Arend said casually.

"I'm not usually around." Danni took the exotic drink from the bartender and sipped at it. "Want to give me a tour?"

"Ah… normally I would, but my uncle doesn't want people wandering the place."

"That's disappointing for you," Danni said in a hushed voice.

Arend was suddenly emboldened with confidence. "Later on, come and find me."

A group of young people approached the bar and Arend was swept up in conversation. He casually introduced Danni, earning barely concealed smirks from his friends. Danni made polite greetings, then, when the attention was off her, disappeared back outside.

Arend was sweet but a little dweeby. He wasn't really Danni's type. She grinned when she figured her type now was probably a supernatural monster.

Danni couldn't see Mel in the garden anywhere. Harry was off with a bunch of professors discussing a statue.

Danni spun around, only to splash her drink as she bumped into someone.

She gasped when she saw it was the archbishop whose clothes she'd just ruined.

"I'm so sorry!" Danni said.

"It is quite alright. This is what I get for wearing my robes to a party," the archbishop responded.

Danni laughed nervously. She could see the archbishop had kind eyes.

"Why did you wear them then?" Danni asked.

"I am never off work, so I always wear my uniform."

"Makes sense," Danni shrugged.

"Who are you, my child?"

"Sandra. I'm a big fan of...you know... God, and stuff."

Danni cringed as the words left her mouth, but the archbishop just continued smiling.

"Couldn't have put it better myself," he nodded.

There was a moment of awkward silence.

"So, how does an archbishop compare to a cardinal?" Danni asked, struggling to find conversation.

"Well, they are above us in the order of things. It is complex, but let's say a rung above."

"So, if you went for promotion, you'd be a cardinal?"

"I suppose. Though I am happy where I am. I would hate to end up in Rome and become a part of that infighting. The message is lost when the holy men turn on each other."

"What do you mean?"

"Well, it wasn't long ago that a cardinal came here to Amsterdam. You arrived with Harry, did you not? I thought you'd know. He lost favour with the others, and I helped put him back on his feet. We all lose our way sometimes. That is why God forgives."

"Which cardinal?" Danni asked curiously.

"It matters not. He and Harry met a lot, having long talks about the nature of things. That's why I thought you'd be familiar with the story."

"Harry and I aren't that close. That is interesting, though."

"Harry is a good man. He helped me bring that cardinal back around. Gave him the answers he sought. You find yourself in good company."

Danni frowned. Harry had helped out a cardinal recently? That didn't bode well.

"You know about The Old World?" Danni asked quietly.

"Of course. Much of what they believe is not really within the realms of the Church, but it is interesting to follow. I personally don't think much of ghost hunting as a hobby."

"But this mysterious cardinal might have," Danni thought.

She had to find Mel. Their enemy in the Catholic Church, Cardinal Vasilije Markovic, was the only cardinal she knew of that had been on the outs with the Pope. If he had come here and spoken to The Old World, who knows what information they may have given him. Or, even worse, could still be giving him.

"Does anyone from The Old World still talk to this cardinal?" Danni asked quickly.

"I have no idea –"

There was a commotion up ahead. Two young men across the patio had started jostling with each other.

The larger of the two grabbed the other by the scruff of his collar and threw him across the tiles.

The smaller one, adequately incensed, got to his feet and began throwing punches. One went wild and knocked an old lady's drink to the floor, shattering the glass.

Danni had an instant flashback to the Hell's Horns Tavern.

Another violent push thrust the larger man straight towards Danni.

She acted on instinct and jumped right into the fray.

Like a striking snake, she wrapped one hand around the larger man's wrist and pointed his fingers towards the sky. She applied pressure on the joint, putting him in a simple yet very effective wrist lock.

He grimaced and gasped in shock.

The smaller man lunged forward, and Danni threw a devastating front kick into his chest.

He collapsed to the ground, winded.

The circle that had quickly formed around the fight stood silent, then a round of applause rang out for Danni.

Standing amongst the circle was a very nervous looking Ernst Carter. He quickly vanished from view then reappeared with a microphone.

"Hello, everyone," he said nervously, his voice electronically magnified. "I'm glad to see some people have over-indulged in the alcohol a little too early in the evening."

There was a smattering of laughter.

This was perfect; Ernst didn't want such unsavoury behaviour tarnishing his event. He was going to do his speech now. The timetable on their plan had just been moved up.

"If everyone could turn their attention to the screen -"

Danni felt a tapping on her shoulder. Arend had reappeared.

"That was cool; how'd you do that?" he asked.

"Karate?" Danni answered unconvincingly.

"Listen, my uncle's speeches are long and tedious. I can show you around the house now if you want?"

"That... sounds like a great idea!"

"Let's slip away."

Just like that, Danni was being pulled away from the crowd and through a side door into the Carter manor. With any luck, she was headed in the direction of the hidden black book.

16

A RATHER SIMPLE HEIST

Danni felt like she was a teenager again, sneaking through a house with a boy she didn't know too well. It would've been far more exciting if Ernst Carter's home wasn't so plain.

Sure, the furniture was expensive, the grandfather clock was ancient, and the kitchen was made of the finest materials. Still, it felt like it was missing something.

Danni had been envisioning suits of armour and libraries abundant with dusty tomes. This was just the dwelling of a reasonably well-off single guy.

Arend, who was quite obviously unsure of what he was

doing, led Danni through an awkwardly formal tour of the kitchen and dining area, then upstairs to the study.

Mustering his confidence, he took Danni into the master bedroom. Danni was smiling internally. She knew that he was trying to create a scenario where he could kiss her and perhaps get something more in his nervous wreck of a mind. The way guys bumbled their way through romance (or the lack thereof) was amusing.

"Nice room," Danni yawned.

Arend looked alarmed. "I don't know what you expected; it is just a house…"

"I don't know! Aren't you guys the descendants of some renowned explorer. I thought there'd be cool stuff around."

Arend nervously adjusted his shirt.

"Is there cool stuff around?" Danni asked, leaning in close.

"Okay, I will show you some of my uncle's collection, but promise not to tell anyone."

Arend led Danni out of the master bedroom, through a door in the hall into a small library. The library contained a couple of bookshelves and an expensive leather chair.

The last bookshelf on the far wall was surprisingly sparse. Arend approached it and pushed it out of the way with a sharp heave.

A secret metal door with a keypad was revealed.

"This is too easy," Danni thought.

"You can never be too careful. Ernst has pretty good security. My great-great grandfather's stuff is pretty valuable," Arend said.

"Ohhh, I'm excited!" Danni exclaimed. "This isn't the entrance to a dungeon you're gonna lock me in, is it?"

"No," Arend inhaled sharply, looking horrified at the mere thought.

"Just kidding," Danni beamed.

She tried to move into a position where she could see the young man punch in the door code, but he deliberately blocked her view.

Danni scanned the room, seeing a small security camera on top of the other bookcase. It was looking right at the door.

"Hey, Arend," Danni started. "What's the wi-fi password?"

"Oh, it is 9-0AD120."

"How'd you know that off the top of your head?"

"My uncle has it set so that you have to put it in every time you leave the house. Very annoying."

Danni pulled out her phone and sent a quick text to Teva. With the wi-fi password, he'd be able to hack the security system a little easier.

Arend pulled the silver handle on the door and held it open for Danni. She could see it was well lit on the other side.

A very short flight of stairs descended into a room chock-full of glass display cases.

It was cold, with ducts spaced periodically along the roof blasting chilled air. The floor was a dark blue carpet that ran up the walls to the black roof. It was like being in a museum.

The room was relatively large, too. There was no way this place was a well-kept secret. All a person would have to do was find the building's floor plans on the internet to see that a sizeable chunk of the house was missing.

"Now, this is cool," Danni marvelled, soaking in the mysterious atmosphere of the hidden room.

Arend propped the door open while Danni looked in the first display case. It contained a primitive wooden spear with a sharp rock point fixed to the top. The rock had simplistic carvings along its face. The twine that tied the rocky blade to the shaft also wrapped a leathery substance to the spear's lower half. It looked like a giant bat wing had been fixed to the wood.

"Used to have bright feathers on it, feathers like you've never seen apparently, but my grandfather failed to preserve them properly," Arend said, looking nervously at Danni to see if she approved of the object.

"What is it?" Danni asked.

"A spear from a primitive tribe William found in South America. Family legend says William used this spear to kill a flying monster."

"Cool," Danni said.

They moved onto the next display case, which was raised a few feet off the ground with steel bars. It contained an immaculate golden sarcophagus.

"That one you do have to pretend you didn't see, because technically it is the property of the Egyptian Government," Arend chuckled.

The following display was an impressive dinosaur skull.

"Awesome T-Rex head," Danni marvelled.

"Actually, not a T-Rex. This species is unknown to palaeontology. According to my father, tests say this animal died in the 1930s."

"Impossible," Danni said dismissively. The irony did hit her that she was the last person who should determine whether something outlandish was possible or not.

Arend shrugged.

They moved across the room to a mannequin dressed in outdated clothes. They looked familiar. Danni had seen William Carter wearing them in the black and white pictures on the internet.

Next was something that looked out of place. A metal chest with an electronic keypad sparkling on the front.

"Uncle says gold and jewels and stuff are kept safe in there," Arend mumbled quickly.

"Open it up," Danni urged, gripping him tightly around the arm.

"No way," Arend said, blushing slightly. "I don't know the code and Ernst would kill me."

The last remnants of a round of applause echoed into the room from outside. Ernst must've been done with his speech.

"We should go," Arend suggested nervously.

Danni begrudgingly agreed. She'd found the secret room fascinating and was confident the Necronomicon was inside the locked steel chest.

When the pair rejoined the party outside, none had noticed their absence, save for Mel.

She casually slid next to Danni and asked, "What did you find?"

"The location of the book. I'm ninety-nine percent sure," Danni replied, barely masking her excitement. "It has a pretty serious looking electronic lock, though."

"So, we need the code…" Mel murmured.

"Teva has the wi-fi password; we will see what he finds."

"I have total faith in him," Mel said. She was looking at Ernst from across the patio.

"What's on your mind?"

"Ernst obviously knows a lot about the Necronomicon. It seems a shame to waste this opportunity. He'll never give us the code, but maybe we can get some information."

"How can you get him to talk?"

"Alcohol."

Mel made for the bar and ordered two drinks. She then moved in the direction of Ernst Carter.

• • • • •

AN HOUR LATER, ERNST WAS caught in the embrace of a good time. The party was pumping. Young and old had moved onto the dancefloor.

The food kept appearing from its seemingly magical place of origin and the liquor was bottomless.

Danni had mingled with everyone. All of the people were really nice. She'd even let Arend have a cheeky dance with her. He'd stepped on her toes and been completely flustered the whole time, but it hadn't been too bad.

Earlier, the air had been full of classical music. Then there was a swift change to booming electronic house. It was becoming a rave.

A disco ball flicked on as the lights went off and showered the place with a myriad of spinning colours. Ernst Carter certainly had a wild side. One thing was unquestionable, the man knew how to throw a party.

Mel had been plying the professor with drinks, and he'd taken quite the shine to her. It wasn't long before she'd dragged him to the dance floor, and they'd pulled off some spectacular moves together.

What was surprising was that Ernst's hands never strayed to an area they shouldn't, and he treated Mel with the utmost respect.

Danni was starting to think he wasn't a seedy old professor. Perhaps he was just desperate to reconnect with his lost youth.

For a brief and refreshing moment, Danni forgot her objective and became immersed in the party. She was having such a good time.

It wasn't until she tipped over the precipice of exhaustion that she snapped back to her objective. It had been a long day of travelling, cultists and experimental physics weapons. She wanted to get the book and go to bed.

She withdrew herself from the group of university girls she'd been chatting with and went to find Mel.

Danni found her boss standing beside a tall potted green shrub, wrapped in conversation with Ernst. It looked intense. Danni moved within earshot.

"No, no, no, my lady," Ernst muttered. "The Necronomicon is said to have been written by Abdul Alhazred. But I don't believe he is the original perceiver of the book's dark truths. There is another figure shrouded in secrets and myth. Some of us believe

Alhazred was a pupil to a greater and darker mind."

"Alhazred himself is shrouded in secrets and myth. How can you know there was someone before him?" Mel shot back.

"It isn't written, but there are carvings of a figure depicted as a broken man being taught by the outer things. Carvings that aren't known by those in archaeological fields. I have always believed, as my great grandfather did before me, that there is a grand cover-up."

"This originator of the teachings of the Necronomicon, does he have a name?"

"The Sundered King. A name only heard in ancient whispers. The Sundered King sought a power greater than that of the gods who betrayed him. His call was answered from the infinite cosmic void."

"It is a captivating story, but you say the only evidence of this Sundered King is kept hidden by what? A secret world order?"

"I don't know," Carter shrugged. "Most who seek the Necronomicon aren't interested in its history. They seek the power contained within its pages. Many years ago, I dabbled in the spells and incantations of that book and only just escaped with my life. Heaven and Hell, gods and angels, all of these things are so small compared to what the black book tells us."

"I'd love to see it. Shame it is so hard to find," Mel said as she twirled a finger through her hair.

Ernst rubbed the back of his neck and said, "Well, such things should remain out of reach of the ordinary person. I'd love to discuss the Necronomicon more, but it really isn't a topic for polite conversation."

"Oh, come on!" Mel urged, grabbing Ernst on the forearm.

"You said you've dabbled in it. How'd you find a copy? The university?"

"Few universities have copies anymore. It is one of the secret banned books. There are copies out there, usually poorly translated and hand-scribbled. Rumour has reached my ear that the Vatican has the original in its secret archives now, though how that came to be, I don't know."

"You work at the University of Amsterdam, don't you? Didn't they once have a copy?"

"It was destroyed long ago," Carter mumbled sheepishly. "I really must go."

Danni approached just as Ernst vanished into the crowd.

"He really doesn't want to talk about his copy of the book," Mel said, apparently aware Danni had snuck up.

"I spoke to the archbishop," Danni remembered suddenly. "The Old World here played host to a Vatican cardinal. I think it was Markovic."

Mel frowned. "I don't know what to make of that now. Maybe the other team has some answers. Like I said, Altior Fulgur has his fingers in every pie."

"You don't think The Old World would sell us out?"

"We don't know what Fulgur wants in all this. To steal the power of Zeus for himself? To make money from exploiting the supernatural? Your guess is as good as mine," Mel sighed.

"None of this feels right," Danni said.

"I know what you mean. Unfortunately, if we are going to find a sunken city potentially holding an artefact of Zeus, we need The Old World's help. The Australian Navy isn't going to take us there, not for this mission."

Danni's phone buzzed. Teva had, at last, got the code.

"Teva, be ready with the van. We are going to extract the book now."

Mel ended the call without waiting for a response.

"Lead the way," she whispered to Danni, making sure no one was watching them.

The revelry was reaching fever pitch. Danni suspected that there wasn't anyone sober enough to pay attention to them in any great detail.

Danni navigated the halls and rooms with focused precision. She quickly came to the metal door with the keypad by the handle. Arend hadn't bothered to push the bookcase back into position, something Danni took a mental note to remember to do.

Danni punched in the code, and the door opened.

"I bet Teva watched the security footage. Ernst never would've thought it'd capture him entering the code all the time," Danni guessed.

"Well, this room certainly is interesting," Mel said.

Mel had no interest in the display cases housing priceless artefacts. She went straight for the steel chest.

Mel assessed the lock, then hit the second set of numbers Teva had sent. The lock beeped and opened.

Mel pulled the lid up. There was only one object inside.

Sitting flat against the grey base of the box, the black face of the book stared up at them. This version was different, entirely void of detail across its covers and spine.

Danni thought it was her imagination, but the room seemed

to get colder.

There was a sense of foreboding about the book. Danni's skin prickled and she felt her heart thumping in her ears.

Mel reached out and touched it.

She withdrew her hand.

"This book doesn't feel right. It feels… evil."

"That is just Ernst talking," Danni said, leaning into the chest and picking it up.

She flicked through the pages. The alien writing and horrific drawings, so vividly described by those who'd encountered the book, were present.

"I'll text Teva," Danni offered. She passed the book to Mel.

Mel's eyes flashed gold. Her oracle powers were activating.

"What do you see?" Danni asked, not willing to touch her this time, lest she be dragged into another nightmarish vision. One experience in the city of black stone was enough for her.

"I see a creature," Mel started slowly. "He… I know its a he, I can sense it… he stands tall above a dark forest, but the trees don't look right. Neither do the stars."

"Go on," Danni urged.

"He has arms in the wrong places and three twisted legs. Tentacles, long and short, spring from his body in all directions. In fact, his head is just one long tentacle with a vertical slit for a mouth. There are egg sacks on his chest and strange orifices opening and closing on his limbs."

"Is it a mythological monster?" Danni asked.

"I don't think so… He doesn't see me. Oh! But now I see me! I see us on the bridge in Niflheim. Artemis is performing the spell and giving life to Sigurd. Now the monster is turning. He is watching us leave Niflheim; somehow, he can see us. He is changing focus again. Now he is looking right at... me."

Mel gasped and collapsed, flinging the book to the floor.

Danni reacted quickly, breaking Melissa's fall.

"What happened?"

Mel rubbed her head. "It moved so fast, on all fours, crawling towards me. I had to get away."

"Any idea what it was?"

"It didn't appear like anything in myth I've ever studied. It must be connected to the black book, though it felt so far away... impossibly far away. Across the stars..."

"Look, we already have gods, angels and demons involved in this. Aliens are too complicated," Danni joked, though semi-serious.

Mel stared at the book on the ground. "Is Teva coming?"

"He will be driving by the front any moment."

"Take the book and give it to Teva. He will know this already, but ensure you remind him to delete all of Ernst's security footage from tonight."

Danni nodded. She picked up the book and followed Mel out of the room.

• • • • •

ALL IN ALL, EVERYTHING HAD BEEN surprisingly easy. They'd successfully retrieved the book and passed it to Teva. Any moment now it'd be arriving in the hands of Malcolm and Randall.

All that was left was to make a casual escape, something that was proving very difficult.

Arend had become like a lonely puppy, following Danni around. The boy was nice enough but a bit clueless towards projected signals.

Evidently, Ernst had bragged to some of his friends of Melissa's impressive mythological knowledge, and now several of the drunk older gentlemen were intent on having conversations with her.

When the indoor lights finally came on and the music stopped, Danni was struggling to hold her eyes open.

She breathed a sigh of relief when a very drunk Harry began bidding fond farewells.

Ernst approached Melissa. He'd been avoiding her ever since their conversation about the Necronomicon.

"Listen, I know you won't want to hear this, but forget learning about the Necronomicon. Only bad things are found in its pages. That book will never lead you to any kind of happiness."

"It's just a book," Mel said, playing dumb.

"No, it's not," Ernst said, looking concerned. "It is a key and a gate to things beyond this world. Things that don't belong."

Ernst scanned left to right before leaning in close.

"I've heard through my old network the Cult of Cthulhu is active again. Mentioning the Necronomicon will put you in danger. They seek the complete book as they can only get their hands on incomplete poorly translated copies."

"The cult of who?" Mel asked.

"It doesn't matter," Ernst said quickly. "If the cult is active, it means something is coming. Getting involved will only have a bad ending for you and everyone you care about. Don't take this warning lightly."

Ernst turned around and embraced one of his guests in a hug.

Mel turned to Danni, "Cult of Cthulhu?"

"We have a name at last for the people in Florida."

Harry walked up to the women, swaying slightly, and put his arms around both of their shoulders.

"Shall we go, ladies?"

"Yes, we shall," Danni answered hastily.

Before long, they were back in the fancy car headed back to the fancy manor. Who knew how long it would be before Ernst checked his silver chest for his prized stolen book.

Guaranteed, at the very earliest, it wouldn't be till tomorrow afternoon, and by then, their group would be out of Europe and en route to the scenic mountains of New Zealand.

17

THE MOA AND THE OCEANUS

The Old World manor was hauntingly quiet upon their return.

Mel checked on Malcolm and Randall while Danni embarked on the long trudge upstairs.

She collapsed into an instantaneous deep slumber for the second night in a row, out before her head hit the pillow.

It only felt like moments had passed before the obnoxious beeping of the alarm clock violently thrust her into the land of the living again.

She yawned wide and sat up. Danni no longer presented the image of beauty from the night prior. Her hair was a wild mess of knots and she'd left a sizeable smudge of makeup on the pillow.

"6:00 am," Danni groaned.

Right on cue, there was a knock at the door.

Teva was standing there. He looked Danni up and down and forced a smile.

"You look… nice."

"Tired," Danni mumbled, pushing long strands of hair off her face.

"Well, unfortunately, there aren't any sleep-ins today. Randall and Malcolm cracked the code. We have viable coordinates in the Pacific Ocean."

Teva had a level of enthusiasm Danni was too tired to support.

"How long do I have?" Danni asked, rubbing the sleep from her eyes.

"Downstairs in an hour. Then wheels up to New Zealand."

Danni nodded and closed the door. She pulled the dress off and headed for the shower.

• • • • •

AN HOUR LATER, DANNI WAS MET by the team on the ground floor. Everyone was dressed casually and looked equally sleep-deprived.

Mel was wearing a tank top, presumably to let the bandages on her arm breathe. Sigurd was moving a little stiffly. He'd developed spectacular black eyes overnight, which only added to his wild barbarian image.

Kane and Randall were both looking miserable. Randall because he'd presumably been up all night studying the Necronomicon, and Kane because he'd been out all night in Amsterdam.

Malcolm and Teva were wrapped in conversation about the Necronomicon, which Malcolm had under his arm in a very protective grip.

Artemis was there too, having returned from her adventure with Moros sometime during the night. She looked lost in thought.

A very sorry looking Harry stumbled into the room.

"Some party, hey?" he groaned, rubbing his head.

"It was successful," Mel smiled.

"I have some good news for your team. Cancel your plane tickets, Altior Fulgur's private jet is arriving at the airport now."

"When did this happen?"

"Moments ago, hence why I am awake. The same limo that brought you here will take you to the airport. Now, if you'll excuse me, I am going back to bed."

Harry bowed curtly, then exited.

"Well, this is all working out well," Danni said cheerily.

"As long as these guys on the other end actually have a submarine…" Teva said.

"Oh, I've spoken to them," Mel grinned, her eyes sparkling. "And they have a hell of a submarine."

• • • • •

AGAIN, THANKS TO THE PRIVILEGES enjoyed by the

ultra-rich Fulgur, they didn't have to line up in long queues or go through security screening at the airport. They were whisked onto the tarmac through a private gate and driven up to their waiting jet.

Altior's Gulfstream 650ER was spectacular with its blue cockpit and black racing stripes. It was a modern, sleek aircraft that screamed wealth beyond measure.

"This is going to be rather comfortable, I suspect," Malcolm yawned, caressing his new prized possession, the Amsterdam Necronomicon.

"We're just playing catch-ups. Team one already got to fly in this from Japan to Israel," Mel reminded them all. Danni noticed a hint of bitterness in her voice.

"We did get to go in the fancy helicopter, though. I'd say we're one up on them," Danni added enthusiastically.

"This holiday keeps getting better and better," Kane marvelled in awe, his eyes running the length of the plane.

"I wish this was a holiday," Mel said.

Randall spoke up, sounding somewhat nervous. "I'm not going back to Geneva, am I?"

"Not just yet. They were at the heart of a demon attack and have a lot of questions. My boss, Brett Sayer, is working to straighten things out. For now, you are stuck with us."

Randall didn't look particularly pleased with this response.

"Come on, Randy," Kane started, slapping him on the back. "Embrace the adventure of it."

"I don't like adventure," Randall mumbled.

"Think of the positives, Mr Dare. There are several passages in this book that your knowledge can help me decipher," Malcolm interjected.

"I will admit, that book is fascinating, and it was satisfying to solve that puzzle last night."

Sigurd now hobbled up to Randall and pointed at a departing plane on the taxiway.

"You are a man of learning, so explain to me how these objects travel through the air!"

Randall's eyes widened. He was terrified of speaking to the fearsome Viking. Everyone else laughed, Danni chortling along with them.

"He can explain it to you on the plane. Looks like the pilots are here," Mel vocalized, pointing at an approaching vehicle.

An electric buggy zoomed up beside them. A dark-skinned man with a thick beard stood up and waved at the group. He was clearly the pilot.

Beside him was the co-pilot, a Caucasian and clean-shaven individual, speaking in a thick Yorkshire accent. The co-pilot approached the group while the pilot moved to open the door.

"New Zealand?" he asked.

"Yep, specifically Dunedin on the South Island."

"We will require a couple of stops for refuelling."

"Not a problem; we just need to be there before tomorrow."

"Easy done, ma'am." He tipped his hat and moved toward the plane. A waiting engineer opened the luggage hatch, and the co-pilot assisted him in placing their bags inside.

The group ascended the stairs inside. The plane's interior was certainly luxurious. Danni was ecstatic to see the abundance of couches, easily long enough for her to sleep on. This was going to be a good day.

Mel walked the length of the plane up and down several times. Danni knew she was looking for bugs. Not the insect kind, but the kind that recorded conversation. Once Mel was finished, Danni performed her own sweep of the plane. It seemed secure.

It wasn't long after takeoff that Danni's eyes closed of their own accord.

• • • • •

DANNI WOKE ONLY A FEW TIMES during the flight. Once due to the booming laughter of Sigurd and another time to go to the bathroom.

As she stumbled in the direction of the toilet, she walked past Malcolm fixed to the Necronomicon, studying its grotesque images. Randall sat beside him with a notepad, drawing symbols and matching them to parts of well-known equations.

Danni didn't bother to make chit-chat. She had a lot more poor quality plane sleep to get before they landed.

The last time Danni woke up was during a brief refuelling stop in Singapore. Unable to instantly fall back asleep, she went in search of some light conversation.

She found Mel sitting by herself staring off into space, and a question triggered in Danni's mind.

"Hey, Boss. I was wondering something about the party."

"Shoot," Mel said, turning towards her.

"You and Ernst Carter were talking about Alhazred or something. Just who is that? You mentioned him in Florida too."

"Abdul Alhazred is known in occult circles as the Mad Arab. A name that by modern standards certainly isn't politically correct. He is the one accredited with writing the Necronomicon."

"How did you know about him, though?"

"In 2019, I ended up in the Vatican Secret Archives with Apollo and Moros. While down there, I saw a fascinating black book amongst all the other artefacts. When I approached it, Moros warned me not to read the writings of Alhazred. At the time, I'd never heard of the Necronomicon, but obviously, I realise now that is what the book was.

"The name Alhazred stuck in my head. After that mission was over, I researched him. Sometime around 730 AD, he wrote the Necronomicon, then succumbed to some horrifying and unspecified fate shortly after."

"Was he a rich or powerful man?" Danni asked.

"No, he was a poet from Yemen. He certainly found some success during the Ommiade caliphs and travelled widely throughout the Arab world. Written records exist of him visiting the ruins of Babylon and being in Egypt, where he dabbled in stories of monsters and death. Though according to our friend Ernst Carter, he was also under the tutelage of this so-called 'Sundered King'."

"Still doesn't seem like there is much detail on him."

"No," Melissa sighed. "I am worried that we are barking up the wrong tree altogether by involving the black book. Still, we are committed to this course."

The history of the Necronomicon was fascinating. Danni wondered what other secrets its pages held.

She bade farewell to Melissa and returned to her lounge for

another long nap.

• • • • •

DANNI MANAGED TO OVERSLEEP, which left her feeling terrible when they finally arrived in the small airport of Dunedin, New Zealand. It had taken far longer than expected, with the aircraft needing to make a stop for mechanical checks. Still, everyone aws in high spirits upon arrival.

Mel explained to the group that the Kiwi Sinkers (the group with the submarine) operated out of a private facility on the nearby Cape Saunders. It was remote and would require a half an hour drive. They'd be headed out there tomorrow morning.

It was a pleasant seventeen degrees Celsius outside and Danni was relieved to at last be in summer again. She'd had enough of winter in the Northern Hemisphere.

Dunedin seemed like an adventure town, full of mountain biking and walking enthusiasts. It was pleasing to the eye as they drove past troves of Victorian and Edwardian architecture.

Mel had booked them all into a decent hotel, even if the rooms were a little cosy.

There was very little socialising amongst the group, as many hadn't slept well on the day-long flight.

Mel had tasked Danni with researching the Cult of Cthulhu. But there was nothing; not a whisper of this group could be found online. Danni didn't want to let her boss down, but she gave up after an hour of searching

Feeling bored and defeated, Danni decided to chat with

Kane and Randall. They'd been abducted by the AST, and Danni wanted to know how aware of current events they were. Also, she wanted to get to know them better.

The two Dare brothers had been forced into sharing a room, as the government's policy was to always save money where applicable.

Kane had been sure to make his grumbling about the situation well heard.

Danni sat across the bed from Randall while Kane attempted to connect his phone to the wi-fi.

"So, what happened between you and Josh?" Randall asked.

"The government got in the way. I guess you could say he got a new job, and so did I," Danni replied bluntly.

"Since we are stuck on this mission with your team, do you think we will see him?"

"I don't know, maybe…"

Kane threw his phone down and snorted, "Stupid internet in this place!"

"Chill out," Randall snapped, shooting his brother an annoyed look.

"Hey, I'm the one here who has been abducted from my holiday. I should get basic creature comforts."

"What do you two actually know about our mission?" Danni asked the pair.

"Well, Malcolm and Melissa filled me in on a lot last night," Randall said.

"And Melissa spoke to me on the plane," Kane added. "We understand that Josh is apparently a 'werewolf', which is the most ridiculous thing I have ever heard. And that we are in New Zealand because you think you've found coordinates to the lost city of Atlantis in the Pacific Ocean."

"Oh good. You're all up to date," Danni laughed, knowing how silly it all sounded.

"Josh isn't actually a werewolf, though, is he?" Randall asked cautiously.

"He is, I've seen it. The night the Australian Government got him was the full moon."

Kane rolled his eyes.

"Hey, if you stick with us long enough, you will see some pretty amazing things," Danni pointed out to him. "Turns out there is no real way to tell what is real and what is simply a story."

"Well, if Josh gets to be a werewolf, I want to be a vampire," Kane argued sarcastically.

"I'm not sure if vampires are real," Danni wondered aloud.

"But they are always in movies together."

"I don't think that's relevant."

Danni found it pleasing that Kane had the same sense of sarcasm as Josh. They were undoubtedly two apples from the same branch.

"Well, I do hope we get to see Josh," Randall said.

Danni didn't want to tell either of them that Josh was currently missing.

Danni sat and laughed with the Dare brothers for hours. They discussed growing up in Cairns and swapped stories about the Dare family's heroic old cat named Maow. It was another instance of normalcy in the crazy week that had been.

Feeling refreshed, Danni left and made for bed. Tomorrow they could very well be on their way to the mysterious sunken city, so she figured she'd better get some quality sleep.

• • • • •

CAPE SAUNDERS WAS THE EPITOME of a windswept landscape. While there were thick clumps of trees, most of what they could see from their hired Landcruiser was grassland lining rocky mountains.

When they caught glimpses of the yellow sands beside the jewel blue ocean, Danni once again found herself feeling like she wasn't here for work.

A winding road took them down a hillside into a secluded bay. They came to a rocky pass blocked by a flimsy mesh gate.

Mel got out of the car and pushed it open.

After another short descent, they came to the Kiwi Sinkers compound.

Mel had told the entire group not to speak openly about their mission. She would brief the Kiwi Sinkers in person and provide the coordinates they'd found.

The compound itself was walled by another, much more solid fence. The area consisted of several long demountable buildings fixed to the rock and a large grey warehouse stretching into the ocean. A thick concrete building with no windows sat beside a wide parking area packed with four-wheel drives of all makes and models.

The road was narrow and the bay looked treacherous, so

how they'd set this place up, Danni had no idea. She figured these guys had some serious engineering skills.

They pulled up in the parking area, and a group of people emerged from a nearby demountable to greet them.

Mel got out of the car first and shook the lead man's hand. "You must be the captain."

"Call me Steve," the captain smiled.

Danni immediately liked him. Steve was a Maori man with light brown skin and tribal tattoos on both arms. He stood about 5'8 and had an undeniably cheery personality. With his backwards All Blacks cap and charming accent, Steve looked the part of a genuine Kiwi entrepreneur, out to make his mark on the world.

"These are two of my crew: Jason Topeca and Samantha Newsome."

Jason was another Maori man, shorter than Steve and extremely thin. Similar tattoos lined his arms beneath his tank top.

Samantha was Caucasian with long blonde hair and bright blue eyes. She was young and extremely beautiful. For some unknown reason, Danni could've sworn she'd seen her online social media profile's pop-up on her feeds.

"Nice to meet you both. You are aware of why we are here?" Mel asked.

"Yep, sure am. You want to use the sub? We call her the Deep Sea Moa."

"Why the Moa? That was a gigantic flightless land-bound bird, wasn't it?" Malcolm interjected.

"Haha, every time bro!" Jason laughed, slapping Steve on the back.

"That question gets asked a lot. I just like the Moa," Steve sighed.

Malcolm chuckled slightly.

"So, you are all prepped and good to go?" Mel asked.

"We will have to assess these coordinates of yours. It would've been easier if you'd just e-mailed them over."

"Bit of secret project, I'm afraid. Tell me, what is your association with The Old World?"

"Never heard of 'em," Steve shrugged.

"What about iHeal Genetics?"

"They were one of our recent financial backers, stopped me going broke."

"And why'd they do that?"

"We captured footage of an unknown species of giant squid off the west coast of New Zealand. Bigger than the colossal squid, I reckon. Somehow, iHeal got word of our discovery before we could publish anything. They wanted secrecy in exchange for funding and rights to any discoveries, in partnership with me."

"Woh, you guys aren't cops, are you?" Jason winked.

Danni thought Mel had come on a bit strong, but at the same time wondered what possible interest Altior Fulgur had in giant squid. Mel also looked quizzical.

"So, this is all of you then?" Steve asked, breaking the awkward silence.

"Yeah. Oh, where are my manners? Let me introduce our group. This is Danni."

Danni waved a curt hello.

"Then we have Artemis."

Artemis barely acknowledged the man.

"Malcolm Selleck, PhD."

Malcolm shook Steve's hand vigorously.

"The tall fellow is Sigurd Volsung."

Sigurd also shook the man's hand a little too hard. Danni could've sworn she heard finger bones pop.

"The other two, Kane and Randall, will be remaining on dry land with Sigurd."

"What a shame. Being on a submarine is kind of spooky. It's a unique experience," Steve said.

"I have no desire whatsoever to drown deep underwater," Kane said dismissively. Randall watched on silently.

"I too do not wish to venture into the depths patrolled by Jormungandr, the world serpent," Sigurd informed the New Zealanders. "Besides, the brothers Dare have much yet to teach me about the modern world. I relish the opportunity!"

Neither Kane nor Randall looked particularly enthusiastic about their newfound friendship with the Viking warrior.

"I'll introduce you to my crew when we set sail tomorrow. It's a big ship, but we can run the Mao on limited staff. Oh, and don't worry about paying. The secretary to the president of the board of directors assured me iHeal Genetics would cover this whole expedition."

"Excellent," Mel said.

"You're the leader, then?" Steve asked.

Mel nodded.

"If you step into my office, we have some paperwork to go over. Samantha and I will assess the coordinates now, and we can have an informal chat. If everything works out, we should be able to set sail this afternoon."

"Excellent. All of our gear is in the car."

"Jason," Steve started, "take the other guys here for a tour. Show them the Moa."

Mel disappeared into the nearest demountable to talk business, while Jason led their motley group towards the large warehouse that stretched into the sea.

"I'm guessing there is a deep water channel right there where the submarine is docked?" Randall asked.

"Correct. Wait till you feast your eyes on her. She is a beautiful piece of machinery," Jason babbled enthusiastically.

The submarine dock was a sizeable open-faced shed that started on dry land and ended in the ocean. Wooden jetties ran alongside it, designed with sharp right-hand turns so a person could walk along the external and internal perimeters of the warehouse.

The main access door was kept latched with a simple padlock. Jason opened it up and directed them inside.

"Here it is!" Jason beamed, proudly puffing out his chest. "The Moa!"

It was a hell of a submarine.

At one hundred metres long and thirteen metres high, the bulk of the vessel was submerged beneath the water.

From beneath the splashing waves, they could see the underside of the Moa was painted red, while the top was entirely white.

Danni's group faced the craft's rear and saw an open hangar door lined with supplies. There were four large hydroplanes with a series of skylights in between them. Just past the end of the hangar were two large jet propulsion engines fixed to the side of the sleek machine.

Danni saw the main entry a little further up, a circular door beneath the sun deck on the submarine's fin. The periscope and radar mast were fully extended while a worker performed maintenance.

"This is a two billion dollar piece of equipment. How can you possibly own this?" Malcolm breathed.

"When Captain Steve got his hands on this beautiful beast, it was a wreck. A bloody expensive wreck to fix. Between us, we had the know-how, but the cost was a factor. Almost all of the crew are former engineers, most of us military. We all have a background in oceanic treasure hunting. We went all in to find our one big hall, and when we did, we agreed to put it towards the Moa."

Jason pointed out the floodlights and sets of expensive cameras lining the ship's beam.

"It was with those we caught the footage of the giant squid."

They moved to the watercraft's front, where Jason then explained the location of the smaller deep-sea sub.

"You see the little circles on top?" Jason asked the group. "They are the vents for the ballast tanks. Just in front of the folding hydroplanes. Directly below them is the launching point for the Oceanus."

"Can we see it?" Danni asked.

"Yes, I'll take you onboard shortly. The Oceanus is a high pressure, extreme depth craft with two mechanical arms on the front. Perfect for your mission."

"You know our mission?" Malcolm asked.

"Barely!" Jason laughed. "Our sponsors told us they had a bunch of people coming who need a submarine. Then we spoke to your boss who said you were looking for an underwater city, something we are very much interested in. Who are you guys anyway?"

Danni and Malcolm exchanged glances.

"We come from The Old World," Malcolm answered. "We study paranormal phenomenon."

"That is not the answer I expected, but fair enough," Jason replied.

"How many can fit inside?" Danni asked. "The Oceanus, I mean."

"Two can go inside."

"How can you launch it from inside the submarine?"

"Specially designed water-lock system. Kind of like an airlock. We seal the door; the room fills with water and the latch releases. Then, when the Oceanus comes back, the process happens in reverse. The Oceanus can launch at the Moa's maximum depth."

"Is it safe?"

"As safe as it can be! Come on, I'll show you inside."

Jason led the group across a metal bridge onto the submarine's fin.

"We can operate the main sub with about six staff," Jason explained. "Steve, myself, Samantha and three others will be coming with you."

Jason opened the top hatch and disappeared inside.

Danni went last, climbing into the depths of the submarine. First, they moved into the control room, which looked very Star Trek. There was a central chair facing an array of monitors. Other stations for the crew to monitor sonar and who knows what else were off to the side.

Jason explained that the rear of the submarine was luxury cabins and storage. Their group would be staying in the multi-share dormitory near the front.

Their journey towards the nose of the Moa was interesting. Danni didn't like the echoing clunks of their boots on metal stairs as they passed rows of air flasks and fuel cells.

There were blinking lights and glowing control panels everywhere, creating a dizzying array of colour in the otherwise dark rooms. Danni ran her hands along the bars of a cage of thick yellow steel that housed an enormous deisel generator. It was stressful for her to imagine that her life would soon be in the hands of all this machinery in the depths of the cold ocean.

The crew area was far warmer in look. Showers, bunks and a generously proportioned mess made up the upper and middle floors of the submarine. These areas almost looked homely, painted in bright colours.

A room packed with deep-sea diving equipment was directly below the bunks, including scuba suits with bulbous circular heads and oxygen tanks. Powerful torches and spear guns hung on a myriad of hooks on the wall.

Then, there was the airlock. They had to pass through a solid metal door into a circular tube, then through another metal door with a complex control panel.

They entered into the room housing the Oceanus.

The bright yellow sub had a wide dome around its two operator seats, allowing for a 360-degree view. Behind the dome sat the primary propulsion system, with two powerful spotlights fixed to the top. Its arms were several metres long and ended in fearsome pincers. Danni imagined operating them wasn't an easy task.

Malcolm seemed happy. "Looks state of the art."

"Yep. You guys are lucky you had friends in high places to get in touch with us."

"How very modest," Artemis frowned. It was the first time since they'd got here that the goddess had said anything.

"I'm just playing with you," Jason laughed. His Kiwi enthusiasm was infectious. "Although, all things considered, you will have a comfortable journey."

"Let us hope so," Artemis scowled, causing Jason to gulp nervously.

"The Moa is fast too, so we should reach your destination in the next couple of days," he added, composing himself.

"We are in the perfect launching spot. Your boss will confirm with you soon, but the coordinates we found are east of New Zealand. Actually, they seem to be right in the middle of the world's loneliest place," Malcolm said.

"What does that mean?" Kane asked.

"It is the point of the ocean that is furthest from any continent," Malcolm explained.

"Alright, guys. We will get out of the Moa and get all your gear from the car. If our destination is that lonely place, there is no reason why we can't get moving ASAP," Jason said.

With that, the gang clambered out of the sub and back to the front of the shed.

Melissa and Steve met them there.

"That was fast," Jason said.

"Everything is when money isn't a problem. Here mate, coordinates are as follows: 49°51'S 128°34'W. Round up the crew and finish the load. We have a city to find."

"A city?"

"Yep, when you brief the team, tell them we are looking for Atlantis."

• • • • •

JUST LIKE THAT, THEY SAID temporary farewells to Sigurd, Randall and Kane.

All of their luggage was transported onboard, and they each chose a bed in the dormitory.

Steve, Jason and Samantha, along with three of their other engineers, worked like madmen to get everything up and running.

It was difficult not to get wrapped up in the excitement of it all. The only person who seemed slightly down-trodden was Malcolm, who'd been forced to give the Necronomicon to Randall.

It was in the early afternoon that the submarine's engines sprang to life, and the vessel departed for its destination in the mysterious depths of the world.

Who knew what they'd find down there?

With any luck, their mission would be a success, and they'd be returning to land with an artefact of Zeus.

18

THE DEEP AND
THE DARK

I t had only been a day of underwater travel, but Danni wasn't
enjoying the experience in the submarine whatsoever.

The claustrophobic underwater coffin had spirited them
far east of New Zealand into unfathomable stretches of empty
ocean. They'd been blessed with an eastward oceanic current that
significantly improved their speed through the water.

Somewhere to the south lay the frozen continent of
Antarctica, and somewhere below was the city pin-pointed by
Malcolm and Randall.

The submarine was remarkably quiet. Occasionally Danni
heard mechanical whirring and sometimes thought she heard

banging on the outer hull, but other than that, there was nothing.

They glided forward through the deep and the dark.

Danni couldn't help but think of the underwater nightmare city she'd seen in the shared vision with Mel. There had been some unspeakable evil in that place. It was a feeling in her soul like it should be avoided at all costs, lest they wake the nameless thing that slumbered there.

She kept her fears to herself. Everyone else was optimistic about the chance of finding something.

Again Danni felt that the events of the week were beginning to take a toll on her. She felt exhaustion in every cell of her being. The journey through Hell, then the events in Amsterdam, and now this quiet undersea adventure had been a lot. All she could hope was that it'd be over soon.

Malcolm was suffering withdrawals from being temporarily removed from studying the Necronomicon. He gushed about the wealth of knowledge it offered and hoped Randall could gain an understanding of some of the passages he'd highlighted.

Artemis was her usual cold, distant self. Though Danni did understand the frustration she must feel at not being able to use her powers. The goddess walked the silent halls dressed in overalls with her hair in a ponytail. She looked very human.

Melissa was resigned to the fact that they wouldn't have the artefact of Zeus by the time she had a conference call with her boss and the head of USSOT. She'd been keeping the details of this big meeting to herself as to not put undue pressure on her team. Unfortunately, they'd just run out of time and despite knowing it wasn't her fault, Danni still felt a little guilty for letting Mel down.

Half an hour ago, the submarine had begun to pick up readings of large structures beneath them. Any moment now, they'd reach the exact coordinates provided by the black book. The rest of the team was assumedly already in the control room.

There was something about their quiet ride through the black abyss of the Pacific that made Danni hesitant to embrace the adventure. That ceaseless current was pushing her further and further forward into the timeless emptiness of the sea, into a world of forbidden knowledge and perilous danger.

Yet, sooner or later, she knew she'd have to face her fear of the abyss.

• • • • •

A CALL CAME ACROSS THE SUBMARINE'S PA SYSTEM, "All staff report to the command area. We have arrived."

Danni jumped out of her single bed and made for the door to the dormitory. She paused before she pulled it open. She just couldn't help but let the wave of unexplainable dread she felt wash over her.

"God, I hope this is uneventful," she thought, before grasping the handle and leaving the cabin.

The command centre was buzzing with activity. Steve was excitedly reading from one of the monitors while the crew shuffled back and forth. The central monitor showed the sonar read-out. Several objects were clearly present below as they bounced off the ship's pings.

Danni walked over to Mel, who was staring intently at the

screen. "What's the word?"

"Seems our black book has found a sunken city," Mel said. She was emotionless, perhaps even concerned.

"Can you use your prophet vision to see what's down there?" Danni asked.

"I have tried but have been unsuccessful," she sighed. "It's strange... I have this feeling of... I dunno, dread maybe. Like we shouldn't be here."

Danni gulped. So it wasn't just her.

Steve approached and nodded curtly at the two women, "We are prepping the Oceanus now. It'll take two of your people down. The seafloor here is unexpectedly deep, and we are picking up evidence of abnormal seismic activity."

"How so?" Mel asked.

"It almost appears as if the seafloor here has been monumentally thrust upwards, at least in the last hundred years, then descended again. We'd need an undersea geologist to confirm, though. Never seen readings like it."

"What does the city look like?" Danni asked.

"Can't know that until someone has a look," Steve replied. He turned to Mel, "Who is going down?"

Artemis spoke first. "I am. However, I require no human contraption. The depth and pressure will have no effect on me."

Danni still couldn't quite get over how Artemis looked in her blue overalls and long ponytail. She hadn't even noticed the goddess standing in the corner.

Mel then added, "Professor Selleck and Danni will go in the Oceanus."

"Me?" Danni blurted out, alarmed. "I thought you'd want to?"

"I have a hook-up with Brett Sayer, Fiona Shear and the other team in about an hour, as you know. Hopefully, the connection works at this depth."

"It'll be spotty," the captain said.

"How long will the descent be?" Danni asked nervously.

"About thirty minutes straight down, we estimate," Steve replied. "The subs not going any deeper. Rendezvous in about five minutes at the deployment bay."

"Shouldn't one of your crew go down? Neither myself nor Malcolm has operated a mini-sub before."

"Don't worry, I've done a bunch of dry-runs with Malcolm over the last day. Plus, the Oceanus is tethered to the Moa; we can take control remotely if needed."

"Any chance this is Atlantis?" Mel asked Artemis.

"I don't know. The location doesn't seem right. This place has a strange energy to it. It could be a lingering effect of the ancient civilisation, but I am not sure," Artemis said.

"Well, wherever we are, let's hope some artefacts are waiting for us. How good will comms from the Oceanus to the Moa be?"

Steve caressed the command console lovingly as he answered. "They will be fine. We will get a full video display here. So you won't want to be too long on your conference call, or you'll miss the excitement of discovery! Ah, now Artemis… when you say you are going down without a 'human contraption', what does that mean?"

"I am not trapped within the limitations of a squishy human

body. While I do breathe in and out, I have no real need for air."

Steve laughed, thinking she was joking. When no one else joined in, he turned to Mel for answers.

"Well, you already signed the paperwork, so I guess I can reveal that Artemis here isn't a person. She's a god." Mel stated.

Steve had a blank, sceptical look on his face.

"So, you swimming in the depths of the ocean won't attract angels to us?" Malcolm asked Artemis.

"No, I am not using any divine magic. I am a goddess; it is my right to move freely through all spaces in the mortal plane. Even in the physical world, I don't think the angels would detect me flying. The other gods have just been avoiding it as a precaution. Swimming is different, as no wandering mortal eyes will see it."

"Just making sure," Malcolm responded.

"Well…" Steve said, rubbing the back of his neck. "Let's go and get you set up in the Oceanus. I'd think you guys are all crazy the way you talk, but we are looking for Atlantis so… I'll just ignore it for now."

Teva, who was glued to a nearby monitor displaying a red graph spoke up. "Based on what I'm seeing here, the city below is huge. Like, insanely huge."

"Is there a location we should focus on?" Malcolm asked him.

Teva spoke as he pointed at the display. "Yeah, it appears just east of us is a raised area with a singular monolithic structure right in its centre. Perhaps a citadel of some kind? I'd suggest you take the Oceanus there first, then fan out."

"Well, a citadel is the kind of place an artefact would be

kept," Danni shrugged.

"I will also go in that direction. I will be much faster than your mortal machinery," Artemis added.

"Right," Steve began, still giving Artemis odd looks, "let's go."

Malcolm and Danni followed the captain to the Oceanus' loading bay. They both pulled their designated heavy-duty dive suits on and ensured the attached oxygen tanks were functional.

Artemis also put a thick orange dive suit on and fastened the bulbous helmet down, more out of curiousity than need.

"Put the helmets on," Steve instructed Malcolm and Danni. "It is a necessary requirement in case something goes wrong when we launch the sub."

Danni and Malcolm slowly walked through the metal tube and into the launch bay, where Samantha waited. Artemis followed, casually leaning against the side of the room.

"She's not seriously going to stand in here while we release the sub?" Steve asked Malcolm. "The pressure will squash her."

"Trust me, it is fine," Malcolm tried to reassure him.

Steve opened his mouth to protest, but Danni butted in.

"She knows what she is doing. You aren't liable for anything that happens here, so just relax, okay?"

"Her funeral," Steve grumbled, looking incredibly uncomfortable. It was clear that he still thought this was a prank being played on him.

The dive suits were cumbersome, and Danni imagined they were similar to what astronauts had to wear.

With some difficulty, they climbed the ladder and took

their seats inside the Oceanus. Malcolm hit the start button and the console lit up like a display of Christmas lights.

Samantha lowered the half-sphere of glass down, and with a series of clicks, they were locked in.

"All the pre-launch checks are done!" Samantha beamed. "Good luck!"

She exited the room behind Steve and sealed the circular metal door.

"I hope you can drive this thing," Danni murmured.

"It seems really easy, and the tethering will allow them to take control at any time," Malcolm comforted her.

Danni noticed the long wheel of thick black cabling spooled against the wall, running from somewhere behind them.

"Comms check," the voice of Steve spoke into the console.

"Loud and clear," Malcolm replied.

"Okay, we are opening her up! Last chance to choose life, Artemis!"

There was a pause. When Artemis didn't move, they heard a distinct sigh.

Then there was the sound of sliding metal and water began rushing in from two open hatches on either side of the room.

Danni felt a pang of anxiety. She wasn't trained for this.

In less than a minute, the Oceanus was fully engulfed in the freezing salty water of the deep sea.

Danni looked over to Artemis. Her dive suit was withstanding the pressure.

However, finding it inhibiting, the goddess detached the helmet and tossed it away.

Her auburn hair fanned out behind her. Artemis didn't look remotely phased by the cold or pressure.

There was a whirring, and the doors below the sub opened up. The latch above them released, and the mechanical arm holding them in place withdrew. They were left to the ocean's mercy.

Malcolm fiddled with the primary joystick, jerking the sub back and forth.

"Hey, don't do that," Danni blurted out. She was wracked with nerves.

"Sorry, sorry. Just getting my bearings…"

The propulsion system spun to life, and in a shower of bubbles, they left the confines of the launch room.

Like an orange bullet, Artemis blasted down at phenomenal speed.

Danni turned to look back at the Moa through the glass above them as they descended.

Bright spotlights illuminated the dark shape of the submarine in the desolate emptiness.

"You can remove your helmets now, guys," Steve informed them through the intercom.

Both Danni and Malcolm pulled them off.

"Thirty minutes and you should be there. I don't think you'll be able to see much until you are right on top of it."

"Roger," Malcolm replied. He was giddy with excitement.

Danni understood why. They were on the precipice of seeing something no human had seen for potentially tens of thousands of years. History was being made.

The spotlights on the Oceanus were incredibly powerful,

shooting intense beams through the dark water.

The black abyss was all-consuming.

There was no beauty in the sinister depths. It was lonely in the cold embrace of the deep and Danni was unsettled by the endless gloom.

Occasionally, something flickered in the light.

"I really hope we don't find any giant squid," Danni murmured.

"We would be incredibly lucky to see one," Malcolm replied. "It is a privilege not many people get to experience."

"Isn't every creature that lives in the deep sea some sort of monster?" Danni asked sarcastically, but with a trace of earnestness.

"No. Like with all remote places of the Earth, there is beauty to be found in the life that survives down here."

He pressed a sequence of buttons, and the Oceanus's external lights went out.

Other than the dim glow of the console, they were smothered with darkness.

A school of bioluminescent fish swam past. The swiftly moving array of colours was dazzling.

"Incredible," Malcolm awed.

Malcolm kept the lights off as they kept sinking.

The sub fell through a swarm of large jellyfish pulsing with light. The creatures eerily flapped in a hypnotic display.

They were in a world of alien beauty, unlike anything on the surface. The flashing lights were a minefield of stars surrounding the Oceanus.

"Wow," Danni breathed.

Once the long tentacles of the jellyfish disappeared, Malcolm turned all the lights on again.

"So, what did you learn about this place from the book?" Danni asked.

"Not much, honestly. It was jarring, really. The page containing the coordinates was jumbled amongst pages of images detailing unheard-of mythology that I couldn't make sense of."

"What does the Necronomicon actually have in it?"

"All sorts of occult rituals and spells. They talk about summoning creatures from the voids beyond space and time. Then, there is a complex history of the world with the aforementioned mythology attached to it. If my translations were correct, the book talks of civilisations older than anything recorded. Civilisations so old that they can't have any basis in truth."

"This ancient civilisation Artemis talks about is meant to have existed around 100 000 years ago, right?"

"I haven't been able to discuss it with her, but all I can gather is that the ancient civilisation were there during the cognitive revolution, around 75 000 years ago. Then sometime around 10 000 years ago, their decline finished and their cities were all but gone from the world."

"And how old are the civilisations the Necronomicon talks about?"

"Hundreds of millions of years," Malcolm sighed. "The book speaks of elder things and chthonic horrors that came to our world long ago. It mentions their cities of black stone designed to befuddle the mind, and speaks of the creatures that built them."

Danni gulped. The underwater city she'd seen was mostly

black stone.

Malcolm continued, "Say we indulged in this fantasy and these cities still linger, this is where we'd find them. The deep places of the world hold untold secrets and are mostly uncharted. While I don't believe it, to think that right now we are headed towards an alien ruin, built by things so foreign to us they seem like living nightmares… it is just fantastic."

"Do you think this is actually Atlantis? Or do you think this is somewhere else?" Danni questioned. Had the professor genuinely believed that this place was their best shot at finding an artefact of Zeus? Or was it all a ruse to satiate his own fascination with the book?

"I think we will find something of value down here. No matter what the city actually is."

Danni could only pray that he was right.

19

LEVIATHAN

"Guys, you should be reaching the tips of some huge spires of rock from when the ground was upheaved," Steve's voice sounded through the intercom.

Malcolm spun the sub around, and they were confronted with a thick black pillar standing like a skyscraper not far away.

"It looks smooth…" Danni said.

"The pressure down here does funny things, make shapes and tricks the mind," Steve's voice replied.

"If this place does end up being Atlantis, what do you think it will look like?" Danni asked Malcolm.

"I expect an enormous temple to Poseidon. The lover of

fiction in me sees white buildings in the style of Athens and huge statues to the gods. Realistically, I have no idea."

They soon found themselves in the grip of several high pillars. As the lights hit them, it became clear the towers around the Oceanus weren't shards of rock that had been violently thrust upwards.

They were monoliths of gleaming black stone inscribed with endless hieroglyphics.

"Let's enhance the lighting, shall we?" Malcolm asked, pushing a big green button on the central console.

The viewing orb lit up like a small star in the dark depths. The powerful spotlights on top shone a blinding glow hundreds of metres ahead.

Both Malcolm and Danni gasped.

Below them stretched a city.

It was huge.

Impossibly huge.

Buildings of twisted green and black stone stretched as far as the eye could see.

Malcolm turned the sub 180 degrees.

"You guys seeing this?" Malcolm asked.

"Yeah," the voice of Steve replied. "Our sonar is barely picking up a portion of what's down there."

"The towers we've been descending beside, they must be taller than the largest modern skyscrapers."

"Do you recognise the writing?" Danni asked.

"I've seen those hieroglyphs only in the Necronomicon," Malcolm whispered.

"Look at the buildings," Danni awed.

Her eyes were having a hard time adjusting to what she was seeing. It was like the place had been designed with the illusion of flatness, yet every surface seemed to warp at concave and convex angles.

Buildings in the shape of spheres and strange bends in the architecture seemed designed to confuse the mind and inflame the senses.

They were still at least a hundred metres above the city proper.

"We are descending further."

With a blast of bubbles, Artemis crossed their vision, moving at extreme speed across the city.

Danni tapped Malcolm on the shoulder and said, "Look at that…"

The rising bubbles were acting strangely. They twisted and contorted when they hit a certain point below the submarine. Then, once they passed the invisible line in the sea, they resumed their usual appearance on the upward journey.

"There is some kind of barrier around this place. Doesn't seem to be impacting the sub at all," Malcolm noted. Danni heard a distinct lack of confidence in his voice.

Malcolm and Danni sat in amazement at what they were seeing. Out here, in the loneliest place on the planet, was a city of unimaginable scale.

It must've been built in long eons past when this portion of the world wasn't underwater. The sheer amount of stone used would've taken thousands of years to transport by ship. It was just impossible for this to have been an island nation.

"When was the last time this part of the world wasn't covered by ocean?" Malcolm asked the Moa above.

"Millions of years ago," Steve answered.

"This isn't Atlantis, is it?" Danni asked quietly.

Malcolm shook his head. "This couldn't be the work of the ancient civilisation. It's too old."

"Then what is it? Who built this place?"

"I dread to speculate. I read in the Necronomicon of a city that fell from the stars. A loathsome place of terror, shaped by creatures from dark worlds in the measureless ages before history. The book called it the nightmare corpse city," Malcolm frowned.

The Oceanus floated just above street level. Not all of the buildings were made of black stone, yet all were complex. Several districts were built of the same slimy green that had composed the monstrous statuette in Florida.

Marine flora and fauna were absent, except for the shells of small molluscs littering the pavement and sporadic growths of seaweed that strangled some of the buildings.

Everything was multi-storied, springing into networks of alleys, roads and bridges.

The geometry of it was hard to comprehend. A person at ground level could never navigate their way through this place.

Yet, it wasn't entirely alien.

There were statues in the streets and murals on the sides of buildings. Though the statues displayed odd creatures and the murals showed some monstrous being on a mighty throne.

"Up there," Malcolm said, pointing ahead.

The ground climbed higher and higher to the east until it reached a plateau with a dark tower in its centre.

Though tower hardly did this structure justice. It was repellent in its design.

As the Oceanus slowly pushed closer, they could see the monolithic building was wrapped in a strangling vine of stone. It was like the skyscraper was flesh with pulsing veins as decorative architecture.

The most concerning feature of this sunken citadel was the gargantuan black doors. Those doors... Danni had seen them before.

Fearsome carvings of unknown creatures adorned their faces. Amongst the intricate designs was the repeated image of a bat-winged monster with a cephalopod head. Its staring stone eyes were terrifying.

The closer they drew, the more those eyes seemed to look into Danni's soul. She saw the wild chaos of the Florida ritual in them. She could hear the beating drums and piping flutes.

This was the city she and Mel had seen in the shared vision after they'd encountered that cult leader. And in that vision, there'd been something behind those doors...

Danni could remember the fear she'd felt when that nameless slumbering mass had stirred.

Artemis was already there. She was floating in front of the citadel with her legs crossed and eyes closed. The goddess was meditating.

"This looks like the place we'd find an artefact," Malcolm smiled, activating the sub's mechanical arms.

"I don't think we should try to get inside-"

There was a booming metallic crunch from above that carried through the water. The Oceanus' small speaker sprung to life.

"We are under attack!" Jason's voice cried. "We are going to have to reel you in Oceanus!"

"What is attacking you?" Danni asked.

"I don't know! It appeared out of nowhere!"

There was another huge clang from above.

"It is like a giant serpent!" Jason cried through the speaker.

"A sea serpent?" Malcolm asked.

"Leviathan!" Danni spat. The fallen angel had found them again, and this time they were in his domain. He'd said his true form was a monster of the deep.

Artemis blasted away from the central citadel, back towards the Moa.

The metallic shrieks from the battered submarine echoed through the dead city below.

Danni didn't know if it was her imagination, but she thought she kept seeing things move in the darkness near the penetrating beams of the lights.

They were being reeled up very slowly.

Again, Danni saw something swimming among the black buildings.

"What else did the Necronomicon say about this place?" Danni asked anxiously.

"Nothing I have deciphered yet... except one thing. If this is the city that fell from the stars, it has a name. R'lyeh."

The Oceanus shook violently. The tether that was pulling them up was swinging them back and forth.

"Mel, do you read me?" Danni asked.

There was no response.

"Mel, if you can hear me, the city is not Atlantis! I repeat, it is not Atlantis! It is called R'lyeh! I repeat, R'lyeh!"

Still nothing.

If something had come through to Mel, who right now should be in her meeting, she could tell the other team, perhaps warn them of this place...

Malcolm had turned his gaze away from the city and towards the Moa.

"Danni, brace for impact!"

A vast scaly body plummeted down towards them, just missing their glass dome but banging into the sub's mechanical arms. They sparked and shuddered.

The small figure of Artemis followed it, throwing a devastating punch into the serpent's body.

The goddess had blasted up to defend the submarine and was now pushing the enormous sea serpent towards the city below.

"Artemis shouldn't be pushing him down like that, should she?" Danni panicked. "She's going to push him into the main citadel!"

Malcolm looked horrified as the coiling body of Leviathan adjusted itself. His long tail knocked the phenomenal black stone blocks of the streets askew. They boomed as they slowly collapsed in clouds of grime dislodged from the seafloor.

Artemis continued her assault, dodging the giant jaws of

the serpent and landing a blow straight in the side of his face.

The sea serpent groaned.

Leviathan was at least as long as the Moa, with a thick serpentine body of blue scales and bright red fins along his back. He had a hooked beak lined with tall sharp teeth. He was every bit the ship sinking monster of legend that went with his name.

Artemis clapped the water, sending a powerful shockwave through the city. Leviathan was pushed back, his head landing against the doors of the alien citadel.

There was a booming crack as the stone broke.

Leviathan reared up, ready to strike back at Artemis.

A new sound carried through the water.

From inside the twisted building came a cry like nothing on Earth.

The slumbering darkness inside had woken.

Both Artemis and Leviathan paused and focused on the door.

Danni thought she could see fear in the great sea serpent's eyes.

Then it happened.

Danni watched in horror as the gigantic door of the black stone temple was pushed away. A dark silhouette of impossible proportions came through the open space and reached out with an enormous humanoid arm.

It looked like tentacles were dangling from the monster's octopus-like head, but it was hard to tell in the gloom.

What she did see clearly was its webbed green hand clench around Leviathan's tail. The great sea serpent screamed when it turned to see what had grasped it.

A deep, unsettling rumbling echoed through the sunken city. It was the unearthly groan of the woken monster.

Goosebumps rose across Danni. She felt Leviathan's dread. The sea serpent squealed as the shadow pulled it inside the citadel.

As the Oceanus rose higher and higher, Danni longed to turn her eyes away from that dreadful sunken citadel, but she just couldn't. She wanted to see the monster in more detail.

Suddenly, Artemis' small orange body sped towards the temple, aiming for the webbed hand gripping Leviathan.

"What is Artemis doing?" Danni asked.

"It looks like whatever that thing is, it's the greater threat. Maybe she's decided she needs Leviathan to fight it..."

Leviathan was nothing to this thing; he was utterly powerless.

"Do you feel that?" Malcolm said over the buzzing alarm of the Oceanus.

Danni nodded. What she felt wasn't like anything she'd experienced, not even in the presence of Lucifer himself. Whatever had slumbered in the temple was new. Just trying to comprehend it was giving her a headache.

They should've never come here.

Artemis, Leviathan and the monster disappeared inside the citadel.

It was dead quiet as the tether kept reeling them up. Danni hoped the Moa hadn't been too damaged in Leviathan's attack.

Malcolm's gaze was fixed on the citadel.

Without warning, Artemis emerged from the darkness behind the broken door. She zoomed toward the Oceanus. Her speed seemed to falter as she reached out for them.

Danni was horrified to see the goddess's face when she drew close. In the bright spotlights, she looked battered. Her eyes were wide with fear.

Danni directed her gaze back at the citadel. The creature had left its dreadful tower. Standing on the raised mount, staring up at them with its red eyes, was a primordial fear. It was a god of a forgotten time, worshipped by inhuman things.

A vast swathe of tentacles carried from its head down past its chest. Two wings stretched wide in the darkness from its back. The light caught hardened ridges of bone, dividing regions of pulsating green flesh.

Fear radiated from it. It had to be as tall as a skyscraper.

"What is that thing?" Danni whispered.

Malcolm remained silent.

The light moved on from the creature. The Oceanus's spotlight system couldn't be angled any further down.

Artemis woozily continued willing herself upwards until she was out of view. She didn't look good.

Another few minutes passed. The city was fading from view in the murk of the deep.

"There!" Danni said, pointing to the right.

Floating just to the side of the Oceanus was the battered body of Artemis, completely unconscious and sinking slowly.

Malcolm pulled on the control handles for the arms. In their damaged state, they struggled to move. Malcolm bashed the controls. They were rising towards the Moa too quickly.

"We can't let Artemis fall into the grip of whatever that thing is!" Danni shouted, wrenching the handles away from Malcolm. She toggled the handles back and forth. There was a whirring as more power was diverted in the arms.

Just in time, Danni managed to extend them both beneath the sinking body of the goddess, catching her in a perilously loose grip.

"Good work –"

Malcolm was cut off by a shrill, horrific wail from below.

The sound was unmistakable.

It was the dying gasp of the fallen angel Leviathan.

"Moa, come in! Get us out of here!" Danni screamed into the mic.

Only crackling static appeared in return.

"Don't worry, the tether is still pulling us up. It means the sub hasn't been destroyed."

Their speed did seem to increase.

Before long, they were back in the deployment bay. The Oceanus was reattached and the water was drained.

Mel and Steve burst into the room just as Danni flung herself down from the small submarine.

"We have to get out of here!" Danni said to Mel, her face alive with fear.

"What did you see down there?" she asked.

"A monster. Something worse than the Devil. Something worse than anything in this world. Leviathan didn't stand a chance!"

Mel turned to Steve, "Get us out of here, now."

Steve nodded and moved to the intercom, where he began issuing orders.

"Your message came through," Mel said. "Hopefully, the others picked it up that this wasn't Atlantis but R'lyeh; if I'm saying that right. Leviathan hit the Moa right as the conference call started."

"Is everyone okay?" Malcolm asked.

"Yeah, a few water leaks in the sub but no major damage. We will have to surface and assess properly, though."

Before she could reply, Mel clutched the sides of her head and fell to her knees.

"What is it?" Malcolm asked, kneeling beside her.

"I hear him... in my head..." Mel cried. Her voice was riddled with anguish.

"Who? Who do you hear?"

"The dead one in his sunken city... is no longer dreaming... he is awake... and he sees... us! AHHH!" Mel released an ear-splitting scream then collapsed to the floor.

Her eyeballs turned black.

"PN'NGLUI MGLW'NAFH CTHULU R'LYEH WGAH'NAGL FHTAGN!" Mel began chanting.

Her voice was lifeless.

"PN'NGLUI MGLW'NAFH CTHULU R'LYEH WGAH'NAGL FHTAGN!"

Danni felt the submarine shudder as the engines roared to life. They were moving.

Mel stopped chanting and lost consciousness.

"Come on," Steve instructed Malcolm, "we will get her to the med bay."

Danni pulled the unconscious Artemis over her shoulder. It

was tough but she could manage the goddess.

A new foe had entered the game. Angels and demons didn't seem to matter so much now. Danni wasn't sure how she knew it, but she could feel it in her bones. That thing was evil and the Necronomicon had led them straight to it.

In the dark depths of the sunken city, a horror had been awakened.

It was all they could do to get out of there.

The mission had failed and now they had something new to contend with.

PART TWO

Part Two takes place after the events of In the Shadow of The Old World.

DATE:
30 JAN 2021

AST TEAM ONE	AST TEAM TWO
CURRENT LOCATIONS:	CURRENT LOCATIONS:

AST TEAM ONE

CURRENT LOCATIONS:

Canberra, Australia:
- Liam Sager

Adams Base, Ukraine:
- Matthew Pyne
- Joshua Dare
- Haruka Masunaga
- Jesse Billiau *(new addition)*

Europe:
- Ingrid Horjen

AST TEAM TWO

CURRENT LOCATIONS:

Pacific Ocean:
- Melissa Pythia
- Teva Henry
- Danni Quinn
- Malcolm Selleck

Dunedin, New Zealand:
- Randall Dare
- Kane Dare
- Sigurd

SIT-REP:

Archangel Michael has returned to Heaven, meaning the gods have gone into hiding in the Dreamscape. Josh sacrificed his hand to Fenrir to gain control of the werewolf form. Hephaestus built him a new magical hand. Josh then travelled to Siberia to rescue Haruka from the clutches of Belial and Cardinal Markovic, where he was captured and experimented on. He bit Haruka, passing the werewolf curse onto her. Molochtech purified Josh's curse, but in the chaos of the full moon, both Josh and Haruka had to be saved by the newly formed Taskforce A. Josh, Haruka and a rescued Jesse Billiau were taken to a US military base in Ukraine. They tuned in for a conference call, where Melissa appeared in distress, stating *'it isn't Atlantis'* before disconnecting...

20

A NEW PLAN

The Moa surfaced with a splash of seawater far above the lonely city and its sunken monster.

After an external structural assessment, the crew concluded that the submarine had come out of Leviathan's assault pretty well. A few holes needed immediate patching and some significant dents would require considerable effort to fix. However, the sub was still very much in working order.

Everyone on board wanted to get out of there as soon as possible, but still, they couldn't risk the Moa unexpectedly falling apart.

The thought of the monster below was of the utmost

concern for the crew; however, the ship's sonar didn't show anything rising towards them. Very apprehensively, the team decided to stay where they were and begin repairs.

Danni, feeling a little shaken by the ordeal, took the opportunity to soak in some sorely missed sunlight before heading back into the sub. She'd watched as Jason and Samantha, draped in expensive scuba gear, disappeared into the blue depths to check everything out. A new fear of the deep had radiated through their masks.

Artemis still hadn't woken from her coma an hour after the escape.

Malcolm was pacing back and forth in the medical bay, waiting to question the goddess about the city. She'd seen it better than anyone else had.

Still flabbergasted that Artemis had swum unprotected, Steve began to accept the idea that she was more than human. He sat in the med bay and watched Malcolm nervously wander about.

There was an air of paranoia onboard, an unspoken dread that the monster from the temple could rise up and swallow them whole at any moment. The sonar monitors diligently watched and waited, but nothing came from the depths.

It was eerily still both above and below the Moa.

After Danni climbed back into the metallic shell of the submarine, she sat beside Mel's bed for a long time. A quick assessment in the med bay showed she was okay.

They needed the space for Artemis, so Melissa had been left in the crew quarters to wake up of her own accord. However ghastly the vision she'd seen was, the med bay was needed for the bruised and battered goddess. Danni thought it was silly, as there was nothing they could do to help a god heal.

It only took a couple of hours to complete the essential repairs. Danni held her breath as the engines roared to life and the Moa began its return journey to New Zealand.

Samantha was tasked with collating all of the data, including the video footage from the Oceanus. Due to the fallen angel's electrical interference, the video became a mess of static when Leviathan appeared.

Dark clouds gathered above and a torrent of rain fell into the sea. As lightning forked and cracked in the sky, the Moa dived back into the black abyss.

Right as the last audible booming clap of thunder burst through the metal hull of the Moa, Melissa woke with a sharp inhalation of breath and a panicked look.

"Mel, you're okay!" Danni exclaimed, alarmed at her sudden revival.

Mel rubbed her head.

"What happened?" she groaned.

"You don't remember? Leviathan attacked the submarine, then got dragged into that ancient temple by some gigantic octopus-man."

Mel's eyes lit up as memory came flooding back to her.

"I saw a glimpse of events around the world. The Cult of Cthulhu was celebrating; they were everywhere! On every continent, conclaves of them were coming together to dance around bonfires, like you saw in Florida. And I saw him… in that undersea temple. Leviathan was there, in the dark. He was dead…"

"That monster must've been Cthulhu, right? That's his name? If the cult is mobilising after his waking, it makes sense."

"I suppose. Hopefully, with a name, we can find some information. Like what religion he came from and who originally worshipped him."

Mel continued to rub her head. Despite her long period of unconsciousness, she looked dreadfully tired.

"How is everyone else?"

"We all came out of it fine, except Artemis. She still hasn't woken."

"Artemis saved the sub. We owe her one," Mel said, lying back down. "If you don't mind, Danni, I might go back to sleep. I have a killer headache. We can assess the situation later after I've had some time to think on things."

Danni left Mel to rest. She was sure the ever-increasing complexity of the mission weighed heavily on Melissa. And they were still no closer to finding an artefact of Zeus.

• • • • •

THE SUBMARINE CRUISED THROUGH THE calm sea uneventfully. The sonar detected swift pods of dolphins that danced around the cold metal tube.

Teva spent a good deal of time observing the marine mammals through the sub's spotlights. He said that something was unnerving about them. The dolphins, in his estimation, were too quick and possessed ghostly green eyes. Captain Steve put this down to the deep playing tricks on Teva's mind, though after the events over R'lyeh, even he wasn't entirely sure.

When Artemis woke up, she had surprisingly little to say. Much to Malcolm's disappointment, she had no idea about the city or the monster that dwelled within.

Danni could hear the disappointment in Malcolm's voice when he reported his brief conversation with the goddess.

Melissa spoke for a long time with Artemis in private. Whatever they discussed was kept between them, despite Danni's burning curiosity.

Unfavourable currents and worrisome noises meant the journey back was a slow one. They stopped and surfaced several times with begrudging caution.

Within a day, Artemis was completely healed of her injuries. The goddess stated the fact she'd been that badly hurt was a sign that Cthulhu was immensely powerful.

Considering all that had happened, Danni found it odd that there was so little to discuss. The mission had thrown them onto the very fringes of knowledge, and she dreaded the road it might lead them down.

• • • • •

EARLY ON THE SECOND OF FEBRUARY, the Moa drifted back into the Kiwi Sinker's base of operations.

Everyone scrambled out of the dented and scratched machine as fast as possible. Danni decided she would be quite happy if she never set foot on a submarine again.

There was a flurry of movement as luggage was collected

and data compiled.

On Mel's orders, Danni was separated from the rest of the team and joined the final meeting with Steve.

Sitting in the rock-bound demountable, Danni sat slightly to the right of Mel as she spoke to the captain.

"Don't report your findings to iHeal Genetics," Mel commanded authoritatively. "Talk to Altior Fulgur himself. We don't know what we found down there. I don't think telling corporate bigwigs is the best way forward. Fulgur is already involved; speak to him directly."

Steve opened his mouth to protest, then changed his mind. He nodded. His eyes remained joyous and kind, yet Danni saw distinct confusion and scepticism in their depths.

"The discovery of that city could re-write human history when made public," Steve mumbled.

"That monster making landfall could write a new history. I think the city should be left alone. I will ask my boss to arrange for the Australian Government to begin watching that area for unusual activity. I'm sure they will contact you to assist," Mel stated.

Steve smiled, presumably at the thought of a lucrative foreign government contract. "Deep-sea sensors should be able to detect if the monster is on the move. A creature that large will have a noticeable impact."

"Oh, and remember the secrecy paperwork you have signed. Any mention of us, our mission, or Artemis will land you in hot water."

Again, Steve nodded. He seemed unwilling to voice his agreement. Overall, the Kiwi entrepreneur had come out on top, and Danni was sure he'd honour his word.

Mel, Danni and Steve stood up. They all shook hands formally.

"This has been interesting," Steve said, rubbing the back of his neck.

"You have my email address. When you can summarise the data you've gathered, I'd like to read your findings."

"It may take some time, but I'll let you know what we uncover. I just wish we'd got a sample of the stone to accurately date the place."

Steve looked physically pained that he'd made such a foolish oversight. Danni didn't understand why, the timeframe between arriving at the city and Leviathan's attack didn't allow for samples to be collected anyway.

"Just go back. I'm sure the octopus man would love to see you again," Danni winked.

"You stay safe out there, Miss Quinn. Don't get too close to any supernatural things, if you can help it," Steve said warmly.

Melissa shut the thin door behind them and turned to Danni. "That was a disaster."

"We didn't get the artefact, but it wasn't a waste," Danni replied cautiously.

"On any other mission, finding alien monsters in ancient cities would be noteworthy, but we need that object of Zeus'."

Danni frowned. "It could be my gut feeling, and I might be way wrong, but I can't help but feel all of this is connected. Cthulhu may not be relevant right now, but I'm sure he will be soon enough."

Mel looked at Danni curiously.

Danni hoped she hadn't said something blatantly stupid, but Mel concluded, "You might be right."

With waves crashing into the cove behind them, Mel and Danni descended to the car park.

They also bid farewell to Samantha, another on the long list of characters they'd encountered.

Jason was the one tasked with ferrying the group back into Dunedin. This time the trip would be made in a clunky seven-seater van, outfitted with comically out-of-place suspension to handle the rugged terrain.

Being his ever-boisterous self, Jason was happy to chauffeur the AST team, as it meant a delay in sifting through all the data the Kiwi Sinkers had collected.

Danni appreciated the drive through the windswept landscape more on the way back, mainly because it wasn't underwater.

• • • • •

WHEN THEY ARRIVED AT THEIR inexpensive hotel, they were met by Kane and Sigurd in the foyer. Jason gave a hasty goodbye and, with a clunking of gears, turned the van back around.

Immediately Danni sensed an air of bad news about the two tall men.

Casually gripped in Kane's right hand was the Necronomicon, the book that had led them on that disastrous mission.

"Give me that!" Malcolm growled, unnecessarily

aggressively.

He snatched the book from Kane and cradled it under his arm, looking adoringly at it like it was his child.

Danni found the sudden snatch and rapt expression on Malcolm's face creepy. She wasn't the only one, as Mel also peered at the professor with an unreadable expression.

"Where's Randall?" Danni asked casually, breaking the silence.

Kane and Sigurd glanced at each other.

"What happened?" Mel asked, sensing the awkward tension.

"I'll tell her," Kane mumbled, "he is my brother after all..."

Sigurd took a step back.

"So, yesterday, we took Randall to the local university with the Necronomicon. He wanted a proper facility to study another part of the book he identified as 'mathematically significant'."

Kane held his fingers up as he made sarcastic air quotes.

"Anyway, Sigurd forced me to go to the gymnasium in his ridiculous mission to make me a warrior," Kane continued, shooting the Viking a dirty look. "When we came back to the study room, I saw-"

"Out with it!" Mel ordered.

"I saw Randall finish writing an equation on the blackboard. Then, there was like this rushing of air, and a kind of black hole opened in the board. Randall stretched out and got pulled into it, then the hole closed up, and he was gone."

"Randall used the Necronomicon to open a portal somewhere?" Malcolm mused, amazed.

"That's what it looked like," Kane sighed.

Sigurd stepped forward. "The portal disfigured the writing, meaning we couldn't replicate what he'd done. We searched the place up and down, but the man is gone."

Danni felt a wave of sadness wash over her. She hoped Randall was still alive and that he hadn't warped himself into the cold expanse of empty space.

"You don't sound very upset, Kane," Danni noted. She was worried he was in shock.

"I don't know how to feel about anything! I went on a holiday, and now there are cultists, Vikings, and black holes... if anyone can tell me exactly what's going on, I'm all ears," Kane answered, exasperated.

Danni walked up and gave him a reassuring pat on the back. A thought occurred to her. What if the portal had opened at the exact moment Chtulhu had awakened? It would be foolish to think these were two independent events.

"Well, that does it. We need to regroup. Our mission to find an artefact has failed utterly," Mel said, sounding defeated.

"Not entirely; we have discovered an impossibly ancient city and learned the cult's name in Florida. The Cult of Cthulhu," Teva corrected her. "And if my suspicions are anything to go by, I suspect the monster in the deep was this Cthulhu."

"Discovering more mysteries doesn't help anyone," Mel said sourly.

Teva didn't say anything more; it seemed Mel wasn't in a mood to be argued with. Danni had never seen her like this.

"What's the plan?" Danni asked tentatively.

"We fly back to Canberra tomorrow and meet with Brett.

I've told him we are coming. He can direct us where to go next."

The group stood in silence.

Mel was radiating an aura of failure, which Danni thought was undeserved. She'd done her best with the information available to them.

As Danni did frequently these days, she nervously flipped the angelic seal of Astaroth around in her pocket.

She seemed to find a bizarre comfort in her fingers touching the cool metal of the medallion.

"Take me to the university," Mel directed to Kane. "Show me where Randall was. I understand you've already searched, but I have to be thorough."

"I'll help," Teva said. Danni stepped forward too.

"No, stay. After what we just experienced, I have no trouble believing that book has the power to open portals. I'll go with Kane and Sigurd; the rest of you get some rest."

There was a general murmuring of a good night as they collected their keys from the reception desk and trudged up to their individual rooms.

Danni got changed and brushed her teeth. She lay down, staring at the ceiling as sleep evaded her.

She felt her eyelids sagging and dreams flitting into the corners of her mind. Yet, she remained stubbornly awake. Randall's fate now sat beside the monstrous visage of Cthulhu in her head.

After Mel was completely satisfied that Randall had disappeared and wasn't just hiding in Dunedin somewhere, she sent out details of the flight to Canberra.

Danni understood why Mel seemed a little more irritable

than usual. She'd been given a team leader's position and failed in her mission. Where, on the other side of the world, the other AST team leader had apparently succeeded.

Liam Sager was still in Canberra and was sure to be part of their meeting with Brett Sayer in the coming day.

When sleep eventually found Danni, visions of black holes and sunken cities consumed her mind. Her rest was neither deep nor sound.

• • • • •

INSTEAD OF NAVIGATING A NIGHTMARE of layovers, Altior Fulgur's private jet got them into Australia's capital city with ease.

A strange feeling washed over Danni when she set foot again on Australian soil. She was home, back in the sunburnt country that had treated her so well.

Even though she was sure it would only be temporary, Danni bathed in the relief of being somewhere familiar.

"We have arrived in the great southern continent, then?" Sigurd boomed as they walked into the terminal.

"Yep," Danni smiled.

"Home sweet home," Melissa muttered, still looking stressed.

"I am curious to see this land you have all come from. Kane has told me it is a place of monstrous land creatures that bounce across arid plains. Where great aquatic lizards strike the unsuspecting from the water. It sounds thrilling!"

"You may be a little disappointed, Sigurd. I fear we won't be here for long. Certainly not long enough for sightseeing," Mel said quickly.

Sigurd looked disappointed.

From the back of the bunch, Artemis spoke up. "I, too, am curious about this region. I don't know anything about it. I am ashamed to say I didn't even know it existed until recently. Who are the gods of this land?"

"I don't think Australia had gods like the Greeks or Egyptians," Teva answered.

Danni looked at him curiously.

"Well, not in the same way. Australia was dominated by culturally and linguistically diverse tribal groups for most of human history. They never had unified pantheons of gods like other cultures. However, I'm sure the individual groups worshipped beings akin to gods."

Artemis seemed to understand.

"I wasn't around for the early days of humanity, yet I know the stories from the older titans and gods. Early humans worshipped nature spirits and lesser beings when they lived as clans. These spirits directly helped small groups in the endless struggle to survive against the cruelty of nature. It was larger societies that turned towards beings such as myself to maintain order."

"Makes sense," Teva said.

A pair of bright red police cars waited for them outside the terminal. It was a game of Tetris to fit all of their luggage in, then squash themselves into the rear seats.

They drove past the spectacular war memorial and over the

peaceful Lake Burley Griffin.

The AST operated in an unassuming building in central Canberra. As they were a secret government branch, it was only fitting that there be no identifying features in sight. The AST office was a blocky brick structure surrounded by other blocky brick buildings. The only giveaway that something of importance was in the area was how frequently police cars could be seen driving past.

This was the first time Danni had been here, and she was enthusiastic to see what was held inside. After all, this could be her office one day. Perhaps there would be legendary artefacts and stuffed monsters lining the halls in awe-inspiring displays.

Mel drew an unassuming ID card from her pocket and swiped them in with practised precision.

Even if Danni's hopes had been low, they still would've been dashed as she faced the sterile white walls.

There was no reception desk. Inside, glass doors going left and right were locked with further swipe pads.

The AST office was bigger inside than it looked from the outside. Halls were lined with doors that led into more halls. Danni caught glimpses of abandoned dusty offices through the occasional glass viewing windows.

It wasn't surprising after all. The AST had never had to do much, so Danni wasn't expecting a thriving population of employees. Still, she found the ghost town confronting. It didn't fill her with much hope for her career development.

Melissa led them to the waiting room in front of Brett Sayer's office.

His name was spelt out in shining golden letters on the

plain wood door.

Melissa knocked three times, then waited.

Danni distinctly thought she heard the sound of hastily shuffling papers before footsteps on the carpet.

Brett appeared and greeted the group. He didn't look to be his usual carefree self – instead, seeming tired and stressed. Clearly, dealing with the admin side of Operation Thunderking wasn't an easy job.

"Hello everyone!" he beamed.

There was a murmur of greeting in response.

"We will all speak shortly. I am enthusiastic about getting to know those of you who have unexpectedly joined our mission."

Danni thought she saw the boss shoot Melissa a sideways glance.

Brett had short black hair, thin square glasses and pale skin. He was solidly built, and while he had a pleasant demeanour, he struck Danni as the kind of man who could hold his own in a confrontation.

Brett ushered Mel and Danni into his office while the rest waited outside.

It was surprisingly homely. The boss kept small potted plants by a rectangular window to catch the afternoon light. He had several framed photographs displaying his family on the various shelves, desks and stands in the room.

Danni quite liked the vibrant circular purple rug dominating most of the floor. The space was there for the whole gang to speak in an open forum if needed, with chairs scattered about the sides of the room.

"I'll invite this little team you've assembled in once the three of us get some things established," Brett started, whipping open his diary. "First is money. You've spent a bit, and I need receipts."

"I've got them all on my phone. Emailing them to you now," Melissa replied promptly.

"Good, ASIO wants you back, Mel. They are short-staffed, and it is becoming a real thorn in my side."

"I'm guessing they still haven't been made aware of Operation Thunderking, then?"

"No, they haven't. I've had the Minister for Home Affairs in here berating me about the money I've been spending getting you around the world. ASIS wants Matthew Pyne moved out of Ukraine for undercover work, and the bloody phone won't stop."

"Maybe it's time to brief up about the gods, the angels and the power of Zeus."

Brett sighed. "Even with a god here, I will never be believed. Artemis looks plainly human, and if I were to use her or Apollo for a little show and tell, they can't use any of their powers. We had that advantage in Japan, but not any more. The funny thing is, after the other team's mission to Heaven, USSOT have had money thrown at them. Different culture over there."

"How come you didn't show off Apollo when you first found out about him?" Danni asked.

"Despite Australia being a non-religious country, we continue to elect conservative Christian ministers. I could have Apollo nuke Sydney with a fireball, and they'd still dive into the AST archives and label him a shape-shifter or a hoax. I've worked with these people all my life, and trying to convince them that old gods are real would've seen our budget halved out of spite."

"Right," Danni said.

"Look, I'd like to have an in-depth brief with you both, but we don't have the time. So instead of playing catch-ups, we will do a bit of forward planning. Mr Pyne can get you up to speed on the finer details when you get to Ukraine. Now tell me, what happened in New Zealand?"

Danni gulped. They were going to Ukraine? A bit of forewarning about this turn of events would've been nice...

"We found a city underwater that we believe is impossibly ancient. We got attacked by the fallen angel Leviathan, and in his fight with Artemis, he woke up some monster that slumbered there. Now, said monster may be on the loose," Mel stated, as if she was completely non-plussed by the revelation they were to shortly fly back to Europe.

"And the Necronomicon led you to this city?" Brett asked as he fidgeted with his glasses.

"Yes, with Malcolm and Randall deciphering it."

"And what happened to Randall again? Just so we are crystal clear."

"According to Kane and Sigurd, he seems to have opened up a black hole, or a portal, and been sucked through it."

Brett pressed his hands to his face, "And we are no closer to an artefact of Zeus?"

"Not unless someone gets a bright idea soon."

"USSOT is doing a lot of work with the Florida Necronomicon. Since the book seems to have a lot of unknown potential for disaster, I will get agent Ingrid Horjen out of Europe to the US to liaise with them. We need to know what they learn."

"Where's Liam?" Mel asked suddenly.

"Arriving soon, he will be going with you."

"To Ukraine?" Mel asked.

Brett hadn't exactly said it plainly, but that did indeed seem to be their next destination.

"Yep, down to business. An Australian military flight will depart from here in two hours. I've been assured there is room. It will be a long, painful flight with plenty of stopovers, but it won't cost the AST a damn thing, so you're going to be on it."

Danni groaned. They'd just come from Europe and now were going back.

"We have Fulgur's private jet..."

"Altior Fulgur is not be trusted," Brett stated. "He is playing every side in this. No more using his toys. Cardinal Vasilije Markovic revealed quite a lot to Joshua Dare. The company Molochtech, which was working to purify the werewolf curse for the Vatican, is owned by Fulgur."

"Well, we knew from that meeting in Japan that something was off with him," Mel said very matter-of-factly.

"Keep in mind that the Operation Thunderking documentation was shared with Fulgur and The Old World. It has also been shared with Jesse Billiau, who resides in Ukraine with Joshua Dare."

"Harry Raatikainen, the head of The Old World Europe, didn't seem to know or care about Operation Thunderking," Mel said.

"Regardless, despite the fact we asked Fulgur to sign

secrecy papers, we need to operate under the assumption that the information is out there and the Vatican knows what we are up to. Trust no one."

Mel and Danni nodded.

"Now, I've also received word from Moros, as you have," Brett continued. "ASIO looked into the Pope's movements in North East Africa and have discovered a base of operation in the Tanzanian town of Moshi. As of very recently, a Vatican convoy has started making daily trips from Moshi towards a secluded monastery on the lower slopes of Mt Kilimanjaro. This has to be the entry to the city inside the mountain which houses the angel's detector."

"Why aren't we going there right away?" Mel asked.

"Moros insisted that we must have the artefact before destroying the detector. Once it is down, she intends to move on Olympus right away. We have no time to stuff around."

"We still need a bomb or something from Moros, too, don't we?" Danni asked.

"Moros said she will meet you in Moshi once you have the artefact and provide you with what you need. Our problem is the bloody artefact."

There was a knock on the door.

"Come in!" Brett yelled.

A handsome man with a face lined with stubble and a small bun of bright blonde hair entered. He looked like a surfer.

"Good to see you, Mel. And you, Danni," the newcomer smiled.

He offered her a hand to shake.

Danni got up, slightly abashed. Liam Sager didn't look at all how he had in 2019 when Danni had first encountered him.

"Ah, Liam, good!" Brett said.

"Boss," Liam nodded, taking a seat beside Mel.

"Now, you three. This conversation stays between us, okay? We have a lot to do at the request of these old gods, but we don't exactly know how. In fact, it has struck me that there are many unknowns in this mission. Circumstance has aligned us with the old gods, but if you have any mythological knowledge at all, you know they aren't exactly good. I will admit, just based on Belial's physical appearance, I suspect that Lucifer's side in this isn't the right side. And the Catholic Church is responsible for so much blatant evil I don't think we want to strengthen their deities. I want you to keep your heads about you when dealing with these beings. Don't trust them just because we're helping them."

"There is still the big question, too," Mel murmured.

Danni looked from her to Brett, confused.

"Just who is claiming the lost power to Zeus," Liam said, answering Danni's unasked question.

Brett nodded. "Moros told me explicitly that she doesn't think the gods can do it. It has to be a being an order removed from the divine. The gods will want to make it a person they can control. I know that much."

"According to Operation Thunderking, Josh carries the legacy of Zeus' power within him. Do they mean it to be Josh?" Danni asked.

Brett sighed, "Josh may be a tool in this. An item to be used and discarded. The point is that we don't know, so stay sharp."

They sat in silence for a moment.

"Bring everyone in, Liam," Brett ordered. "Let's have a round table about this artefact. You never know what little bits of information people might have that could give us an idea."

The rest of the crew trudged into Brett's office and used the available seating. Sigurd chose to lean against the wall, his face cast with long shadows.

Brett cleared his throat. "Alright, team, where do we find an artefact of Zeus?"

21

TALES FROM THE POETIC EDDA

CANBERRA, AUSTRALIA
- FEBRUARY 3 -

Every head turned in Teva's direction. Finding an artefact had been his task, after all.

"I don't know what to tell you... I can't find one. I can't find anything in any museum around the world, nor in any private collection or black market, that is remotely close to an artefact of Zeus."

"What could a possible artefact of Zeus be?" Kane asked. It was actually a good question from one of the outsiders in the room.

"I'll go through my approach," Teva stated. He pulled out his notebook and flicked to a page almost black with scribbled words.

"First, I started with the goat Amalthea. This was the animal that nursed Zeus as a baby in myth. I figured such a creature would've been supernatural or immortal. I searched USSOT and The Old World's records for any reference to a divine goat, but the closest I got was stories about the God Pan."

Danni was happy to see that it wasn't only her face screwed up incredulously towards Teva. Hopefully he'd started with the longest shot possible.

"Next, I looked for any artefact that had its discovery in the Cretan mountains. Both Ideon Cave in Mount Ida and Dikteon Cave in south-central Crete are attributed as the possible birthplaces of Zeus. Again, I got nothing.

"Zeus' direct symbolism was where I went next. The eagle, the bull and the oak offered me very little that was tangible. His last, and possibly his most well-known symbol, the lightning bolt, was where I focused my effort. But again, the lightning bolts seem purely restricted to myth. They are said to be the most powerful weapon ever constructed and prized among all supernatural weapons. The Old World files reference the lightning bolts as divine energy weapons, though they still classify them as purely mythical. I suspect if any of Zeus' lightning bolts survived the assault of the angels, they'd be under lock and key in Heaven."

Sigurd loudly cleared his throat.

Brett looked at him calmly and stated, "Something to say?"

It certainly conveyed Brett's relaxed attitude that a legendary Viking hero stood in the room, and Brett looked at him like a petulant child.

"Yes, I believe I may be able to assist you."

Sigurd stood from his chair and moved towards Brett's desk. After positioning himself slightly to the right of Brett, he loudly addressed the group.

"As I learned in New Zealand, my life is detailed quite accurately in your Poetic Edda, though not all details are present. There is one missed journey that could prove to be very important now. It is the story of my journey to the magical castle of Skrymir in the land of Utgard."

"Oh god," Danni thought. *"More mythology to remember."*

"Does anyone here know the story of Thor, Loki and Skrymir?"

Several heads nodded.

Danni looked like a deer caught in the headlights.

"You'd best catch me up," Brett said. Danni was relieved that the boss wasn't across this tale either.

Sigurd, apparently resigned to the fact that this would be a long story, pulled up a chair from a corner desk behind Brett and sat down.

"We begin in the time of the gods –"

Melissa exhaled sharply.

"What happened?" Brett asked.

"When he started talking, I flashed backwards in time… I think I can see the story he is about to tell!"

"If you can, then we all can!" Danni exclaimed. "It worked in Florida, after all. People who touch you can see your visions."

"Can you tap into that power again?" Brett asked.

"I think so…" Mel said hesitantly.

"Excellent. Sigurd, get talking. Everyone else, get in close and touch Mel."

Kane snickered.

"Touch her appropriately," Brett clarified.

Danni shuffled her chair in close and grabbed Mel on the right shoulder.

Sigurd began again, "In the land of the giants…"

Danni's eyes closed as she was swallowed by visions from Melissa's mind. Tall frosted peaks stood mighty in a frozen landscape. She was seeing Sigurd's story come to life.

"The land of Jotunheim was home to the giants. The God of Thunder, Thor, and the trickster, Loki, travelled east through these lands, accompanied by their servants Pjalfi and Roskva. Why the humans were with the gods is another story that I will not go into. Still, it is important to note that the boy Pjalfi was one of the fastest runners to have ever lived."

As the words left Sigurd's mouth, Danni saw the party of four standing on the edge of a dark forest.

Thor and Loki looked like powerful Asgardians, dressed head to toe in armour, while the human children were dressed in what appeared to be layers of warm rags.

Danni was seeing these events as they were happening. She was actually looking at the ancient God Thor in all his glory. He looked different to how Danni had imagined him. He was beefy and broad-shouldered with a wide chest. The god was by no means shredded, instead looking like a middle-aged man in strong shape.

He had a long red beard and eyes that glowed with the fierceness of a hardened warrior. They looked somewhat similar to Sigurd's eyes. His famous hammer, Mjolnir, the symbol of his power, was hitched to his belt.

On the other hand, Loki had mischievous eyes and a cunning grin. He was incredibly handsome, with a face like it was chiselled from stone. His hair was bleached blonde and his silver Asgardian armour glistened in the evening light.

Sigurd's voice was lost to the booming chatter of Thor.

"We will journey through the forest, Loki. Shelter will appear before dark," Thor muttered.

"Have the boy run ahead," Loki suggested. "I do not wish to wander through the night with no guarantee of safe lodgings. We are in the land of giants after all."

The boy, Pjalfi, dressed in his oilskin rags, looked to the two gods, then bolted into the forest. He was amazingly fast.

He returned quickly, stating that just to the north was a strange cave in a smooth mountainside.

Thor and Loki found this perplexing and set off to investigate.

The vision moved forward in time.

Now the party of four stood before an enormous cave mouth that looked eerily like it was made of leather.

"Strange," Loki said, rubbing his hand along the rock.

"We do not know what foul sorcery the giants cook up here that twists the land, brother," Thor stated. He lit a torch from his belt and worked to establish a larger fire.

Their two child servants huddled around it to stave off the cold of Jotunheim.

Before long, all were asleep.

A deafening sound rang out. It was like a meteor impacting the Earth, repeating in a steady rhythm, driving Thor from his slumber.

The red-bearded god tried to cover his ears but to no avail.

By the time morning approached, his eyes were bloodshot and his mood was sour.

"I will find the source of that sound and destroy it," he murmured angrily.

The origin of the nighttime explosions was revealed when their cave rose from the ground into the sky.

As it turned out, the smooth mountainside was actually a glove - a colossal, impossibly enormous glove worn by a creature of such magnitude it was difficult to comprehend.

The glove belonged to a giant, though the word 'giant' didn't do this being justice. His head stretched well into the clouds. The world looked too small for such a creature to exist.

Both Thor and Loki were caught in utter shock and amazement as they peered up at him.

"Oh, good morning!" the giant boomed happily as he spotted the ant-like gods on the ground below. He knelt down, causing the world to shake as he did so. "Anyone care for breakfast?"

The giant introduced himself as Skrymir, bowing graciously toward the gods.

The scene flashed forward again to the next night. It appeared Thor and his companions had travelled in the shadow of the giant all day.

As they slept beneath a tall oak tree, the cause of the previous night's earthquakes was revealed to be Skrymir's snoring.

Each breath rumbled the world.

Growing incredibly agitated at the giant's ceaseless noises, Thor walked onto Skrymir's head and raised his hammer high. He brought it down, intending to kill the giant.

Nothing happened. Thor looked confused. His hammer never failed to kill an enemy, no matter their size. He struck again.

Skyrmir groggily opened his eyes and muttered, "I think a leaf hit my head."

He promptly fell back asleep.

Thor, looking crestfallen, returned to the oak tree and tried to rest.

Skrymir parted ways with Thor, Loki, and the children the next day.

"If you continue on your course east, you will come to the castle of Utgard. Heed my advice, little gods, do not act cocky in the presence of Utgarder-Loki, or see his men treat you with contempt," Skrymir warned them.

"The King of Utgard is also called Loki?" Loki asked.

Skrymir nodded and went on his way, shaking the world with his every step.

Thor and Loki were curious about the castle of Utgard, so they continued into the east.

Again, the vision jumped ahead in time.

Now the party of four were standing by the gates of a towering castle. It was so large that they had to crane their necks to their spines just to see the top of the gate.

Thor, a being of incredible strength, attempted to lift the gate and found he couldn't. Instead, Loki directed them to climb through the bars.

They entered a great hall so high that wisps of cloud lay across the roof.

At the end was a throne of pure opulence and magnificence. Atop it was another giant, similar to the friendly Skrymir, though this one was even bigger. This giant was dressed in kingly attire, with a rather simple gold crown on his flowing white hair. This was Utgarder-Loki, the lord of the castle.

"Who enters castle Utgard?" Utgarder-Loki demanded of the four newcomers

"Thor, God of Thunder and Loki, God of Mischief. Plus our servants, Pjalfi and Roskva."

"Gods in my hall. I long suspected a day would come when I'd be graced by the Aesir. I know stories of you, Thor. Never had a problem you couldn't hammer into submission. And you Loki, tricks and deceptions; childish things. I do not permit those who are unexceptional to pass through my hall. Therefore, if you wish to linger in Utgard, you must prove yourselves worthy."

Thor snorted, incensed by Utgarder-Loki's words.

"He dares question our ability?" the storm god muttered.

Loki looked equally annoyed and stepped forward. "I can eat faster than any man alive!" he boasted.

Utgarder-Loki grinned.

"Prepare a feast," he ordered. An old woman, also astonishingly gigantic, shuffled through a door at the side of the hall.

Before long, Utgarder-Loki led the party into his expansive dining hall. He set a seat (that was far too large) for Loki before a trough filled with the meats of giant animals. Another chair was placed for Loki's challenger at the other end of the trough.

A giant with wild red hair and an enormous belly entered the hall and took the other seat. He laughed stupidly at Loki, then licked his lips as he observed his smorgasbord.

"Begin!" Utgarder-Loki decreed.

Loki set to work demolishing his end of the long bowl of food. In seconds, he stripped the meat from the bones and broke them to suck out the marrow. The trickster god ate faster than any giant could possibly hope to replicate.

The two contestants met in the middle.

Content with his efforts, Loki leaned back, leaving a trough full of bones. He was horrified when he turned his head to see that the red-haired giant had eaten everything. Meat, bones and even his side of the trough were wholly gone.

Loki was utterly dismayed to have lost so resoundingly. Utgarder-Loki turned his attention towards the boy, Pjalfi.

"What is the one thing that makes you exceptional, little mortal?" the giant boomed.

"Well, I don't want to boast," he squeaked, "but I am the fastest person I've ever met."

Time jumped forward again. They stood in an oblong stadium made of wood and coated with coarse red fabric. A simple running track had been marked out along it.

While Pjalfi stretched, Utgarder-Loki fetched his competitor, another giant named Hugi. Hugi was large, muscular and cumbersome.

To make the match fair, the Lord of Utgard shrunk Hugi

down to the same size as Pjalfi.

They raced.

Despite Pjalfi's best efforts, becoming a blur on the track, he was beaten considerably.

Two of Thor's party had failed.

Now, the king turned to the God of Thunder himself.

"What will it be?"

"Drinking!" Thor demanded. "No one out drinks me!"

Utgarder-Loki invited them all back into his great hall, where he produced a spectacular carven drinking horn.

"All of my thanes can finish this horn in one gulp. Some of the lesser giants take two. But no one is pathetic enough to require three," Utgarder-Loki smiled.

Thor dismissively brushed the Utgarder's boasts aside and balanced the giant horn in his hands. He pressed it to his lips and began swallowing its disgustingly salty contents.

He sucked in the largest swig he could, but the horn was barely depleted. He took two more mighty gulps, and while it was lower, hardly a dent had been made in it.

Even the great Thor was humbled before Utgarder-Loki.

"I sense treachery! I demand another challenge!" Thor burped.

Utgarder-Loki looked around his hall. His eyes fixed on the fireplace. Before it slumbered his cat. This was no ordinary cat but a giant's house cat. And as such, it was many times larger than Thor.

"Very well, pick up my cat," Utgarder-Loki suggested.

Thor slapped his palms together and moved to the furry beast's belly. He squirmed under it as far as possible and attempted to push the cat off the ground. He strained and strained, pushing the slumbering feline up as high as he could manage. Eventually, one paw dangled off the ground.

Thor gave up.

"Another challenge!" he demanded, his pride almost beyond repair.

Utgarder-Loki's eyes sparkled at the suggestion. "I do love a good brawl. Elli, come here," the giant king ordered.

The hunched, withered old giantess who'd prepared Loki's meal earlier approached.

Using his magic, Utgarder-Loki shrunk her down to Thor's size.

"Pin her or knock her down, and see your pride restored."

Thor looked dumbstruck to be fighting an old woman. Regardless, he pressed on, launching himself at her like a raging bull. She absorbed Thor's blows as if they were nothing.

She effortlessly pushed him to the ground. But Thor got back up, endeavouring to fight on. He fought with all the effort he could muster and managed to land some good hits on the woman. Again, she knocked him to the ground and pinned him there.

Thor was defeated.

"The three of you have performed admirably. You will be permitted to spend the night in Utgard and enjoy my hospitality." Utgarder-Loki beamed.

The other child-servant, Roskva, was also allowed to stay, despite not competing.

Thor and Loki drank through the night, if only to ease the pain of their bruised egos. In the morning, Utgarder-Loki escorted them from the castle.

It was then that the giant knelt down and revealed his secrets.

"I am a powerful sorcerer, yet I had not seen the strength of the gods and now know I have much more to learn. Thor, you are too powerful, and our games threatened the planet. Because of this, I am removing Utgard from the world, so that no gods may stumble upon it again without my invitation."

"But you humbled us," Loki said, evidently confused.

"I will reveal to you the truth of yesterday's challenges. As I said, my magic is strong, particularly with illusion."

The giant shrunk in size until he was about sixteen feet tall, the regular size of a giant in Jotunheim. His face changed too, so that it mirrored that of Skrymir's.

"You were Skrymir," Loki said, impressed.

"I wanted to test your powers, so I made myself a size I thought unchallengeable. Yet, Thor still struck at me with his hammer. To negate those blows, I magically shifted mountainsides between myself and Thor. So powerful were your strikes that new valleys have been created."

"And the challenges in Utgard?" Thor huffed.

"Loki, the red-haired giant you faced, was a wildfire I transformed, consuming everything in its path. You could never out-eat it. And Pjalfi, you ran against the concept of thought itself, so fast it can never be beaten."

"And me?" Thor asked.

"That drinking horn was connected to the ocean. So deep were your three swigs that the world's sea level was lowered. My cat was no cat; he was actually your mortal enemy, Jormungandr, the serpent wrapped around the world. The fact you raised his paw almost ripped our planet in half."

"And the old woman?"

"Entropy," Skyrmir answered. "The fact that you could fight at all is a miracle in itself."

Thor's face was red with anger and indignation. He raised Mjolnir to the sky and storm clouds gathered.

"I have seen your power and will learn from it. I thought mine was so great as to be unchallengeable. I am glad you have proven me wrong."

Thor summoned a blast of lightning down on Skyrmir, but the giant and his castle vanished in that instant. Never to be seen in the world again.

· · · · ·

DANNI RUBBED HER EYES. It had been quite the complex and detailed vision.

"That was a nice movie, but what does it have to do with anything?" Teva asked.

"Now, we must talk about me, in brief. I understand most of you have researched my life in your quiet moments. While we were in the land of New Zealand, I asked Kane to show me what the world recorded. As I mentioned before, one significant part of my life is missing from the story.

"Shortly after I killed the dragon Fafnir, I met the giant Skrymir, the very same from the story I just told you. Near the day of my death, I travelled to Utgard. The same Utgard we all just saw. And it was in Utgard, I believe I saw an artefact to this god, Zeus."

With that, everyone in the room was much more interested in hearing mythology.

22

SIGURD AND SKRYMIR

They all waited with bated breath for Sigurd to continue.

"I wanted to tell you the story of Thor and Skrymir to prepare you for what the giant may ask of us if we enter Utgard. He will not hand over his treasure without a price, and it could well be a test. Since we are not gods, the same deception will not be involved. I suspect our challenge will be simpler. When I went to Utgard last, he made me fight."

"You're suggesting you know how to access this magical castle?" Brett asked.

"Yes, when I killed Fafnir, I gained ownership of his fabulous treasure horde. Several enchanted items were in it, and I was approached by Skrymir, who desired one for his own collection.

"At this point in history, Utgard had long been hidden from the eyes of mortals and gods alike. It was the bastion of the last elves and dwarves from the Nordic realms. It was so absolutely unfindable that you could never get to it if Skrymir didn't approach you himself. Perhaps only Odin could've seen it floating somewhere beyond Midgard.

"When Skrymir came to me, I was hesitant to part with anything too quickly. He offered me a trade as he greatly desired a ring that amplified distant power. It wasn't Norse in origin; I know that much. I told him I'd think on it, and the giant left me with a token. A small bronze horn shaped like a wolf. Not just any wolf, mind you. It was carven in the image of dread Fenrir, the destroyer. He told me to take the horn to a quiet place and blow.

"When the time came that I wished to look upon the giant's home, I took the ring and horn deep into the woods, to a place where sound left me. I put the horn to my lips and was transported through space to a new world, a world of Skrymir's own creation. In the light of a foreign sun stood mighty Utgard, tall and proud.

"The castle wasn't magically deceptive as when Thor had seen it, yet it was still a fitting home for an incredibly powerful wizard-giant. There were also foreign gods in his court, those in hiding for misdeeds done in the forgotten past. Clearly, Skrymir's experience with Thor made him seek gods to teach him their powers.

"Skrymir offered for me to stay in Utgard, to be his champion, yet I declined. Still, he showed me his treasury and spoke warmly of his collection of artefacts belonging to far-off gods. I found a suitable trinket to exchange for the ring. After completing a combat challenge for the giant's entertainment, I went on my way."

"If you didn't know Zeus then, how could you recognise an artefact of his in the treasury?" Brett asked.

"Memory is a funny thing. Despite my long years in Hell, Teva's story of Zeus' lightning bolts triggered a memory in me; a memory of such a weapon in Skrymir's collection."

"You think it's still there?" Mel asked excitedly.

"It has to be," Sigurd smiled.

The most silent person in the room at last spoke up. Artemis stepped from the shadows beside the door and said, "This course will be favourable to us. I remember a foreign being visiting Olympus in my youth that looked much like the giant Skyrmir from that story. Zeus would have wanted to earn the favour of a being that powerful, and he would've done so by offering a mighty gift."

It wasn't the first time that Danni had forgotten that Artemis was even there.

"Great, the only question left is this: if Utgard is in a pocket dimension no one can get to, not even the gods, how do we get there?" Melissa added on from the goddess.

"The horn of Utgard, of course," Sigurd smiled. "When I returned to Midgard, I buried the horn. If it is still there, then we can blow it and return to the castle."

"Excellent!" Brett shouted, slapping the table.

"Just like that, we are back in the game," Teva smirked.

Danni knew the only reason he was so happy was that he could take a break from researching. The proverbial weight of failure had just been lifted from his shoulders.

"We have operatives in Ukraine now. I'll call and see if we can get a team to go and dig up this horn. Hopefully, it'll be waiting by the time you get there," Brett said enthusiastically. "Oh, and an hour and a half till wheels are up on that military flight. You all need to get going right now!"

"Can I ask why we were going to Ukraine in the first place?" Danni interjected. She worried her question might be interpreted as rude.

"Oh, of course, I should've said. We are reuniting the team around Joshua Dare before we press on with the mission. As he is in currently in Ukraine, that will be your starting point."

"Right," Danni gulped.

"Sigurd, do you know where the horn is now? Could you locate it on a map?" Liam asked the Viking.

"Find an ancient map of my home country, and I can point it out."

"Give me a location to work with," Brett demanded.

"I buried it at the spot I killed Fafnir the dragon. A place in my time called Gnitaheath on the River Rhine."

Brett pressed the intercom on his desk. "Sandra, I need you to pull up every ancient map of Germany we have access to, as quickly as possible. Sigurd, Teva and Mel, you stay here. Oh, and you too, Doctor Selleck. We will pinpoint a location and send it to our man in Ukraine. He can make the travel arrangements and go ASAP. Liam, it's on you to organise everyone else. Pack your stuff. Utgard awaits."

23

THE FULL TEAM ASSEMBLES

Malcolm told Danni later that there had been a bit of guesswork involved, but they'd been able to determine a rough location for the burial site of Sigurd's horn. During the meeting, the professor had been so quiet Danni forgot he was even there.

Brett contacted USSOT representatives in Ukraine right away, calling in unknown favours.

It was now up to someone to fly to Germany and dig up the wolf-shaped horn.

Danni was glad she wasn't on the receiving end of an order to find a historically significant archaeological site at a moment's notice. It sounded impossible.

Danni hadn't been concerned about why there was such an American military presence in the Eastern European country, but that didn't stop Teva from explaining the geopolitical strife in the region.

Liam then told them how the location of the US base had been fortunate for their cause. It was the closest place to Siberia, where Joshua Dare had been recently rescued from the mysterious genetics research company Molochtech.

A weary boredom fell over the group as they were all shuffled back to Canberra Airport, where a C130-J Hercules sat waiting for them. Groups of police and military personnel were already boarding as they pulled up.

With several stops along the way, the military aircraft would take them to Ukraine. Brett had made a special mention to Danni that Joshua Dare would be there waiting when they arrived, which had set her nerves on edge.

Danni had no idea what her relationship with Josh was anymore. She wasn't sure if she was ready to see him after everything she'd been through. The flight would be unpleasant, with all of that running through her head.

Still, no matter her feelings about her relationship with the werewolf, she noticed she wasn't the only one looking lost in other thoughts. She overheard Melissa venting her frustrations to Liam Sager on the tarmac about the underwater disaster and how her prophetic sight only worked randomly.

Kane sat by himself, looking stressed. Malcolm also kept his distance from everyone else, perpetually flicking through the black book.

When Liam and Mel separated, he moved to the spot in the shade where Danni stood.

"We should get to know each other. We didn't meet properly back in 2019, and I was too busy to check in with you during training," Liam said apologetically.

Danni waved her hand dismissively and said it was fine.

"It's important that we get to know each other, as it sounds like you might become the third permanent member of the AST."

"Really? I assumed I'd be going to ASIO after all this was over."

"That could be a possibility. The werewolf appearances in 2019 could mean that the AST gets expanded after the next election. You've basically walked into a hard-to-get position due to luck."

Danni frowned. Being a full-time monster hunter did sound cool.

"How did you end up working there?" Danni asked.

Liam sighed and looked towards the big aeroplane. "I was Icarus, I flew too close to the sun. I was an investigator before this, and I was good at it. Had the sort of record it takes people a lifetime to achieve. My coworkers were jealous, to put it mildly. They conspired to have me moved somewhere out of the way."

Danni felt a pang of sorrow for Liam.

"Regardless, I was already in the AST's pool of short notice operatives and had headed a mission in 2016. Actually, it was in Cairns, where you are from."

"Cyclone Bolton?" Danni asked.

"The very same," Liam nodded. "That cyclone was no

ordinary weather event. We never got to the bottom of it. Still, fishermen who'd survived said creatures from the deep attacked vessels beyond the Great Barrier Reef. Some kind of fish-men."

"That explains the big cages my uncle pulled from a fishing boat!" Danni exclaimed.

"Ah, yeah," Liam said in surprise. "Some foreign groups were there to try and hunt the fish-men. The Old World was there investigating, too, as it turns out. I'm still working on that file."

"Well, I can help you out, if I do end up being a permanent member," Danni grinned.

"And the help would be greatly appreciated. The funny thing is, some of the ruins we dredged up look strikingly similar to what's written in that book." Liam nodded towards Malcolm, still flicking through the Necronomicon.

Danni looked again at the professor with concern.

"Are you happy? Working for the AST?" she asked.

Liam pondered on the question for a moment. "On the whole, yes. There is a certain thrill in diving into the unknown, though the lack of tangible data can be frustrating."

Danni looked at him blankly.

"Well, when I was investigating criminals and taking them down, I always got a sense of satisfaction. Both with the job and myself. After a few years, that didn't happen so much. I watched as some terrible people got off on technicalities or received slaps on the wrists for evil crimes. I have often wondered if our justice system, based on the idea that people can be rehabilitated, is entirely wrong. You won't have to worry about that in the AST."

Danni didn't have the knowledge or experience to continue

down this line of dialogue, so she quickly changed the subject.

"So, you spent some time at Down Under base with Josh, right?"

"Yes, I did."

"Did he ever talk about me?"

As soon as the words left her mouth Danni looked away, her cheeks turning scarlet. This wasn't very professional of her.

"Relax," Liam laughed, noticing her discomfort. "He asked about you several times, despite knowing we couldn't tell him anything. I think he will be very pleased to see you."

Danni felt like a weight had lifted from her chest.

Liam looked back to the plane and said, "We are boarding. Come on, Agent Quinn, destiny awaits."

Danni decided she quite liked Liam.

When at last it took off, the military flight to Ukraine surpassed all negative expectations. It was long, loud and painfully uncomfortable.

Danni had grown accustomed to sleeping through flights, but here it was impossible. She missed the luxury of Altior Fulgur's private jet and its long comfortable couches. As predicted, the thought of her impending reunion with Josh was playing through her mind on repeat. Scenario after scenario washed through her head, inflaming her emotions.

Somehow, most of the Australian soldiers and support staff occupying the rows of seats were out cold. It must've been an acquired military skill to sleep through the noise of the Hercules.

It was so noisy that Danni couldn't even make small talk with the people next to her.

On her right was the enormous muscular frame of Sigurd, and on her left was the almost-as-large Kane Dare. Their shoulders were pressed against hers, making her the meat in a sinewy sandwich.

Fortunately, the plane's first stop in the Solomon Islands arrived quickly.

After the heavy plane touched down, Danni's group disembarked. At the same time, the bulk of the Australian servicemen collected their bags and headed off into Honiara. The pacific island nation was going through a period of unrest so the government was supplying soldiers and police to quell the rioting.

Liam talked with a few of the grizzled old police members, many of whom he'd worked with before his full-time move to the AST.

The air was thick with moisture, and just being outdoors made Danni begin dripping with sweat. Malaria-riddled mosquitos appeared in clouds to pester the Australians.

Sigurd, ever curious about modern weaponry, discussed the soldier's guns with unbridled enthusiasm. Danni noticed that the army guys eyed the giant Norseman distrustingly.

A forklift moving heavy pallets off the plane died mid-operation. Annoyed at waiting, Artemis strode back on board and began lifting the pallets out herself. She balanced them high over her head as she effortlessly carried them from the cargo hold and dumped them at the soldier's feet.

The look of sheer disbelief on the soldier's faces made Danni laugh. Mel looked annoyed; Artemis wasn't meant to be drawing attention to herself.

When the soldiers questioned Sigurd about the woman's

absurd strength, he offhandedly mentioned she was a goddess, causing Mel to storm over and pull him away.

As was typical, Malcolm still had his head buried in the Necronomicon. He loudly muttered to himself as he sat in the shade beneath the plane's wing.

Danni was growing more and more worried about the professor; he really didn't seem himself. Malcolm looked unnaturally pale like he was caught in the grip of perpetual tiredness.

When Kane wandered up to ask if Malcolm had made any progress in discovering what had happened to Randall, he received a rather sharp and rude response. Kane walked off in a huff.

Danni wondered if she should make her concerns about the professor known to Mel. Though Mel looked occupied with other business.

As soon as they'd landed, her phone had rung, and she'd been stuck on it ever since. The pieces of the conversation Danni picked up on didn't sound good. Mel spoke about seismic activity where their submarine had been. Hopefully, that deep-sea monster wasn't on the move...

At least when they all shuffled back on board, there was more room to spread out.

The C-130J Hercules took off and soared through the sky towards Europe. Several brief stops later, they finally got words of their descent into Ukraine. Relief like Danni had never felt washed over her, though it was short-lived when she remembered who she would meet at the US military base.

With a spray of dust and the squealing of brakes, the big Aussie bird touched down at Poltava Air Base in North-Eastern

Ukraine. The airbase sat adjacent to a second public airfield around ten kilometres out of the town of Poltava.

This time, it was only the AST crew leaving the plane. Danni collected her bags and found herself standing in the open air. Unlike the day earlier in the Solomon Islands, it was freezing cold here.

"We will have a Ukrainian military escort to the Adams Military Base. It is a semi-permanent military complex to the southeast of here. Should only be a couple of hours," Mel said, addressing the group.

"Watch what you say," Liam added.

"Yes," Mel continued. "In fact, it is best you say nothing to anyone."

"Any word from USSOT in the USA? Have they re-interviewed Dean Oswald about the Cult of Cthulhu?" Malcolm asked.

This was news to Danni.

Evidently, they'd discussed this with Brett while locating Sigurd's horn. She paid extra attention to Mel's answer, hoping for some information about Cthulhu or the Necronomicon.

Danni couldn't help but notice that even Mel looked shattered. Her hair was a mess, falling over her face, and she had distinct bags under her eyes.

"No word yet. I suspect when Ingrid gets there, that's when we will get some real information."

Kane let out a huge yawn.

"Once we get settled at the base, we are taking two days off," Mel said decisively. "This mission has been non-stop travelling. We will be assigned sleeping facilities, and everyone can have a break. It's not like this mythical Utgard castle is going anywhere."

Liam looked quizically at Mel, then nodded in agreement.

There was a murmur of approval. Everyone seemed to think a genuine rest would be fantastic.

Danni pushed her suitcase onto its side and promptly sat down on it. The lethargy being spread by her coworkers was contagious.

"An excellent idea. Skrymir will test us; this you can all be sure of. We will need to be ready to think and to fight," Sigurd stated.

"You are certain you know how to get to Utgard?" Teva asked Sigurd.

"If nothing has changed, yes," Sigurd answered simply.

Danni put her head in her hands. Thor had been given impossible challenges in Utgard; what chance did they have? She shook her head as a physical gesture to remove the negativity from her mind. Thinking like that wouldn't get her anywhere.

Artemis spoke up from the back. "If this giant doesn't hand over his artefact of Zeus, I will simply obliterate him."

"Mighty Artemis, I suspect the court of Skrymir will still be home to many gods who sought refuge from their foes. Even back in my time, he had allies from afar in Utgard. In my bones, I feel we have to play the giant's game."

A low rumbling filled the air as two impressive military vehicles roared into view. Two v-hulled Kozak Ukrainian armoured personnel carriers sped towards the Hercules alarmingly fast. The cars looked like bunkers on wheels, purpose-built to take a beating.

The greenish-grey and very imposing vehicles stopped just shy of them, and a dozen men clambered out. Several of them had M4A1 Carbines slung around their necks.

They were all dressed in military fatigues with black helmets and balaclavas. Without bothering to introduce themselves, they waved Danni's group towards them.

"How do we know this is us?" Teva asked quietly.

Mel looked concerned and Danni knew why. Eastern European countries often had strong military ties to the Vatican. Mel didn't want to get them all caught in an ambush.

Suddenly, another man emerged from behind the second vehicle and waved enthusiastically. He was broad-shouldered and beefy, wrapped in civilian clothing. He had a square jaw and hair that had been meticulously gelled.

Both Liam and Mel had wide grins on their faces as he approached.

"You're both thinking 'Vatican ambush', am I right?" the stranger beamed.

"Nah, bro," Liam replied.

He shook Liam's hand enthusiastically, then Teva's, and lastly Mel's.

"Everyone," Mel said, addressing the crowd, "this is Matthew Pyne of ASIS. Matt, meet Danni Quinn."

Danni got up from her suitcase and shook his hand as well.

"Heard a lot about you. When I told Josh you were coming, I swear he almost had a mental breakdown."

"That makes two of us..." Danni thought.

"Then, we have Sigurd the Viking hero, Professor Malcolm

Selleck and Kane Dare. Oh, and Silver Artemis, sister to Golden Apollo."

Matt greeted all of them, pausing to size up Sigurd. He looked displeased. Then, upon reaching Artemis, Matt was met with his own look of disdain. The goddess had a withering gaze which he promptly withdrew from.

"Matt fancies himself an action hero. He's probably afraid Sigurd will steal his thunder," Teva whispered to Danni.

She giggled.

"I heard that!" Matt called, scowling at Teva.

"In fairness, I did once see him take down an Italian attack helicopter with a grappling hook and explosive sheet," Teva said, begrudgingly.

"You guys will get all caught up when we're there," Matt said to Mel, loud enough so everyone could hear. "But in short, the US has funnelled some money towards our mission. The Taskforce A team leader will fill you in properly."

"What is Taskforce A?" Mel asked.

"Navy SEALs and Army Rangers, all specialists in a new USSOT team. We can't really talk about it now. Adams Base isn't far."

And with that, they piled into the Kozaks and began moving toward the US outpost.

Danni was assigned to the front vehicle with Melissa, Liam, Artemis, Teva and Matt. The back was dark, with light coming in through six small rectangular windows in the heavily armoured sides.

Matt looked from Melissa to Teva and said, "Look at us, the

Golden Apollo crew back on mission together again."

"Time has really flown by," Teva yawned.

"It was you three who discovered this whole 'missing power of Zeus thing'?" Danni asked.

"Yep," Matt said proudly. "We were there in Afghanistan when Apollo and Moros beat Michael and Belial."

"Not really beat, though," Mel interjected.

"How much did Brett brief you on?" Matt asked her.

"Not much; we discussed Utgard and got out of there."

"Well, then you won't have heard the good news. Belial and Cardinal Markovic are both dead."

"What? How?" Mel asked, astonished.

"It was Joshua Dare. On the mission to Heaven, he lost his hand, so the god Hephas...Hephea... I can't say his name. Some god built him a new magic one. Pulled Belial's heart right from his chest."

"Hephaestus," Artemis corrected him, not impressed.

"Josh lost a hand?" Danni asked, alarmed.

"And Markovic?" Mel said, accidentally talking over both Danni and the goddess.

"There is another new werewolf that Josh bit. A Japanese girl named Haruka Masunaga. She got Markovic."

"Yep, three werewolves now," Liam added. "Apologies, I thought you were already aware."

For some unknown reason, Danni felt a pang of jealousy. Who was this Haruka girl that Josh had bitten?

"How did this Haruka survive the bite?" Mel asked.

"Oh, that is the other piece of big news. Josh can now

control his werewolf transformation. He can transform at will. He bit Haruka so they'd have a distraction to escape from a Siberian research facility."

"These are all astonishing developments," Mel said, lost in thought.

"Except on the full moon," Matt added. "Josh can't control the werewolf on the full moon."

Artemis frowned. "The curse has been purified, then?"

"Yes, my lady," Matt said awkwardly.

Teva stifled a laugh.

"Joshua Dare is now the completed link to Zeus. We will get this artefact, which I hope is there, then make for Olympus."

"I have some information for you," Mel said. "We can't make for Olympus, even if Moros is ready in time. We have a new mission, to destroy the angel's god detector in Africa."

Matt raised his eyebrows.

"I know what you're thinking. It just doesn't end," Liam sighed.

"Moros is still gathering the information needed for the ritual. In recent days, what has become clear is that the gods will need to use their power freely to perform it," Mel said.

Artemis nodded.

"Brett hasn't passed this on to USSOT. So let's not mention this part of the plan to our US contemporaries until it becomes necessary," Mel added.

"The Taskforce A guys are very good. They will be helpful," Matt stated.

"This will be a stealth mission," Melissa said, her voice

stern. "We say nothing until I've assessed the situation here."

"Have you met Patrick Leeson? He's a good bloke," Matt said.

"We met in Nagoya."

"Oh right, I forgot. I think he will be doing the full brief with you once the admin stuff is taken care of."

"Admin stuff?"

"Adams Base is a big place. Unfortunately, you will have to sign some forms when we arrive."

As the Kozaks crunched through the snow across the sparse Ukrainian landscape, Liam told Matt his tale from the recent mission to Heaven.

Matt then told Liam how he and Ingrid Horjen had escaped from Jerusalem while being pursued by the Cult of Belial.

Danni thought it would've made quite the movie if it had all been fictional. It was an exhilarating tale.

They soon stopped at a series of thick steel gates and were waved into Adams Base by a surly looking American soldier.

The base was buzzing with activity and far more extensive than Danni had imagined.

They drove past large sheds with tanks inside. There were multiple helipads with military aircraft scattered about them. Despite the cold conditions, lines of US soldiers were doing PT in the open spaces.

Potential global conflict aside, the thing that was troubling Danni was her imminent reunification with Josh.

She'd done her best not to think about it during the flight and Kozak ride. Every time she did, a wave of butterflies fluttered through her stomach. Her training was meant to have made her tougher than this, so why was she so nervous.

What would it be like to see him again? This was the man who'd, in some ways, changed her entire life… Danni was fully aware of how much she'd accomplished; she was here due to her own drive and ability. She'd overcome difficult odds and swam well out of her depth due to her perseverance and fortitude. Yet, it was inescapable that Josh had put her on the path here…

Danni nervously flattened her hair. She was sure she looked tired and dishevelled from the flight.

When they finally stopped and the back doors opened, Danni's paranoia about her appearance was getting the best of her.

She desperately wanted to find a mirror before she saw her ex-boyfriend.

In the usual way the universe offers only poor timing, a US marine approached the group before she had the chance.

"AST party?" he asked.

Mel nodded.

"Right, we need to get you to the check-in facility. We will get some ID badges made up for you."

"ID badges? Really?" Mel asked.

"Yes, ma'am. Lot is being run out of this operating base. Hordes of intelligence people and soldiers working on all different projects."

"I understand," Mel replied curtly. "Lead the way."

"We are using an old Ukrainian barracks as our admin centre. It is about a five-minute walk. In the time it takes to get your badges set up, I'll be able to find someone from Taskforce A to speak to you."

"Leeson?"

The marine nodded.

They walked past long rows of tents, the mess hall and a series of demountable buildings with tall antennas on top.

The marine told them that the staff here had tripled in the last couple of months, and the base's incoherent layout was due to the rapid expansion.

Now that USSOT and Taskforce A were here too, more space had to be appropriated for their mounds of specialist equipment.

Danni nervously scanned the crowds for familiar faces.

They came to what appeared to a be series of portable armouries set up in shipping containers. The admin centre was just behind them.

The building was a one-story square slab of concrete that looked very old. Sitting against the perimeter fence, the admin centre was abundant with cracks, discolourations, and mould clinging to its sides. Menacing black bars protruded over its rectangular windows. Snow had piled up on its flat roof, and two US servicemen were shovelling it off.

Their marine escort swiped them into the waiting room.

It wasn't luxurious inside.

Plastic fold-out chairs lined the dank little room. There was a reception desk protected by bullet-proof glass, with a military policeman on the other side. He waved them over and then spoke into his microphone.

"Line up and enter the booth," he sighed, sounding

completely bored. "I will take a picture and process your card. Your government has sent all your forms pre-filled, so that will be all that's required of you."

Sigurd had to crane his neck forward to fit under the low roof. He promptly took a seat, and his chair splintered and cracked, collapsing beneath him.

Kane let out a hearty laugh at the Viking's expense.

"Mock the humiliation of others and find yourself equally humiliated," Sigurd stated knowingly.

"Is that the wisdom of an ancient Germanic king?" Kane asked, rolling his eyes.

Matt looked at Kane and said, "At least now I know your sarcasm runs in the family."

The receptionist scanned the group and said, "There is one missing - a Randall Dare."

"Oh, he won't be joining us," Mel informed the man.

"What happened to him?" Matt asked.

"Got sucked into a black hole," Kane answered.

"Right, so he's... dead?" Matt continued, rather callously.

"No," Kane replied. "At least Professor Selleck doesn't think so. He reckons that Randall accidentally opened a portal somewhere."

Everyone looked to Malcolm, who was sitting alone in the corner of the room, still pouring over the Necronomicon. He was furiously turning pages and saying strange phrases like 'Yog-Sothoth'.

"What's up with him?" Matt asked.

"He's enamoured with that book," Mel whispered, her voice

betraying her internal concern. "We need all the information we can get, considering the events of the past few days."

Matt shrugged. He was a man of action, happy to let the reading and learning be done by others.

Danni stepped forward and had her picture taken. She then went and sat beside Artemis, who looked lost in thought. She didn't really want to sit next to the goddess, but it was the only free seat.

The goddess turned to Danni, "This building represents everything I despise. A cold grey block made the home of process and order. This entire land we now sit in seems tarnished. The drums of war beat distantly but regularly. The forests have been poisoned. I loathe it."

Danni forced a smile and said, "We shouldn't be here for long."

"I feel the approaching footsteps of fate. I dread this quest to Africa to destroy the watchful eyes of the angels."

"Why?"

"Victory can only come at great cost. Even I am but a fly to be swatted by the Archangel Gabriel. We cannot afford to lose any gods, myself included, as each of us is essential for ending the reign of the angels. But more than this, do you remember the bridge in Niflheim?"

"Of course," Danni replied.

"Ever since I gave life to Sigurd, I have felt something... a presence drawing closer and closer. It is here now; I feel it. I am no longer a hunter but prey being stalked."

Danni thought about the vision Mel had at the party in Amsterdam. Of the creature that watched from an alien world.

"Is there any way we can get clarity of these laws of the gods?" Danni asked.

"To access one who has answers and knowledge from those times is impossible. I remember that not so long ago Zeus himself sought answers on the old rules of the primordials, and even he failed in his task."

Talking to Artemis was stressing Danni out. She had her own problems to worry about right now. Sure, they were tiny in comparison, but all of Artemis's issues would have to be faced when they arrived.

Fortunately, Artemis was then called up for a picture.

Soon, the entire party had white cards swinging on new lanyards around their necks.

The military policeman cracked open an internal door and ushered them towards a classroom.

Like a procession of oversized school children, they all sat behind desks in front of a grubby whiteboard and waited.

No one really talked much except Matt and Liam. They were like a couple of university guys abusing the term 'bro' as they discussed a failed date Matt had gone on with one of the US support staff. Danni giggled as she eavesdropped. Apparently, the night had ended with the woman throwing her drink in Matt's face. Matt, in his cultural ignorance, had been talking about how he missed his thongs, which American's called flip-flops. Thongs meant something else to them, and Matt had realised this after the fact.

There was a groan of old hinges as another new face entered the room.

It was a tall, muscular American with medium length brown hair and prominent sideburns. He hadn't shaved for a few days leaving a sprawling swathe of dark stubble coating his sharp rectangular jaw.

This man was dressed in PT gear darkened with sweat. His blue tank top and white basketball shorts sat in stark contrast to the dull colours of the classroom.

He was puffing and dabbing his face furiously with a towel.

"Sorry, guys. Didn't think you'd be here so early."

Liam shook the stranger's hand warmly, and Mel nodded a curt hello. Once again, Danni felt like the only AST member in the room who didn't know who this person was.

"My name is Lieutenant Commander Patrick Leeson, but everyone calls me Neanderthal," he said.

Danni was surprised to hear that he barely had a trace of an accent.

"I know you guys didn't get much of a chance to get caught up in Australia, so I'll try to be as thorough as possible. I recently joined your mission as a representative of the USA… and ended up flying around Heaven in a pair of winged Greek shoes.

"Needless to say, once I returned from the Dreamscape, my subsequent report generated some waves. Supernatural occurrences are one thing, but angels, gods and demons weren't accounted for. By executive order, Taskforce A was established. I hand-picked the team, and our first mission in Siberia was successful, with the help of Matt here, of course."

Matt looked smug.

"The mission ended with the known agents of Lucifer dead

and three werewolves taken into custody. Though it was unintended, we also achieved the purification of Joshua Dare's curse. Thanks to Brett Sayer, we know that was a goal for Operation Thunderking. The other goal of securing an artefact of Zeus is where we're currently at."

Sigurd spoke up. "These warriors of yours, Taskforce A, you say they are capable?"

"They are some of the best the US military has to offer," Neanderthal said, eyeing the massive Viking curiously.

"I would test them. I do not know what awaits in Utgard, but we will need warriors, I am sure."

"I'm guessing you are one of the late additions to the team, the Viking Sigurd. Just by looking at you, you couldn't be anyone else. If you have the time, we can arrange something. But I suspect you won't, as we have a helicopter waiting to get you to Germany to assist our team in uncovering this Gnitaheath," Neanderthal proposed as he glanced at Mel.

"We are standing down for the next two days for rest and recovery, so take him. He has been dead for a long time, so I think he can do without the break."

"Good," Neanderthal affirmed. "If the scenery hasn't changed too much, your knowledge will help us unearth it. Now, I know there are some civilians among you. Adams base is happy to accommodate you as long as you need."

"Woah, hold up, I am coming to Utgard," Kane stated.

"As am I," Malcolm added.

Sigurd laughed and slapped Kane on the back. "We will make a warrior of you yet!"

"Guys, please, this is a dangerous mission," Mel said.

Kane looked deeply offended. "I guess Josh is going on this mission?"

"Josh is probably the most powerful human on the planet right now," Neanderthal remarked, amused. "Based on the resemblance, I guess that you're his brother."

"Yep, the useless brother who isn't a supernatural monster or off in some other dimension fighting aliens with math!" Kane burst out.

Malcolm stood up and closed the Necronomicon for the first time in days. "We are all in this together, Mel. If this castle Utgard is the last free bastion of magic, you will need more than just military skill to unlock its secrets."

"Malcolm, look –"

"It is more than just logic," Malcolm said, cutting her off. "The path we are headed on is significant, and all of us here must walk it together."

Danni noticed Malcolm stroking the spine of the book as he talked. His eyes were sunken. The professor didn't look healthy.

"I agree with him," Artemis said simply, commanding the room. "Not for his words, but his obsession with that book. That book led us to the monster in the sunken city, whatever that thing was. And now, in the way dark magical items affect mortals, the book is using this man as a conduit. I'd heed his words if he says we should all be there. It means it is a place of significance for someone or something."

Malcolm looked offended, but Artemis was making his point, so he didn't interrupt.

Mel sighed. "Well, that argument actually makes me think it could be too dangerous… Malcolm, you are still you, right? You haven't been possessed or anything?"

"I am still very much me," Malcolm said, giving Artemis a dirty look. "The Necronomicon isn't alive. It has no will to manipulate me. It just holds information and secret truths. I can't tell you why yet… but I know all of this is linked. The power of Zeus, the sunken city, the sacred rules of the gods, that monster that was awakened in the temple… all of it. I feel that the answers are waiting for us in Utgard."

"Fine, all of us going. None of you had better die there." Mel pointed her finger straight at Kane, sounding defeated.

"How many Taskforce A members can we take?" Liam asked Neanderthal.

"Four. Captain Shear has reassigned the rest."

"I will take them to the old haunt of Fafnir with me. I will test their worth at Gnitaheath," Sigurd declared.

Neanderthal gave each of them a card assigning them to a tent. He assured everyone that they were perfectly warm and featured proper beds.

Then, Mel dismissed them.

Danni didn't even wait around to see if she had to sit in on her meetings with Liam and Neanderthal. There was someone here she wanted to find.

24

HARUKA AND JESSE

A s Danni left the sterile grey admin centre, she couldn't help but think it wasn't much of a briefing.

It had been more of a chance for this Neanderthal fellow to say hello. The team had already grown quite large, especially with the unexpected edition of Sigurd, and then Kane Dare.

Now, they'd added Matt Pyne and Neanderthal, too. Where would it end?

Her head buzzing with nervous energy, Danni decided the best thing to do would be to find her designated tent.

Teva headed off to the comms area while Kane and Sigurd made for the mess hall. Malcolm didn't bother to say goodbye, disappearing to continue his obsessive reading.

"16A," Danni muttered as she crunched through the light snow beside the rows of brown tents. She couldn't discern markings anywhere.

She paused by the nearest tent and began searching the flapping canvas for any indication of which number it was.

"Ah, excuse me," a small voice said.

Danni turned, and her eyes fell upon a stunningly beautiful woman wrapped in a warm khaki windbreaker. With her long black hair, vibrant green eyes and soft pale face, she looked quite out of place as a convoy of bulky military vehicles rumbled behind her.

"The numbers are on these little signs out front," the woman said, kicking the snow away from the tent's base. Her english was very good, though it didn't entirely hide the trace of a Japanese accent.

Sure enough, pegged into the ground were wooden stakes with letters and numbers burned into them. The snow had piled around most of them, making them almost invisible.

"Oh, thanks!" Danni beamed.

She brushed the white powder away with her hands to reveal this tent was 8A. Hers must've been a bit further down.

The stranger approached and offered a handshake. Danni grasped the black mitten with her bare hand and shook it vigorously.

"Danni Quinn, AST."

"Are you Australian?" the stranger asked, giving Danni a funny look. Danni got a distinct impression that this person knew exactly who she was.

"Yep, how can you tell?"

"Your accent is very strong. My name is Haruka."

Danni's mind lit up in an explosion of curiosity and jealousy. This was the werewolf, the one Josh had bit.

At once, an air of awkwardness sprung up between the women.

"So, you know Josh then?" Danni asked casually.

"I know him, yes. And I know of you. You are his ex-girlfriend. He has been very excited knowing you're coming, wouldn't stop talking about it actually…"

"Where is he?" Danni asked.

"Around somewhere. He likes to train with the Taskforce A people."

"How do you know Josh?" Danni asked abruptly.

She was thrown by just how gorgeous Haruka was, with her hair like silk and emerald eyes.

"I met him in Japan. We went on a date, and I got dragged into this world. Much like with you."

"A date?" Danni questioned.

"That's right," Haruka smiled. Her lips were twisted upwards, but her eyes were cold.

An uncomfortable silence hung in the air as Danni scrambled for something to say.

"I am lucky that Josh is here," Haruka said at last. "He has helped show me just how strong the werewolf curse makes you. I am stronger and faster than I ever could have imagined."

"Good for you," Danni thought.

"Why did he bite you?" Danni asked.

"He went to Siberia alone to rescue me, but they were

waiting for him. He knew they would experiment on him during the full moon, so he gave me a bite. It was my idea. The Molochtech people didn't expect it, and my werewolf allowed us to escape."

Haruka sounded quite proud of the whole affair.

"But didn't Taskforce A come in and rescue all of you?"

Haruka didn't respond, looking annoyed at the question.

"I'm so glad you both got out okay —" Danni said, with snide undertones, until she was cut off by a man's voice.

"All three of us, actually," the new person said from behind her. The voice was so familiar. She'd last heard it back in 2019.

Danni spun around to be confronted with the beaming face of Jesse Billiau.

"Jesse!" Danni gasped, jumping up and giving him a big hug.

Taller than Kane but still shorter than Sigurd, Jesse was a mountain of a man. A former Queensland cop, Jesse fought the Vatican's werewolf in Cairns and killed it with a silver bullet, but not before receiving some cursed bites.

Despite the cold, Jesse was wearing a tank top. His poor choice of attire displayed the horrendous scarring he'd received that night.

His right bicep showed rows of teeth marks and pulled flesh where jaws had clamped down on his skin. His left shoulder was much the same.

Danni remembered that the werewolf had broken his collarbone, but Jesse had healed and fought on.

Jesse was sporting an unkempt blonde beard and untamed hair. He wore blue sweatpants with socks and sandals. Something in his eyes showed he'd had a rough time last year.

"It's good to see you again, Danni. Look at you, working for the Australian Government."

"I know, times have changed," Danni laughed.

Jesse's eyes also radiated an unspoken kindness from them. That's how Danni knew that if he hadn't become involved in all this werewolf business, he would've been an excellent police officer.

"What are you doing now?" Jesse asked.

"I guess… looking for my tent," Danni responded. She didn't want to say 'hoping to find Josh' like some lovesick school girl.

"16A, you're just down there," Jesse stated, pointing to the right. "Let's go to the mess hall and catch up. Josh won't be done with his training for some time."

Jesse gave Danni a knowing look.

"Trust me, if he knew you were here, he'd come sprinting over."

Jesse's words seemed to sour Haruka's mood. She gave them both a curt farewell and wandered off.

Danni was quite glad to see the back of her.

"Haruka is lovely," Jesse said as he directed Danni towards the mess hall. "Although I worry she doesn't always understand that the werewolf curse is a curse, not a blessing."

"How has it been for you?" Danni asked softly.

"Tough," Jesse said.

"What happened that night? When you hit Liam and fled?"

"I had the Greek in the back of the car. He had two plane tickets on him, meant for him and the werewolf. They were taking some long-winded route back to the Vatican, assumedly to avoid detection. We made a deal and he kept his mouth shut. He wanted to take me as a replacement monster for the one I killed."

Danni hadn't actually met the Greek, but knew who he was. He was the other half of the duo who'd hunted Josh in 2019, trying to stamp out the werewolf curse. Danni didn't actually know his name, and based on Jesse still using 'the Greek', neither did he.

"We landed in Vietnam first and I made a break for it - into the forests away from civilisation, before the government could track me."

"You could get on a flight just like that?"

"No, the flights were for the next day. But I had my police ID on me, and the check-in person was more than happy to change them to a flight departing that night. It was all up to luck. I did my best to lose the government cars tracking us before going to the airport."

"Wow," Danni said.

They climbed some steps and entered the warmth of the mess hall. There was a line before a bain marie full of steaming hot dishes.

"Yeah, I went deep off the map, as remote as I could go. I was scared of what the curse had done. The Greek wasn't happy to be there with me, but he didn't want to let me go. He had to return to the Vatican with something."

"What happened to him?"

"He didn't survive my first full moon transformation," Jesse said sadly.

"Oh," Danni mumbled.

"I was horrified at what I'd done. I decided to stay as far away from innocent people as I could... though the Greek certainly wasn't innocent. Still, it wasn't easy. With each full moon that passed, I would wake up with no memory. Sometimes it was in small villages where the people had been massacred. On better occasions, it was in armed compounds where drugs were being manufactured. The werewolf can travel colossal distances in a night."

Danni could feel the weight of Jesse's guilt in his words.

"Hey, the werewolf isn't you, you know that right," Danni said softly.

"I've grappled with that a lot," Jesse said.

The mess hall was lit with warm orange lights. It was filled with white round tables that easily fit seven or eight people.

Jesse nodded to an elaborate looking self-serve coffee machine beside a plethora of mugs and foam cups. Danni shook her head; she didn't want anything that would keep her awake unnecessarily.

"I'll make you a hot chocolate. Trust me, you can't beat it in this weather," Jesse convinced Danni as she sat down.

It did sound like an excellent idea.

Jesse was right. When that warm chocolaty liquid touched Danni's lips, new life was breathed into her.

"Was I right, or was I right?" Jesse laughed.

"I'll give you this one," Danni smiled.

"This last week or so has been the first taste of freedom I've had in such a long time..."

It looked like the shaggy man was going to burst into tears, but Jesse regained his composure.

"On the positive side, at least you get to be a part of these big events with the rest of us," Danni reassured him.

"Yeah, I suppose it's for the best that the story of the werewolves in Cairns didn't end up being a simple tale of monsters in the moonlight."

Someone coughed loudly beside them. Both their heads turned to see the tall slim frame of Liam Sager standing just behind them.

The air was palpable with tension.

Jesse stood up and the two squared off.

"Constable Billiau," Liam said.

"Detective Sager," Jesse replied.

"I'm no longer a detective," Liam said. "Full time with the AST now; we don't really have titles."

"I figured you'd moved away from the feds. Can't do much police work when you're chasing me through the jungle."

"I almost got you so many times too. How you managed to slip away must've been down to sheer dumb luck."

"You were on his trail then?" Danni asked Liam.

"For most of 2020. I had to go back to spend periods at Down Under, but my primary mission was hunting Jesse through South East Asia." Liam rubbed the side of his head while he spoke. The memory of Jesse slamming it into the side of the car clearly lingered.

"It's funny. I was so desperate to avoid the AST I fell right into Molochtech's trap. They took me to Siberia and began experimenting on me," Jesse grumbled.

"You look fine, at least," Danni said.

"You should see my werewolf transformation. It is bizarre and mutated. I look like a proper monster, like I've been pieced together from different sized werewolves."

"Taskforce A secured samples of the God Particle and several Molochtech scientists. We can potentially purify your curse if we can get them to talk," Liam suggested, as if being a science experiment was a pleasant idea.

"No, it won't work. My curse is too distant, as you can guess. The God Particle will only serve to mutate me further. I overheard Viktor Petrov discuss it at length while I was chained up in Siberia."

"Well, regardless, I am glad to see we are on the same side," Liam stated.

"For now," Jesse mumbled, eyeing him suspiciously. "What will the AST do with us once Operation Thunderking is complete?"

"That is yet to be determined. This has been a learning experience for everyone. Rest assured, we will do right by you and Josh."

"What about Haruka?" Danni interjected.

"She is a problem for the Japanese Government."

"Isn't The Old World quite close with the government in Japan? Surely they will look after her?"

"The Old World can't be trusted," Liam said plainly. "We know Altior Fulgur personally assisted Vasilije Markovic. The cardinal told Josh everything. Altior doesn't know that we know yet, so we still have cards to play. The Old World doesn't know Haruka is a werewolf, and we will keep it that way for as long as possible."

Danni thought back to Ernst Carter's party and her conversation with the highest-ranking member of the Catholic

Church in the Netherlands. He'd stated that The Old World had helped Markovic out after the Church distanced itself from him. That must've been when Altior and Markovic met.

"On the plus side," Liam continued, "thanks to our werewolf friends here, now that Markovic is dead, Lucifer has lost most of his players from the board."

Danni grimaced. Lucifer's kiss still lingered in her mind. Was she his only remaining way back into this? No, it wasn't just her, there was still one Knight of Hell out there too.

As usual, when she thought about the experience in Hell, her fingers dived into her pocket to touch the smooth surface of the coin Astaroth had given her.

"All these plots and conspiracies. I'm happy to work with the AST for now, just because I don't want to see the world ending. When this is all over, don't make us enemies again," Jesse said, shaking his head.

Liam absorbed his words and answered, "I'll do my best not to."

The two men shook hands.

Liam turned and walked away as Jesse sat back down.

"You seem quite mistrusting," Danni observed.

"You should be too. Think about it. In this mission, there is a chance that anyone could swoop in at the last minute and take the power for themselves, assuming the ritual is all set up. The Americans, the Australians, The Old World, Altior Fulgur... who knows what any of them want? Even the old gods, who are apparently behind all of this, aren't to be trusted. What are they in it for?"

Again, Danni's mind snapped to Artemis, instructing her not to tell anyone about Lucifer's kiss. Maybe Jesse had a point.

"We just don't know, though," Danni shrugged.

"I'm worried about Josh," Jesse said quietly.

"Why?"

"Because he is the pure curse. I've read the Operation Thunderking documentation, as you have. It says the gods will designate a person to perform the ritual and take the vacant position of Zeus. What does that mean for Josh? Will he be destroyed as part of the ritual? Or will he have to perform it himself and become a pawn in a godly game?"

Danni hadn't thought about that element of it.

If the archangels got a hold of Josh so that one of them could perform the ritual, they wouldn't hesitate in sacrificing him. Danni knew that none of the Greek gods thought they could complete the ritual themselves, but the angels and humans could.

"Josh could be in great danger," Danni murmured.

"Keep eyes in the back of your head," Jesse said, barely louder than a whisper.

Danni accepted Jesse's warning. They were small fish in a game with sharks.

The pair drained their mugs in silence.

"Alright," Danni said, standing up and pushing her chair in. "I'm gonna go find my luggage and set up my tent."

"They are surprisingly comfortable," Jesse informed her, leaning back in his chair. "It's great to see you again after all this time."

Danni repeated the sentiment and strode out of the mess

hall, feeling rather uneasy about that conversation.

Melissa was doing her best to lead them down the right path. After all, she had godly sight. The Oracle of Delphi could literally see any conspiracies happening around them; she was sure Mel wouldn't lead their small AST team astray.

Finding her way back to the tent rows, she quickly found 16A and was relieved to see her suitcase sitting in front of it. She brushed the snow off and thrust it inside.

Danni stepped in to see a quilted single bed standing on patchy brown grass.

It'd do.

Of all the exotic destinations they'd visited these last few weeks, Ukraine certainly wasn't ranking highly on the accommodation front. She closed the zip to keep the warmth in.

As soon as she sat down on the bed, she heard her zip sliding back up.

Like a booming echo from another life, a voice pierced her tent.

"Ah, hello… Danni?"

Danni froze. She knew that voice all too well.

A head peeked into her tent.

"Hi," Danni breathed. "Come in."

The man awkwardly fumbled inside, battling with the zipper before sitting across from Danni.

"Josh," Danni stuttered.

Joshua Dare looked straight into Danni's eyes, lost for words.

They were reunited at last.

25

REUNITED

ADAMS BASE, UKRAINE
- FEBRUARY 5 -

anni and Josh stared at each other for a long moment. Neither spoke. A lifetime had passed by in the year that they hadn't seen each other. Both were responsible for the triumphs, misfortunes and adventures of each other's lives.

"I have missed you," Josh said at last.

"I've missed you too," Danni stammered. A small tear ran down her cheek. "Everything has been so surreal since I met you…"

Danni felt like she was looking into a mirage. Josh had clearly gotten a haircut sometime in the last month, with the sides being too short and the top way too long. A light beard had formed around his jaw, with a few of the hairs already turning orange among the sea of black. It was in his eyes that he looked different. Those sparkling brown eyes held a confidence in them that Danni hadn't seen before. While on the outside they looked sunken and tired, within their depths were the embers of a great fire. Joshua Dare, it seemed, had finally adjusted to his life as a monster.

Josh moved from his seat opposite Danni and sat down right next to her. He wrapped his arm around her while Danni leaned in close to him.

Instantly, she was back on the banana farm in Tully, laughing with Josh after a hard day's work. Everything about him, his warmth and even his smell seemed so familiar; so welcoming.

"Where do we even begin?" Josh asked slowly.

"I don't know," Danni replied.

They sat just like that for a long moment.

"Let's go back to the start. That night in Cairns, the night they caught me," Josh suggested.

Danni suddenly felt a burst of anger well up in her chest. She pulled away from Josh and slapped him across the face with a resounding WHACK.

"How could you go without me? I became a criminal and fugitive for you!"

"Woah!" Josh said rubbing his face. "It was dangerous! I wasn't going to put you in harm's way again."

"So, you just drive off and leave a note! I can't believe you!"

Danni crossed her arms and looked down. She knew she must be giving off the impression of a pouting child, but she didn't care.

"Well, what happened?" Josh asked carefully, hoping not to anger her again.

"I got an offer from Mel to join the ASIO and ASIS training program because of my exposure to the supernatural. The AST cleared my name with the local cops and I got left with nothing. The Green Cap wouldn't take me back. The banana farm stopped production for a while after Ellen's death and I felt too responsible to go back there."

Danni saw a pang of guilt cross Josh's face. She was sure he felt somewhat responsible for the Tully farmhand's death in 2019.

"So, you did the course, obviously?"

"Yeah, it was tough but I got through... then Brett Sayer came along and put me on this mission."

"So... you aren't seeing anyone?"

Danni smiled. It was funny that of all the things Josh wanted to know right away; that was it.

"No," she answered. "Are you?"

"No, I don't really meet people too often," Josh laughed.

"That Haruka girl is very pretty," Danni stated, frowning.

"Haruka is a werewolf too," Josh said, sounding a little uncomfortable.

"You bit her?" Danni asked.

"I did," Josh mumbled, rubbing the back of his neck.

"I hope that was all the biting involved," Danni proclaimed sharply. She didn't know why she was suddenly so aggressive. She had a year's worth of pent-up emotions that were spilling out.

"I put Haruka in this situation, just like I did you," Josh replied solemnly. "But we are all in it together now."

"Yeah, I guess so… What happened to you in the time we've been apart?"

"It is crazy to talk about. I've been to Heaven. Like, real Heaven in the sky with angels and everything."

"Wow," Danni smirked. "I've been to Hell. Met Satan. Rescued a legendary Viking warrior, no big deal."

Josh laughed. "Well, I met the embodiment of Ragnarok in Heaven, the destroyer wolf Fenrir. It's a pretty big deal."

"WELL I helped discover an underwater city that is hundreds of millions of years old."

"Really?" Josh's eyes were burning with curiousity.

"I don't know about hundreds of millions… Malcolm is the person to talk to about that. I did see Artemis punch a fallen angel into the city though."

Josh laughed. "I saw Apollo fly down from the sky and impale a fallen angel with his sword."

"Are we just going to sit here one-upping each other?"

"Its just interesting. Who would've thought this would be our lives?" Josh said.

"We are lucky in a way, aren't we?" Danni mused, leaning back against Josh.

"Maybe," Josh shrugged. "Though we aren't at the end of this story yet, and the situation seems to be evolving rapidly."

There was a pause in the conversation.

"I thought about you all the time. You've been in the back of my mind for years. I tried to push you out. I thought that was the only way I could commit to this life. But you wouldn't go," Josh said at last.

A huge smile washed over Danni's face.

"I'm glad you're back," Josh grinned.

"Me too," Danni whispered. She looked up at him.

Danni saw concern in his eyes that hadn't been there a moment ago.

"Can I tell you something? Just between us?" Josh blurted.

"Okay…" Danni answered cautiously.

"I made a deal with Fenrir, the destroyer I met in Heaven. No one knows about it but me, not even the gods. He gave me the power to control the werewolf form outside of the full moon."

"That's pretty cool," Danni said. "Matt Pyne said you'd somehow gotten mastery of it."

"Yep, when Taskforce A raided Molochtech in Siberia, they downloaded all of their security footage. They saw I could bring on the transformation of my own accord.

"I can pretty much transform whenever I want. But that's not the concerning part. Fenrir also gave me a choice. You know the mission, to take the position of Zeus? Fenrir told me I could perform the ritual and take his place instead. I already have all the pieces… but it would mean I become a destroyer like he is."

Danni let that all soak in. "When you assume the empty position of a god, I didn't think you became like them, you just got their power or something."

"Well, if I can explain it how I understand it; Zeus was the king of the gods. All this power was flowing up to him, and when he vanished, it just kind of pooled there in the cosmos. If someone takes his empty position, they'll get all that power without any defined purpose. Fenrir is different, he had a destiny. If I were to assume him, I fear I would have to adopt that destiny. Or, it would adopt me."

"But you don't have to take the place of Fenrir, right?"

"No."

"Then don't," Danni said simply. "Don't overthink these great cosmic choices until you are faced with them."

"You are the only one who knows this. I've been dying to get it off my chest."

"Okay, in the spirit of sharing," Danni said nervously, "I have a similar situation."

Josh raised his eyebrows.

"When I was in Hell, Lucifer kissed me."

Josh's jaw dropped.

"Its not like what you think," Danni continued. "I felt a strange energy wash over me. He said when the time comes to perform the ritual, I need to call on him. I think Lucifer made me a vessel for him. I'm afraid that if I'm there when the ritual is performed, a giant three-headed demon will come out of me."

"Three heads? And no one knows about this?" Josh murmured.

"Artemis does, but she told me to keep it to myself and I'm not sure why."

"Great, potentially the fate of the world hangs in the balance and there are secrets everywhere," Josh said sarcastically.

Danni smiled. Same old Josh.

"Who is going to perform the ritual?" Danni asked.

"I got told they would find someone suitable, but I think because I carry the pure curse, it will be me."

"Don't forget us little people when you're a god," Danni laughed, punching Josh playfully.

Josh wrapped his arms around her and she squirmed in his grasp. Danni managed to turn herself around so she was face to face with Josh.

They looked into each other's eyes; two long lost lovers reunited. Danni leaned in and kissed Josh passionately and deeply, then, noticing something odd, she withdrew. Josh had one hand wrapped in a thick leather glove.

"What's with the glove? You think you're a pop star or something now?" she asked playfully.

"Oh, right," Josh said, his eyes lighting up. "That's how I gained control of the werewolf curse. I had to sacrifice my hand to Fenrir for his blessing."

Josh pulled the glove off. Sitting on his wrist was the most unusual appendage Danni had ever seen. It was shaped like an ordinary hand, though it was bronze and entirely devoid of all but the simplest detail. It looked heavy and very fake.

Then, Josh wiggled his fingers, and the metal moved like it was living flesh.

"Pretty cool, hey?" Josh smiled.

"How did you get this?"

"A god made it for me; specifically, Hephaestus, God of the Forge. Watch this!"

Josh nudged Danni off him and stood up. Danni stepped back as he stretched his arm out.

His bronze hand began to vibrate. Without any warning, a shining silver sword burst forth from Josh's hand. He gripped it around the hilt.

"This is Vargr Muor. I named it myself," he remarked happily.

"That is one fine looking sword you somehow have hidden in your hand," Danni joked, suppressing her shock. It was an impressive magic trick. She moved in close to study it.

It looked devastatingly sharp and had Nordic runes inscribed along the blade. The ancient symbols were identical to the tattoos Sigurd had on his ribs. The metal was otherworldly, with a similar sheen to Apollo's golden sword.

"This belonged to an unknown Norse god. It was jammed in Fenrir's mouth so long it has become an artefact of his. I pulled it free."

"If only it belonged to Zeus," Danni muttered.

"I did hear that you guys haven't gone too well in your mission," Josh said, swinging the sword back and forth.

"Yep. We have been going the wrong direction pretty much the whole time."

The sword sunk back into Josh's magical hand, and he sat back down.

"It's okay, we can all do it together."

"You said that sword was an artefact of Fenrir, but what about the other things we need? Like his blood and a link to his power?"

"When I pulled the sword free from his mouth, I got spattered with his blood. I've still got the clothes in my luggage. And my ability to transform at will is my link to his power."

"Hmm, easy as that, hey?"

"Yeah, easy as that," Josh smiled. Danni could tell he wanted to kiss her again.

"Got much on over the next two days?" Danni asked him.

"Not a gosh darn thing," Josh replied.

"I guess we will have to use our time wisely."

They kissed again, though this time it was like some blockage had shifted. The second Danni's lips touched his, there was an explosion of fireworks in her brain. Her senses went into overload. She could feel the rough hairs of his beard against her face. Her nostrils were filled with a forgotten but comforting scent. It was the smell of Joshua Dare, a smell unique to him.

Their embrace carried all the passion of star-crossed lovers in it. Moments ago there relationship had been a quiet ember, but now it was a roaring flame.

Danni could feel Josh pushing against her. Her hands ran up and down his muscular frame.

This was the man with the monster inside; the man who'd dragged her into this life. She could feel from the way he breathed that he'd missed her as much as she'd missed him. Not even the raw power of time could dull the passion in that moment.

Danni withdrew and looked into Josh's eyes. She didn't see the shadow of a monster behind them. She saw something else. She saw the flicker of destiny. Danni knew she was where she needed to be.

· · · · ·

THE TWO-DAY REST PERIOD was the most welcome break

from work Danni had ever experienced.

The only person who didn't get to enjoy any time off was Sigurd, and he didn't desire it anyway. The US military were able to find an appropriate sling so that the Viking could carry Apollo's golden sword on his back. Both Mel and Artemis had been fine with him bearing the weapon, as he was the only one could effectively use it.

It was late on that first afternoon that the Viking had been whisked off to Germany with four Taskforce A members to aid the search for the lost location of Gnitaheath.

The USSOT representatives in Ukraine made no secret that they were happy to lend people to the search, as long as they could take possession of any dragon bones they uncovered.

Both Mel and Liam happily agreed. They decided they wouldn't even report the discovery of any remains to Brett, it was too much hassle and not relevant to the mission. Plus, once they considered the amount the Americans had done for them, it seemed like a fair trade.

Mel spoke to everyone individually over the break, not wanting to hold any group meetings. She stated that once the horn was found, they'd all rendezvous with Sigurd in Germany. Until that happened, their time was totally their own, to use as they saw best.

It seemed Danni was the only one who hadn't done any research into Sigurd's life, so, when at last she was willing to seperate herself from Josh, she corrected that. What she found was very intriguing. Sigurd was one of the most celebrated figures in Germanic and Scandanavian legend and his legacy still lived on into the modern day. His story was weaved through European history.

When the German empire was founded in 1871, they used Sigurd as a unifying figure, as his story offered several parallels to the German cause. They directly equated Sigurd re-forging his father's sword in myth to Otto von Bismark reuniting the German nation.

Several articles Danni read tried to identify Sigurd with a few well-known Viking age figures, but the dates were all wrong. Since Danni knew Sigurd had been in Hell before the angel's attacked in 337 AD, he couldn't have been a person with a different name in the sixth or ninth centuries. Regardless of how he'd been adapted, it was undeniable that Sigurd was a true leader and warrior who'd died at the hands of those he'd trusted. Hell hath no fury like a woman scorned, and Sigurd had scorned a couple of women in his time.

While Danni researched Earth's mightiest warrior, there was another who spent all of his time with his face buried in a book. Malcolm was getting more and more sickly, reclusive and paranoid.

Late one night, Danni had walked past his tent to hear him softly repeating the phrase, *"The crawling chaos is coming… Nyarlathotep…"*

While that was certainly worrisome, Danni's reunion with Josh had pushed all other concerns from her mind.

Being with Josh again made Danni feel like she was stepping into the past. She was taken back to a time when her life was simple, with no gods, angels or devils lurking about. They laughed together and fell right back into old patterns. The best thing about Josh was that Danni genuinely enjoyed his company. His sarcasm always made her laugh.

Josh and Kane's reunion was also amusing, with Kane being

unable to hide his envy as Josh transformed back and forth from his werewolf form, calling upon his divine sword while doing so. The brothers spent a lot of time reminiscing; though Josh seemed quite shaken when he learned of Randall's odd disappearance. His experience with the supernatural wasn't positive, and he was deeply concerned for his youngest brother.

After two days of almost normality, the call came in.

The US military team, under the guise of being amateur archaeologists, had dug up some ancient stonework in an area Sigurd had identified. Buried deep below the ground, in a locked strong box, was a peculiar golden horn fashioned in the shape of a wolf.

Melissa sent out word for everyone to kit up. She issued orders for all operatives (who were legally allowed to carry a gun) to have regular rounds and silver bullets on them. The Taskforce A soldiers also had bullets designed with holy water tips, but they weren't willing to share them.

Matt Pyne had a sniper rifle disassembled in a purpose-built case, and Neanderthal had more weapons on him than any person could ever need. The rest just had handguns.

Josh, Haruka and Jesse had supernatural powers at their disposal.

Kane had nothing, and Malcolm, as always, clutched the Necronomicon close to his breast.

Bracing against the winter wind, they waited for three HUGHES OH-6 Cayuses to spin up. The small, sleek helicopters were owned by USSOT, and had been given specifically to Taskforce A for their operations in Ukraine.

Once they'd clambered on board, facing the freezing gale produced by the whirring blades, the helicopters zoomed them towards Germany. They crossed spectacular rivers, valleys and streams. There was beauty beyond parallel in the landscape that raced below.

It took a few hours, but they soon arrived at the impromptu archeological site by the River Rhine.

The site was in remote Germany, so they could fly in and out without attracting too much attention. Something all of them were banking on. Awkward encounters with the German Government would only serve to slow things down.

The River Rhine wove its way through mountainous countryside thick with vegetation, north of the city of Cologne. Towards the south it flowed beside grasslands and areas cultivated for farming.

It was in this southern region, near the Pulsbachklamm walking track, that Sigurd had remembered the site of his legendary battle with Fafnir. The trees were less dense here making excavation work easier.

Judging by the extent of the digging Danni saw on approach; it had taken quite a while to find the exact spot. Danni was horrified to see half a dozen shovels plunged into the dirt, meaning it had all been done by hand.

They zoomed low over a series of tents and a large grey marquee sheltering the cooking area from the elements.

Sigurd, shirtless and coated with sweat, despite the cool temperature, enthusiastically waved as the helicopters circled, searching for a suitable clearing to land in.

Danni noticed a small object glinting in his right hand. Sigurd had the horn.

At last, it was time to secure the artefact of Zeus and complete the mission.

26

THE JOURNEY TO
UTGARD

Aslight drizzle had begun, causing most of the military diggers and Taskforce A soldiers to take cover under the marquee. A few of the workers, wearing dirty overalls, scrambled to place plastic sheets over long white objects they'd unearthed. They must've found dragon bones.

The helicopters didn't wait around, dropping Mel's team and soaring off to refuel. The AST operatives rushed to join the others undercover as the sudden shower intensified.

Neanderthal pulled his four Taskforce A men aside to speak to them in private, as Melissa addressed her team.

"First, excellent work with the horn, Sigurd," Mel nodded.

"This land has changed much, yet the hills by the river have forever been imbedded in my memory," he replied.

"Looks like you had to dig quite deep," Liam noted, surveying the various holes around them.

"It was in this spot, untold years ago, that I dug a hole and waited for the slithering beast Fafnir to journey towards the river. The dragon spewed poison, making him unapproachable from the front. There is always a way to defeat an enemy, no matter how overpowering they seem."

"A good lesson to remember as we embark on a journey into the unknown," Melissa stated, taking back control of the conversation. "We are not going to Utgard as hostiles to its leader, nor are we going to rob him. Whatever we encounter there, keep your composure and do not accidentally insult our host."

She shot a sharp look at Matt, who feigned hurt.

Josh moved next to Danni and put his gloved hand in hers.

Other than the Taskforce A soldiers, the rest of Mel's gang was dressed in civilian clothing. Melissa was explicit that they shouldn't go in looking like an army.

Matt had his sniper in its long case at his side. The rest of them didn't have any baggage, other than the weapons equipped to their covert belts, sitting snugly beneath their shirts and sweaters.

Sigurd addressed the group. The hilt of Apollo's sword stuck out at a diagonal behind his head. "Remember, Skyrmir wanted to test Thor's powers when the Aesir arrived in Utgard. He will not do the same for mortals. The giant will use us for entertainment, but he will not make his challenges impossible. Keep your wits about you and fight strong!"

Neanderthal approached Mel and asked, "Where are we going from here?"

"Somewhere quiet," Melissa said, looking to Sigurd.

The rain was falling harder now. The small rays of sun that had been poking through the clouds were entirely blocked by ominous grey clouds.

Danni noticed Sigurd's eyes kept flicking to Josh. The pair hadn't met yet, so Danni moved to make introductions. Sigurd, however, beat her to it.

"Who are you?" the imposing Viking asked Josh.

"Josh," he responded, looking unsure.

"You look incredibly familiar. Like a vision from another life," Sigurd mused as he studied Josh's face.

"I get that all the time," Josh winked at Danni, who chuckled.

"Memories of old conquests came back to me, though I can't quite place them. I am certain we have met!" Sigurd said, his face etched with frustration.

"I can assure you we haven't. I'd remember you," Josh stated dryly.

A clap of thunder from above brought an abrupt end to the odd exchange.

"Will this rain matter?" Liam asked above the steady downpour plummeting into the tarp above them.

Sigurd frowned. "When I used the horn, it was in a far distant land in a moment devoid of the wind or any sound at all."

"Can we loophole this?" Danni suggested.

"What do you mean?" Melissa asked.

"Well, if you only need to hear silence; if the silence is

subjective, we can just put soundproof headphones on. I can see a container full of them just over there."

Everyone turned and looked across the grass to one of the nearby tents. Sure enough, it was chock-full of military grade headphones.

"Good idea, Danni," Liam said, looking very impressed.

"Do we each need to blow on the horn?" Jesse asked from the back of the group.

"No, the horn creates a runic circle a few metres in diameter, then everything in that circle will get pulled through. We will just need to huddle together," Sigurd answered.

"Alright, let's do this," Mel ordered.

Moments later, on a flat expanse of damp grass by the marquee, the group stood wet and uncomfortably close together.

Sigurd stood right in the middle, with multiple people pressed up to him.

The Viking pressed the small horn to his lips and blew.

A piercing sound came from it, temporarily overpowering the rain. Despite the high quality of the sound-proof headphones each of them wore, the noise cut through like a knife in butter.

Black lines began burning into the grass beneath the party, weaving around each other and intersecting as they created an elaborate Nordic pattern. It seemed the entire group just fit within the small confines, though the huddle got tighter as Kane struggled to keep his toes within the circumference.

When the intricate drawing was completed, rainbow-coloured energy began fizzling from the lines. After a few seconds, it became a waterfall of energy, flowing upwards to the sky. It was beautiful, like they were embraced by the northern lights in all their glory.

Danni's feet lifted from the ground as she started floating upwards. As she climbed higher, her speed increased.

The sky shattered like glass, and Danni unexpectedly fell a few feet into a sea of tall wild grass. The grey skies of Germany were gone, replaced with bright blues stretching as far as the eye could see.

The uncomfortable compression returned as the huddle arrived. Sigurd lost his balance, toppling over and triggering a domino effect. Half the party fell flat on their faces.

Danni, being one of the people knocked over, stumbled to her feet after pushing the heavy body of Jesse off her.

"Wow," she breathed.

Standing tall and proud in the endless grass ocean was the castle of Utgard. Other than its smaller size, it looked identical to how she'd seen it in Thor's story.

Castle Utgard had been built on a polygonal plan, with circular towers on each angle, topped with sapphire blue domes. Teva whispered that it looked inspired by Renaissance era architecture. Danni admired the thick walls of grey brick that sparkled in the blazing sun. It was enchanting. Its front gate (looking a bit too tall for human entry), however, was made of black iron and appeared supremely uninviting.

There were no trees, just the infinite sea of wild grass. The castle stood singular and beautiful against the blue and green backdrop.

Danni removed her headphones and heard the soft rustling

of wind through grass. She breathed the clean air in deep, which was ripe with magic, and let it flow into her.

Teva had a compressed hiking backpack in one of his jacket pockets. He pulled it from its small casing and unfurled it. It was just large enough to fit everyone's headphones inside.

Sigurd moved to the front of the group. "Follow me. Allow me to speak first with the Lord of Utgard, Skrymir. Goddess Artemis, please walk with me."

Artemis moved up next to Sigurd.

The goddess was once again dressed so startlingly like a mortal it was easy to forget she was even there. Ever since the events under the sea, she hadn't said much. It was like there was an internal dread constantly eating at her.

As they approached the giant's gate, it began to raise. Someone knew they were coming. The Taskforce A soldiers were alert, constantly scanning for any sign of a threat.

The gate led them into a wide grey courtyard. Giant gargoyles leered down at them from their perches atop tall Romanesque columns.

Another giant door, looking like it was cut from an unblemished slab of a singular gleaming stone, creaked open to reveal Skrymir's grand hall. Much like Thor and Loki had done an age ago, the AST team entered with looks of amazement.

The entire hall was arched, with upper balconies and off-shoots leading into distant parts of the castle. The roof was lined with gold and decorated similarly to the Sistine Chapel. Only these images showed the stories of giants in a frozen land.

A very real giant sat impressive and foreboding on his

throne not far ahead, curiously observing the strangers.

The court was abuzz with activity, all of which ceased when the party entered. Odd humanoid creatures stopped their chatter and gawked.

Danni recognised some as dwarves, and different types of elves from Norse mythology. Some wore long hooded robes and others were dressed in elaborate finery. Whispers began following Danni's troupe down the hall.

There were also several humans present, and judging by their dress, they were preserved from a time long since passed.

Sigurd confidently marched them forward towards the giant's throne. They passed another door, one that looked rather out of place in the side of the hall. It was a magnificent blue, as blue as the sky, but didn't seem to have a handle. Danni thought she felt an ominous energy coming from it; felt that its shining exterior masked a forbidden interior.

Her attention was swiftly drawn from the blue door to the figures flanking the Lord of Utgard.

One was a human, so perfect in shape and proportion, that he looked cut from stone. He had no veins, moles or freckles. He also had no irises or pupils in his blank eyes, and the only imperfection on him was a terrifying scar over his lower abdomen. All he wore was a patterned loin cloth with a golden belt. There was something else, too… Some unseen factor that made him difficult to look at it; almost as if the air warped around him and the light bent in unnatural ways. Danni had to look away to preserve her sanity.

The other figure was far more threatening. This man looked South American, like he was Aztec or Mayan. His face was decorated in blue war paint. He had a royal diadem on his head and nose ring jutting from this left nostril. He wore a waistcoat and cape and was armed with primitive feathered weapons.

Danni noticed that Artemis couldn't pull her gaze from the man in the loincloth. She must've known him.

Skrymir himself looked much as he did in Sigurd's story of Thor and Loki. He wasn't dressed like Utgarder-Loki, instead like the wandering giant they'd encountered in the woods. He was about sixteen feet tall and draped in an unblemished white robe. He had long silver hair and a matching beard. His eyes were as blue as the sky door they'd just passed. He had simple sandals on his feet and his fingers were decorated with an assortment of large rings, each with gems so large they had to be magical in nature.

Skrymir got to his feet and beamed at Sigurd.

"Sigurd, slayer of Fafnir! You have returned at last to become my mortal champion!"

"Lord Skrymir," Sigurd bowed formally.

Following his lead, everyone else knelt before the ruler of Utgard. Danni, Jesse and Josh were very awkward about it. This kind of royal protocol wasn't common place in regular Australian society.

"Rise, Sigurd. Such formality is not needed here! Who accompanies you?"

Artemis stepped forward. "I am Silver Artemis, Goddess of the Hunt. I journey with these mortals in pursuit of a common purpose."

"Artemis, your name has reached me through legend. Always good to see the old gods. You would know my dear friend

Prometheus here?"

The man with the vacant eyes walked towards Artemis and embraced her.

"Dear Artemis, I have not seen you since the wedding of Peleus and Thetis. It pleases me to know you survived the long dark years we've faced."

"Prometheus, I am surprised to see you here. You vanished without a trace so long ago."

"After I was saved from my tens of thousands of years of punishment, Zeus never truly welcomed me back among the gods. The ancient people who worshipped me were long gone; their halls quiet and their cities emptied. I left the Greek lands and journeyed across the world. Life took me to the Aesir, and eventually I found Utgard and Skrymir. We have been firm friends ever since."

"A titan, standing at the side of a giant's throne doesn't look right," Artemis whispered.

"I have my reasons for lingering here," Prometheus said reassuringly, but also quite cryptically.

"*So, this a titan, one level above the gods,*" Danni thought. No wonder she couldn't perceive him properly.

Danni noticed that Mel was observing the titan sourly, with her hand pressed on her gut.

"Let me introduce the other fellow standing here," Skrymir announced.

The silent Aztec warrior didn't step forward.

"This is the Aztec God Quetzalcoatl. While in my hall he must exist in human form, as per my rules."

"You would command gods?" Artemis asked incredulously.

Danni suddenly heard a hoarse whisper in her head. It was Prometheus, and by the looks of it he was speaking telepathically to the entire group.

"Skrymir is more powerful than you can imagine. Tread carefully in this place."

The warning in his voice was powerful.

Sigurd quickly changed the topic. "Skrymir, we have come with a request. We seek an artefact of the God Zeus. I believe you have one in your collection."

The giant raised his bushy eyebrows and pondered the request.

Danni felt the hairs stand up on the back of her neck. There was an unfriendly gaze in here, but it wasn't coming from the giant.

She scanned the hall and saw someone out of place.

Standing in the shadow of a tall pylon was a brown-skinned bald man wearing jewelry reminiscent of the Egyptian pharaohs.

Everything was off about the Egyptian. He had a demonic presence and his stare clouded Danni's mind. He looked from her to Josh, then to Artemis. Danni thought she saw the hint of a smile cross his face.

Skrymir's booming voice caused Danni to turn from the unfriendly figure back to the conversation.

"I am willing to part with my artefact of long missing Zeus, for a price…"

Sigurd nodded. He'd been spot on with his assessment of Skrymir.

"Who are these mortals?" the giant asked.

Sigurd took a step to the side and Melissa approached.

"Lord Skrymir, my name is Melissa Pythia, the Oracle of Delphi. My team includes people from the lands of Australia and the United States of America. We primarily work in fighting the supernatural and paranormal. I –"

Skrymir held up his hand to silence her.

"Supernatural, eh? I have an idea. Quetzalcoatl, prepare the stadium! Prometheus, send word to all who dwell in Utgard. Today, we have games!"

A cheer went up from the elves and dwarves in the great hall.

"I sense something of the old gods about some of you. Lycanthropes, I'm guessing. Werecreatures always have a stink to them," Skrymir said, scanning the group. "This will be a lot of fun."

"What would you have us do?" Artemis asked Skrymir.

"I'd have one of you win my challenge. That person can take my artefact, you have my word."

Everyone looked incredibly nervous. That was everyone except Malcolm, who had the Necronomicon open and was muttering quietly.

"What can we expect, Sigurd?" Danni whispered as she inched over to him.

"I do not know."

"Preparations will be made quickly; I will send you to the antechamber to wait for the arena to open!" Skrymir said, very enthusiastically.

"Arena?" Haruka squeaked from the back.

The giant snapped his fingers, and the entire group warped from the great hall into a walled chamber. They were trapped.

27

THE GAMES OF SKRYMIR

UTGARD
- FEBRUARY 8 -

The high chamber was lit with blazing torches. The room was semi-circular, with its only distinguishing feature an ominous black gate on the far wall. It looked like the antechamber had been constructed entirely out of large slabs of roughly hewn grey stone. Its dark interior sat as a stark contrast to the perfect exterior of the castle they'd seen from the grass sea.

Danni had the irrational fear that the gate could open up and spew out unknown horrors. This must've been how the ancient Roman gladiators felt all those millennia ago. When the gates to the Colosseum opened, did they know if they would face men or beasts? Here, in the hidden lair of the giant Skrymir, anything could be waiting for them.

Danni steeled her nerve. She was not alone in this and took comfort in that.

"We can all get through this. He said arena, so I expect a battle. Take the time to analyse your foe and fight smart," Mel addressed the room.

"What if he sends foes we can't beat?" Matt asked.

"There is no sport in that. He said the victor could claim the prize, so there has to be a way to win."

"That is the most optimistic outlook," Josh mumbled, perhaps louder than intended.

"When Thor came here, he was given impossible challenges. For us, it will not be so. I trust in the goodwill of Skrymir," Sigurd stated.

There was a pop, and the divine figure of Prometheus appeared in the room. He moved towards Artemis and whispered something to her. He then turned and addressed the crowd.

"Skrymir will make good on your request to claim his artefact of Zeus. He will allow the winner or winners of this game to take it. If you do win, that is."

"What waits for us on the other side of that gate?" Sigurd asked.

"As per your introduction, you are all trained to combat the supernatural. The Lord of Utgard wishes to give you a fighting chance. Just do your jobs."

There was a sound in the background. Malcolm was pacing back and forth, still muttering to himself. His eyes were bloodshot and sweat dripped from his brow. The professor looked worse than ever, though everyone was now more concerned with the upcoming battle.

Danni looked at Malcolm. The Necronomicon's negative influence was still growing, sending him mad.

"At least we have Artemis," Liam murmured. "She should be able to obliterate whatever we face."

A few of the Taskforce A soldiers beside him nodded.

"Artemis will not be competing," Prometheus informed them, his empty stone-like eyes snapping to the blonde Australian.

"But she is part of our mission to get the artefact of Zeus," Mel protested.

"She is a god. She does not have to prove her worth. The rest of you do."

"Well, then we fight together. We are all highly-trained; we can do this."

Danni suspected Mel was trying to reassure herself as much as the rest of them.

"You will fight in pairs," Prometheus stated. "The last pair standing will have the opportunity to run the gauntlet and claim the artefact. Should your partner fall and you succeed, you will continue alone."

Danni gulped. Who would she get? And what did 'run the gauntlet' mean?

Prometheus scanned the room. "I have all of your names. When you are called, approach the gate. If you attempt to enter when you are not called, you will die. The rules are simple; win and continue, lose and see your journey end. You may use whatever you have on you. Good luck."

Prometheus disappeared.

Josh moved over to Danni and whispered, "I hope we get each other."

Danni nodded. Josh's ability to transform at any time would give him a considerable advantage.

"Hey guys," an unfamiliar voice said.

One of the unnamed Taskforce A agents had unclipped his military helmet and removed his balaclava.

"My name is Chris, callsign Rathbone. I don't know what we will face on the other side of the gate, so I guess you should get to know us before we do."

Everyone murmured hello. The other three heavily armed soldiers did the same.

"Troy," the second one said. He had a square face, a short military haircut and grey bags under his eyes. He looked like a no-nonsense kind of guy.

"Fomiatti," the next one said. He was only young, but had the severe expression held by those with an old soul.

The last soldier kept his helmet on, "Everyone calls me Saxby. Nice to meet you all."

Neanderthal, who was casually leaning against the wall, stated, "These guys are the best."

"Thanks, boss," Chris said.

"Ah, I just want to point out that I am a huge liability, as I'm not a monster hunter," Kane stated.

"Just follow the instructions of whoever you're with," Mel said. "Stay calm, and don't let fear overwhelm you."

"Easier said than done," he murmured in response.

The booming voice of Skrymir flowed into the room, magically magnified from outside, "First pair! Liam Sager and Matthew Pyne!"

There was a cheer from the other side of the gate. Apparently, this was a spectator sport, and the denizens of Utgard had rallied for it.

The two old friends nodded at each other. Mel gave them both a big hug.

Matt still had his sniper rifle case firm in his grasp. "You will have to distract whatever's in there while I get set up," he grinned.

"Better be quick, or I'll have to win without you," Liam laughed.

Danni felt a swell of sadness. While she didn't really know either man, she hoped they would come out of this okay.

Liam and Matt approached the gate, and with the creaking of rusty chains, it began rising into the stone wall above. The space behind the bars was entirely black.

Without looking back, both men stepped forward into the darkness.

• • • • •

THE MINUTES PASSED QUIETLY. No one spoke. Everyone was listening intently, hoping for any sign of what was happening.

Then, there was a roar from the crowd and a smattering of applause.

Danni nervously spun the angelic seal of Astaroth around in her pocket. It had become something of a good luck token to her. She used to wear her grandmother's silver cross around her neck and considered it a lucky charm, but ever since her spy training she'd learn necklaces could be liability and had gone without it.

There was another whooping cheer.

Ten minutes went by with frequent shocked gasps and sighs of relief flowing into the room.

Danni wondered whose side the crowd was on. She also thought it odd that they could hear the audience but couldn't hear the sound of an announcer.

Perhaps Skrymir didn't want to give anything away?

Then, final applause rang out, and Skrymir's voice again filled the antechamber.

"Approach the gate, Danni Quinn and Jesse Billiau!"

Josh gave Danni a hug. It was a tight, squeezing embrace that was filled with emotion. For a moment, Danni was lost in it.

Jesse walked up and shook Josh's hand. He gave Haruka a curt nod. She was looking sullen.

"Me and you, hey?" Jesse said, forcing a smile.

"Yep. At least I have a werewolf on my side. That super strength and healing will come in handy." Danni did her best to sound calm and collected, but inside her stomach was a hurricane.

"I'm guessing you have some spy skills and silver bullets on you? That will come in handy, too," Jesse laughed nervously.

Danni felt the pouch with her spare mag on her belt. It was still there, loaded with silver bullets.

Melissa approached and grasped Danni on the arm. "You've done the training and been to Hell and back. You are fully capable of this challenge too."

It wasn't much of a pep talk, but Danni did feel slightly better.

"Let's do this," Danni said to Jesse.

Side by side, Jesse and Danni walked toward the raised gate. She took one last look at the group behind them. Mel gave her a thumbs up.

Haruka scowled. All of the Taskforce A guys shouted some words of encouragement.

"Once more into the abyss," Jesse said before stepping into the darkness.

Resolved in facing her unknown destiny, Danni followed.

• • • • •

THE CLAUSTROPHOBIC ALL-CONSUMING blackness of the passage only lasted a few metres. It was as if an invisible curtain lifted when Jesse and Danni stumbled into the natural light of the outdoors.

They came out into a walled cage surrounded by grass.

The dark opening behind them sat in the towering outer walls of the castle. As far as the eye could see, a sea of wild grass flowed from the grey brick out to the horizon.

Directly in front of the pair was a procession of floating steps, climbing higher and higher until they reached a wide platform.

The platform was held up by magic alone. On either side of this structure were tall wooden towers, where the crowd's chatter could be heard. It was tough to tell from Danni's vantage point, but she thought she could make out levelled stadium seating.

The door to the cage opened.

"Should we make a break for it?" Jesse joked.

"You give it a go, and I'll watch," Danni smiled.

Jesse laughed. His jovial attitude was certainly helping alleviate Danni's tension.

"What do you think is waiting up there for us?" Danni asked him.

"Who knows? Skrymir probably collects biological treasures as well as artefacts. Could be anything."

"Great..."

"Come on," Jesse said, holding out a hand for Danni.

She took it, and they both began climbing the magical floating steps.

It only took a minute for them to reach the stadium, which was revealed to be an oblong flat surface coated in a coarse red material. It was as long as a football field, and on the other side was a wide gate before a pit of blackness.

Danni and Jesse stepped into the stadium, and the crowd cheered. They'd reached fever pitch already. Evidently, Liam and Matt's challenge had been exciting.

The significant figure of Skrymir took up the entire middle portion of the left-hand stand. Sitting on his elaborate throne, flanked by Prometheus and Quetzalcoatl, the giant raised his arm and silenced the crowd.

The only one who wasn't excitedly muttering was the small figure of the mysterious Egyptian man Danni had noticed earlier. He seemed to be looking directly at her with a cold penetrating gaze. He sat alone on the uppermost level of the seats.

The other spectators were all the elves, dwarves and humans of Utgard, some of which they'd seen when they first arrived.

"I now present our next two challengers!" Skrymir boomed.

The crowd clapped enthusiastically.

"Now, here we have Jesse Billiau, a police officer from Australia. But he is more than he seems. He is a werewolf! But not like one you'd know; he is mutated and deformed. The result of experimentation with what humans have called the God Particle."

The spectators murmured excitedly.

"And, we have Danni Quinn. A human spy, though only a rookie. She signed up to fight the supernatural… so let us see her do it!"

A roar bellowed from the other side of the stadium, so loud it made both Danni and Jesse jump in fright.

"Don't die," Jesse gulped.

Danni quickly drew her pistol, hit the mag release and replaced her regular rounds with the magazine holding silver bullets. She now had one regular hollow-point round in the chamber and fifteen silver bullets to use.

"Walk forward, challengers, and meet your monster!" Skrymir commanded.

Danni and Jesse strode forward until they reached the centre of the stadium. A rather conspicuous pool of blood by Danni's feet was alarmingly fresh.

There was a metal creak, and the huge chains attached to the far gate began moving. The iron squealed as the gate raised.

Silence filled the floating arena.

A growl came from the open gate.

Jesse shifted into a fighting stance.

At incredible speed, a creature emerged from the darkness, running right at them.

It was as large as a bull African elephant, but much more bizarre.

With a human head attached to a lion's body, the monster bounded forward. It had a long mane of drooping brown hair and sharp pointed teeth. The thick maroon scorpion's tail protruding from its rear was its most dangerous quality.

"What the hell is that?" Danni gasped.

"Manticore," Jesse breathed. "Split up!"

Danni bolted right, while Jesse went left.

The manticore paused, confused, then darted after Jesse.

Seizing her moment, Danni raised her gun towards the beast's rear. She fired, sending a round into the scorpion's tail. It harmlessly bounced off.

Jesse was fast but couldn't outrun the lion's body. Fortunately, the manticore was somewhat cumbersome due to its size, meaning agility became Jesse's weapon of choice. He turned abruptly and dived beneath its high pounce.

The manticore roared as it landed and swung around. Its tail flicked quickly, the deadly stinger narrowly missing Jesse.

Danni breathed out and fired again. This shot was a silver bullet, and it hit the manticore right in the side. There was a spurt of steaming toxic blood as the small projectile buried itself in the manticore's ribs.

The crowd cheered. Skrymir looked displeased.

Feeling the stinging bite of the bullet, the manticore turned toward Danni.

Its oversized human face had a perpetual dopey smile on it. The distorted eyes, nose and ears, and wide lips, made the manticore look like an abstract painting come to life. It was cartoonishly goofy looking.

It lunged, and Danni dived left.

A paw thundered down beside her.

Danni rolled right to avoid the thrust of its stinging tail.

Jesse, running as hard as he could, slammed straight into the manticore's right hind leg. The manticore swiped at him, while its tail attempted to pierce Danni again.

Danni didn't know what to do. Even with Jesse's enhanced strength, it was just too big. Jesse jumped and threw a punch into the manticore's bullet wound.

It howled in agony and re-directed its stinger towards Jesse.

Jesse caught the tail in mid-air, wrapping his arms and legs around the thickest part. He held on for dear life as it waved wildly back and forth.

Danni, now lying on her back, pointed her gun up at the monster.

Its eyes met her eyes.

They were blueish-grey and didn't display the slightest hint of intelligence. It opened its mouth, revealing three rows of pointed teeth in its upper and lower jaws.

As the teeth came towards Danni, she fired.

Her second silver bullet whizzed right into the roof of the manticore's mouth, going up into its brain.

With a groan, the monster collapsed.

Yet, it did not die,

The manticore panted heavily as it lay on its stomach.

"Finish it!" Jesse bellowed.

Danni scrambled to her feet. She was just off to the right of the big cat's heaving body. She pointed her gun towards its head and moved her finger to the trigger.

Long pale spikes erupted from the manticore's body. It was like it was suddenly covered in porcupine quills.

"Now!" Jesse yelled.

Danni fired. The manticore expelled its quills as the bullet left her gun. The deadly arrows flew in all directions.

"Oh," Danni gasped as three quills impaled her.

Everything went black.

Danni Quinn was dead, or so she thought.

In the blink of an eye, Danni left the stadium and magically appeared in the spectator seats not far from Skrymir.

"What a shame," the giant beamed at her. "You were so close. Those guns you humans have make fighting these creatures too easy."

Danni felt herself up and down. She was definitely still alive and not injured in any way.

Down below, Jesse had dodged the deadly explosion of toxic arrows and stood alone beside the dead manticore. He appeared to be frantically scanning the arena for Danni.

"Jesse moves on alone!" Skrymir boomed.

The crowd whooped and cheered. Then, just like that, Jesse vanished from the arena, along with the manticore.

"If you die, you get to watch?" Danni asked.

"Yes," a voice answered from behind her. It was Artemis in the next row up.

"Wish I could tell the others that…"

"Then no one would win the artefact. The two men before you succeeded in defeating their monster, though with great difficulty. I am intrigued to see what else Skrymir has in his zoo."

"Every team has to kill a monster?" Danni asked.

"It appears that way. When we are left with one person, he or she will be offered an opportunity to claim Zeus' lightning bolt."

Danni was privately disappointed that she was the first one knocked out of the tournament. But now, knowing this wasn't life or death, she was very excited to see how the others did.

It wasn't long before the next pair wandered up the floating stairs and into the stadium. The crowd of robed figures cheered fervently as Kane and Sigurd stood ready to face their monster.

Sigurd had Apollo's golden sword in the sling on his back. This would surely be a cakewalk for the Norse hero.

"It isn't the manticore every time, is it?" Danni asked Artemis.

"No, Skrymir is all about the spectacle. The denizens of Utgard have spent long years in isolation. They want a show."

She saw Sigurd speak to Kane and then give him a hearty slap on the back. Even from her high vantage point, she could see that Kane looked petrified.

Sigurd drew Apollo's golden sword from the sling and held it at the ready.

This time, heavy thudding footsteps emerged from the darkness behind the gate.

Skrymir again rose to his feet and spread his arms wide, addressing the crowd with his magically magnified voice.

"Before you stands a legend! Earth's mightiest warrior! A long time ago, I met Sigurd of the Volsung line. Now, an age after his death, he stands before me again. Let us see him face a monster of his era!"

Danni noticed that the giant neglected to mention Kane at all. She also picked up on all the excited gossiping around her about Sigurd. Many of the elves and dwarves spoke his name with the highest regard.

The thudding footsteps drew closer and closer. The gate squealed open, and a hideous creature emerged.

It was sixteen feet tall and resoundingly wide. The creature had a comically long flat nose on a squashed head, with boils and warts lining its cheeks. It had ribbons of matted brown hair and wore a simple hide tunic. Much like the manticore, it had a distorted human face.

Danni's first guess was that the creature was a giant, much like Skrymir. Though, it looked far sillier than he did.

"What is it?" Danni asked Artemis.

"Troll," the goddess replied.

The troll laughed stupidly as it observed Sigurd and Kane. It broke into a run, its wildly hairy feet shaking the stadium.

Danni saw Sigurd shout something but, strangely, couldn't hear what he said.

Kane moved backwards, looking terrified, while Sigurd sprinted forward to meet the beast head-on.

The troll slammed a fist down, splintering the stadium floor.

Sigurd dodged.

The troll tried to grab him, but Sigurd thrust the golden sword straight into its outstretched palm.

The troll reared up and screamed in pain. Still grasping the sword's hilt, Sigurd was flung into the air.

With its other hand, the troll reached out and gripped Sigurd tight, catching the man like he was a baseball.

It then used its teeth to remove the sword from its palm. It spat the golden blade away and grinned maliciously at Sigurd, who began to turn blue from compression.

The sword clanged to the ground just feet away from Kane.

He heaved it up, and seeing Sigurd's predicament, made a move.

The troll didn't even notice him at first, but it certainly saw Kane when he implanted Apollo's sword into its foot.

The troll dropped Sigurd, who drew in a deep breath before falling to his knees, coughing and spluttering.

The troll hopped, wailing in agony.

Danni saw Sigurd mouthing commands, then Kane knelt down and held his arms at the ready. It was lucky Kane was such a big guy because no one else would've been able to give Sigurd the flying boost he'd apparently requested.

After sailing upwards gracefully, Sigurd landed on the hopping troll's knee. He spun around and ripped the sword from the monster's foot.

The troll lowered its leg right as Sigurd jumped again, holding the sword high above him.

There was an explosion of blood as Sigurd buried the sword

into the troll's neck.

The monster's eyes went wide with shock.

It stumbled a few feet until it was standing directly over Kane, who instinctively ducked.

A wet sloppy sound emanated from the beast.

Somehow, everyone watching knew what was about to happen before it did.

A mountain of defecate rained down on Kane. It sat like a perfect steaming cone on the stadium's floor.

The troll fell backwards with a thud.

Danni grimaced as she saw a hand burst forth from the mound of faeces. Thoroughly coated in brown muck, a queasy looking Kane emerged to the roaring laughter of the crowd.

He shot Sigurd a deathly glare.

Danni clasped her hands over her mouth. She was shocked that he'd survived. Kane had done better than she had.

Like a deflating balloon, the troll released a wave of gas that washed over Kane.

Returning the golden sword to his sling, Sigurd raised his arms triumphantly. The crowd roared its approval.

He'd made short work of the troll.

"Sigurd and Kane advance," Skrymir announced to a cheer.

Then, the two men vanished from the stadium.

Danni heard Skrymir mumble to Prometheus, "The next one needs to be a bit harder…"

She wondered who would be next.

That question was quickly answered when Melissa and one of the Taskforce A agents stepped onto the stadium. While the troll had disappeared, its mountain of excrement hadn't, leaving Mel looking confused and disgusted.

Skrymir identified Melissa as the Oracle of Delphi. The crowd murmured excitedly, loudly chattering about how well-equipped the Taskforce A member, Chris, was with a plethora of modern weaponry.

The mighty gate opened again, and a very familiar-looking beast emerged. It was similar to the manticore, though half as tall and slightly longer. This creature had a beautiful woman's head on a lioness's body. There was no scorpion's tail, but she did have glorious wings folded on her back.

Danni recognised this being.

Much like the great stone statue that guards the pyramids of Giza, this was a sphinx. She was golden and sparkled as the sun's rays hit her unblemished skin.

The sphinx extended her long golden wings and a waterfall of shimmering powder fell from them.

Unlike the goofy manticore and the defecating troll, this was a regal being, a symbol of pride and royalty.

Her feminine sculpted face would've been quite beautiful if it weren't attached to such an odd creature.

The sphinx surveyed the stadium with mild interest. Her eyes blazed with intelligence. They narrowed as they fell upon Mel and Chris.

Chris had his rifle raised, pointing right at the creature. Mel ushered him to lower it.

The sphinx yawned and took to the air. Danni felt the powerful downward draught its wings generated as it soared past her. It circled the stadium a few times in a mesmerising golden display, then landed in front of the two combatants.

Melissa stood her ground, cautiously surveying the sparkling creature.

"Lower the sound barrier," Skrymir commanded Prometheus.

The titan waved his hand, and suddenly they could hear the sounds of the conversation below.

The sphinx casually licked her paw.

"My name is Melissa," Melissa said.

"And I'm Chris," the Taskforce A agent stammered, hesitant to lower his rifle too far.

The sphinx peered intently at them.

"A soldier tried and tested. Your feats unknown, yet your perseverance noteworthy," the sphinx said in her melodic voice. It was entrancing.

The sphinx's eyes darted to Mel.

"Eyes that see more than mortal eyes should. Answer my questions and see your challenge fulfilled."

Still focused on Mel, the sphinx spoke its riddle.

"There is a building one enters blind and leaves seeing. Name it?"

The crowd was silent, waiting for Mel's answer.

"A school, of course," Mel said. It barely took her thirty seconds to deduce the answer.

The sphinx smiled, then bowed low. Mel returned the gesture.

It then turned to Chris and spoke its second riddle.

"Out of the eater, something to eat; out of the strong, something sweet?"

Chris looked to Mel, who just shrugged.

"Ah... ah... tomato?"

The sphinx snarled and leant forward, wrapping its mouth around Chris so fast Danni barely saw what happened. With the loud crunching of bone, it bit him in half.

His legs flopped down while the sphinx consumed the rest of him.

Looking satisfied, the sphinx turned its head to Skrymir.

Chris appeared in the seat next to Danni, completely intact.

"What the hell just happened?"

"You lost," Danni smiled.

Skrymir announced Mel's success, and she disappeared.

Danni wondered if Jesse and Mel would be teamed up for the next round.

Skrymir loudly voiced his displeasure at the riddles, stating that the sphinx was always 'too boring'.

Prometheus raised his hand and the sound bubble appeared again over the stadium.

"For some reason, Skrymir doesn't want to hear people talking down there," Danni said to Chris.

"Probably ruins the spectacle," Chris shrugged, unslinging his rifle and leaning it against the railing in front.

Some dwarves in the rows behind were loudly muttering their displeasure at the manticore and sphinx looking too similar.

"So, what's the go?" Chris asked. "Is each team facing a monster?"

"Yep. The first three had to kill it. You got weird riddles, I guess to shake things up."

Chris leaned back, looking very eager to enjoy the show. "I must say, I'm glad I didn't just die."

"Me too," Danni agreed.

• • • • •

THE FOLLOWING TWO CONTESTANTS were a pair of the Taskforce A guys. Danni thought there was no way they could lose.

After all, they had rifles, handguns, different types of ammunition and gadgets galore. Both were specialists, war veterans, and highly trained.

Yet, when they faced their monster, they were hopelessly outmatched.

From the darkness came a humanoid moth-winged creature with large red orbs for eyes. It was utterly black and coated with thick fur.

It was part man, part insect and made a horrifying screeching noise as it took the air.

Despite some good positioning and skillful acrobatics, the mothman was impervious to everything they threw at it.

After swapping bullets and trying different weapons for a few minutes, both men collapsed and began spasming on the floor.

Danni could see the men's eyes rolling backwards in their skulls even from her high vantage point. It looked unpleasant as they twitched and foamed at the mouth. The mothman never touched them, yet both quickly appeared in the spectator stands.

Skrymir wasn't happy this time either, berating Prometheus for choosing a monster that was too hard. The titan, with his vacant stone-like eyes, was obviously uncaring.

Chris gave the two new failures the rundown of what was going on. They both looked thoroughly relieved to be alive, unclasping their helmets and removing their goggles for a better view.

The next pair also failed to defeat their foe.

Teva and the final Taskforce A agent, Fomiatti, came up against a kurita. Danni learned from Artemis that it was a monster from the Philippines. It looked like a giant chimpanzee, only with eight extra arms emerging at random points from its hairy torso.

It used the ring of arms as its primary form of locomotion, rolling around like the monster was stuck in a perpetual cartwheel.

The battle was relatively long, with the two men finding a way to disorient the rolling kurita, pausing it for long enough to get a clean shot off. They just didn't factor in the kurita falling right on top of them, squashing them both.

Once Teva realised what had happened, he was quite embarrassed. At least Skrymir seemed pleased; that match had been a rollercoaster ride.

None of the Taskforce A agents were pleased either. They'd all been knocked out right away.

"I hope Neanderthal gets knocked out," Chris muttered darkly. "Otherwise, the mandatory training he brings in will be endless…"

Danni was chuffed to finally have someone on her team up

in the stands with her.

"This is actually a great show," she said to Teva.

"Well, even though I lost, I am glad to be out of that waiting room. Things are starting to get a bit tense down there."

"Yep, much better to get it out of the way early," Danni laughed.

The next two combatants stepped into the stadium.

Danni's laughter was cut short. Something was wrong.

Malcolm Selleck, clutching the Necronomicon to his breast, was standing hunched.

His head twisted back and forth fearfully. It was like he could see something no one else could. His mouth was also endlessly moving like he was muttering a long string of gibberish out loud.

Neanderthal, his partner, stood well back from him, looking nervous. In fact, Neanderthal looked more concerned about Malcolm than whatever was moving in the darkness behind the large gate.

"What's wrong with Professor Selleck?" Danni asked Teva.

"I have no idea…"

The gate at the far end slowly opened.

All hell broke loose.

28

THE MADNESS OF
MALCOLM SELLECK

A series of shrill screams echoed as a flock of harpies flew from the darkness into the stadium.

They carried with them the foul stench of decay. Each was about a metre tall and equipped with deadly talons. Their upper half was in the form of a woman, however with wings instead of arms, and their lower half appeared as a brown feathered bird.

Neanderthal began firing at the swift birds, failing to land a shot as they swooped and dived.

Malcolm looked at the swarm and dropped to his knees. He began frantically turning pages of the Necronomicon, looking for a passage to help them (or so Danni assumed).

Neanderthal expertly predicted a dive toward Malcolm and landed three shots on a harpy, sending it careening into the ground in a mess of feathers.

This drew the flock's attention while Malcolm began sounding out a spell.

Sweat was pooling around the professor.

Neanderthal reached for the assortment of grenades on his belt and picked up a flashbang.

He threw it straight up into the cloud of circling bird-women and closed his eyes.

A blinding explosion filled the stadium, earning an 'oooh' from the spectators. Most of the harpies, disorientated, fell from the air.

At once, Neanderthal began picking them off with his rifle.

Malcolm threw his arms up unexpectedly, and there was a sound like rumbling thunder.

The professor gasped, slamming the Necronomicon shut and pointing toward the far-left side of the stadium.

Danni followed his finger but couldn't see anything but empty space.

"This is no good," Skrymir mumbled, frowning.

Suddenly, the few harpies still in the air began screeching in panic.

Neanderthal picked up on the warning signs and scanned the stadium for a new threat, but like Danni, he couldn't determine it.

A harpy began moving strangely in the air. It was as if it was caught in the grip of something unseen. It shook violently, whipping back and forth. Then the harpy disappeared entirely.

"There is something else down there, and judging by Skrymir's expression, it isn't part of his games," Teva deduced, looking towards the giant's throne.

The Tahitian was right. Skrymir looked deeply concerned.

Another two harpies were caught and quickly vanished in the same manner.

Neanderthal ran towards Malcolm and kicked the Necronomicon away.

While Danni had noticed that Malcolm hadn't looked himself recently, she didn't really perceive the extent of his transformation until she saw him there beside Neanderthal. He looked shabby and noticeably dirty, like he hadn't washed in days. His hair poked out at odd angels and a patchy beard had formed around his jaw.

Gone was the prim and proper professor they'd left in Florida. Here stood some hobo addicted to a particular drug; the Necronomicon.

Even Skrymir noticed Malcolm's odd appearance.

"Lower the sound barrier. I wish to hear the discussion below. I feel I may have seen the ailment afflicting that man before."

As it had with Mel and Chris, the voices of Malcolm and Neanderthal filled the spectator seats.

"It's coming, it's coming... I can feel it... it's coming," Malcolm was frantically muttering.

"What is coming?" Neanderthal asked, exasperated.

"It's coming, coming from the void. The crawling chaos... Nyarlathotep..."

"Pull yourself together, man. Tell me what's killing the

harpies!"

The remaining harpies squealed as they tried to escape the stadium.

The invisible creature went after them one by one, pulling them down and ripping them apart.

Neanderthal began following the attacks with his rifle, trying to shoot at the invisible monster, but wasn't finding any success.

Malcolm was still kneeling in place, muttering loudly. He'd gone completely mad.

A harpy swooped by Neanderthal and was seized mid-air. Neanderthal gulped. The attacker had to be close.

An invisible appendage hoisted the Navy SEAL up and threw him across the stadium. He landed with a bone-shattering crunch.

He fired blindly in the direction he'd been flung from.

Some of the bullets didn't embed themselves in the far wall; they disappeared into the unseen thing.

It was then that Danni noticed the unfathomable new smell. It wasn't the stench of the harpies. This was a singular rotten odour that's mere existence boggled the mind. Danni had to pinch her nose, as did Teva and the Taskforce A soldiers.

"Enough of this!" Skrymir roared, clearly annoyed.

He pressed his hands towards the stadium. "Let's see if I can force this creature to reveal itself!"

Runic circles of glowing energy manifested around Skrymir's hands.

An alien wail filled the air, silencing the crowd. It was a sound unlike anything Danni had ever heard.

The creature came into view, piece by piece.

It was an eldritch horror from another plane of existence.

The sounds this thing made were like nothing the organs of a human could produce. Danni was chilled to her core as its acoustic perversions flowed over the spectator seats. They were less like the sounds of organic life and more like vague ghastly renditions of nature - like this thing was speaking the distorted language of an echoing thunderstorm.

And then there was the stench, which only seemed to grow more apparent when the monster became more visible.

"FATHER! YOG-SOTHOTH! FATHER!" Malcolm screamed, kneeling before the whipping tentacles of the eldritch horror.

Of all the monsters they'd seen, this one clearly didn't belong. It was abstract and unshapely, made from matter not of this dimension.

The creature was a conical wall of flesh standing on four spindly legs with cloven hooves.

It was a mass of eyes, large and small, piled on top of one another. Interspersed between the eyes were pockets of bubbling flesh that contained oozing orifices. Dozens of female breasts were flopping from random places all over the creature. Long grey tentacles ringed with suckers stretched out up and down its body and flailed.

The horror didn't look like it should be able to stand. It had no discernable head or torso. It was just a mismatch of different parts.

It galloped for the last harpy, pulling it from the air and

absorbing it into its mass of oozing, pulsating flesh.

Then, it turned on Neanderthal again, who was struggling to get to his feet.

With a look of great pain, Neanderthal plucked an incendiary grenade from his belt, pulled the pin with his teeth, and threw it.

The subsequent engulfing flash of fire made the creature squeal and barrel away from him.

Neanderthal looked temporarily relieved until Malcolm crash tackled him from nowhere.

"LEAVE IT ALONE!" Malcolm screamed, sounding completely unhinged.

Neanderthal kicked the professor and pointed his rifle right at him.

"Stay down!" Neanderthal ordered.

Malcolm lunged, wrapping his arms around the American's legs.

Neanderthal kicked him off again, tearing Malcolm's long-sleeved shirt.

Danni gasped when she saw Malcolm's skin. It had gone purple and also seemed to be coated in large boils.

The eldritch horror cried its unearthly cry as the flames continued to lick at it. Its tentacles tore gashes in the stadium's walls.

Malcolm got to his feet and sprinted towards the monstrosity. The creature paid him no attention while it was on fire.

Then, the flames died.

Neanderthal had his rifle raised and pointed at the professor, though he hesitated to shoot.

A grey tentacle reached out and wrapped itself around

Malcolm. It drew him towards the mound of eyes and breasts. Much like the harpies, Malcolm sunk into the monster's body and disappeared.

The creature paused.

There was a soft tearing noise. A horizontal gash appeared right in the middle of the monster, cutting across its eyes and orifices. With something akin to a vomit, it spat Malcolm back out.

Only it wasn't Malcolm anymore.

The professor's right arm had become a writhing tentacle, and his right leg was horribly engorged. Half his body had turned purple, and his left eye had magnified dramatically in size. He was completely deformed, taking on eldritch characteristics of his own.

The crowd murmured, and Skrymir shook his head sorrowfully.

Malcolm limped towards Neanderthal, rivers of slime flowing from his snarling mouth.

"You should end this," Prometheus said. "If you know this magic, send that creature back into the abyss from whence it came."

"Fortunately, I do, though I regret that I do. It has been a very long time since I've had to speak the words of elder things and great old ones. No good comes of these spells. That mortal was a fool to dabble in such ancient horrors."

Artemis looked toward Prometheus and said, "What is this? I cannot feel this creature in my domains, and I feel all things in the hunt."

"I wish I could tell you, goddess. This is something very, very old," Prometheus replied.

Danni grew even more concerned. Just what the hell was

this Necronomicon? What powers was it channelling that even a titan didn't know it."

Skrymir spoke slowly and carefully.

"Ygnaiih ygnaiih thflthkh'nha Yog-Sothoth…"

At once, the creature below spun in a circle and reared up, the way a startled horse would.

"No!" Chris bellowed, as he saw one of its long appendages wrap around Neanderthal.

The Navy SEAL struggled to free himself from the suckers, but he was too badly hurt. Blood dripped from his lips.

"Ngh'aa yaheeha…"

Another tentacle caught the monstrous Malcolm Selleck in its flailing, causing him to bellow in frustration.

"H'yuh n'gaih YOG-SOTHOTH!"

The wind stopped.

For a split second, Danni thought she saw pockets of green flesh laced with eyes appear all over the stadium and up in the air. She thought she saw giant tentacles reach up into the sky on the horizon. But she blinked and they were gone.

The eldritch horror in the stadium had vanished, seemingly taking Malcolm and Neanderthal with it.

It was completely quiet.

Even Skrymir looked flabbergasted. All that remained was the splintered wood of the abomination's rampage and the spent shell casings from Neanderthal.

Prometheus turned and looked at Danni.

The shimmering, blinding visage of the titan messed with her senses too much for her to meet his gaze.

"He's not looking at you," Teva whispered. "He's looking at Artemis."

Danni felt a stream of air on the back of her neck.

Prometheus had just teleported into the seat next to Artemis, right behind Danni.

"Explain how these mortals have accessed this dark magic," Prometheus demanded.

"The book. I dismissed it as some magical token from a distant pantheon of gods. It appears that I was wrong."

Danni swung around to look at the Greek deities and noticed something odd. The Egyptian sitting high in the far back row was gone.

"I haven't felt power like that since the early days. Well before your time. In my youth, during the reign of Ouranos, I recall feeling the echoes of that power."

"You don't know what it is, then?" Artemis asked, sounding very surprised.

The loud voice of Skrymir cut across their conversation. "I know it. Utgard is supposed to be impenetrable to foreign magics, yet that mortal used a book to summon that horror. You, goddess, will come with me. The games will be on hold while we discuss what just happened."

The anger in the giant's voice was unmistakable. Artemis, Prometheus, Skrymir and Quetzalcoatl vanished.

"That book has been nothing but trouble. First, it leads us to that nightmare city where we accidentally awaken some underwater monster. Then it sucks Randall into a portal to who knows where. Now it summons an invisible monster that is a bunch of eyes, breasts and oozing body parts," Danni said quietly to Teva.

Teva's response was barely audible. He whispered right into Danni's ear. "Did you see it? In that second before they disappeared, there were eyes in the sky."

Danni gulped. So, it wasn't her imagination. The clouds of green matter with their innumerable eyes had been there.

"What were those things?" she asked.

"Malcolm called out to Yog-Sothoth. That name was also in USSOT's notes. I think it must've been Yog-Sothoth."

"But there were so many of them. Different pockets of eyes all around."

"I think they were all part of the one being," Teva said darkly. "Like whatever Yog-Sothoth is, Malcolm was trying to pull it in. But it doesn't belong here... or it's too big and needs something more to come through."

"Great, so now we have Cthulhu somewhere in the Pacific and Yog-Sothoth floating all around us. Creatures apparently hundreds of millions of years old that not even the gods have heard of."

Teva shrugged. "Well, Prometheus seems to have a vague idea, at least. And somehow, Skrymir knows that magic. There is a lot more to the giant lord of Utgard than meets the eye."

"We should've never let Malcolm keep that book," Danni sighed.

"The book is still down there," Teva said, pointing to where it had fallen.

Just as he did so, Prometheus appeared in the stadium, picked it up, and vanished again.

"Is that the same book USSOT is working on in Florida?" Chris asked Teva.

"A more complete version. When we get out of here, you will have to tell your boss that extreme caution needs to be exercised around it."

"That creature was one of the most disgusting things I've ever seen," Chris stated.

"Yeah, its shape and proportions were all wrong. And the way it moved didn't suit its body. It was how a creature might appear if it was extra-dimensional."

"How do you mean?"

"Like it came from a dimension higher than ours that we can't perceive. So, when it's pulled into our world, we see some distorted mess of things we can recognise."

"Still not sure I get you," Chris said, scratching his head.

"Okay, imagine you are a two-dimensional person looking at a three-dimensional being like us. A human can't be perceived properly in two dimensions. The two-dimensional being would see a flat cross-section of a human, depending on where they view it. Suppose they got caught inside one, for example. In that case, they'd face an outline of pulsing internal organs, flowing blood, bone, fat and arteries. It'd be a nightmare vision. The 2D creature wouldn't know about the skin coating it. All they'd see is a horror like we saw."

One of the other Taskforce A guys leaned back casually and asked, "Why all the breasts, though?"

The discussion about multi-dimensional space lasted for some time before Skrymir and the gods reappeared.

All of the Taskforce A soldiers looked uneasy. They'd just lost their decorated commander. Someone would have to tell Fiona Shear that Neanderthal was gone. It was an unpleasant job.

Danni and Teva were also racked with guilt about Malcolm. What would they tell Mel?

The crowd was growing restless.

Skrymir addressed the population of Utgard in his magnified voice.

"My people, apologies for the delay. We only have two more competitors before we move on to the second round."

Everyone's eyes darted to the stadium.

Two new people had walked up the stairs and onto the red expanse.

Josh and Haruka stood side by side.

The splintered wood, shell casings, pile of faeces and pools of blood must've created a frightening first impression. Josh looked at the ominous gate at the other end and murmured something to Haruka.

He then doubled over as if he had a bad stomach cramp. His entire body shook as he transformed from man into beast.

Josh's werewolf form looked different to the last time Danni had seen it. He no longer had short grey hairs on his chest, stomach, snout and around his eyes. He was shaggy black all over, looking sleeker and less bulky.

His bronze hand had also turned into a claw, and from it sprung Josh's prized Norse sword Vargr Muor. The pure werewolf was certainly impressive to behold.

"Make this a fair match," Skrymir said to Prometheus.

The titan paused to consider his options, then a small smile twisted his lips.

Danni guessed Skrymir wanted the audience to forget about what had just happened as quickly as possible. He was going to put on a good show.

The far gate began to open, and Josh's monsters emerged.

They were five naked people. Four men and one woman, looked dazed and confused as they ambled into the natural light.

Instantly the curiosity of the crowd was piqued.

"What is this?" Teva asked.

Danni peered down at the strange assortment of people wandering towards Josh and Haruka. They were a mix of ethnicities and seemed totally lost.

Then, Josh snarled.

It reverberated up the wooden stands and gave Danni goosebumps. Obviously, his enhanced werewolf powers could sense what was going on.

"Do it," Skrymir ordered, his eyes wide with delight.

Prometheus snapped his fingers.

The five people went rigid. They began to spasm and contort, either writhing on the ground or falling to their knees.

Each screamed until their voices were lost.

The sound of breaking bones and tearing skin rose from the platform to the seats.

"Surely not..." Teva said, amazed.

"What? What is it?" Danni asked.

"They're supposed to be mythical, but I think we are about to see the other five known werecreatures..."

29

WEREBATTLE

Danni thought back to her two-week AST course. They'd covered lycanthropes in depth because of the recent appearances in Australia. It was mentioned, albeit very briefly and somewhat sarcastically that other cultures had werecreatures much stranger than the wolf.

What was it that they'd covered?

Werebears from North America were in there. Maybe werelions in Africa, too… She couldn't remember the others. It was more of a footnote than an actual lesson.

Haruka spoke to Josh, but the sound barrier was swiftly raised again, so the audience couldn't hear the conversation.

Josh, brandishing his gleaming sword Vargr Muor, sprang into action. He wasn't going to wait for the agonised humans to transform; he would put them out of their misery before they could fight back.

"Clever," Teva breathed as Josh pounced.

Josh raised the sword high. It sliced through the air, a devastating shimmer plunging towards its target.

The werewolf came down on the closest person, whose skin had turned a sleek blue.

"No, no, no!" Skrymir said, pointing a figure at the black werewolf.

Josh froze in midair. His wolf's head barked and snapped as he looked around, confused.

"I want to put on a show. You can't kill them before they all become their inner monsters."

Danni privately agreed with Skrymir. She wanted to see what they all became.

Haruka ran towards Josh at phenomenal speed. She was fast.

Josh's bronze claw dropped the sword, and without missing a beat, Haruka caught it as it fell.

She aimed a deadly blow at the nearest werecreature instead and was also met by the magical constriction of Skrymir.

"These two," Skrymir laughed.

Haruka squirmed on the ground while the werewolf howled above her. It was an odd sight. But even odder were the finishing transformations of the naked people.

Danni soaked in each creature's strange appearance.

The person closest to Josh and Haruka looked awesomely terrifying and mind-bogglingly absurd. It was a wereshark, a part man, part shark hybrid.

Its body was hunched forward, balanced on human legs with dangling long arms falling from its front, ending in webbed hands. It had a tall fin and the head of a great white.

Slightly further down, in all its feathered glory, was a wereeagle. It would've looked majestic if it weren't for its deadly yellow eyes. This bird-man had the torso and arms of a human, yet its hands and feet were talons. From its back spread two wings. Its head was entirely white like the American bald eagle.

The next two monsters sized each other up.

They were a werebear and werelion, both physically large and looking rabid. The werebear appeared similar to an ordinary bear, but with a longer, leaner midsection and a cross between paws and hands.

The werelion had a striking red mane on a muscular orange body. He had thick legs that ended with paws and hands equipped with deadly claws.

The last was the most bizarre. It was the werecreature the woman had become. With a long serpentine neck and the broad head of an anaconda, she was a weresnake.

She had a human body with green scaly arms below her neck and a long powerful tail. She had no legs at all and slithered along the ground.

Chris leaned over the railing to better look at the assortment of monsters and stated, "This is the most awesome thing I've ever seen."

The denizens of Utgard were also suitably impressed, wagering amongst themselves which werecreature would reign victorious.

The wereshark fixed its black beady eyes on Haruka and spread its jaws wide. Faced with the rows of large triangular teeth, Haruka's face lost its focus and succumbed to fear. She frantically tried to scramble back.

Skrymir released his magical hold on them.

Josh crashed to the ground next to Haruka, then quickly scrambled to his feet. He flexed his arms and wriggled his fingers. The deadly black claws on his biological hand caught the light, looking menacing. His bronze hand had matching daggers more than capable of slicing any creature apart.

Josh turned his head towards Haruka and whimpered. She nodded, finding her courage.

They had a plan.

But, as with all best-laid plans, it was quickly dismantled in the talons of the wereeagle.

Screeching in faster than they could've predicted, its claws dug into Josh's shoulders while its wings beat furiously. The black werewolf was pulled into the air.

Josh was caught totally by surprise and reached up fruitlessly towards the eagle's humanoid torso.

Haruka suddenly looked very alone as she faced down the gnashing jaws of the shark.

At least, from Danni's vantage point, the five werecreatures didn't know they were on a team against Josh and Haruka.

The werebear and werelion were caught in a vicious

exchange of blows. The werebear had formidable strength on its side, but the werelion was faster. Its red mane flashed as it dodged clumsily thrown paws before implanting its teeth in the bear's fur.

The weresnake slithered along the wall, its malicious eyes searching for prey. Its emotionless prehistoric head had a cold reptilian dignity.

Danni imagined that if the dinosaurs had lasted long enough to evolve like humans, they could've looked like the weresnake.

The wereshark ran at Haruka, slamming its jaws open and closed. It had to use its elongated arms to keep its hunched frame upright, the tips of its webbed fingers dragging against the ground.

It looked comical from the spectator stands, though Danni was sure it wasn't from Haruka's vantage point.

Haruka rolled and avoided a thumping bite.

The wereshark fumbled for her with its gangly webbed hands.

Perhaps this thing was fast and deadly in the water, but it was borderline useless on land.

Haruka, it seemed, was also realising this.

She sprang to her feet and dodged another bite by cartwheeling to the left, planting one foot into the side of the wereshark's face.

The shark didn't budge. Its hunched disposition and heavy top half gave it a solid centre of gravity. It lunged again, but Haruka was too quick. She wrapped her arms around the tall top fin and spun herself onto the shark's back.

She straddled it, holding the fin with one hand for support. The other hand still gripped the hilt of Vargr Muor.

The crowd whooped and cheered.

The shark reared up furiously like a bucking bull, trying to dislodge the girl. The blade's edge nicked the wereshark just above the eye, making it angrier.

Haruka tried to raise the sword high enough to thrust it down through the shark's mouth but was having too much difficulty maintaining her balance. She needed both hands free.

"I'm not sure it's right to say this, but knowing they can't really die down there makes this awesome!" Teva stated.

The Taskforce A guys murmured their agreement.

Danni turned her attention from Haruka to Josh, who was being carried through the air by the wereeagle. He was now well above the spectator seats, hanging limply from the bird's gleaming talons.

The eagle screeched when it realised it couldn't go any higher, being magically confined to the stadium. It let out another piercing cry, then released its grip.

Josh fell.

The monstrous black werewolf usually didn't display much emotion on his canine head. Still, as he fell past the spectator seats, all watching could see the look of pure dismay etched on his face.

When the werewolf impacted the ground, every elf, dwarf and man alike turned their heads away simultaneously.

"That's gotta hurt," Teva muttered.

Josh's legs were clearly broken. He was splayed out in a small crater of splintered wood, breathing heavily.

He caught the attention of the weresnake, which raised its serpentine torso high, balancing on its long powerful tail. It surveyed Josh with a look of hunger.

The weresnake's forked tongue flicked in and out.

Of all the werecreatures, the weresnake was easily the most threatening. It had whip-like reflexes and, by its length alone, was easily the largest of the monsters. Despite its human elements, it still exuded the cold alien aura of snakes, lizards and all things that slithered and crawled.

The weresnake slithered towards Josh, gruesomely extending its jaw. Its fangs were impressively long yet didn't appear to be dripping with venom.

Josh's healing factor had already kicked in, snapping his broken bones back into place. Rolling, just in the nick of time, he narrowly avoided the first stinging strike of the serpent.

The snake attempted to wrap its thin muscular arms around the werewolf, but Josh was too fast.

Palms pressed against each other, the werewolf and weresnake were locked in a battle of wills. The werewolf was strong, but the weresnake was powered by metres of thick muscle.

The scaly arms of the snake still displayed the thick sinewy muscle beneath. Josh was in danger of being quickly overpowered.

Danni wondered what was going through each creature's mind. Josh's lycanthropic form was as fearsome as impressive, and the weresnake looked like a dinosaur.

Its tail flicked around and swept Josh off his feet.

The weresnake bore down, implanting its long stinging fangs into Josh's neck. It hissed as two jets of crimson blood exploded from the werewolf's skin.

Josh twisted his body and tried to kick the weresnake away.

The snake quickly coiled its tail around the werewolf, wrapping him in a tight embrace.

Josh whimpered as the air was squeezed out of him.

Salvation came in the most unlikely form possible.

Haruka, still riding the wereshark, barreled teeth-first towards the snake.

It was clear from the swinging sword and Haruka's look of sheer fright that she had no control over the situation.

Still, the crowd gasped and awed when the shark's jaws clamped down on the snake's tail, tearing a chunk of flesh clean away.

The snake immediately released Josh and violently spasmed.

Josh woozily got to his feet, looking battered and broken. His black fur was now matted with blood.

Once he'd composed himself, the fire of determination flashed in his haunting orange eyes.

He sprang into action. First, he braced, then pounced for the weresnake, catching its head in his jaws as he sailed past.

Josh tore it clean off.

The weresnake's body spasmed for a few seconds, then lay still.

Josh howled in victory, catching the attention of the werebear and werelion briefly. However, it wasn't enough to distract them from their increasingly bloody fight.

The shaggy black werewolf then faced the wereshark. Josh bolted towards it, slamming straight into the demented fish like a charging bull. The shark stumbled and turned.

Haruka tossed Vargr Muor and Josh grasped the sword in

his claw. The magical sword instantly morphed in size to fit his palm.

As the wide-open maw of the shark rushed towards Josh, he thrust the sword straight up through its lower jaw. The shark paused, its mouth hanging open. Josh reached up with his natural claw and moved his dagger-like talons into the roof of the wereshark's mouth. They plunged straight into its brain.

Haruka collapsed off the shark in an elegant summersault, before it fell dead to the stadium floor.

Josh pulled the sword from the shark and rearranged his grip. He held it above his head like it was a javelin.

Josh spotted the wereeagle, still squawking and attempting to escape the stadium.

With a mighty heave, Josh catapulted the sword through the air.

It hit, penetrating the eagle right through its chest.

The eagle screamed and began zooming down, crashing into the ground. Its hollow bones had spared the stadium another crater.

Three werecreatures were dead.

This moment of intense action had the crowd on their feet and roaring. Thunderous applause rang through the stand.

Even Danni jumped to her feet and cheered.

The werelion and werebear were physically larger and much more imposing than the werewolf.

The question now was; how would Josh overcome these impressive foes?

Haruka ran to retrieve the sword from the bird man's

corpse.

The werebear picked up the werelion and tossed it across the stadium. The lion crashed into the floor and rolled towards the gate.

Danni wondered if all werecreatures had the same healing ability because the lion looked pretty beaten up.

On all fours, Josh bounded towards the werebear. This was his chance to take it one on one. The bear saw his approach and stood tall, releasing a bellowing roar that even the sound barrier couldn't suppress.

Josh circled the bear and dug his claws into its back. Despite their unworldly sharpness, they didn't penetrate far into the wall of fur and meat.

The bear rolled, throwing Josh away, then turned and pinned Josh in a display of impressive speed. It raised its right paw and swiped, taking a chunk of Josh's flesh from his chest.

Danni clutched her own hand to her chest. She'd felt that blow.

The werewolf spat out blood as the bear went for the killing blow.

But then, the werebear paused, and its weight on Josh lessened. It reared up, giving Josh the chance to pull himself away with some difficulty.

Haruka had thrust Vargr Muor into the bear's back, catching it entirely by surprise.

Haruka, struggling to remove the sword from the thick mass of flesh and brown fur, pressed a foot against the monster's back. With a grunt of exertion and a splash of blood, she ripped it clean of the bear and threw it to Josh.

With his bronze hand, Josh caught the sword. His natural hand covered the bleeding wound on his chest.

Panting heavily, he aimed the sword at the bear's heart.

It found its mark and the bear collapsed.

The lion was still unmoving by the gate. Apparently, it couldn't heal the same as the werewolf.

Retrieving the sword, the crowd was ecstatic as Josh stalked towards the lion, leaving a trail of blood behind him, and quickly buried the blade in its back.

Josh howled victoriously.

"What a match! How mighty stands the legacy of Lycaon!" Skrymir cried in joy. "The most famous of the weremonsters stands tall over its kin! Both Joshua Dare and Haruka Masunaga advance to our next round!"

"Wow, that was pretty epic. I'm going to have a big job updating the AST's database after all this… or actually, you will. You've watched almost all the matches, haven't you?" Teva said to Danni, barely hiding a smirk.

Danni nodded hesitantly. She didn't want to do that; she'd just been watching for fun, not paying attention in any great detail. Suddenly, she was trying to remember the important aspects of the sphinx and kurita, in case she had to write about them.

Haruka gave Josh a hug, and then they vanished, leaving Danni with a pit in her stomach. She didn't like Haruka.

"I wonder what round two will bring?" Teva asked.

"I don't know, but I'm super embarrassed to be one of the few who didn't make it through round one…"

"Such is life," Teva said simply.

Artemis, who'd been eavesdropping, turned her head towards Skrymir's throne. "What is the next challenge?"

"I had intended on a series of puzzles; however, after that last match, I feel like we should continue with the theme," Skrymir stated quite enthusiastically.

The giant turned his head to the ever-silent god Quetzalcoatl. His war paint and fierce eyes still gave off an air of intimidation.

"My dear Aztec friend, reshape the stadium. Make it a colosseum! The winners do not yet know that they cannot die in the ring. Let us see them fight each other to earn my favour."

The Aztec god bowed silently.

Danni had to hold on to the handrail in front as the entire stadium shook.

The far metal gate exploded. The stadium split in half repeatedly, turning into thousands upon thousands of wooden planks. They began re-forming themselves into a new shape through the god's magic.

The stadium became round, and the spectator stands stretched and twisted to encircle it. It only took a couple of minutes for the stadium to become a miniature replica of the Roman Colosseum.

The audience chattered excitedly at the change. Danni, Teva and the Taskforce A soldiers were in the first row, about three metres above the stadium proper. They'd have a great view.

"Prometheus, ready our victors for battle against each other. Tell them the winner claims the artefact of Zeus. Quetzalcoatl, use your magic to ensure the combatants can't see the spectators. We don't want them knowing that this isn't a life or death game."

Prometheus vanished, and Quetzalcoatl nodded.

Danni gulped. She didn't envy Mel, Josh or any of the others. This was psychological torture of the highest degree.

Surely none of them would fight.

A horn blew, and Skrymir stood to address the crowd.

"Let the battle begin!"

30

THE VICTORS

T he crowd was still high on the adrenaline rush from the weremonster battle.

Heated debates broke out, and hastily made wagers cemented the Utgardian's pick for the greatest warrior.

Sigurd was a strong contender for victor by his legend alone, though Josh had also developed quite the fan base.

They didn't just vote for the overall winner; many also seemed intent on gambling on all facets of the coming match. Kane Dare – or the 'troll defecate man'- as the audience described him, was the overwhelming pick for the first elimination.

The Taskforce A soldiers were adamant that had

Neanderthal not been drawn into oblivion by the eldritch beast, he would've taken the victory.

The audience all seemed to overlook the fact that none of them would fight each other. Danni was confident of that point.

The AST were a team, and they were all good people. None of them would kill their colleagues to win an artefact.

This created a new problem in Danni's mind. If they didn't fight, Skrymir would lose his afternoon of entertainment. The giant might deny them the artefact out of annoyance alone.

"We have to find a way to show the others they aren't going to die when they enter the arena," Danni whispered to Teva.

"I was thinking the same thing, but how?"

Danni scratched her chin as she pondered their predicament. She knew that the combatants wouldn't be able to see her and Teva when they appeared. Still, as far as she could tell, they weren't blocked from interacting with the arena itself...

A childish yet brilliant idea formed in Danni's mind.

"Teva, do you have a notebook on you?" she asked excitedly.

"I always do," Teva replied.

"Write a note. Say: *It isn't real; you can't die - Teva.* That should send the message, right?"

"How do you intend on getting it to them?"

"You'll see," Danni smiled.

Teva wrote the note and passed it to Danni. She creased it down the middle and folded the sides inward to make triangles.

"A paper plane? Really?" Teva scoffed. He sounded both sarcastic and impressed.

"Simple solutions are often the most effective," Danni

stated, remembering a lesson she'd learned in her spy training.

Danni sat in nervous anticipation, holding the paper plane gently in her hand.

Quetzalcoatl's simple re-imagining of the Colosseum lacked the grandeur of the real thing. The arena floor was still the same coarse red material that had made up the stadium, though at least the re-model had shaken all of the faeces and blood from the platform.

Prometheus returned to his position beside the giant seat of Skrymir.

"Everything is ready," the titan confirmed.

Danni imagined them all in that dark antechamber now; Mel would be rushing to improvise a plan to get them through this.

Skrymir addressed the crowd again, "Today, you have seen mortals overcome monsters far beyond them. Their skill is undeniable, but now they must face a greater foe. Themselves!"

The crowd whistled and applauded.

"Will one have the courage to tear his allies apart in the pursuit of my prize?"

Skrymir sat back down and nodded to Prometheus.

Silence fell in the arena.

Each member of the AST party appeared, spaced equally far apart on the circular platform, just in front of the wall. They all looked surprised, as if the teleportation had come mid-conversation.

The unseen horn blew again, signalling the start of the battle royale.

Each person looked around the circle nervously.

None moved.

The closest to Danni was Matthew Pyne. He was just off to the right and well within range of the small paper plane.

Next to Matt, further along the circumference, was Mel. Then was Kane, followed by Haruka, Liam, Jesse, Josh (still in his werewolf form, his chest wound now healed) and Sigurd.

Skrymir's eyes were fixed on Sigurd, on the far left of the arena.

Danni seized her moment and threw the plane forward.

It looped and zoomed sideways before being caught by a lucky gust of wind and landing beside Matt's foot.

The ASIS agent had his complete sniper rifle held in his left hand, so he knelt down and picked up the note in his right. He unfolded it and read it.

He swivelled his head around, looking right at Danni.

His blank expression showed that he couldn't see anything. Teva shouted out to him, but the sound barrier was in effect.

Skrymir was already growing agitated. Obviously, he didn't think much of humans if he'd presumed they'd all begin killing each other right away.

"Why aren't they fighting?" he demanded of Prometheus, who didn't answer.

Skrymir stood up and, in his earth-shatteringly loud giant's voice, ordered the combatants to begin fighting or see the artefact of Zeus be forever lost.

Matt looked at the note again, then down to his sniper.

With a sigh of resignation, he moved into the prone position. He set his rifle forward and lined up a shot. Yet, he hesitated to shoot.

Danni understood why. This was a hell of a gamble to take.

Another paper plane landed beside Matt, and Danni turned to Teva in surprise.

"I wrote a message that he would know could only come from me," Teva said. Again, Skrymir hadn't seen the plane fly into the arena.

Matt read the note, then looked down his rifle's sights.

The rest of the circle looked at him curiously. None of them could've possibly thought he'd fire.

"Complete this challenge, or all of you will die!" Skrymir yelled.

That was enough for Matt. He had no choice but to trust the magical paper planes.

He shook his head as his finger moved to the trigger.

A bullet whizzed across the arena, slamming into Liam's forehead, which exploded in a spray of grey matter and blood.

A second later, a very shaken Liam appeared in the row behind them, next to Artemis.

"What the hell?" he breathed, rubbing his temple up and down.

"Welcome to the loser's circle," Danni laughed.

"So, it's not real? We suspected that was going to be the case," Liam frowned. "How did Matt confirm it, though? I mean, come on, him of all people."

"With a little help from us," Danni winked.

Back in the arena, the others were reacting to Liam's unexpected execution.

Melissa ran at Matt, crossing the gulf between them at a

sprint. Matt saw her coming and rolled onto his back. He pulled his pistol and fired three shots at her.

Mel dodged the first two by falling into a running slide, but the third hit her clean in the shoulder.

She gasped in agony but didn't stop moving.

Mel kicked the pistol from his hand and screamed something. It looked to Danni like, 'what are you doing?'.

Matt swept her legs and got to his feet, but Mel was too fast. She controlled her fall and landed right-side-up, so her pistol was easily accessible. She drew it and thrust it into Matt's stomach with her one good arm.

Matt wrapped his arms around Mel in what looked like a bizarre, and poorly improvised, defensive bear hug.

Matt then whispered something into her ear. He was passing on the message!

They saw the air rush out of Mel as the bulky man compressed her, leaving her no choice but to squeeze the trigger. Two rounds flew out of Matt's back as the bullets passed right through him.

Matt collapsed to his knees, gasping for breath. Mel also stumbled, attempting to suck in lungfuls of clean air.

Jesse and Haruka arrived to pull the pair off each other. Matt had been grievously wounded and appeared to be dying slowly.

He shouted something, then began moving his mouth frantically. He was rushing to explain the situation to the others!

Even though Danni couldn't hear him, she knew that was what was happening.

Of all the people to launch into action upon hearing that

death here was fake, Danni never expected the first to be Haruka.

The Japanese girl had a seemingly meek disposition, but she hadn't held back so far in this battle.

Haruka picked up Matt's gun and aimed a shot at his head. She fired.

And faster than anyone else could move, she shot Mel, too.

The whole audience went quiet upon seeing the violent and unexpected display. Then, they cheered harder than ever.

The two AST operatives appeared next to Liam, both looking dumbstruck.

Mel observed Danni, Teva and Liam, then promptly slapped Matt hard across the face.

"Hey! I was doing you a favour!" Matt said, holding his bright red cheek.

"You tried to kill me!"

"Guys, shut up. You're distracting me from the action," Chris, the Taskforce A soldier, said.

Jesse and Haruka were in an all-out brawl. Jesse spun Haruka around and threw her with colossal force towards the arena wall.

Haruka positioned herself to land on the wall feet first, her fingers digging into the wood. She hung there for a moment, like a spider, then pushed herself off and back into the action.

Sigurd, Josh and Kane still hadn't cottoned on to the fact that death didn't matter here. Kane had pushed himself as far back against the wall as he could.

Josh stood, snarling, as he watched everyone else.

Haruka rushed towards Jesse at speeds so fast it didn't look real, like her movement befuddled the eyes.

Jesse grinned and set himself into a fighting stance. Then stopped. He shouted something at the oncoming blur of silky black hair, and she hesitated.

The pair of them turned to face Sigurd.

"I think they want to test their mettle against Earth's mightiest warrior," Mel deducted.

Sigurd appeared to share the sentiment. He drew Apollo's sword and held it at the ready. He laughed heartily and ran forward to meet the two human werewolves.

Haruka and Jesse exchanged sly glances, and Danni immediately knew they'd been training together.

Sigurd brought his blade down towards Jesse, who ducked and tackled the mountainous Viking. Sigurd saw the attack coming and side-stepped, re-directing Jesse's momentum.

That's when Haruka struck, coming in from the side and kicking out the back of Sigurd's knees, causing him to buckle forward.

Jesse threw a powerful back kick right into Sigurd's gut.

"Oh damn!" Teva exclaimed.

"Money's on Sigurd," Liam said quickly.

Sigurd absorbed the blow and dropped the sword. He wrapped his hands around Jesse's ankle and spun him, tossing him away.

Haruka leapt high and wrapped her arms around Sigurd's meaty neck in a clumsy choke-hold.

Sigurd jumped backwards, smashing Haruka into the arena floor and causing her to release. Danni assumed the broken ribs

Haruka surely now had were quickly healing.

Sigurd grabbed Haruka around the neck and heaved her up, before slamming her across his knee.

His eyes went wide when he realised what he'd done.

He'd gotten temporarily caught up in the thrill of the fight. Putting Haruka down gently, Sigurd looked to be furiously apologising to her.

Haruka's spine had already righted itself, and she grabbed Sigurd's head from the front, using him as a pivot to launch a double legged kick into his chest. It was enough to knock the wind out of the Viking.

Right as Sigurd began gasping for air, Jesse approached from behind, wielding Apollo's golden sword.

With an insane reaction time, Sigurd tilted his neck to the left just as the point of the blade sailed towards him. The attack missed by millimetres.

Jesse instantly dropped the heavy sword and lunged back at Sigurd, wrapping his arms around the Viking's midriff. He was strong enough to lift Sigurd off his feet into the air. Haruka began launching a volley of lightning-fast punches into the Viking's gut, causing the Viking to spit blood.

Jesse suddenly dropped Sigurd.

He looked down at his chest and saw a golden point poking through it. Blood was trickling down his clothes.

Kane, the only other man physically large and strong enough to wield the heavy weapon, had run up to help Sigurd, impaling Jesse from the rear.

"This is so epic," Teva giggled.

Kane looked both shocked and horrified at what he'd done.

"That won't be enough to kill a werewolf," Mel murmured.

Sigurd kicked Haruka away and faced Jesse. He spun the Australian police officer around and pulled the sword from his back.

Then, in a powerful sweeping motion, he removed Jesse's head from his body.

Jesse's corpse thudded forward while his head rolled a few feet away, still carrying a startled expression.

Artemis looked mildly annoyed as her row was populated with another defeated combatant.

Jesse placed his hands on his neck and sighed in relief. He then looked at Danni.

"Thank god you're alive!" he said, tears welling in his eyes. "I felt like I'd failed you."

"Nah, we did good!" Danni beamed, reaching out and ruffling his hair.

"We could never have predicted those quills coming from the manticore."

"How did you even know it was a manticore? I was very impressed."

"In my long isolation in Vietnam, I read a lot of books. My mythological knowledge is on point."

"Guys, you're missing it!" Teva hissed.

Sigurd was waving and thrusting the sword at Haruka, who was ducking, dodging and weaving with her own inhuman reaction times.

Kane tried to sneak up behind her, but she hit him in the

face with a spinning tornado kick.

Kane stumbled back, his eyes watering. His jaw was definitely broken.

"Haruka is pretty good for someone who's only just started training," Jesse murmured.

"How can she dodge so well?" one of the Taskforce A guys asked.

"The werewolf curse gives you physical and mental speed. Her perception is superhuman. In a fight, you can feel everything; changes in the air as body parts move, your opponent's heartbeat increasing and decreasing. The curse makes you a weapon."

"I did a lot of training with Josh at Down Under," Liam added. "He is an outstanding fighter now, even when in human form."

The menacing black werewolf was still watching the three-way battle between Sigurd, Haruka and Kane from the far side.

Haruka let loose a volley of punches into Sigurd's chest. He absorbed them and threw a right hook at Haruka, who flipped backwards to dodge it.

Kane, clearly in shock, stumbled away, nursing his jaw. He found a damaged part of the arena's outer wall and climbed up the splintered wood, heaving himself up into the spectator seats.

There was a pop, and Kane teleported to Danni's row, wholly healed.

Much as everyone had done, he gingerly touched his injury. He looked amazed to see everyone else sitting there.

"I have no idea what's going on…" he said slowly.

"Can you move away a bit?" Jesse said to him, shuffling

away. "You stink."

Kane's clothes still had splotches of brown on them from the troll incident.

Skrymir looked towards their group.

"Congratulations on your disqualification," he said sourly.

Kane just shrugged and whispered, "What do I care?"

Sigurd had gone on the defensive, expertly rolling and twisting around Haruka's kicks. He was laughing. The Viking avoided every attack with ease.

He was an experienced warrior and had already figured out Haruka's attack pattern.

Haruka was growing more and more frustrated, and Sigurd was using that to throw her further off-kilter.

Sigurd side-stepped an ungainly punch and pushed Haruka to the ground.

Haruka tried to get up, but Sigurd pinned her down with his foot.

He looked unsure about what to do. There was no way the noble warrior would coldly execute the beautiful Japanese woman, even if he understood it was all just a game.

The elves, dwarves and humans of the audience leant forward in nervous anticipation.

Sigurd raised Apollo's sword, paused, and returned it to his back sling.

He released his foot, and Haruka scrambled to her feet, panting. She looked dishevelled, with torn clothes and hair flopping over her face.

"Oh, so he lets her go but slices my head off," Jesse

muttered.

Haruka raised her fists defiantly but then turned and looked at the ruined wall Kane had escaped from. Not wanting to be killed, she ran for it and quickly pulled herself up.

She popped into place with the rest of them.

"Well fought, Haruka," Jesse beamed.

"Yep, you put on an excellent showing against one of this planet's most well-known warriors," Liam said.

Haruka blushed slightly. Danni felt even more annoyed that she'd been eliminated right away. She could've put up a good fight too, despite not being a supernatural monster.

With only two warriors remaining things had slowed down significantly in the arena.

Sigurd fixed his eyes on Josh.

Earth's mightiest warrior and the pure werewolf faced each other. The greatest among them was about to be determined.

31

JOSH VERSUS SIGURD

Seconds stretched into minutes as every person in the arena held their breath. All were expecting a fight of epic proportions.

Here stood Sigurd, legendary hero of old, against one of the world's most well-known supernatural terrors. A terror that was, unusually, in complete control of its own faculties.

Mel broke the silence by asking, "Hey, where's Malcolm and Neanderthal?"

Danni had forgotten to fill her in.

Teva answered, having some difficulty framing his response. "Ah, well... it seems Malcolm reached a breakthrough in his research into the Necronomicon. He summoned an extra-dimensional monster into the stadium, and it… sort of… transformed Malcolm and pulled Neanderthal into whatever realm it came from."

"What," Mel stated incredulously. "Please explain what 'transformed Malcolm' means?"

"He grew a tentacle and got somewhat purple and swollen," Teva explained.

"So, they are both gone to realms unknown?"

"Yes, it seems so."

"The same as Randall Dare?"

"That is a good assumption to make."

"This is an absolute nightmare," Mel muttered, leaning back.

Danni was surprised by the emotional maturity of the team. Moments ago, they'd been killing each other, and now the focus was back on the mission.

The games of Skrymir had been so distracting that Danni hadn't yet processed what had happened to Malcolm. The professor was such a kind, diligent man, yet the black book had consumed him.

"Where is the Necronomicon?" Mel sighed.

"Prometheus has it," Teva answered.

"A problem to add to the ever-expanding list of problems _"

Mel was cut off by a wave of enthusiastic chatter rolling through the crowd.

Josh and Sigurd had moved towards each other.

The sweat dripped from Sigurd's veiny muscles. The gigantic Norseman was as tall as the werewolf. The fighting had left significant tears in his t-shirt, revealing the runic tattoos on his side. With his braided beard flowing in the breeze, the man was indistinguishable from a god.

On the other hand, Josh looked demonic as he stood hunched on his hind legs, his arms forward with his dagger-like claws outstretched. One swipe from them could end any mortal's life. His fur was matted in the places blood had spilt.

His bronze hand contrasted significantly with the rest of his thick jet-black fur.

Despite the primal fear Josh exuded, he also held a kind of dignity. The dignity of a being so imposing and frightening that a person couldn't help but be impressed.

The two men bowed as a sign of mutual respect.

Sigurd didn't draw Apollo's sword and Josh didn't summon Vargr Muor. This was going to be a brawl.

There was a flurry of clattering metal as gold coins changed hands in the seats. The elves and dwarves were betting heavily on the outcome in what appeared to be a 50/50 split.

Either way, the AST had won. Skrymir was enthralled; that artefact was as good as theirs.

While Sigurd was a dragon slayer and a renowned fighter, Danni was sure he'd have nothing on the pure werewolf.

Josh howled and Sigurd roared.

Sigurd threw a straight punch, and Josh caught it with his bronze claw. Josh shot his other arm forward, his nails ready to impale Sigurd.

Sigurd had planned for this, turning his arm and shifting his weight. On his thin hind legs, the werewolf was thrown off-balance for the briefest moment.

With a sweeping tactical low kick Sigurd forced Josh to jump, releasing his grip.

The Viking launched an uppercut, powered by his entire body.

It connected with Josh's lower jaw with a sickening crunch. A long sharp tooth flew out of his mouth and across the arena.

One of the Taskforce A operatives turned to his fellows and said, "Did I just see a Viking punch a werewolf's tooth out? This is a crazy mission, but I love it."

Both Danni and Teva chuckled.

Josh had been knocked flat on his back. Sigurd pinned his total weight against Josh, wrapping his arm around the wolf's neck. However, the look of surprise when Josh easily pushed him up showed that Sigurd hadn't expected the immense strength of the monster.

The werewolf raised itself as tall as it could, lifting Sigurd onto his tiptoes. Sigurd applied pressure, but the werewolf flipped forward in an awkward gangly summersault, slamming the Viking into the ground.

Josh dug two of his claws into Sigurd's meaty forearm, causing him to yell out and release his suffocating hold.

The werewolf rolled and sprung onto all fours. It lunged jaws first at the Viking.

Sigurd met the bite with a head-butt straight into Josh's snout.

The crowd let out a synchronised gasp of sympathy. They all felt the crunch that followed.

Josh reeled back, blood dripping down his jaws.

Fire burned in his eyes.

He stretched his arm out at a forty-five degree angle and summoned Vargr Muor from his magic hand. He quickly swapped the sword from his bronze left hand to his natural right one.

Sigurd laughed and drew Apollo's sword.

There was a flashing flurry of strikes, parries and blows, in which Josh was hopelessly outmatched. The werewolf body was too ungainly to wield the sword effectively.

Sigurd fought less like a swordsman and more like a dancer. His movement flowed with sublime precision and effortless elegance.

It only took twenty seconds for Josh to be disarmed.

Apparently, Josh decided that the gimmicky sword-slicing werewolf wasn't the best approach for this fight.

He touched the sword with his bronze claw and let it sink back into the hand.

Sigurd, being a perpetual man of honour, once again sheathed the golden blade.

Liam looked disappointed. "Josh is thinking like a man. He is in a monstrous animal body and should act accordingly. The werewolf is a *mindless* effective killer."

It was as if Josh could hear him because his demeanour changed as fast as a shifting wind.

He pounced at Sigurd with ravenous fury. A black mass of teeth, claws, and fur was furiously swiping on top of the Viking.

Sigurd managed to hold his arms high enough that the gashes in his chest didn't go too deep. To hold the killer werewolf back at all was a sign of spectacular strength.

He bent a leg up into a small gap between their torsos and kicked at Josh's knee. It connected with immediate effect, reversing the joint.

Josh yelped and hobbled back in agony, his knee quickly righting itself.

A new fierceness crossed Sigurd's face, probably due to the dozens of deep wounds enveloping his upper body. The Viking was soaked in his own blood.

He went on the offensive, dodging a slash and grabbing the werewolf on the left shoulder. He began delivering knee strike after knee strike into the werewolf's ribs, completely shattering them.

Somehow, the battle had quickly turned in Sigurd's favour. The barrage of injuries was beginning to slow Josh's healing process.

Josh spread his jaws wide and clamped down on Sigurd's left shoulder, ceasing the Viking's relentless assault. Sigurd's collarbone snapped very audibly.

Sigurd wrapped his right arm around the werewolf's neck and pulled his body backwards, slamming the werewolf's head into the arena floor.

This attack finally dazed Josh enough for Sigurd to finish the fight. Even with his broken collarbone, Sigurd was able to sit on Josh's upper back, grip both sides of his head and twist.

Smiling with victory, Sigurd performed the movement.

Only the horrible sound of breaking bone didn't fill the stadium.

Josh transformed back into his human self so fast that Sigurd's hands slipped off his head as he made his neck-twisting final motion.

Josh pushed forward, slipping out from under Sigurd's legs.

It was all so quick Sigurd barely had time to turn to see Josh rise in his fully naked glory.

Again, he summoned Vargr Muor. Now it was he who was ready to end this fight.

The Nordic silver blade whistled threw the air. The clean blow found Sigurd's neck.

Much as the Viking had done to Jesse, his head departed his body.

The crowd exploded.

Even Danni jumped to her feet, screaming with joy.

Josh had done it. The artefact was his. Considering the mission they were on, there wasn't a more perfect winner. Danni couldn't have been more proud.

The geeky bartender she'd met in Cairns had just bested Earth's mightiest warrior in one on one combat.

Standing there, holding his blood-drenched sword high, Josh didn't bother to cover his shame. He embraced his victory in nothing but his own skin.

The elves, dwarves and humans rose to their feet in resounding applause for the champion.

"Excellent!" Skrymir boomed. "Absolutely excellent!"

The wall in front of the giant melted and morphed into a set of red stairs. Skrymir descended them into the arena. He approached Josh, his footsteps shaking the floating ground.

Artemis looked to Prometheus and said, "Clothe the man. I do not desire to see his manhood dangling in the sun."

Prometheus nodded, and the clothes Josh had been wearing before his transformation reappeared, stitching themselves together in midair, and wrapping around him.

Sigurd thumped into the row behind Danni's.

"I cannot believe I lost. Defeat is not a foe I've known in a long time."

"Bloody good fight, though," Danni said.

Everyone else murmured in agreement.

Skrymir stood beside Josh and addressed his watching citizens.

"Utgardians! My friends, see here this day the winner of my games! His victory will reward him with the item requested, an artefact of mighty Zeus. From my treasury, I present this!"

There was a sound like clapping thunder, and an object appeared, floating in front of Josh.

It was roughly a metre long and entirely without detail. It was a jagged cutting of metal, in the shape of a zig-zag, like a cartoon thunderbolt.

Josh gripped it.

"What is it?" Josh asked the giant.

"One of Zeus's weapons. His legendary lightning bolt, capable of obliterating titans and gods alike. This is a weapon of unimaginable power, obtained a long time ago. It is now yours."

Josh looked to where the AST gang were seated. Apparently, he could now see them. He smiled and waved.

He then scanned across the still cheering spectators.

Danni saw him frown slightly. She followed his eye-line to see that the strange Egyptian man had reappeared. His gaze was relentless, staring right into Josh.

The Egyptian's head snapped towards Danni, his haunting eyes boring into hers.

Then, the world went black.

32

NYARLATHOTEP

D anni stumbled as the seat beneath her vanished. She stood in an endless sea of nothingness.

There was someone else here too!

Josh was not too far in front of her, turning back and forth in confusion. Danni called his name and ran over to him. Her feet splashed like she was running through very shallow, invisible water. Josh looked at her, his face etched with concern.

"I don't think this is Skrymir's magic," he called, his voice echoing and distant.

"This place feels like the sunken city... it feels like the Necronomicon!" Danni replied, startled at her own oddly magnified voice.

"The nightmare city was a place of danger, you said," Josh replied. His neck veins pulsed as he let the werewolf transformation take him over again. He summoned his silver sword from his bronze hand and stood at the ready, expecting an attack.

No one else was here other than herself and Josh. Why had the two of them been transported to this empty place?

From the nothingness came a sinister voice, "R'lyeh is a city designed in foreign worlds. It confuses the human mind, and you interpret that as fear and dread."

Josh growled and sniffed the air.

Then, Danni saw the speaker appear.

His footsteps sounded like singular drops of falling water hitting the surface of a pond. In all his ancient finery, the Egyptian was walking toward the pair.

"Who are you?" Danni called across the black abyss.

"A granter of wishes," the Egyptian sneered.

Every hair on the back of Danni's neck stood up. She could smell the ill-intent dripping from the man. Every time he spoke, it was as if Danni could hear a quiet scream in the back of her mind.

Clearly, Josh felt the same way.

The werewolf rushed towards the Egyptian. His deadly bronze claw was wrapped around the hilt of Vargr Muor.

The wolf leapt, raising the gleaming blade high.

He thrust the blade down, aiming to split the Egyptian in two.

The Egyptian didn't flinch. He didn't even blink. The sword collided with his temple and violently dislodged itself from Josh's grip.

The metal clanged as it bounced away.

Josh didn't miss a beat, thrusting his claws at the stranger's torso.

The Egyptian stood completely still as the daggers attempted to pierce his stomach.

Despite Josh having the face of a monstrous black wolf, the concern his eyes showed when his claws did nothing was entirely human. Any other creature would've been impaled, but this man just stood there, looking disdainfully at the monster.

"Enough," the Egyptian commanded. His voice was coarse and quiet. It sent goosebumps across Danni's skin.

"I see you for who you are," the man said.

Josh was blasted away at astonishing speed. He smashed into an invisible wall with a deadly thud and collapsed in a heap.

The Egyptian snapped his fingers. The long shaggy fur that coated Josh retreated. He shrunk in stature, turning back into a man.

Josh whimpered as he sat naked against the wall.

Danni ran towards him.

"Stop," the Egyptian ordered.

Danni froze in place, losing all control of her own body.

"I knew you were coming here," the Egyptian whispered, his eyes fixed firmly on Josh. "The destroyer. You who will unbalance everything."

The Egyptian's words magnified as they travelled through the air. Every time he spoke, Danni could hear that high-pitched wail in her head. The sound was maddening. She wanted to scream along with it.

Josh looked up. His eyes were bloodshot and a red trail dribbled from his mouth.

"Name yourself," Josh gasped, clutching at his ribs.

The Egyptian said nothing as he slowly moved towards the human werewolf.

Danni thought back to the ramblings of Malcolm Selleck. He said the crawling chaos was coming; the monster called Nyarlathotep. She'd heard that name repeatedly, Nyarlathotep, and now it had just clicked. This must've been the creature Mel had seen standing on the alien world when she touched the Necronomicon.

The Egyptian's head snapped to Danni.

The entire room changed. The floor became an endless ocean of blue flame.

It was like she and Josh were floating high enough to see the curvature of a world of fire.

"You know my name," the Egyptian said.

"Nyarlathotep," Danni breathed. She felt like she was trapped in a cocoon of thick air.

"Let her go!" Josh demanded.

"You two together," Nyarlathotep smiled, "are balance before chaos and the chaos before balance."

He drew a yin and yang symbol in the air in front of him.

There was a flash of the most brilliant light, and for a terrifying second Danni saw the Egyptian's true form. Skinless, faceless and covered in writhing tentacles, the man's true being floated before them.

"Why are you here? Why have you come?" Danni asked,

her voice riddled with panic.

"I walked across space and time to see the beginning of the end. Forward and back and round and round goes the cycle. Men should not look upon the faces of the gods, let alone try to join their ranks."

"We are doing what needs to be done," Josh spat.

"What needs to be done..." Nyarlathotep mulled that statement over.

Josh and Nyarlathotep disappeared.

Danni squirmed against her invisible bindings. The blue planet of fire was growing smaller and smaller below her. She was soaring across the cosmos.

"You know why I am here," Nyarlathotep's disembodied voice said. "You were there when the goddess broke the old laws. She played with life against my command."

"If she has the power to do it, why shouldn't she?" Danni said aggressively.

"Why should Eve not eat from the Tree of Knowledge?" Nyarlathotep sneered back.

"If it's Artemis you want, why are you speaking to us?"

"You two are part of my punishment. You are like pebbles rolling down a mountainside before the avalanche crushes all in its way. You cannot avoid your fate, much as she cannot change the path she now walks."

The planet of blue fire was now a marble-sized spec in the distance.

Danni crashed into something. It was the naked writhing form of Josh, apparently also fighting invisible bonds.

"Danni," he said, relieved.

"This creature is from the Necronomicon! Everything in that book is evil!" Danni yelled to Josh.

"Evil," Nyarlathotep stated, sounding intrigued.

Suddenly, he appeared towering like a titan against the black backdrop. His vertical slit mouth and eyeless tentacle head twitched.

"I am the Necronomicon," he laughed. "I taught the Sundered King how to dance with the gods. I led him to Abdul Alhazred, who gave my knowledge to the world. I sat in desert storms and waited for a traveller to take my book on its long journey to the angels."

"What are you?" Josh demanded.

"An outer god, they call me on your small world. I am the only one of my kind who walks among you."

"What about the monster in the sunken city? Was that an outer god too?" Danni asked.

"Cthulhu's rise will be a blessing. Long have I whispered into Archangel Michael's ears from the dark, making him dread slumbering Cthulhu. They have become too powerful; their existence is an affront to the order of things. The great old one will swipe them from the skies."

"You spoke through the Necronomicon, didn't you! You drove Malcolm insane!"

"I have no plan. I just set things in motion and hope they end up the way they should. The Necronomicon reveals many things to those who read it, as was Alhazred's design. The true power of this universe isn't found in gods or magic; it is found in piping flutes and beating drums!"

Something moved in the dark.

Danni saw a swirling black mass in the centre of all things, pulsing with red lightning. Distant galaxies were tiny compared to it. They must've been so far away, but the dread visage was all-consuming. The sound of drums and flutes assaulted their ears, deafeningly loud.

"MAKE IT STOP!" Josh yelled.

Danni saw something else; things were shifting in the darkness of space between the swirling galaxies. Like colossal cosmic larvae, the hideous slimy creatures as black as emptiness were pressed upon one another, squirming and writhing.

Danni felt like she was losing her mind staring into the horror of the darkness.

"I wanted to see you two now," Nyarlathotep said coldly. "As I have watched Artemis since you arrived. The gods lost their way and lost their position. I do not see their use anymore. Do you?"

Josh cried in agony. The noise, the lightning, and the creatures were all too much.

The pair of them began spinning through the darkness, faster and faster. Danni thought she was going to be sick.

She could hear something else now. There was a faint song in her ears. Nyarlathotep was singing.

"In the shadows of mountains and in the wind of mountain-tops, she loves to take her bow..."

Danni grimaced and braced.

"Her bow made of silver, and shoot off her shafts of woe..."

Then, with a thud, they landed on solid ground. Blinding

natural light flooded into the arena and the crowd continued cheering.

It was like they'd never vanished.

Danni was still in her seat, and Josh was holding the jagged piece of metal. The Egyptian was nowhere to be seen.

Danni felt renewed purpose; she had information no one else did. Nyarlathotep was clearly a force well beyond that of Earth's gods. He had set things in motion to destroy the angels and punish the gods. Now that they knew that was happening, they could make a plan.

Danni was sure the plan to take the empty position of Zeus was pivotal to all this.

Josh looked across the arena to Danni, his eyes brimming with fear.

33

THE CAVERN OF
THE SKY

THE CAVERN OF THE SKY
- FEBRUARY 8 -

The lightning bolt in Josh's hands was rather plain.

In fact, if Danni hadn't been assured of its authenticity, she would've thought Skrymir was pranking them.

Burying his concern over the startling encounter with Nyarlathotep, Josh continued playing his role. He raised the prize high above him, and the crowd cheered again.

Skrymir stood up and bowed deeply.

Then the world blurred.

Danni was no longer seated in the spectator stands. Josh, too, seemed dazed by the change of location. Just how many sudden snaps across space could the human body handle?

For a long second, Danni feared they were back in the black abyss again.

Fortunately, she'd returned to the great hall before Skrymir's throne. In front of her stood Josh, Skrymir, Prometheus and Artemis. Danni figured the stadium's architect, Quetzalcoatl, had stayed to return the arena to its original design.

"Consider it payment for an entertaining afternoon well earned," Skrymir said.

"It's so simple," Josh said, studying the artefact closely. His voice was shaky, and Danni could tell he was trying to ground himself back in the present.

Artemis walked up and took the lightning bolt from his hands.

"It has been an age since I've seen one of these."

"It is genuine, then?" Josh asked, quietly enough that Skrymir couldn't hear.

"Yes. Watch."

Firm in the grasp of the goddess, the metal sprung to life. It became a twisting arching line of pure electricity, explosively crackling.

Artemis raised it like a javelin, as if she was about to throw it, but stopped. She lowered the weapon and it returned to its motionless metallic form. She handed it back to Josh.

"One of these could obliterate a titan," Artemis said with hushed awe.

"How did you activate it?" Josh asked.

"It is designed for the divine. You could never use it."

Danni watched Josh and Artemis' conversation with

mild annoyance. Had he forgotten their bizarre encounter with Nyarlathotep so quickly? Or had she just dreamed it?

"Artemis, we need to talk to you. In that arena, something happened… we met a creature named –"

"Nyarlathotep," Prometheus interjected.

"How did you know?"

"I felt his energy come and go for a split second. It was so fleeting that it almost wasn't real, but I was paying special attention after the incident with the book. That is why I have brought both yourself and the girl here back before the others."

"What are you talking about?" Skrymir boomed, leaning in.

"Old mysteries and dark stories," Prometheus answered.

"I do love a good story," the giant stated, taking a seat on his throne.

"This story is so old its truth is beyond my knowledge. I know the name from my youth; a name associated with secret laws and fearful words from the primordials," Prometheus stated.

"He's coming for you, Artemis," Danni interjected quickly.

Josh nodded. "He said it directly. You broke his laws, apparently."

Danni was elated that Josh had spoken up. It meant she wasn't going crazy.

"Where was he? What did he look like?" Artemis asked.

"He was here the whole time. He was that Egyptian-looking guy. We saw him when we first arrived and he watched the games," Danni answered.

"I never saw such a man," Artemis frowned.

"Melissa also saw him in a vision when we were in

Amsterdam, only there, he looked like an alien monster," Danni added.

"If he was here, and he intends to punish me for breaking the old laws, why didn't he?" Artemis asked.

"He said he'd put things in motion to punish everyone on Earth, basically, and a comment about training the Sundered King, or something..." Josh answered hesitantly.

"What do you know of the Egyptian who lingered in your court?" Prometheus asked Skrymir.

"Very little. Long ago, he taught me powerful magic in return for a place to rest when he visited this world. I always suspected there was more to him than the image he presented. He takes particular joy in cruelty and misfortune. Everything is a game. He appears here from time to time, but we do not speak much. I dread his loathsome company."

Danni exchanged a glance with Josh.

This giant was so powerful in magic that he had a Greek titan and an Aztec god working beneath him. Yet, Nyarlathotep was a source of fear for him. That didn't bode well with Danni.

"That black book has something to do with him," Danni added on from Josh. "He said he taught the Sundered King how to dance with the gods, and the Sundered King helped Abdul Alhazred write the book, I think."

"This magic he taught you, do you use it still?" Prometheus asked Skrymir.

"No, or I try not to. I did today, actually, to send that creature back into the void," Skrymir replied darkly. "That magic comes from a forbidden place. It is foreign, dangerous, and I do not trust it. I recognised it when the professor summoned the abomination in the games. There are dark things in the voids beyond our world that are always trying to get in, and I was always concerned I'd accidentally do just that if I tampered with it too much."

"The old laws of the gods, most of which were lost to time, could've been designed to keep this being, this Nyarlathotep, away," Artemis said, unsure.

"He must be a primordial of some kind, though he doesn't seem like one… at least his energy and how he interacts with mortals are nothing like the primordials we know," Prometheus said slowly.

"Is there a primordial we can speak to? Concern fills my mind that a trap is being set for me. I need information."

"There is no primordial that can be called upon without tearing the planet asunder, although…"

Prometheus looked down the great chamber to the fantastic blue door they'd all marvelled at on entry.

"The sky door? That doesn't open," Skrymir bellowed, following the titan's gaze.

"Yes," Prometheus nodded.

"What is that door?" Josh asked.

A dreamy gaze wrapped Skrymir's face. "My masterpiece. Magic so profound that I don't think Hecate herself would've been able to manifest it."

"A door that doesn't open is your masterpiece?" Josh asked sarcastically.

Skrymir paid him no heed. "Even when I was young in Jotunheim, I felt something in me. It was a pull in my very soul. I was found an orphan, you know, blessed with magic beyond anything the giants had ever seen. As I grew older and more powerful, I felt the pull grow stronger. After I built Utgard, I couldn't resist any longer. I let the magic take my hands and it slowly began creating this door. Thousands of years it took... it was like there was another force resisting it, but I didn't stop. Now the door with no key stands radiant in my hall. Where it leads, I don't know. How it opens, I don't know. I just know it's part of me."

"For a being that isn't a god, your power is unnatural," Artemis stated plainly.

"What can I say?" Skrymir smiled.

"In the years I've resided in Utgard, I have developed theories about that door. Theories we can now test," Prometheus remarked.

"Where do you think it goes?" Artemis asked.

Prometheus snapped his fingers and time stopped. Skrymir was caught mid-yawn. It seemed only Josh, Danni and Artemis were unaffected.

"I would speak without Skrymir listening," Prometheus said.

"How can you freeze him if he's that powerful?" Danni asked.

"He still needs time to react and apply his magic," Prometheus answered.

"What is he?" Artemis asked, staring quizzically at the frozen giant.

"I have, for a time, suspected that Skrymir is an unknowing avatar of the Sky-Father Ouranos. That is why I have lingered here for so long. And due to this, I suspect his Sky Door is a gate to the

Cavern of the Sky."

"The Cavern of the Sky?" Josh asked.

"The deepest point of the Underworld holds a prison so perfectly hidden that it can never be found. Inside it is Ouranos, father of Cronus and grandfather of Zeus, eternally chained inside a pit of pure darkness, or so the legends say. Apparently, it can only be accessed by the Lord of the Underworld. Even then, the path to take is almost impossible to find."

"I'm guessing Ouranos is super powerful?" Danni asked.

"He is the first titan and the last primordial. His anger and hatred have bled into the rocks of the Cavern of the Sky and towards the surface. You humans now mine this product as uranium. He is so powerful that his will still asserts itself on the world, unknown even to him.

"Beings like Skrymir are manifestations of Ouranos, though they would never know it. Across cultures, stories pop up every now and then of creatures with power beyond that of the gods. They are all avatars of Ouranos, his influence manifesting in physical form."

"If any being would know about the old laws, it would be Ouranos!" Artemis exclaimed. "Can we open the door and speak to him."

"I actually believe we can, with you three."

Artemis, Josh and Danni all looked at each other. What did they have that could allow them to enter the perfect prison?

"Joshua Dare, you are a link to the power of Zeus, the grandson of Ouranos. Artemis, you're his descendant, as I am, though you are closer to the line of kings. And Danni Quinn, I don't know what it is, but I feel something of Lucifer about you."

Danni thought about the kiss of Lucifer. Both Artemis and Josh knew about it, and they were the only ones here.

"Lucifer did something to me. He said that if I called upon him, he would come."

Prometheus continued, "Lucifer is the current ruler of the Underworld and the only being that could potentially call on the Primordial Tartarus. Also, he is the only being that could visit the Cavern of the Sky, if he knew the way."

"These three separate links are enough to enter the cavern?" Artemis said.

"Not on their own. However, I believe if all four of us exist in the same space at the same time, the union of these elements could allow one of us to pass through the door."

"Doesn't make sense to me," Josh murmured.

"You must remember that this door isn't really a door. It is a manifestation of the avatar of Ouranos. It is his power trying to return to its source. If we can connect to that flow of energy through our shared links, we may be able to move through the door into the cavern."

"What did you mean 'in the same space at the same time?'" Danni asked cautiously.

"I can combine our physical forms and essences into one being," Prometheus stated.

"We will split apart, though, right?"

"Most certainly. A titan, a god and two mortals will make an unstable mix. We must be in and out before the spell breaks down. Control your minds, do not let Ouranos talk us in circles. His long years of imprisonment may have left him more than eager to answer our questions."

Prometheus teleported them to the threshold of the huge Sky Door. Its shimmering light blue façade was as entrancing as ever.

Then, something uncomfortable happened. Danni felt her body turn into fleshy jelly, and she sped towards Josh. They slammed into each other with a wet slap.

Danni felt every uncomfortable second pass slowly as their bodies were molded into one. Then Artemis zoomed in, too, though she didn't feel like a squishy human. Her part of the union made Danni feel giddy and light-headed.

The squirmy pyramid of flesh they'd become wrapped itself around Prometheus in a grotesque display of body horror.

Although Danni had lost all sense of her body, she was still thinking. The sensation was so strange. It felt like a twisted drug-induced hallucination. Like she was just a disembodied thought floating in the air.

She felt a mix of other voices in her head. Josh, Artemis and Prometheus were all chattering loudly in her mind.

Then, she only felt one voice, but it wasn't Danni Quinn's. This was a new voice. She decided that she would call herself 'the entity'. A fitting name for a being that shouldn't be.

The entity looked at her body.

It was both masculine and feminine.

All four of them had blended together into one creature that balanced all of their features equally. She was a hybrid of gender and being.

The entity approached the door and placed her hand against

it.

Yes! She could feel it not as metal but as cascading energy moving through dimensions!

Without a second thought, the entity dived through from Utgard, frozen in time, to the Cavern of the Sky.

• • • • •

THE RIVER OF ENERGY PROPELLED her through darkness, water and molten rock, going faster and faster towards the roots of the world.

It was hot.

If it weren't for the divinity of Prometheus and Artemis, she would've melted during the journey down.

The rapid descent slowed, and the entity found herself falling through a mighty cave somewhere near the Earth's core.

The air was cool and a serene blue glow lit the place up.

The entity landed on the ground and immediately felt woozy. All the dirt, rock and stone were poison, so she took to the air and surveyed the place. It was simultaneously a surprise and something always known that she could fly.

A dark chasm ran the length of the cavern. Huge stalactites hung from the roof, and around them, hundreds of glowing primordial wisps danced and whispered secret things. It was them who gave off the unholy light flickering in the depths.

In the dark chasm, where the light didn't penetrate, was the eternally bound Ouranos. The entity feared getting too close. Every cell, both mortal and divine, wanted to flee from that black pit.

Rage and hatred emanated from it in an endless tidal wave of pain. The enmity of Ouranos choked the air.

"Who has come to my prison?" a deep voice called.

"I have."

"How are you here?"

"Luck and circumstance," she replied.

Ouranos growled in the darkness below. The entire cavern shook.

"I sense familiarity, though I cannot place it," Ouranos said.

"Some of my blood is your blood," the entity replied.

She didn't want to linger here. She needed to ask her questions and go.

"Hades came down here when the angels attacked the Underworld, then he died," Ouranos said solemnly.

"I have not come to talk about the diminished gods of old. I desire knowledge that only you can tell."

"Speak and let your request fall on willing ears."

"The ancient laws of the primordials, which say you cannot transfer life between beings, where did they come from?"

"A strange question. Higher beings shouldn't dabble in life and death unless it is in their domain."

"Why not?"

"Because life is sacred above all things."

"Is that your decree? Or the decree of something beyond the Sky-Father Ouranos?"

Ouranos went silent for a moment. Apparently, even for a being such as him, this was a complex topic of conversation.

"Do you know the history of the divine?" he asked from

his dark prison.

"Yes," the entity answered. "From Chaos came the primordials, then the titans and then the gods."

"Chaos, yes. What is Chaos?" Ouranos asked playfully.

"To my knowledge, it is the original lifeform, birthed into the universe when it began. The origin of magic and divinity," the entity answered.

"Have you met Chaos?"

"No... I thought Chaos was more of a concept than anything. Some force that spewed out the first primordials then vanished."

"I have seen Chaos. There is a storm in space where black clouds pulse with red lightning, hiding the truth beneath. Drums beat in the dark at the centre of all things, and flutes play an unhinged melody. Chaos sleeps, as he will for the life of the universe. When he wakes, everything will end, including me..."

"This sounds like a myth among the primordials," the entity thought.

"But the laws around life and death? What do they have to do with Chaos?"

"The primordials of Earth are of the unnumbered children of Chaos. But none are his true children. His true spawn knows him by another name. A name I dare not speak for it summons their gaze. They spoke the ancient laws, and they enforce them."

"The name Nyarlathotep, what does it mean to you?"

Ouranos laughed. "And so you speak a name I dare not. Though it is the name of a lesser evil than what Chaos hides."

"Who is he? What is he?" the entity asked.

"He is the heart and soul of the outer gods. He is their messenger and it is from his words the ancient laws spring. His kind are cold and distant, some existing beyond the boundaries of this universe, waiting in the dark to be let in. He plays with mortals and gods alike for his amusement, calling on his family from the infinite void to bring madness. He is the chaos that crawls across millions of worlds. Do not bring him here!"

"He is here," the entity replied. "Your great-great-granddaughter, Artemis, broke the sacred rules and he came. How do we defeat him?"

"He cannot be defeated," Ouranos stated absolutely. "He can be distracted, that is all. He will make bargains and deals, but they cannot be trusted! Artemis must pray that Nyarlathotep forgets her, or she will face the consequences of her actions. Do not repeat the mistakes of Zeus."

"Wait, Zeus?"

"Before Hades travelled down here during the Battle of the Underworld, Zeus came. It can't have been more than a couple hundred years beforehand. He asked similar questions to you. Questions about knowledge that should've been forgotten."

"Then he was pulled from time and space," the entity thought.

"Why has knowledge about these outer gods like Nyarlathotep been hidden and not passed down through the titans to the gods?" the entity demanded.

"Because we pretend they don't exist in the hopes they ignore us. Nyarlathotep could blink our world out of existence with a thought. The divine perform their roles as their nature indicates. I have not lived in the world of mortals like the gods currently do, but I suspect that when Nyarlathotep comes now, he leaves seeds of his power for mortals to find. Teaches them some of his tricks. Connects them to the monsters in the cosmic void, all for his own entertainment."

"Like Abdul Alhazred! Leading him to the knowledge that allowed him to write the Necronomicon! What about the monster in the sunken city, Cthulhu? That place was hundreds of millions of years old, and the Necronomicon led us to it. What interest does Nyarlathotep have in ancient alien cities?"

"Along with the outer gods were lesser beings in their order called 'the great old ones'. Some of them came to Earth with armies and made war with us, and amongst themselves, in our early days. The great old ones are mighty foes. If one has arisen in your world, you will need considerable power to defeat it."

"Perhaps you know this one? He is named Cthulhu from the city R'yleh. He is awake."

"I know his name as a dread whisper. He is a foe equal to the primordials. As he was called in my time, the great dreamer will have long been infecting the minds of mortals in his slumber. They will use the seeds of Nyarlathotep to wake his army."

"Yes! The Cult of Cthulhu has been using the Necronomicon! What does Cthulhu want?"

"To rule your world, both the physical and the divine. If Cthulhu is awake, your petty wars between gods and angels must cease in preparation for a greater foe."

The entity felt a wave of sickness wash over her. She doubled over in pain.

"Our time is at an end. I feel the magic that brought you

here fading. Do not bring an end to this world by angering the outer gods, for I wish to one day escape my bonds and reclaim my position as king," Ouranos boomed.

The entity screamed out in pain. She fell backwards, letting the river of energy flow back the way she'd come. Through fire, rock and darkness, she soared, turning into gelatinous goo and splitting apart.

The entity burst through the Sky Door and slid along the stone tiles of Utgard's great hall. Her bulbous unshapely body separated, turning back into the four beings that had formed her.

Danni inhaled a huge breath. Her entire body ached.

With a groan, she stumbled to her feet and wiped her eyes.

She was thoroughly coated in a slimy layer of mucus.

"Gross," she muttered, wiping it away.

"Hey!" Josh said as the gooey load landed on his face. He was equally sopping and disgusting.

Both Artemis and Prometheus looked immaculate, free from the residue of the merger.

"Well, we have an answer and a further problem," Prometheus said.

"Yes," Artemis frowned. There had been a lot to take in during that brief talk.

"If he truly wishes to punish you, it could be a game with devastating consequences for all of the gods," Prometheus said.

"Don't forget about Cthulhu in R'lyeh," Danni added. "We probably haven't heard anything from the Pacific because he is awakening an army. Ouranos said the great old ones came here with armies."

"Let us hope he is. The armies of Heaven will be met by an unknown and difficult foe. We can use that to our advantage," Artemis grinned.

Artemis picked up the artefact of Zeus, which had been left lying on the floor.

"It is now more important than ever that we destroy the angel detector. If I have any hope of combating Nyarlathotep's schemes, I need to be free to use my power."

"Ouranos made it sound pretty hopeless," Danni murmured.

"He has been in chains for millions and millions of years. He does not know the world and he does not know us. No matter what an outer god is, we are still gods all the same."

Danni nodded.

"Let us find the humans. We make for Africa immediately. Are you coming, Prometheus?"

"No. I have confirmed that Skrymir is an unconscious manifestation of Ouranos' desire to be free. He has built the Sky Door, and while he cannot pass through it as we just did, he must be watched. The Sky Father's freedom would be just as deadly as any of the current threats."

Artemis nodded, and Prometheus teleported them back to Skrymir's throne. He snapped his fingers and time resumed.

Skrymir observed Josh and Danni dripping with mucus.

"I do not know what trick you have just pulled, Prometheus, and will not ask," he sighed.

A side door to the great chamber burst open. The entire gang walked in, all looking perfectly healthy after the ordeal in the arena.

Skrymir stood up and addressed the crowd. "Thank you all for your participation today. Your reward from my collection is well-earned."

"It was kind of fun," Matt joked.

"Except that we lost Selleck and Neanderthal," Mel responded, her eyes like daggers.

"You are free to leave with nothing further asked of you."

"Can you do us a favour, Lord Skrymir?" Melissa asked the giant.

"Ask and see it considered."

"Give us some time to prepare, and then transport us to the town of Moshi in Africa. We have another mission to complete right away."

Artemis grunted her approval of Mel's request.

"Very well, but I will ask something in return," Skrymir smiled. "Give me Sigurd from among your ranks. An age ago, I asked him to become the champion of Utgard, and I will ask again now."

"He is not mine to give," Mel replied, looking at the Viking hero.

"What would you have with me?" Sigurd asked.

"A mortal champion of Utgard. The fact that you have all come here signals our time in isolation is over. If the castle is opened to others, we will need a representative and defender."

Sigurd looked to Mel, who shrugged.

"I reluctantly agree. It seems my path has been leading here for a long time," Sigurd said with a heavy sigh.

Danni ran up and gave Sigurd a big hug.

"Save your farewells for your departure!" Sigurd laughed.

"Let's make it quick. Africa awaits," Mel said.

Danni felt a sense of finality in the air. Their team was depleted, and the mission ahead was tough, but she was sure they could do it.

34

THE NEXT STEP

I n truth, they didn't have much to prepare. None of the team had come with any luggage (except Teva and his bag of headphones), and all the ammunition spent in Skrymir's games had magically replenished.

Mel ordered Danni, Matt, Liam and Taskforce A to discuss the pending mission to Africa in an impromptu meeting.

Josh, Haruka, Jesse, Kane and Sigurd were left to their own devices, though they couldn't be bored in the magical castle. Prometheus let slip that there were several magical rooms to find that contained wonders he could barely describe. He hinted that if they found tapestries that seemed out of place, they would discover hidden pathways to Utgard's most secret areas.

While Danni was well aware of her duties, she struggled to suppress her annoyance at having to be in the 'planning team'. She would've liked nothing more than to go on a fantastical treasure hunt with Josh. She longed to explore the realm hand in hand with him, breathing in the enchanted air. It wasn't to be, though.

The giant's dining hall was well equipped with normal-sized seating. Mel sat at the head of the table and addressed the congregation.

"First thing, Taskforce A, how are you going to report the disappearance of Lieutenant Commander Leeson?"

The older member, Troy, spoke up. "We will report it as we saw it. Since that monster came from the Necronomicon and USSOT is currently studying the same book, it's operationally relevant."

"I will be doing the same in my report about Malcolm," Mel stated.

"Though leaving out the part where he became a monster, I assume?" Matt asked.

"No, that will go in, too. It needs to be made known just how dangerous the Necronomicon is. We need to be on the same page as the US regarding that book."

Danni hadn't yet told Mel about her meeting with Nyarlathotep. That all-powerful outer god was a trickster and seemingly responsible for everything recorded in the Necronomicon. She wanted to broach the topic as soon as possible but in private.

"Next," Mel continued, "will you be joining us in our mission to Africa?"

"No, we have orders to return to Ukraine. However, after we speak to Captain Shear, I don't think she would be against us assisting you in whatever your mission is. That being said, without magic, I don't see how we can get there. Your mission will be over before we arrive. I think it best that we wait for the next step."

"To be expected," Mel said, looking somewhat disheartened. Though Danni didn't know why. This mission was more likely to succeed with fewer people, not more.

"Where is Artemis?" Danni asked.

Of all the people that should be here, she was one of the most important.

"She went off with Prometheus. Danni, you were in the spectator seats with Artemis for most of the games. Did something happen? She seems off..."

Again, Danni's mind instantly jumped to Nyarlathotep. Artemis knew she would be punished soon, and the outer god's words implied that all gods would feel his wrath as a consequence.

"I don't know... she's still worried about the bridge in Niflheim."

Mel looked at her curiously. She could tell Danni wasn't telling her the whole story.

"You and I can discuss it later," Mel said.

Danni felt guilty as Mel's gaze pierced her.

There was a creaking of rusty hinges as Sigurd burst into the hall, unaware that he wasn't invited to this particular meeting.

"My friends, the Lord of Utgard has offered one night's lodgings and a magnificent feast tonight. Be like Loki, an age of the Earth ago, and eat until your heart and stomach are full to bursting!"

"I don't want to seem rude, Sigurd, but time is not our friend," Mel said slowly.

"I'm afraid you have no choice but to accept Skrymir's hospitality. There is no way out of Utgard without him, and he has decided on a feast. Besides, was it not you who allowed your team to rest recently for several days? After that tournament, I think one night's recovery is well earned."

Mel seemed unable to combat his logic.

"Well, I could use a break after that tournament," Matt yawned happily.

"A blessing in disguise," Liam said, rising from the table. He looked at Mel and added, "We can't fight fate. I'm sure everything will fall into place tomorrow."

"Thanks, Liam," Mel smiled warmly. She stood too.

"Danni, I will find you later. Everyone, make sure you are in the great hall at sunrise tomorrow. Spread the word."

Danni scanned left to right and concluded that the meeting was over.

Maybe Josh hadn't found any of the castle's secrets yet, and she could still join him.

Grinning slightly, Danni rose and made for the great hall.

Before she left, she saw out the corner of her eye that Matt and Liam had spotted a stack of enormous barrels. They disappeared using stairs that looked conspicuously like they led to a wine cellar. The two professionals, both accomplished in their fields, acted like rowdy teenagers in each other's company.

The Taskforce A members bid curt farewells to those still around and went to find Skrymir. They needed to request an early departure. Danni figured that reporting Neanderthal's disappearance was a matter of urgent priority. She was sure USSOT would dive into the Necronomicon to try and find him. Perhaps they'd locate Randall in their search. That'd be a win.

Danni found Josh waiting inside an alcove that led to a high winding stair.

"I have a surprise for you," he smiled, grabbing her by the hand and whisking her upwards.

Danni laughed as all thoughts of outer gods and great old ones were swept from her mind.

Their footsteps echoed on the shimmering marble as they climbed up and up.

Josh lifted the corner of a tapestry showing a blonde warrior fighting a smokey creature holding a hammer. Behind it was a crawl space that fresh air was blowing through.

Ushering her in, they both got on their hands and knees and crawled out.

The day had been long, and its ending was greeted by a spectacular purple and orange sunset. The clouds were ignited high above the endless sea of grass around Utgard.

They skipped along the ramparts and finding a high arched gate, entered onto a viewing platform abundant with tall sunflowers.

"Someone likes sunflowers a bit much..." Danni murmured, running her hands through the plantation of cheery yellow petals.

"Wow, you're so edgy now that you're a spy," Josh said sarcastically.

"You can't go to Hell and not be a little edgy," Danni laughed back.

"Oh, I'm Danni; I made out with the Devil and hate sunflowers," Josh mocked in a poor imitation.

Danni pushed him playfully.

On the edge of a dangerously steep rampart, Josh and Danni sat side by side and soaked in the magic flowing in the artificial breeze. Facing the sunset and surrounded by tall flowers, Danni felt like she was living in a teenager's romantic fantasy, and didn't hate it.

Josh had managed to barter with a serving woman for a wicker picnic basket. He'd then snuck into the kitchen and filled it with whatever he could get his hands on.

Unfortunately, it was only a selection of roasted meats.

Danni wasn't a heavy red meat eater these days but couldn't deny the succulent smells.

"Do you remember when I took you up the Red Arrow for a picnic back in Cairns?" Josh asked.

Danni leaned her head on his shoulder and smiled. "Yep, it rained and rained."

Josh laughed.

"It was magical, though. We stood up high and watched that thunderstorm," Danni yawned.

"Yeah, for a moment there, it felt like we were in a world like this. There was nature in all its raw power, just me and you beneath the storm. I've thought about that a lot."

"Now look at us. We are sitting on top of a giant's castle after battling monsters in an arena. Things have escalated quickly."

Josh chuckled. "Yep, a bit of a change from working in that bar. Remember emptying coins from the pokie machine?"

Danni had never been one to live in the past, but she liked that Josh had such a nostalgic sense.

The last rays of sunlight flickered on the horizon.

"It's not real, you know," Josh said, pulling a hunk of meat from the basket and ripping at it with his teeth.

"What isn't?" Danni asked, retreating from his carnivorous assault.

"The horizon, clouds and distant grass. Utgard is really small. It is all a spell maintained by Skrymir, a metaphor for reality lost in infinity or something. That's what an elf I met this afternoon told me."

"It's pretty beautiful for something that isn't real," Danni smiled.

"Makes me think about Ouranos. The way Prometheus talked about him was like he was a diabolical tyrant. But Skrymir is just a manifestation of him, and look at the beauty he can create."

"What is your point?" Danni asked.

"I dunno… ever since I became a werewolf, I've thought about the duality in all things. The inner darkness and the outer light. Not even the gods are absolute; we are all capable of beauty and terror."

"What terror am I capable of?" Danni asked coyly.

"Getting a dangerous job and making me worry about you," Josh said, half sincere and half sarcastic.

"I've handled myself so far."

"So you have," Josh smiled. "Here, you are letting the pieces of giant roast oxen get cold. Or how about roast giant boar?"

Josh shoved the wad of meat towards Danni, and she batted

it away.

Night engulfed Utgard, and the northern lights began dancing across the sky like they were ripped from the Arctic.

"What are we in for tomorrow?" Josh asked, wrapping his arm around Danni. His bronze hand rested on her thigh.

"Finding a way into an ancient city being watched over by a super-powerful archangel inside a dormant volcano. You know, no big deal," Danni shrugged.

Josh frowned.

During their two days in Ukraine, Josh'd told Danni how he'd been able to fight angels in Heaven by being imbibed with angelic power. Without access to that powerful form, the werewolf inside wouldn't help against these foes.

They sat for a long time in silence, watching the colourful lights sway in the sky. In that moment, Danni felt at peace. Though in the very back of her mind swirled thoughts of Nyarlathotep and the promised doom he was bringing.

· · · · ·

JOSH AND DANNI EVENTUALLY joined the feast in the dining hall. Alcohol was flowing in tall foaming mugs. There was an endless supply of meat, and a group of elves were playing upbeat but strangely ethereal music on odd instruments.

Danni smirked when she saw that both Matt and Liam had gotten drunk and were loudly boasting about their victory over their monster.

A group of dwarves had surrounded Sigurd, who was

deeply embroiled in a drinking competition with Kane. They were beginning to wager gold and weapons on the winner as Kane inhaled yet another goblet of mead.

Haruka, for once, didn't look sour. She had whipped Jesse up to dance with her on one of the long tables while Skrymir watched on, tapping his foot and looking thoroughly amused.

None of the Taskforce A guys could be seen anywhere. Danni learned that Skrymir only granted their request to leave early because they'd performed so dismally in the games. She was embarrassed to think by that logic, she'd be allowed to go too.

Teva had been handed a bunch of old scrolls and was pouring over them with some of Utgard's more scholarly denizens. To say he was captivated by the documents was an understatement.

Artemis and Prometheus were nowhere to be seen. Quetzalcoatl stood ominous and unsmiling by the door.

Sitting in a dark corner were five people Danni somewhat recognised. Though she couldn't pinpoint them in her memory.

She nudged Josh when she realised who they were. They were the five werecreatures he'd fought, now fully clothed and looking grim.

Josh rushed over to introduce himself. Danni didn't follow, watching curiously. They seemed to greet Josh warmly but eyed him suspiciously.

Danni felt a tap on her shoulder and turned to see the unreadable face of Melissa behind her.

"We should talk," she said quite loudly.

"Let's go somewhere else!" Danni shouted above the noise.

They left the hall and followed a wide corridor into a small room, where the noise of the party had diminished enough for conversation to be had.

"Sorry, Mel, I haven't had a chance to talk to you since it happened. When Josh won the tournament, I had a vision. We both did. Only it wasn't a vision, not really. We were pulled from Utgard by a being that called himself Nyarlathotep. He told us that the old rules of the gods, like the one Artemis broke, came from him. And that he was going to punish her and all the gods. He said me and Josh had a role to play in that."

Danni was so nervous that she stumbled over her words.

"This creature was a god?" Mel asked.

"He called himself an outer god. Oh! They have lesser relatives that are similar, called great old ones. The monster in R'lyeh, Cthulhu, is a great old one and apparently a challenge for even primordial deities to beat."

"More need for us to destroy the angel detector, then. If we have to face Cthulhu, we will need the full force of the new Olympians on our side."

"Has your prophetic vision shown you anything since the submarine?" Danni asked.

"No. I haven't seen anything, and it doesn't feel right. I feel like my power is being blocked or inhibited in some way. I thought it had something to do with that Necronomicon; we should've never gotten ourselves involved with that book. But now... maybe Nyarlathotep is the true danger in all this. I seem to be completely cut off from Apollo. I want to warn him that danger could be coming for Artemis and all of them."

"I agree that the book has been a bad omen," Danni sighed.

"Will you ask Prometheus for it back?"

"I asked and he said no. With all the trouble it's caused, I'd say it can just stay in Utgard, but losing Malcolm Selleck is a huge deal. I have no idea how I will explain it to his university or family. Not to mention Randall being dragged away, too. Our hope to find them will now rest in the hands of USSOT."

"Hopefully, we didn't lose them for nothing..."

"Is there anything else I need to know?" Mel asked Danni.

Danni thought about the kiss of Lucifer.

"No," Danni mumbled.

"Good. I hope you realise that a normal intelligence role is nothing like this. Once this Zeus nonsense is sorted, I can begin teaching you how to do your actual job."

Danni laughed. "I'm glad I didn't go through all that training for nothing."

"Go back and enjoy the party. Big day tomorrow," Mel smiled.

"Yes, boss."

Danni felt like the weight of the world was on Melissa's shoulders, but there was nothing she could do to help. The Oracle of Delphi was a leader and, as such, would have to find her own path forward.

• • • • •

THE PARTY RAGED INTO THE NIGHT. By morning's first light, everyone looked a little sheepish and sleep-deprived.

The group all stood before Skrymir's empty throne, saying

their goodbyes to Sigurd.

Danni again gave him a big hug. So did Mel.

Teva shook his hand, and he gave warm nods to the rest.

Sigurd made a special effort to approach Josh and congratulate him on winning. Josh said that in any fair match, Sigurd would always best him.

"My friends, I feel in my bones that your journey will get harder from this point. If you call for aid, I will do my best to answer. I have seen your inner courage, and any of you would be welcome to fight in my army. Though part of me thinks you already have."

"Why did you so easily agree to become Utgard's champion?" Danni asked Sigurd, while Josh looked confused at the odd remark.

"I denied it in my natural life. Now that I have a second chance, I should embrace the opportunity this place presents. Your modern world is so complex. My days as a king are over. In ever-changing Utgard, I have something to offer."

"Good enough for me," Danni said, patting his meaty bicep.

With a pop and unexpected torrent of wind, Skrymir appeared in the great hall and looked at Sigurd.

"I have considered your request, and I will allow it. The mortal can stay."

Danni looked around, confused. Skrymir wasn't talking about her, was he?

"Kane Dare," Sigurd began.

Kane looked both embarrassed and surprised to have been singled out by the Viking.

"You have spoken at length about how your life has lacked

purpose. Both of your brothers seem to be firmly gripped in the suffocating grasp of destiny, while you linger unemployed and useless."

Kane shrugged. "Well, yeah, but…"

"Then you have a choice to make now. Stay here in Utgard and learn the old ways of magic and fighting. Look to the past to find your future."

"Ah, thank you for the offer, but I don't want to be stuck here forever," Kane said nervously.

"You will not be a prisoner here. You can leave whenever you want. This is not a request that I would grant usually, but Sigurd stated that he has seen courage within you on your mission. Sigurd is the greatest of all men, so I trust his judgement," Skrymir interjected.

Kane looked terrified to have been addressed by the giant directly.

Josh approached his brother and put his bronze hand on Kane's shoulder.

"I reckon you should stay," Josh grinned. "This is an opportunity that apparently very few people receive."

"You're just trying to get rid of me," Kane retorted.

"Well, I'm cursed and apparently so is Randall. You will be left out if you don't get a bit of magic about you."

Kane looked to Sigurd and asked, "I'm going to have to train to be a warrior with you, aren't I?"

"And a mighty warrior you will become!" he shouted.

Kane looked across the group.

"I guess you can't fight fate," he sighed.

Kane moved out of the conglomeration of people and stood beside Sigurd. "For what it's worth, it was nice to get to know everyone. And I forgive you for kidnapping me in Geneva."

At least his sense of humour hadn't dimmed.

"And it was a pleasure having you on board." Melissa shook his hand.

"Learn some skills off of Sigurd and the Lord of Utgard here, and we might have a job waiting for you in the AST," Liam added.

"I like the sound of that," Kane nodded.

Kane and Josh embraced each other.

"Technically, you are outside the world. If anyone has a chance of journeying into the void to find Randall, it's you. Next time I see you, I want to see a long grandmaster's beard to go with your ultimate warrior status."

Kane chuckled. He nodded towards Danni and said, "You found a good one. Keep her safe."

Danni beamed at him.

"It has been my pleasure to fight alongside you all," Sigurd said, breaking the silence.

He pulled the sling off his back and handed it to Artemis with the golden sword inside.

Artemis nodded curtly.

"Goddess Artemis, I cannot thank you enough for returning life to me. Long had I languished in Hell, a rat in Lucifer's system. I will honour you with every victory, like I did the Aesir of old."

He bowed before the goddess.

"Rise, mighty warrior," Artemis ordered. "Live well, hunt

nobly and protect those who can't protect themselves, and see your debt repaid."

"We are leaving a little lighter than we arrived," Danni murmured to Mel.

"The fewer people on the next mission we have, the better. We need stealth and subterfuge. Though I wish Taskforce A could've come..."

Skrymir spoke over the top of them.

"Perhaps we will meet again. You have each earned the hospitality of Utgard, so if you can find a way back, you can stay for a while."

With that, the same lines that had appeared in Germany burned themselves into the ground at their feet.

Again, they were enveloped in rainbow energy and began floating towards the roof.

There was a flash, and the group crashed into an unfamiliar place.

When the thudding in Danni's head subsided, she saw they were as far from the glamour of Utgard as possible.

It looked like an extremely run-down motel room with chicken wire over the windows. Broken bottles were strewn about the floor, and it appeared someone had gone out of their way to kick holes in the wall.

And they weren't alone in this dump.

Silhouetted in shadow, sitting on a cheap plastic stool in the far corner of the room, was a familiar face. It was the Goddess of Doom.

Moros was here to brief them on their next mission.

35

THE PLAN

Moros looked different.

If it weren't for her grey storm-cloud eyes, she would've been indistinguishable from any run of the mill eco-warrior.

Danni couldn't quite decide if she thought the goddess was excellently blending in or just having a really rough time.

The Goddess of Fate and Doom was wearing green khaki cargo pants below a blue long-sleeved work shirt. It was splotched with dirt. She even appeared to have started the process of turning her hair into dreadlocks. Instead of being the Goddess of Fate and Doom, she more resembled the Goddess of the Hippies. It was a striking change in the brief period since Danni had last seen Moros in Amsterdam.

"Interesting disguise," Mel noted, approaching the goddess.

Danni could hear the restrained judgement in Melissa's voice.

"I have come to Tanzania with a group of travelling conservationists. I studied their appearances and altered mine to match," Moros said casually.

"I like it. Looks kind of wild and free," Danni remarked.

"Though, true freedom is not a thing any of us has. For we are all bound to the whims of fate."

Moros got to her feet. She and Artemis embraced warmly.

Dani thought she saw a flicker of concern roll across Moros' face when the two gods touched.

"My dear Artemis, I feel the lingering mark of evil on you. I feel you in my domain of doom. What has happened?"

"Dark things from ancient times look upon me. Though I have discussed this predicament with wise Prometheus at length and believe these tribulations can be overcome."

"Fate does also bend to our whims," Moros smiled. "This mission is an important step in ending the reign of the angels."

Josh approached the goddess. "Moros? From the Dreamscape?"

"Joshua Dare, I am pleased to see your curse is purified."

Jesse and Haruka looked at each other confused.

"For everyone who doesn't know, this is Moros. The ancient Greek God of Fate," Melissa stated.

"Hey," Jesse said awkwardly.

Moros surveyed the entire group, pausing to soak in each face.

"My heart trembles looking at you all. In my ears, I hear the marching steps of destiny. A moment of great significance, unknown even to me, approaches swiftly. We must move on the detector right away."

Moros pressed her hands forward, and an object quickly spun into existence. The goddess beckoned Jesse forward.

The object she'd summoned looked like a black crystal bowling ball. Pulsating inside it were a series of purple spikes, growing and retracting in size.

Danni didn't like this thing. She didn't know why, but she sensed it was best to stay far away from it.

Jesse gingerly took the black ball from Moros and stared into its mysterious depths.

"What is it?" he asked.

"A divine-energy bomb, crafted by Hephaestus to destroy the angel detector. The explosion contained inside has a considerable radius. At least a few hundred metres, so you will want to be well-clear when it is activated."

"How does it work?" Mel asked.

"Artemis is the only one who can activate it. The bomb will only interact with a divine being. She must speak to it, and it will begin an internal countdown. Place it correctly, and it should demolish the tower beyond repair."

"What effect will it have on me?" Artemis asked.

"It will incinerate you along with every creature present, if you linger where you set it. Hence why it has a delay, though it is only short. You will need to use godly speed to escape, and the mortals must try to remain well clear of the bomb. During his long imprisonment in the Citadel of Heaven, Hephaestus was forced to craft seven weapons imbibed with magic able to kill the gods beyond any hope of survival. This magic was a creation of the archangels and nigh on impossible to wield, yet Hephaestus mastered it. He looked to humans for inspiration. The terror of your weapons... not even the gods could've imagined your destructive capabilities.

"Failing death, the weapons of the archangels sapped divinity from their intended victims – as in the case of Apollo. Apollo survived due to the direct intervention of Demeter. Even then, it took myself, Hecate and Aion to prevent his death. No other god has met one of these weapons and lived to tell the tale. That same secretive angel magic is contained inside this orb, so nothing will survive this blast," Moros answered.

"Will it be enough to destroy the Archangel Gabriel?" Artemis asked.

"That, I cannot answer. Thanks to prayer and worship, Gabriel's power is beyond comprehension. Whether it will kill an archangel, as they are now, I cannot tell you."

Something Astaroth had said sprang into the forefront of Danni's mind, about how dragons were a nuisance to the angels because they were oblivious to their power fluctuations. If Hephaestus wanted a bomb to kill an archangel, he should probably learn the internal power of dragons.

"So, no two-birds one-stone approach, then?" Matt said, snapping Danni back to the conversation.

"Your target is only the detector," Moros said sternly.

"Gabriel can be distracted, but he cannot be defeated. Avoid the archangel at all costs."

"He is definitely here in Africa, then?" Melissa asked.

"Yes, word has reached me that Michael's displeasure at the archangel's complacency has manifested as punishments for his brothers. Gabriel was sent to Earth to manage the detector. He has only arrived recently, so he is unfamiliar with this place. This is of great benefit to us. Now is the time to strike."

"What other information can you provide, Moros?" Melissa asked.

"A Vatican congregation arrived several days ago to greet Gabriel. Ceremony and lavish honours have followed. The Pope was here for a day but has gone. A party of esteemed Vatican representatives remains in his stead. They travel from here to a monastery at the base of Mt Kilimanjaro. The monastery guards a passage through the mountain into a mighty chamber. This chamber houses a long-forgotten city of the ancient civilisation. The gates are guarded by creatures of Heaven. You cannot get through unless you are part of the Vatican convoy. I do not know if the Vatican party heads that deep into the mountain."

"Okay," Mel started, beginning to pace back and forth. "We need to infiltrate the Vatican group, get past the gate and into the mountain, where we make our way to the tower, set the bomb and get out. This is doable."

"Talk to us about the Vatican," Liam said, stepping forward.

"Ah, excuse me," Haruka's small voice squeaked. She had her hand nervously raised. "I don't really understand what you are all talking about..."

"I'll admit I'd like to be filled in too. What is the Vatican's involvement in all this, exactly?" Jesse asked.

Melissa surveyed the group and sighed.

Danni knew why. They'd done a terrible job of keeping this secret mission secret. Between the gods, The Old World, Altior Fulgur and everyone they'd subsequently told, there was no telling how far the information had travelled. The phrase 'need to know basis' had been completely tossed out the window.

"Let's recap. Firstly, we are in the town of Moshi, Tanzania. As for why we are here, let's go back to the beginning. In 2019, the Vatican sent operatives to hunt down Joshua Dare. Around this time, I discovered I was the Oracle of Delphi reincarnated, and I pulled Apollo from Hell to Earth.

"It was also around that time that someone discovered, or deduced, that Zeus had left a colossal pocket of power in the universe. And that a ritual could be performed to claim it. Though, how that was discovered, we don't yet know."

Danni had a lightbulb moment and cut in. "You said that when you, Apollo and Moros were in the Vatican Secret Archive, you saw a copy of the Necronomicon, right? A copy that someone had clearly been studying. That monster, Nyarlathotep, told us he moves through time and that the Necronomicon originally came from him. I don't think we can assume the outer god did it directly, but what if the book is a loose conduit to his mind?"

Moros furrowed her brow.

"Nyarlathotep?" she asked.

Most of the others also looked confused at this name drop.

"The creature who seeks to punish me. An outer god of the

early universe whose dark thoughts crafted the book which led us so easily astray," Artemis answered.

"My mother spoke once of outer gods and cosmic terrors as things long forgotten from the memory of the waking world…" Moros said, eyeing Artemis with even more concern.

"The gods have always had foes. Danni's idea has merit," Artemis stated.

"Perhaps. I don't think it's likely the book changes depending on the outer god's thoughts. The Vatican began studying the Necronomicon. Maybe, through its words, they learned that the pocket of power from Zeus was there. The Catholic Church had only received the book shortly before all of this started, but I never thought anything of it. If Zeus' power is recorded in the book, I may have missed something substantial," Moros explained.

"Abdul Alhazred wrote the book, right? How would he have known about Zeus' power?" Danni asked.

"Remember what Ernst Carter told us, Danni," Mel responded slowly. "Abdul Alhazred was under the tutelage of someone called the Sundered King."

Josh now spoke up, adding, "And it was the Sundered King that Nyarlathotep taught to 'dance among the gods'. That's what he said! Even if Nyarlathotep created the magic in the Necronomicon, it has filtered through a couple of other sources to reach us."

"The Sundered King is a name I have heard whispered over the millennia, though I have never been able to determine who or what it is," Moros said.

Melissa snapped the group back on track.

"Regardless of the book's origin, I suspect the Vatican

team studying the book included Vasilije Markovic. He was a devil worshipper and would've ensured Lucifer knew about the pocket of power as soon as the church did. Archangel Michael would've learned it from the Pope. All the while, the only link they had to said power was hunting down Joshua Dare in Australia," Melissa said.

"Look at the journey that book has led us on over the past few weeks. I'd have no trouble believing that all of this started with the Necronomicon. That Vatican probably has an expert who can decipher it more easily than us," Danni suggested.

"So, it was from the Necronomicon that the Vatican learned about the power and that they needed a pure link to it?" Josh asked.

"Perhaps it's all in the Vatican's copy of the Necronomicon. The black book might hold all the ingredients necessary to claim the power of a god ripped from creation."

"It isn't just in the Necronomicon. I have travelled the world unearthing tablets and scrolls with pieces of information that have led me to all of the information required to complete the spell," Moros added.

"Who created the tablets and scrolls?" Josh asked.

"I cannot tell. My domain of fate should reveal their mysteries, yet my power is blocked when interacting with these objects. Human knowledge tells me they have a Roman origin," Moros answered.

"If they are older than the Necronomicon, then the book's knowledge probably came from the same ancient source. Whoever created the stone tablets and scrolls later instructed Alhazred to put that same information in the Necronomicon," Danni thought aloud.

Moros frowned and said, "Not Nyarlathotep then, but..."

"The Sundered King..." Melissa finished quietly.

"Okay, guys, you aren't being any less confusing. Why are we here in Africa?" Jesse asked.

"Right," Melissa continued. "Apollo and Michael fought in Afghanistan, and Michael was defeated. In that battle, the Vatican's private army, the Gladius Vaticanus, and a bunch of Italian military gear were destroyed. This left Markovic on the outs with the rest of the clergy. At some point, he came to The Old World Amsterdam."

Moros spoke up again, "I still have ears in the Vatican, and I can tell you this part of the story. I sealed the door to the hidden temple in Afghanistan, though evidently, poorly. I did move the divine flame into the Dreamscape, just in case. During Markovic's banishment from the Vatican, he travelled to the battle site and explored the temple. He discovered the primordial wisps that had been entombed within the walls tens of thousands of years ago. Wanting to learn the nature of the wisps, he researched a place that studied the supernatural."

"The Old World," Melissa continued darkly. "Of course, that wisp would've captured the attention of Altior Fulgur right away. Altior then used one of his companies, Molochtech, to study it. They quickly learned that it had the potential to purify the werewolf curse. That is quite the leap to make without already having a wealth of magical knowledge at your disposal."

"Then they captured and experimented on me during the full moon. I was the test subject while they refined the God Particle, a product of the wisps," Jesse stated.

"But you were too far removed; they needed Josh, whose

curse was almost pure," Melissa continued.

"Altior manipulated me into going to Siberia alone, where Markovic was waiting," Josh added sourly.

"And at this point, Altior was well aware of Operation Thunderking and the mission to claim the missing power of Zeus. Because we'd directly told him," Melissa said.

"But," Josh began, "do you remember the meeting in Japan? He was very dismissive of the idea, even saying it was a waste of time trying to claim Zeus' power."

"Altior's motives are still unknown. As far as we know, Lucifer has lost all of his active operatives in the mortal world, though there still should be one more fallen angel out there. Because Michael was gone for a year, Heaven, and thusly the Vatican, has been out of commission completely. For some reason, it appears that only Michael desires this power. The other archangels don't care."

"The angels are impossibly powerful now, but they will diminish as people stop believing in their religions. The archangels took steps to ensure they'd never fall below the level of a god. When the time comes that belief has fallen enough, the old gods will strike back. Michael is the only one with the wisdom to see this," Artemis said.

Danni thought about this statement. It wasn't entirely correct.

"It's more than that. Nyarlathotep told us he's been whispering into Michael's head warnings about a slumbering darkness in the heart of the world. The same darkness the primordials fought... it has to be the great old one, Cthulhu. Maybe he thinks he needs that power to fight the monster we accidentally awakened in R'lyeh."

"We will take that power and deal with the monster ourselves," Artemis stated.

"This is good," Melissa said. "We now have a clearer picture of what's going on. I guess the last part is why we are here. The angels watch the world for divine power from a facility near this town. If we destroy it, they cannot repair it, and the gods will be free to use all of their divine magic again."

"Right, so the answer was 'destroy a tower'," Jesse ended, looking somewhat annoyed. "How do we do that?"

"A lot clearer for who, exactly?" Danni heard Haruka mutter.

"The Vatican convoy has secured private accommodation here in Moshi that is heavily guarded. There are several esteemed members of the Catholic Church still here. At sunrise, the convoy begins its pilgrimage to Mt Kilimanjaro. They return mid-afternoon. You have already missed it today, so you must strike tomorrow," Moros informed them.

"Who is in this convoy?" Liam asked the goddess.

"Security wise, African militia from the DRC are guns for hire. Then, you have the remaining members of the Cult of Belial. They are few in number, as I believe most were sucked back into Hell in Geneva."

"I would've thought the cult would no longer be operating with both Belial and Leviathan being dead," Liam said.

"Remember, there is one hitherto unidentified fallen angel still on Earth. He will have assumed control of the demon hosts.

Though, there is nothing to indicate that he is here in Africa."

"If the Cult of Belial is here with the Catholic Church, that means Michael must still believe that Lucifer is on his side, not out to take the power of Zeus for himself," Danni noted.

"Next, we have a secretive order of nuns from the Vatican. History calls them the Order of Saint Clare, though that is not entirely true. For years the Catholic Church has hidden radical elements within the order. These nuns are known within the church as the Arms of Deborah. They can fight.

"There are several cardinals here. But the true ranking members are the Patriarch of Constantinople, Neophytus IX, and the Major Archbishop of Fagaras and Alba Julia."

The Patriarch of Constantinople, wasn't he a Nazi?" Matt asked.

"Well, people claim he was an avid Hitler youth member, though those stories have never been substantiated," Mel shrugged.

"The guy is like a walking corpse," Matt said. "A classic example of the mantra 'do bad things and live a super long life'. If you believe the rumours, he volunteered as best he could to help out concentration camp employees."

"I know him from my time in the Vatican. He is not a good man and does not repent for the evil he has wrought," Moros added.

Something else now triggered in Danni's mind. It was again the memory of Astaroth telling her to press his angelic seal into an evil man in a holy place. Doing so would summon the fallen angel. Why would that spring into the forefront of her mind now, though? She still had the wide coin in her pocket and touched the cool metal with her finger.

"How many nuns are there in the Arms of Deborah?" Melissa asked.

"I've counted about twenty-five."

"Enough to get lost in," Melissa murmured.

"Jesse and Josh, if we carve the demonic symbology into your forehead, you can slip in among the Cult of Belial."

"That won't work; we will just heal," Josh said quickly.

"Not if we carve it with a silver knife. That'll take a long time to heal," Mel grimaced.

Jesse and Josh exchanged a nervous look.

"Teva, Liam and Matt, you guys will have to arm yourselves and find a car. Matt has his sniper; he can provide overwatch for our escape."

The three men nodded in unison.

"How are we going to get the bomb in?" Danni asked. Even dressed like a nun, she couldn't see a way to sneak the bowling ball inside the lost city.

"Good question," Mel responded, turning to Moros.

"I could bind the object to one of you, but to unbind it would require a magic spell that would never go undetected. That's proper divine magic."

"I can unbind it at the tower's base. I know the process; I learnt it from Hecate. The second I do it, though, Gabriel and the angels will know we are there," Artemis mulled the idea over out loud.

Moros looked crestfallen, yet resolute. "Hecate and Apollo know everything they need to perform the ritual on Olympus. My part in this story is done. When Artemis is ready to unbind the bomb, I will use my magic and create a distraction. The angels will come for me, and you can do it then."

Artemis made a strangled noise at this suggestion.

"You cannot do that, Moros. You are ancient beyond any of us, and being so close to the detector means they will surely kill you."

"It must be this way. If I do not make this sacrifice, I see only dark roads leaving this place."

"We need you, Moros. For both your wisdom and power in the wars to come."

"Dear Artemis, I would hear no more. This is the way."

"Would you bind the bomb to yourself, Artemis?" Melissa asked.

"It is better that it goes with one of you," Artemis replied distractedly, still staring at Moros. "To have an orb of such intense power linked to my being would invite discovery. A mortal should do it."

"I can do it! I'm the smallest and fastest. If anyone is going to get to that tower first, it's me."

Danni hadn't even realised she'd said it. The offer had left her mouth before she could stop herself. After she failed in the games of Skrymir, Danni wanted to show she had some value to offer the team.

Josh shook his head and mouthed 'no'.

Jesse handed the divine explosion to Artemis, who thrust it straight into Danni's chest. The black orb simply sunk into her and disappeared.

"Do you remember in the Ninth Circle of Hell when I bound myself to you?" Artemis asked.

"Of course," Danni said.

"When we begin tomorrow, I will do the same. I will hide so deep in your soul that I cannot be detected. When you reach the base of the tower, say my name. I will emerge and remove the weapon. When it is set, I will carry you away from the tower so we avoid the blast."

"Wait," Josh started, "so, you can't take the bomb because it will make you detectable. But you and the bomb can go inside Danni?"

"Do not underestimate the power radiating within each mortal soul, lycanthrope," Artemis said.

Josh looked at Danni with concern in his eyes.

"Our mission begins when the Vatican convoy returns from the monastery. We will survey how best to infiltrate their ranks and plant the bomb," Melissa said.

Danni gulped.

She was nervous.

Just being in the same room as the Goddess of Fate made her feel like an indefinable finality was in the air. Now they just had to make a plan.

36

INFILTRATION

MOSHI, TANZANIA
- FEBRUARY 9 -

Mid-afternoon arrived, bringing with it the scorching power of the African sun.

Heatwaves distorted the distant monumental figure of Mt Kilimanjaro as it loomed high over the surrounding landscape. Within the dormant magma chambers of the world's highest free-standing mountain was a city lost to history.

A city they were going to infiltrate.

The ancient civilisation, a race of men born from the gods, had called that mountain home. Then, they'd fallen into ruin, vanishing from the Earth. When the angels rose to prominence, they'd repurposed the city to suit their will.

To most people, climbing Mt Kilimanjaro was a testament to personal triumph. Even those with little mountaineering experience could summit Kilimanjaro with relative ease.

Now that Danni was aware of the secret history of the place, it seemed so much more important than people's small personal victories.

Kilimanjaro was roughly thirty-five kilometres from Moshi, making it a forty-minute drive. Danni's journey wouldn't be so quick. She had to follow a hidden path around the side of the mountain to the secretive monastery via a track that wasn't marked on any map.

After the morning discussion, Danni's team spread out through the town to gather what intelligence they could.

The AST team didn't even look out of place in the Tanzanian town of Moshi. Hikers wandered about in droves, and they even came across several youth leadership groups volunteering in local schools. The awkward zit-faced youths looked perpetually concerned as they tried to embrace the concept of cultural immersion.

Moshi was a typical African town. Generic shopfront banners, provided by popular international soda companies, made all local stores look identical. It had an overgrown village atmosphere, with almost all of its structures old and run down. Some clever business owners had hidden their establishments behind a façade of elaborate decoration to distract the eye and attract tourists.

The main thoroughfares consisted of potholed bitumen. However, most of Moshi's streets were dirt. Overcrowded buses and vans zoomed by without adherence to even the most basic road rules while the brightly coloured Maasai tribesmen performed for tourists. They jumped, danced and sang to the applause of watching crowds. Then they laid out vibrant blankets and began selling myriads of plastic beads and lion's tooth necklaces on the street.

Danni found a leather armband coated with coloured beads in distinctive triangles. She bought it and quickly fixed it on her arm. It'd be a nice trinket to remember this mission by.

Despite the rampant poverty, Danni couldn't help but notice how happy everyone seemed. Moshi was brimming with positivity.

Teva paid off a local shopkeeper to use his internet connection. At the same time, Melissa got on the phone with her colleagues in ASIO. It didn't take much digging to determine the location of the compound the Vatican party was staying in.

Much as Moros had said, satellite imagery made the place look like a miniature fortress. Armed foot and vehicle patrols, plus a total lack of surrounding vegetation, made it impossible to sneak in. Furthering the problem was the Cult of Belial, who walked the internal perimeter with hellhounds at their sides.

A distant hill and his powerful telescopic zoom allowed Matt to scope it out undetected.

Despite being the ranking officer, Liam had been happy to let Mel take full charge, as she'd been leading the majority of the team thus far.

Melissa quickly concluded they'd have to strike the convoy on the road. There was no way the whole team could infiltrate the compound.

Back in Moros' dirty hotel room, a plan was made.

Danni and Mel would commandeer a truck driven by

the Arms of Deborah and replace the nuns inside. They needed a transport that only carried two to mitigate the risk of being recognised as imposters.

Matt identified that the Vatican was transporting pallets of goods into the monastery every morning. It was the nuns doing the heavy lifting. A truck with just a driver and passenger became their target.

Once they'd gathered enough information, they moved back to the hotel to enact the more painful elements of the plan.

Josh and Jesse had it the worst, as their disguises required physical injury.

Liam offered a weak apology, then pointed a silver knife into Josh's forehead. He winced in pain as the five-pointed star and ram's head were crudely cut into his temple. Josh's eyes watered and his skin sizzled while Jesse looked on apprehensively. He was next.

Danni grabbed a cloth and wiped the blood from Josh's face.

"Thanks," he mumbled, shooting her a pained smile.

Teva arrived with a stack of long brown robes from a local vendor and thrust a pair to Jesse and Josh.

"I got lucky with this. I think they look identical to the robes worn by the Cult of Belial."

"We are lucky they don't dress with style," Danni murmured.

Her joke was only met with a groan from Jesse as the blade cut into his head.

Thanks to the werewolf curse, Jesse and Josh could move with the unnerving supernatural speed of the demon hosts. The Cult of Belial seemed to be about ten strong, Matt reported. They were transported in and out of the monastery in the back of a covered flat-bed truck.

The idea was to have Matt take out two with his sniper right as they concluded a patrol, then have Josh and Jesse replace them.

It was a risky plan, but Artemis convinced them the demons wouldn't notice. They were always fighting the pull of Hell, trying to rip them back in. This made them less focused and easier to fool.

Of course, Matt had managed to steal a few holy water infused bullets from Taskforce A back in Ukraine without anyone noticing. That meant they didn't need to worry about the two sniped demons quickly healing and getting back up.

Fortunately, it seemed that the hellhounds weren't permitted to travel to the monastery and stayed to guard the Moshi compound. Since Teva didn't have the time or data to determine when the cult had the dogs with them precisely, it would have to be a big gamble in the morning. They had to take out a patrol without hellhounds, that was imperative to success.

Melissa positioned everyone at discreet vantage points to observe the convoy as it rolled back into town that afternoon.

All the vehicles were old hunks of junk, having lived hard lives. The African militia cars, with roof-mounted machine guns, didn't rendezvous with the Vatican vehicles until they were twenty minutes out of the town and well into the bush. Roaming armed militia weren't a familiar sight in Tanzania and would only draw unwanted attention to the Vatican presence.

Because the convoy had to meet the militia in the bush, it gave the team a window to strike.

Dust and stones flew across the road as Danni watched the

long stream of cars pass. The nuns who made up the Arms of Deborah were all stone-faced and very serious.

The only clean vehicles were a pair of 200 series Land Cruisers that carried the Patriarch of Constantinople, the archbishop and the other cardinals. From his hilltop perch, Matt was able to see that all in the delegation were dressed in full holy attire for their audiences with the angels.

Once the Vatican group had made it safely into the walls of their African fortress, the AST group reconvened for a final briefing in the evening.

"We all know our roles. At 5 am, it begins. Liam, Teva, Danni, Haruka and I will start the walk in the early hours to the rendezvous point for the African militia. Then, we will commandeer a car before the Vatican group arrives. Remember bandanas, sunglasses and whatever else you need to conceal your identities!

"Matt, you will set up a position on the hill nearest the compound. It is quite far away, so you will need to be 100% sure of your shots before you fire. Two headshots, then Josh and Jesse discreetly climb the compound's walls and assume their positions. Just avoid the hellhounds.

"The next part will be the hardest. Danni, Haruka, and I will need to take out the transport truck drivers on the road. We know that the truck driven by the Arms of Deborah is the last vehicle in the convoy, other than two rearguard militia cars. It will be on Liam and Teva to take over a militia car before they join the convoy. Haruka will have to slow the truck for long enough to get the nuns out, for us to steal their garb, and then replace them. Since we have no way to disable the truck without destroying it, it's gonna be on Haruka's werewolf speed and power to get the job done.

Danni shot a sideways glance at Haruka, who looked incredibly excited and terribly nervous.

Josh leaned over to the Japanese girl and whispered some words of encouragement in her ear, which Danni understood, but didn't appreciate.

"Again, luck is on our side. Because the goods truck struggles on the terrain. I am assuming it gets left slightly behind the rest of the convoy. I estimate we have about two minutes to get this done as silently as possible. Josh and Jesse will ensure the rear flap on the tray carrying the Cult of Belial is closed to prevent prying eyes from looking too far back."

"This is a very haphazardly made plan. It'll be a miracle if we pull it off," Jesse murmured to Josh.

"Lastly, Matt will have to meet with Haruka and set up a sniper perch overlooking the monastery. Inside, we have no idea what to expect, so we will all have to be smart. We get Danni in and towards the tower, where she will summon Artemis and set the bomb. Moros will cause a divine distraction, and Artemis will perform the magic needed. If we screw up, and a fight starts in the monastery, Haruka will come to back us up. Matt must stay in place and cover our escape."

"Sounds like a plan," Liam nodded.

"Everyone, get what sleep you can. We have early starts and a long day ahead tomorrow."

The entire group was silent. Everyone was contemplating the difficult task ahead.

Once the room was empty, Josh approached Danni.

"Don't be a hero, okay?" he said.

"I'm naturally a hero," Danni laughed.

"I don't want you anywhere near that bomb when it goes off." Josh looked deeply concerned.

"It's all worked out so far, hasn't it? Have a little faith. After all, we have the gods on our side."

Danni leaned up and gave him a peck on the cheek before retiring for bed.

The Maasai armband she'd purchased earlier slid down to her elbow.

She quickly unfastened it and thrust it into Josh's bronze hand.

"Here you go. This is too big for me. I think it'll make you look more hipster and free."

"Oh, just the look I'm going for," Josh joked, raising his eyebrows. Still, with a slight smile, he clipped it to his wrist. There was still a lot of space, but it wouldn't fall off.

"I actually think this could survive the werewolf transformation," he said.

Danni repeated goodnight and turned away.

Josh watched her go, looking troubled.

She didn't want him to worry. She wanted to show that she was cool, calm, collected and up to the task. Though privately, it didn't stop worry gnawing at the edges of her mind.

· · · · ·

SLEEP DIDN'T COME EASILY that night. Danni lay awake,

tossing and turning, full of nervous anticipation.

By the time her alarm buzzed, she was relieved for the operation to finally be starting.

After quickly tying her hair back, Danni strode down to the lobby to meet with Artemis.

Checking the place was clear, they began.

Artemis placed her hand against Danni's. She then vanished inside Danni's body, hitching a ride in her soul. Danni was privately happy that carrying both a divine bomb and a divine being inside her didn't add any physical weight. Otherwise, the coming stumble through the dark would've been hard going.

Melissa, Liam, Teva and Haruka arrived shortly after. Each wore an expression of determination. Together, they began the long quiet march through the African countryside.

The street outside the motel was devoid of people. They moved like shadows beneath the feeble glow of flickering street lights.

Moshi felt unsafe in the early hours of the morning.

This feeling was only magnified when they left the outskirts of the town and moved into the wilds.

Liam and Melissa frequently stopped to check their map by torchlight. It would've been so easy to get lost out here.

Strange sounds in the night created a spooky atmosphere. A couple of times, Haruka leapt in fright at the distant chattering of hyenas.

The nocturnal chorus of nature was extinguished and replaced with man-made sounds the closer they got to the militia camp. They could see the light of a bonfire and hear raucous laughter. It reminded Danni of her first mission in the Florida swamp. That felt like a lifetime ago now...

The stars were beautiful in the night sky above. Moshi didn't produce enough light pollution to dim the swirling constellations. Danni found an unexplainable reassurance in the eternal majesty of it all, that was until the smoke from the bonfire shifted in the wind and blocked the image of the sky above.

It sounded like the guns-for-hire were at the tail end of an all-night party.

Melissa held her hand up to signal a stop. They were surrounded by thick clumps of shrubs on all sides.

They all exchanged significant glances.

It was go-time. The mission started now.

Liam dropped to his hands and knees and began inching forward through the scrub.

Danni waited with bated breath for him to return.

The minutes passed in total silence as she listened to the intoxicated laughter of the militia. Surely, getting drunk was against their orders, but clearly the men didn't care.

Liam reappeared, looking dirty and covered in leaf litter. Using hand signals, he told the group there were eight people around the fire.

Teva pulled a collection of scarves and bandanas from a knapsack slung around his back. All of this had been purchased extremely cheaply in Moshi the day prior.

Both Teva and Liam already looked the part. They wore cargo pants, brown vests lined with pouches over long-sleeved shirts and bandoliers. Once their faces were covered entirely by bandanas, leaving only slits for their eyes, they screwed long black silencers to their pistols. Liam put on a floppy white wide-brimmed hat, and Teva donned a grey skater beanie.

They waited for Melissa's signal.

Danni wondered how Matt had gone with his difficult sniper task. Had Jesse and Josh made it over the wall undetected?

Mel tapped her watch. Liam nodded.

He and Teva crawled out of the thicket. Moments later, barely distinguishable against the backdrop of music from old car stereos and clanging bottles, two silenced shots whizzed out, followed by two thumps.

If Danni hadn't been listening for the sounds, she wouldn't have known they'd happened.

Melissa and Danni now moved forwards, staying crouched. They saw that Liam and Teva had picked off two stragglers, who must've stepped aside to relieve themselves. Both militiamen were just as wrapped in face coverings as the two AST operatives. It couldn't have been more perfect. It was luck, the luck of the gods.

Liam and Teva pilfered the large magazines full of ammo and slung their AK-47s around their necks. They then wandered in the direction of the party.

Danni grabbed the body of Teva's victim by the scruff of his collar and began dragging him back through the bush as quietly as she could. She and Mel fought against the unyielding environment as they pulled the heavy men into the thicket.

Haruka looked dreadfully uncomfortable, crouched there next to the bodies.

Right on cue, the roar of sputtering vehicles cut through

the music. The rest of the guards were readying themselves for the soon arriving Vatican group. They heard someone begin barking orders, and the music was quickly shut off.

Teva and Liam blended in nicely to the chaos.

Soon, other headlights lit up the bush.

The Vatican convoy was here.

The guns for hire who'd been drinking all night scrambled to their positions. It was such a jumbled mess that the obviously confused figures of Liam and Teva didn't look out of place.

The militia vehicles groaned to life and slid onto the dirt road, waiting for the Vatican officials to arrive. Two cars remained behind, ready to move in when the transport truck passed.

Mel flashed a thumbs-up to Haruka as a loud rumbling moved in their direction. Two trucks came past, the first carrying the members of the Arms of Deborah and the second with the Cult of Belial.

Danni moved closer to the road and peeked around a tree, just in time to see the back flap on the latter track was down. Jesse and Josh had done it. No blank-eyed cult members would be watching the road behind.

A minute passed, and the sound of another truck approached. Accompanying the growl of the engine was a series of rattles and squeaks.

Two more quiet gunshots were heard amongst the noise.

Mel signalled for Danni to crawl forward and see what Liam and Teva were doing. Danni saw that the two men had split up and neutralised the other remaining militia car. They were hard at work propping up bodies in the passenger seats as best they could to make the men look alive. It wasn't a great idea, with even poorer execution. Though, it was still too dark for anyone to notice in any great detail.

The cargo truck lurched over a pothole, and an ominous crunch broke the brief silence. Still, the truck kept going, moving recklessly fast along the dirt track.

Mel tilted her head towards Haruka.

Haruka breathed deep, steeling her nerve.

Melissa gave her a thumbs up.

Haruka sprinted towards the road, launching herself at the truck's cabin. She yanked on the door handle and, not knowing her own strength, ripped the door completely off.

It fell into a bush with a *thunk*.

The nun in the passenger seat barely had time to react as Haruka wrapped her legs around the nun's neck and tossed her from the truck. Danni was ready, running alongside the lumbering vehicle as the nun landed. She quickly put a length of masking tape over the nun's mouth and bound her hands and feet.

Haruka swung herself into the cabin, then, after a tense grapple, pushed the nun driving out the other side. Haruka plopped herself into the driver's seat just in time to stop the vehicle from stalling.

She slowed the truck substantially as Teva and Liam pulled out behind it in their stolen militia cars.

Danni had never felt time pressure like this before as she struggled to get the nun's clothes off and put them on herself.

The seconds ticked by as the nun fought her every movement. Getting more and more annoyed, Danni pistol-whipped her. The job was much easier with the nun out cold.

Time was up.

The cargo truck had to catch up to the others.

Hitching the nun's habit up, she sprinted to catch up with the rumbling truck.

Mel had had similar trouble, arriving breathless shortly after Danni.

Danni pulled herself into the doorless passenger seat while Haruka jumped out. Mel clambered in, took control of the vehicle and put her foot down.

They'd done it, though the missing door might become a problem.

"When we get to the monastery, I'll try to park it so no one can see the missing door," Mel sighed.

"Must've been a hell of a pull," Danni said, begrudgingly impressed.

The sun crested the horizon as Kilimanjaro consumed more and more of their vision. The environment quickly became dense rainforest, and the track became rougher, crisscrossed with thick tree roots and fallen branches. Mel had some difficulty getting the truck over some of the muddy crevices in the road.

Teva and Liam's cars held position well back from the truck. They now had the added difficulty of getting dead bodies out of their passenger seats undetected. Danni hoped they'd thought of this complication before enacting their improvised plan.

They drove up a small rise and were greeted with a gap in the trees. Through they could see the monastery. It didn't look at all how Danni had imagined.

"This is it, I guess," Danni said apprehensively.

"Moment of truth," Mel replied, skillfully navigating a narrow turn and pulling the truck up behind the rest of the convoy. She managed to keep Danni's doorless side pointed towards the rainforest.

The long train of vehicles pulled into a wide dirt circle of cleared vegetation. The rainforest was thick, and unseen monkeys' shrill calls filled the air.

Most of Kilimanjaro was a slow ascent upwards. Here, however, it was like a chunk of the mountain had been ripped clean from the earth. A sheer cliff face sliced into the mountainside, and pressed against it was the monastery's buildings.

Teva had been unable to find a name for this place. Moros told him that local superstition called it Angeli Oculi, or Angel's Eyes. Danni thought that name was a little on the nose. It didn't look like angels would ever live here. It was so old and ruined.

The monastery was rather large and a squashed mismatch of several differently styled structures.

The main building was two stories tall and positively ancient. The brickwork had been done by hand, with several portions of the wall being severely discoloured and unevenly spaced. Massive arched windows dominated the building, and there was a golden door embedded in the front.

Behind this rectangular structure was a series of rock-hewn buildings carved from the removed portion of the mountain. They had long series of windows on steadily rising levels as they climbed the cliffside. This section had a bit more artistic flair, with ancient crucifixes decorating the roof and horrific gargoyles leering from the rock.

Interspersed between the rock-hewn buildings were a series of smaller chapels with circular domes backing onto the cliff face. These were much more modern and looked European in design. Images of angels and the Virgin Mary decorated them in gold and silver. The chapels looked like shrunken basilicas smooshed into the vertical wall.

The militia cars had parked in pre-determined spots all around the clearing. Both Teva and Liam quickly deduced the missing places in the pattern. Furthering their luck, all of the soldiers of fortune stayed in their beat-up vehicles, leaving the engines running. For now, no one paid them (or their unmoving passengers) any special attention.

The immaculately clean land cruisers pulled up closest to the building with the golden door.

The Patriarch of Constantinople stepped out. He had a long black cane to hold his hunched frame upright. The archbishop followed, then the three cardinals. They all chatted animatedly as they moved towards the main entrance.

As soon as the Vatican officials were on open ground, everyone else started moving.

The militia, the Cult of Belial and the nuns moved to fulfil their assigned tasks.

Danni and Mel improvised. Danni knew the basics of lowering a ramp and hit the correct sequence of buttons after one failed attempt. Half a dozen other nuns rushed over to assist them, and Danni made a conscious effort to make sure no one could see her face.

Melissa tapped Danni on the shoulder.

The Cult of Belial had disembarked their truck and slowly made for the main entry. They moved like a shambling horde of zombies, with Jesse and Josh's hooded figures bringing up the rear.

Some of the African militia let their AK-47s dangle as they exited and leaned against the cars. Clearly, everything was running as per normal for them.

It was a good sign.

Two hung well back from the rest, pretending like they were checking out the engine of one of their vehicles. How long Teva and Liam could remain adequately concealed was a pressing concern. The fact that neither of their cars had bodies in the front passenger seats was an astonishing feat. Both Teva and Liam had moved quickly to dump them out of sight.

They all just had to look the part until the convoy (hopefully) moved into the ancient city. Moros had been quite clear that they had to remain invisible among the Vatican host to find the way in. She'd said it would most likely be a long dark tunnel that led deep into the mountain – a guess Danni could've made even with no information.

Somewhere nearby was one of the most powerful beings in existence. A member of the seven archangels of Heaven.

Gabriel had to be avoided at all costs.

Fortunately, a senior nun approached and began barking orders, making Mel and Danni's deception much easier. All of the Arms of Deborah worked swiftly and silently, unloading crates of silver goblets and assortments of jewels. It was like the truck had brought a medieval tribute to the monastery.

Each crate had to be separated by its contents and placed into a series of wheeled carts. They looked like old mining trolleys that usually sat on tracks, and struggled to move over the lumpy ground.

Once they'd sorted and loaded the tribute, each cart was pushed to the most pristine of the mini-basilicas.

This had to be it, the path to the ancient city.

Danni studied the gate to the chapel intently. There was no way she could get in undetected. They had to wait.

Once they'd passed the gate, Danni would do her best to sneak off and make for the tower.

"You can do this," Danni told herself, right as the golden door swung open and the Vatican officials emerged.

37

ANGEL'S EYES

MOUNT KILIMANJARO
- FEBRUARY 9 -

T he Patriarch of Constantinople and the archbishop left the confines of the large rectangular building. They approached the most fancifully decorated of the basilicas.

Danni wiped the sweat from her brow. The nun's habit was hot; it was not practical work attire. It was all black, meaning it attracted endless swarms of mosquitoes from the jungle, yet none of the others complained.

The senior nun ordered them all to hurry up. There were eight carts now full to the brim with elaborate gifts. Eight pre-determined nuns moved behind the carts to push them into the domed structure ahead.

Fortunately, the two Mel and Danni had bound back in the African jungle hadn't been assigned this task.

The African militiamen pushed open the gate to the basilica. One held it open for the two most senior Vatican men. The cardinals, it seemed, were not entering the mountain, stepping back to let others pass.

The ten Cult of Belial members entered next, then the nuns pushing the carts, then the remaining militiamen. Danni looked at Mel nervously. All of the other nuns were moving back towards the trucks.

There was a low whistle. Danni's head snapped to it.

The mercenary continued holding the door open even after the others had passed. Mel and Danni quickly departed the throng of nuns and slipped inside.

The emerald gate groaned as it swung closed behind them.

The militiaman lowered his sunglasses to reveal he was Liam. He gave them a quick wink.

The chapel wasn't anything more than a circular room with a small altar. Old paintings were plastered across the walls, though they were far too damaged to interpret what the ancient images had depicted.

At the back was a golden arch lined with Arabic writing. It led into an ominous passage stretching into the mountain. The air seemed imbibed with a ghostly green hue as refined marble gave way to natural stone.

Danni, Mel and Liam followed the mass of people down the stone passage.

She quickly learned where the green glow came from. Large

emeralds were periodically fixed to the wall. In a trick of the ancient civilisation, they were generating light.

The passage went some distance in a dead straight line before it split into a fork. Danni's group didn't dare deviate from the Vatican emissaries as they took the left-hand path.

Soon, Danni was confronted with architectural majesty.

The passage opened up into a vast tiled chamber lined with thick square columns holding the roof up. Each was widest at the ends and tapered in the middle. Decorative streaks ran the lengths of the columns, converging near the top. Each column had emeralds of enormous proportion decorating its upper portion, giving the illusion of a green sky.

They could hear the buzzing of a generator. Thick black cabling was fixed into the ancient stone, leading to a series of portable lights igniting the ground level.

"This isn't it, is it?" Danni whispered to Mel.

"I don't think so. This looks to be an entry chamber."

The chamber walls were lined with balconies and ledges. Much like outside, many rooms were carved directly into the mountain.

Mel and Danni positioned themselves behind one of the thick columns, within earshot of the main congregation.

Liam walked towards the militiamen, hanging slightly back and using the long shadows of the columns as a cloak.

The nuns were wheeling their carts into a storage room off to the right. Danni could see a glittering mountain of jewels inside, sparkling in the fluorescent blaze of a nearby light pole.

An unknown man approached the group. He had light

brown hair, a stern face with a gaunt complexion and dark shadows under his eyes.

He was dressed like a hiker, but walked with an air of regality.

"You return again at dawn to provide more gifts?" the stranger asked.

"Yes, Lord Camael. Has mighty Gabriel re-considered my request to meet?" the patriarch murmured.

"Archangel Gabriel does not permit humans to speak with him. How many times must I tell you this?" Camael drawled.

"Please… my lord…"

"I will broach the subject once again. Do not hope for a better outcome, mortal."

"So, this is an angel," Danni thought.

He looked so ordinary.

The archbishop ordered the African militia to fan out. They all looked utterly bored (other than the few who were groggy and tired). A few Africans had their cellphones out and were frustrated at the lack of signal.

Before they'd left, Moros had told them that the angel's detector would generate so much interference in the mountain that their phones wouldn't work. Mel had already assumed this. Signal rarely reached the long-forgotten underground places as it was.

They were in this mission totally alone.

The Cult of Belial began slowly walking the chamber's perimeter, much the same as they did at the compound in Moshi.

The archbishop and patriarch crossed the stone tiles with echoing footsteps, heading towards a side room. They crossed right by Danni and Mel, and the patriarch saw them out the corner of his eye.

Danni's stomach did a summersault.

Had they been found out already?

"You, girl, come here!" he demanded, waving a decrepit old finger. Melissa quickly shuffled to the other side of the column and disappeared into blackness.

Danni approached with her head bowed.

"Shouldn't you be sorting jewels?" the patriarch demanded.

"Yes… father…" Danni said carefully.

"Couldn't resist looking around, hey?" the patriarch spat. "You nuns are meant to be beacons of discipline; you do your order a disservice. I will never understand why the Pope holds you in such high regard. Women shouldn't even be allowed in such a place!"

"Apologies," Danni murmured.

"Get out of my sight," the patriarch ordered.

Danni shuffled back into the darkness between the columns.

That was too close.

Making sure to avoid the blank gaze of the Cult of Belial, Danni and Mel began darting from column to column. Long shadows in the green haze proved disorienting. Still, they crossed the length of the chamber and saw something new.

There was a gate on an intricately decorated far wall. The tall images of the seven archangels leered down at them, painted on the enormous sandstone blocks. This whole portion of the entry chamber was differently made. It had to be a later addition.

Flanking the sides of the gate were the watchers.

Danni gasped when she saw them. While they'd seen many

odd creatures during this adventure, they were so bizarre that even she was taken aback.

The creatures were composed of two rotating rings of fire, one inside the other. Across the flaming circumference of each ring was a series of different sized eyeballs, blinking at random and scanning the immediate area. The burning wheels hovered a few feet off the ground.

Danni was pleased to see that the gate was open, and another passage behind it disappeared further into the mountain's depths. This had to be her destination.

It didn't appear as if the congregation was going any further than the entry hall.

"Goddammit, we can't pass as a group to avoid those things, as I don't think the larger group will leave the entry chamber," Mel muttered.

"What do we do?" Danni asked.

"I'm going to have to give myself up. If I try to pass the gate, it should summon the Cult of Belial and the mercenaries."

"But they won't go through the gate, will they? I still need to actually pass those wheels of fire."

"It is a long shot, but if I can touch each wheel and activate my inner sight, I might be able to pull the watchers into my vision. Look at all those eyes. Surely, they can see beyond the physical. You can slip through before everyone else arrives. Hopefully, the watchers won't pick up on it."

Danni thought that was actually a good plan, except for the part about Mel revealing herself. So far, anyone who'd touched Mel when her vision activated saw what she saw. There was no reason to think this wouldn't be the case now.

"Plus, if I get caught, I might get a chance to talk to one of these Vatican higher-ups. I'd like to know what's going on on their side."

"Or they could have the militia straight up execute you," Danni mumbled.

"I doubt it. They'd want to know how an imposter knew about this place," Mel replied.

A pair of cultists were slowly approaching. If they didn't do something now, they could miss their window.

"You haven't been able to control you sight. Will it work now?" Danni frantically asked.

"I can only hope so. Good luck, Danni, you can do this. Prophetic powers don't fail me now," Melissa grimaced.

She then sprinted forward, sliding on the tiles and stopping between both watchers. The wheels of fire turned as Mel outstretched both arms. Her hands made contact, and she screamed as her eyes flashed gold. The spinning wheels froze, and then all of their eyes shut.

Danni bolted for it, running past Melissa and the wheels and into the ancient tunnel as fast as she could, right as electronic alarm bells started ringing, completely overpowering the sounds of her footfalls.

The passage quickly took a sharp right turn, and Danni was out of sight before any of the Vatican's party were the wiser. She was going it alone from here on out.

38

INSIDE THE SLEEPING
VOLCANO

D anni couldn't believe she'd done it; she'd successfully managed to get away in the ancient halls. The Patriarch of Constantinople had spoken directly to her, and she'd still gotten out of there.

Once she was sure she was far enough away from the elaborate entry chamber, she allowed herself to slow down. Her echoing footsteps carried like the endless chime of a ringing bell.

"I'm far enough away," she thought. *"They won't hear me. I'm far enough away."*

The nun's habit made running difficult, but she was so pumped with adrenaline that nothing could stop her.

Danni moved down the tunnel shaped by long-dead hands. She slipped and slid on the smooth stone. The brilliant shining emeralds in the wall provided a cold alien light.

Foreign hieroglyphs showing strange tales stretched down the length of the tunnel, though Danni could hardly focus on them.

In brief glimpses, she saw the carven images of giant tentacled monsters battling with anatomically incorrect beings. The image of Cthulhu in the deep sprang into her mind.

She tripped and fell into a wall laden with an exquisite drawing of bulbous-eyed fish people emerging from the sea. An army of spear-wielding humans was on the shore, and they didn't appear to be offering a friendly greeting.

Danni turned away from the captivating scene and ran. The passage had to be six or seven kilometres long. She didn't pass another living being in the green glow of the mountain's depths.

Then, the tunnel began to widen.

Danni came to an old stone wall laced with the cracks of age. A single brass door, decorated with the images of gods and heroes Danni didn't recognise, stood ajar before her.

Danni nudged the door with her foot, and it shifted backwards. Once she was sure it wouldn't squeak, Danni gently pushed it open and stepped into a cavern of immense proportion.

Before her stretched a city.

A city unlike she'd ever seen.

Domed mansions and high bridge ways stretched across complex multi-level roads and footpaths.

This wasn't like R'lyeh. This city was distinctly human, though its architecture was perfected to use the small space. Instead of building outwards, the ancient peoples had built up. The city was circular, with a diameter of about a kilometre.

Judging by the pockets of rising steam billowing through the cavern, Danni figured the city had once used geothermal power.

Danni's objective was in the middle of the maze of buildings - a simple white tower about two hundred metres high. It looked like the Washington Monument, only at its pinnacle was a golden crescent moon with a statue of a winged person sitting inside.

Visibility was good. Not only was the green glow of the emeralds still present, but thousands of primordial wisps bobbed up and down above the city. The glowing balls danced and zoomed, emitting their shining light like a swarm of fireflies.

High above the central tower was a series of thin horizontal rocky ledges. They moved like long pathways across the cavern, ending in points above the golden crescent moon. Danni identified one right above her target, maybe fifty metres or so, that many wisps had congregated around.

Though the wisps weren't the only creatures floating in this architectural wonderland. Watchers, the same as those from the gate, were everywhere. The balls of fire ringed with eyes were all over the cavern.

More worrying than the watchers were the other guardians. Angels in golden armour with lances and pikes patrolled in and above the city.

Danni could never sneak through the ancient city unseen. There was no way to reach the tower without a distraction.

She nervously flipped the angelic seal of Astaroth around in her pocket. As her fingers gingerly touched the cool metal of the coin, an idea appeared in her mind.

Danni's meeting with Astaroth in Hell flashed back to her for the third time in as many days. The fallen angel had said his angelic seal could tap into his essence, no matter where he was.

But Astaroth had been eaten by the red dragon.

What if... no, it was impossible. But...

Danni was in a holy place, and there was a sinner nearby. If the Patriarch of Constantinople was the evil man Moros had suggested him to be, then he would fulfil the requirements needed to use the angelic seal.

She pulled the coin from her pocket and studied the carven image of the upside-down angel.

She was never going to be able to sneak past the magical watchers, let alone the angels in the city. She needed a big distraction right now.

There was a series of square crumbling buildings just to Danni's right. She ducked beneath a shattered roof and pondered her options.

She couldn't go back down the long tunnel. The patriarch had to come to her. But would he need to be able to meet with Gabriel to do that, then enter the ancient city. And even if that miracle happened, how could she get him alone?

Danni frowned. She pulled her phone from her pocket; there was no reception.

Then, out of nowhere, fate answered her call.

With a small pop, two figures emerged at the entrance to the city. Looking hunched and feeble, the patriarch stood beside a shining, marvellous six-winged figure. It was Archangel Gabriel.

It seemed the old servant of the Church had finally received his audience.

Gabriel radiated divinity. He had a glowing golden disc floating slightly above his head of flowing brown hair. He was dressed in a sparkling green robe and yellow tunic. Bright red gauntlets, patterned with angelic words and symbols in gold, graced his arms.

The archangel was awash with colour. He had piercing green eyes, and in the same way reality had warped around the Titan Prometheus, Gabriel was tough to perceive.

The air seemed to pulse with his general power output. He was handsome too, maybe the most handsome man Danni had ever seen.

Danni couldn't see any weapons on him. She wondered what Hephaestus had forged for this archangel.

"Days of lavishing mortal wealth upon this place has made Camael grow weary of you. He beseeched me to hear your words and let your pleading end," Gabriel said, barely repressing his disgust as he looked at the old man.

"I appreciate this exception to the old rules," the patriarch answered.

"You wish to speak where the ears of your colleagues can't hear you. Then look upon this city, a testament to your people, and speak carefully. Choose your words incorrectly, and see yourself fade as the citizens of this place did," Gabriel yawned, totally disinterested.

"Camael has always expressly forbidden the eyes of the Church here. Its majesty is breathtaking, and I am honoured to see it. In giving me this gift, I hope to give you one, mighty Gabriel. The Pope will not heed my words. The Catholic Church is moving in a most unfavourable direction. Openness, acceptance and tolerance for sin are his way forward. Your brother Michael's way forward. It is unacceptable."

Gabriel laughed heartily. "This is why I grew so tired of mortals. Sin is something invented by you! Your holy books are blatant manipulations of God's words, so twisted through the ages they mean nothing now. The archangels do not care for the interpreted sins of man."

"I have built my life around the teachings of the Church! Served it, served you and your kind faithfully! I do not wish to see it desecrated now! You know the people are losing faith. Too long have the Lords of Heaven been distant and uncaring..."

"And what would you have of me?" Gabriel asked. "You wish for my brothers and I to usurp the place of Michael? To come to the Earth and enforce your warped view of our religion?"

"There are whispers of the old gods assembling. Apollo's return –"

"Means nothing. The old gods may have some tricks on their side and unexpected cunning, but they are nothing to my brothers and I."

The patriarch stood as tall as he could and looked the archangel in the eyes. "You would risk your position so easily? The gods don't have to beat you in a fight. They just need to show the people they are real. Build temples in their names and see the public flock to them."

"We are always watching," Gabriel stated, looking towards

the tall white tower.

"But —"

"Listen to me, old man!" Gabriel's voice shook the cavern. "I can see your soul. I know you. Wealth, greed and power are all you've ever craved. Only a fool would ever trust your plans and schemes! Consider yourself blessed to have had an audience with an archangel. Enjoy the long walk back."

There was a pop, and Gabriel was gone. The patriarch looked dismayed in the ghostly glow of the ancient city.

Good luck had manifested itself again.

The nearest patrol of angels, who'd watched on with curiosity, floated away.

Danni readied the angelic seal of Astaroth in her palm. She scanned the sky as best she could, ensuring the attention of the angels who'd seen the exchange from afar had faded.

She had no idea what would happen next. Astaroth was probably dead, so she would be exposing herself for nothing...

"Place the medallion in the centre of a sinner's chest, inside a holy place," Danni thought, trying to recall the fallen angel's instructions.

Her heart in her mouth, Danni rushed from her hiding place towards the patriarch, who was angrily muttering to himself.

He barely had time to process Danni's appearance as she pressed the coin straight into the centre of his chest.

Danni jumped back, expecting a portal to Hell to open up.

Something far more horrific happened.

The patriarch gasped in pain as the coin sunk into his skin. His black robes sizzled and smoked where a hole had been burned.

He coughed, spitting up a wad of blood.

"I'm... I'm sorry!" Danni squeaked, looking horrified. What had she done?

Danni bolted back to her hiding place and turned around.

The sharp tip of an enormous black claw was gingerly poking through the patriarch's chest.

There was cracking like thunder and the patriarch's body exploded.

Inside the spray of red mist, something dramatically grew in size. A large creature was being pulled from Hell to Earth.

Danni was still so shocked at the gruesome death she'd wrought that she didn't realise her guess had been correct.

The coin was connected to Astaroth's essence. And where was Astaroth's essence? Inside a big red dragon.

The dragon roared and spread its wings.

Its reptilian eyes looked perplexed as it studied its new surroundings.

It snorted, releasing a jet of flame that ignited the cavern.

Shouts of alarm came from above. The dragon searched for the voices and saw angels. It roared a second time and took to the air.

The angelic guards looked dismayed as the beast came careening towards them. Some drew bows and shot arrows of light at the creature, which seemed to just bounce off its magical hide.

The spinning balls of fire wheeled away as the dragon shot an inferno of fire across the city.

The dragon Danni had freed in the Seventh Circle of Hell was just as strong and fearsome as she'd seen it in the wasteland. Brilliantly red all over and with long claws and teeth, it was the distraction she so sorely needed.

Astaroth had neglected to mention that the angelic seal would explode the person it's used on. Danni would have to live with what she'd done. But now wasn't the time to dwell on it. Guilt could wash over her when the tower was destroyed.

She breathed in deep and steadied herself, then sprinted into the city.

Danni bolted into the dense network of buildings that would simultaneously hide and shield her from dragon's fire.

She noticed the tower's magical protection, as an unseen forcefield prevented the flames from reaching it.

Danni also noticed a more pressing problem.

The angelic defenders were sinking into the city to use the buildings as cover. This, in turn, was directing the dragon's attacks toward the ground, filling the streets and alleys with torrents of flame.

Danni paused when she narrowly avoided being consumed by a sudden inferno overwhelming the stonework ahead. She needed another way.

Danni looked straight up.

The long rocky ledges hanging over the city! That was her way around the growing battle at ground level!

There must be a way up there in the outer walls somewhere…

Gunshots began echoing through the chamber.

The host of African mercenaries had arrived through the entry door and were observing the swooping dragon with looks of utter disbelief.

At their head was the angel Camael, who'd clearly teleported the entire group to the city. Danni hoped that included Liam and Teva.

The armed African's appearance worried Danni. Sure, the dragon had protection against magical attacks; but knights had used swords to kill them in the past. A rain of bullets from the soldiers of fortune might be enough to tear the dragon to pieces.

She had to reach the ledge above the tower before they brought the dragon down.

Someone was ordering the African soldiers into position.

In a burst of light, Gabriel returned. He was outraged as he looked at the streets ablaze with fire.

His eyes lingered on the dragon, though he didn't move right away. Of all magical creatures, Danni knew this would be the toughest for him to deal with.

Gabriel flew at the dragon and knocked it out of the air with a devastating punch. The blow generated a shockwave so powerful it blew Danni's hair back.

As the dragon fell, the Africans took aim.

The rapid-fire of the AK-47s rang out, only it wasn't aimed at the dragon.

Liam and Teva, fortunately still hidden among their ranks, started firing at the militia.

Several men fell dead before they had to reload.

Quickly, the militiamen returned fire. Both AST operatives ducked behind chunks of rubble, snaking their way into the city, preparing for a drawn-out firefight.

As Danni travelled back the way she'd come, she saw a new wave of people arrive.

This time it was the Cult of Belial, teleported in by a different angel. The demon-hosts weren't looking at the city. There seemed to be a disturbance within their ranks.

A shaggy black werewolf appeared and began knocking them askew. Another very tall robed figure stood valiantly before the door and halted anyone who tried to pass him.

"Well done, Josh and Jesse," Danni thought.

Because the angels were summoning all forces to fight the dragon, they'd unwillingly pulled most of Danni's team into the fight. Now all Mel had do was escape her capture and run down the long passage and she could help as well.

The dragon bellowed again and launched itself at Gabriel. Its wings were quickly becoming laced with bullet holes.

It swallowed two angels who'd come to aid Gabriel, then destroyed a portion of a building with its tail.

Danni darted through a side street, missing another jet of flame and narrowly avoiding two militiamen searching for Liam.

As Danni flew past, Teva popped his head down from the third story of a bell-tower-like structure.

"Danni!" he shouted.

She swivelled her head around and saw him.

"Two hundred metres to the left! I can see a path with stairs going up through the cavern wall!"

Danni followed his finger.

Teva ducked out of view as a barrage of machine-gun fire found him. The bullets ricocheted off the stone and bounced dangerously around her.

She sprinted again, vaulting over a fallen pylon and darting through an open-planned circular temple. She was back on the outskirts of the city.

Danni saw it! A roughly-hewn arch in the wall with steep stairs going up into the mountainside.

Danni breathed deep and moved, only to be crash tackled by a brown-robed figure.

Several of the Cult of Belial had broken free of Jesse's blockade. It looked like Josh had followed them into the city but had turned his attention to the militiamen.

The blank-eyed cultist violently pinned Danni to the ground, knocking the wind out of her.

She saw two more cultists approaching.

"Help!" Danni gasped.

Someone came charging in with a flying kick.

It was Haruka, who'd rushed into the battle from outside at superhuman speed.

Matt must've also made it to the monastery and would now be set up to cover their escape.

"Go!" she said to Danni, brushing long hair strands out of her face.

The other two cultists leapt at Haruka. She nimbly dodged them, catching one in the stomach with a powerful knee and flipping the other over her shoulder onto his back.

"Thanks," Danni panted, scrambling to her feet.

Haruka kept fighting.

Danni jumped through the arch and began the harrowing climb up. After a minute, her legs started burning, but she didn't let it slow her.

Occasionally she came across a window cut through solid rock that looked out onto the city below.

She had to pause for breath.

Danni leaned against a window and looked at the battle. She saw the black werewolf leap from the top of a building onto an angel's back and thrust Vargr Muor straight through it. The angel brushed off the attack and threw Josh away, refocusing on the difficult-to-manage dragon.

"Everyone is fighting. I have to keep going!" Danni told herself.

Higher and higher, the earthy stairs climbed the side of the chamber.

Danni was beginning to feel woozy from sheer exertion.

When she next stopped, Danni was dismayed to see that the mighty red dragon was finally succumbing to now coordinated teams of angels.

Golden lassos of pure energy had bound its legs and neck, though it still struggled ferociously.

The African militia's bullets had ripped its wings asunder. The dragon was being pulled to the ground, much like it had been in that quarry in Hell.

It seemed that Gabriel's intervention had quickly turned the tide of the battle.

More harrowing was the sight of Liam and Teva, both blindfolded on their knees, guns pointed to the backs of their heads.

Mel was still nowhere to be seen, though the higher Danni got, the harder it was to make out the individuals below.

Jesse was the only one still fighting, single-handedly holding back seven cultists from entering the city.

"Come on!" Danni murmured, literally willing the dragon to keep fighting on her behalf.

It was as if the beast heard her call. There was a colossal rumbling as the dragon rolled and dislodged half the angels holding it down. It spread its wings and shot fire in a glorious tornado, then returned to the air.

Right as that happened, the black werewolf, with its bronze claw and silver sword, slashed its way through all the soldiers of fortune tying up the AST. It was an orgy of blood and gore, as the men were powerless to combat the supernatural terror.

Danni saw the tiny black specs of Liam and Teva pick up AK-47s and begin firing again.

A scream echoed up the stairs.

It was a terrible, cold sound. It might've been Haruka.

There was now a chance something was pursuing Danni.

Gabriel was utterly embroiled in his battle with the dragon. The entire cavern boomed when they crashed into the far wall.

Seconds stretched into minutes as Danni willed herself upwards.

At last, huffing and puffing and with legs like jelly, Danni reached an opening in the wall. The dizzyingly thin rocky ledge above the city was stretched before her.

Unknown symbols were plastered all over the walls that depicted ancient human sacrifices. People in ceremonial headdresses pushed others down to the cheer of the carven crowd.

Danni hoped not to share the grim fate of those who'd come up here before her.

It was about two hundred metres until the ledge reached the

point directly over the top of the tower.

The shimmering crescent moon sat below in all its golden glory. The time was now.

Not looking down, careful to maintain her balance, Danni made the fraught journey.

"Artemis," Danni whispered.

The shining silver goddess appeared before her.

"Send word to Moros now and unbind the bomb! We can drop it straight down. Just make sure we have enough time; the path I took here goes even higher. I'm sure we can avoid the blast if we go up!"

Artemis looked at her coldly.

"What are you waiting for?" Danni pleaded. All of her team could be dying down there. It was a miracle that anyone was still alive.

"I cannot allow Moros to sacrifice herself. She is too important in the coming war."

"What do you mean?"

"Moros is one of the oldest and wisest of the gods. Her life is worth too much, far more than any mortals."

Panic rushed through Danni. She had to get out of here.

"Get this bomb out of me!" Danni demanded.

"I am sorry, Danni Quinn. I truly am. Your sacrifice will not be in vain."

Artemis reached out and touched Danni on the forehead.

Danni knocked the goddess's hand back but paused when she felt energy swelling inside her.

Artemis lightly tapped her foot on the ground, and a

thundering crack tore through the ledge.

Danni didn't dare move. Her shifting weight could cause her precarious perch to tumble away.

Then, Artemis fell.

Like a silver star dropping from the heavens, the goddess dived from the ledge into the turmoil below.

Danni was left standing there, all alone, with a ticking time bomb inside her.

Pebbles began sliding as the rock shifted, losing more of its tenuous hold on the far cavern wall.

Danni raised her arms to keep balanced.

The ledge continued to snap and break. Panic continued to race through Danni. She had no idea what to do now.

A howl rang up from below.

She could see Josh clinging to whatever handholds he could find, trying to jump his way up the internal wall of the chamber. He must've seen Artemis fall and figured out something was wrong.

He must be trying to save her…

"Save me," Danni thought. It sounded funny to her. She was in a situation so helpless that she had to be saved. She almost laughed. How had it come to this?

Even though the shaggy black werewolf was far away, Danni could somehow feel his concern, see the dread in his eyes.

She could also see the silly plastic-beaded armband sitting snug on his forearm. Its bright colours made her feel… unexplainably sad.

Danni was beginning to grow ill. She was trembling all over, and her legs were shaking violently.

Her knees gave out.

She fell forward.

The second her nun's habit touched the ledge, there was a huge crack, and the ledge fell away from the cavern.

The sound of rushing air filled her ears.

Danni tipped over the side of the falling rock and sailed downwards.

She quickly passed the crescent moon and the lifelike angel sitting inside it. She fell beside the steep white walls of the tower.

Danni tried to form words as her chest expanded.

All she could manage was a barely audible gasp.

Then, in mid-air, Danni Quinn exploded.

39

CONSEQUENCES

There was a flash of serene blue light.

A dome of pure energy erupted from the white tower, swallowing everything in its path.

The angel's detector was obliterated as the unstoppable blast of divine power rolled across the city.

The red dragon and Gabriel were caught in it. Gabriel spun himself around and used the dragon's scaly body as a shield. The dragon took the impact first, though it didn't stop the archangel from being swallowed completely.

The angelic guardians were incinerated.

The explosion kept spreading outwards, threatening to fill

the entire cavern.

Liam and Teva, who'd begun a frantic sprint through the city to reach Haruka, turned and looked at each other. They shook hands in the face of the inferno. The furious orange wall of light consumed them too.

Jesse, who was bruised, bloody and finally overwhelmed by the Cult of Belial, collapsed moments before the explosion. He was left for dead as the cultists rushed into the city.

Feeling the sheer heat of the sudden expanding sphere, Jesse pulled his broken body back into the passageway before it could reach him. His werewolf healing factor was utterly depleted.

When the explosion dissipated, all that was left was a crater. All trace of the ancient city was gone, along with every living soul that had been fighting there.

Josh had dived through one of the larger viewing windows into the endless stair. The force of the blast crumbled the rock around him, forming a tomb that saved him from the worst of it.

Still, the intensity was enough to drain all of his healing stamina and force him back into his human form.

Melissa heard the blast from down the passage. She'd just finished her interrogation of the archbishop and had rushed to join the fight.

A silver blur flashed by so quickly she wasn't sure if she'd imagined it, but it was quickly forgotten in the face of the explosion.

She shielded her eyes as she ran forwards, tripping over a severely wounded Jesse Billiau.

"Find the others," Jesse sputtered through mouthfuls of blood.

Mel pushed into the open space where the city had stood right as the light faded.

A thin film of dust clung in the air. The cavern was pitch black.

Mel dropped to her knees in the darkness.

Then, several dozen primordial wisps emerged from cracks in the rock and flooded the emptiness with soft light.

She gasped when she saw the destruction the bomb had wrought. There was nothing left; just dust and rock.

"Danni! Liam! Haruka! Josh! Teva!" she called out, only to be met with her own echo.

A hundred metres to her right, she heard rocks tumbling down a passage.

A naked man emerged, looking significantly burned. It was Josh.

Held in his bronze appendage was the plastic beaded armband.

Mel rushed to him as he stumbled.

He fell, and Mel caught him. She sat him down in the dust.

"What happened?" she asked, unable to strip her voice of fear and panic.

Tears streamed down Josh's face as he punched the ground.

He struck at the rock furiously until his natural hand was raw and bloody.

"Moros and Artemis did this," Josh choked, madness and rage swelling inside him.

"What do you mean?"

"I saw Artemis fall! I saw her flee the city! She set Danni

up!"

Josh struggled to form coherent sentences. His anger was palpable. But more than that, his sadness was absolute.

"Josh," Melissa said, wiping her own tears away, "I know it's hard, but –"

"YOU DON'T KNOW ANYTHING!" Josh yelled at her. His face was twisted with rage.

"You're one of them. The Oracle of Delphi. Is this how the gods are? Huh? They just throw away lives for no reason? Out of sheer indifference. How are they better than the angels? Why are we on their side?"

Josh screamed out again. The huge cavern echoed with his anguish.

"Artemis must've seen the plan wasn't going to work," Mel said, scrambling for an excuse.

Her words were hollow and she didn't really believe them. Clearly, the silver goddess had planned for Danni to be a scapegoat to save Moros.

Melissa put her hand on Josh's shoulder, but he violently brushed it off.

"Fenrir was right," Josh whispered.

With a groan of pain and difficulty, he stood. He tried to fix the armband back to his forearm, but the heat of the explosion had melted its metal buckles.

He threw it at Mel's feet, then doubled over.

With some difficulty, he assumed his werewolf form. The great shaggy black monster ran for the door, quickly vanishing from view.

Joshua Dare was gone.

Melissa collapsed to her knees again and cried. Cried like she hadn't in a long time.

She'd failed her team. They were all gone. Matt would be waiting outside for his teammate Teva and his good friend Liam. There was no sign of Haruka. She'd been innocent in all of this, a helpless victim of circumstance.

And then there was Danni. She'd pulled Danni into this life and brought her here…

What sort of oracle was Melissa Pythia if she couldn't see this horror coming? How could Artemis throw away lives so easily? Was their side the right side...

Suddenly, her phone buzzed in her pocket. The destruction of the detector must've allowed a slither of reception to appear.

"Hello," Mel said in a choked voice.

"Mel, listen, I don't have much time! Get your family out of Sydney!"

It was Brett Sayer, sounding broken and very frantic.

"What's going on?" Mel asked, sniffing.

"It's Cthulhu! He's risen off the coast of Sydney. Get everyone you know out of that city!"

Melissa instantly hung up and dialled her parents.

Nothing.

She tried again.

It didn't even ring. The line was completely dead.

Melissa needed to see what was going on. She concentrated hard on thoughts of her home.

Her eyes flashed gold.

40

A NEW WAR

SYDNEY, AUSTRALIA

I t was mid-afternoon in Sydney. As usual, Circular Quay was buzzing with life. The coffee shops were packed with tourists and locals alike who'd come to see pristine views of the Harbour Bridge and the Sydney Opera House.

A young man who'd flown from North Queensland to Sydney for a job interview stood against the railing beside the sea and observed the hustle and bustle of Australia's most famous city.

The water was blue, the sun was shining and the day was perfect.

A well-known seal honked loudly as it dived from the water onto the concrete walkway nearby, much to the amusement of nearby Chinese visitors.

The young man desperately wanted to visit a fast-food establishment but had convinced himself to only eat healthy while in New South Wales. To secure a new, better employment position meant he had to do everything right, including eating correctly. It was his personal superstition, but it always seemed to work.

The seal once again honked, shaking its head back and forth. This wasn't the same playful call as before. The animal sounded frightened.

Then, every seagull in Circular Quay took to the sky. The mass of birds was suddenly joined by all the pigeons. They shrieked and squawked as they furiously flapped away from the water.

"What the hell…" the young man said.

Was some big weather event about to happen?

Most people were pointing up at the cloud of birds, curiously and loudly wondering what they were doing.

With a splash, the playful seal vanished into the depths of the harbour. The tourists all looked severely disappointed to see it go.

The young man spotted something out in the water. It looked like turbulence. The ocean, just beneath the Harbour Bridge, was violently churning. A series of small waves began rocking the ferries back and forth.

A few people whooped and cheered as their boat rolled over a particularly large swell.

Something didn't feel right. Even the sky seemed to darken as the intensity of the waves increased.

The young man was suddenly overcome with a sensation of

dread like he'd never experienced.

There was a sound like a whale song, and everything went still.

It was eery and beautiful.

It washed over the harbour area, causing every person to pause and listen.

When it ended, the world was silent, before an enormous creature burst from the ocean, right up into the Harbour Bridge. Wires snapped viciously as the monster's head cracked through the manmade structure, crumbling it into a thousand pieces.

Chunks of the bridge cascaded into the water, smashing into boats and crushing everything beneath them.

Most people onboard the ferries jumped into the churning sea and tried to swim for shore. One by one, the people sunk beneath the waves, pulled down by some unseen threat.

The young man couldn't take his eyes off the giant that now walked through the harbour. Just gazing upon the aberration burned his eyes. It was as if just looking upon this sunken beast turned all beautiful things into poison. He wanted to tear his eyes out to never see anything so horrible again.

The towering monster walked towards the Sydney Opera House. It was an equal mix of octopus, human and dragon, all a slimy green and alien.

It had prodigious claws on its huge webbed hands and great bat wings folded on its back.

Feelers, in their hundreds, fell from its cephalopod head, the longest of which drooped well past its navel.

The monster roared. The sound was like the dying groan of

a ship before it crumbled and sank.

Then the young man saw them.

Equally hideous and similar in appearance to the monster (though much smaller, roughly human-sized), thousands of star-spawned creatures were surfacing. They didn't draw close to shore. They bobbed up and down and watched the screaming people run in all directions.

The main creature took a few earth-shattering steps towards the Sydney Opera House.

The young man was so paralysed by fear that he didn't move as the monster slammed one of its webbed hands straight down, pulverising the famous landmark.

The monster groaned, and the young man noticed lines of sizzling black energy running from the crumpled Opera House into the city.

The giant octopus head turned and peered down at the frozen man beside the former home of the arts.

He looked up into those alien eyes. Its pupils were slits and its irises were a yellow-orange. There was no human emotion there. No beings from the Earth had eyes like that.

A voice sounded in his head, saying a singular, horrible word.

"Cthulhu."

Then, Circular Quay exploded.

It was like a small nuclear bomb had gone off. An enormous chunk of the city was gone, wiped off the map in a burst of cosmic energy.

Cthulhu looked at the destruction he'd wrought as his army

began moving towards the city's ruins.

Something drew Cthulhu's attention.

There was a hissing sound. Electric sparks began zapping in the air without a distinct point of origin.

On the wreckage by the shore, a small black dot appeared.

The circle seemed to be spinning astonishingly fast, sucking the air into it. As it spun faster, it grew larger.

Soon the black hole was as big as a person.

The black abyss kept turning and turning, warping the world around it.

At the moment it seemed it was most out of control, the anomaly rapidly stabilised.

A skinny man with short brown hair appeared inside the dark circle. He calmly stepped out from its borders onto the shattered ruins of Sydney's waterfront.

It was Randall Dare. The young physics prodigy was back from wherever he'd gone.

Another man soon followed him through the breach. Wearing a torn black uniform, with pieces of shattered body armour hanging off him, was US Navy SEAL, Neanderthal.

With a defiant stare, he faced Cthulhu beside Randall.

The great old one bellowed his deep thudding groan as the two men stood as guardians of the world against him.

The portal didn't close.

Someone new stepped through.

It was a man in a white robe with long brown hair and a beard. He was very recognisable, perhaps the most recognisable person in history.

The newcomer looked at the churning ocean between them and Cthulhu.

He started walking towards the water, right as Cthulhu's star-spawned army marched onto land.

A new war had begun.

THE STORY WILL CONCLUDE IN:

IN THE SHADOW

OF THE

SUNDERED KING

OTHER NOVELS
BY JOEL PRESTON

SEE WHERE JOSHUA DARE'S STORY FIRST STARTED IN:

THE OLD WORLD SAGA BOOK ONE
IN THE SHADOW OF MONSTROUS THINGS

An epic adventure begins with a single bite.

A European holiday takes a sinister turn when Joshua Dare encounters a werewolf. Feeling its bite, Josh escapes, but soon realises that he is now inflicted with an ancient curse. Having to learn how to manage his full moon affliction, Josh is thrust into a world of secret organisations, government operatives and mysterious strangers hunting him. Josh has entered a larger story of gods and monsters, and this is just the beginning...

THEN JOIN MELISSA PYTHIA IN ROME AS THE LARGER STORY IS UNRAVELLED.

THE OLD WORLD SAGA BOOK TWO
RISE GOLDEN APOLLO

RISE GOLDEN APOLLO follows the two stories simultaneously. Join Melissa Pythia as she searches for a powerful artefact in Rome. More than underworld figures are on her trail as she learns about her connection to a golden sword.

At the same time follow the gods of the Underworld as they wage war against the angels of Heaven. The surprise attack on the Olympians leaves Apollo lost in time. Only Melissa can bring him back...

RETURN TO JOSHUA DARE'S ADVENTURE IN:

THE OLD WORLD SAGA NOVELLA ONE
THE WENDIGO INCIDENT

Something has angered a supernatural terror in the forests of Minnesota, and the US Government needs help dealing with it. Fortunately, rumours have reached them that the Australians have captured a werewolf. Sometimes to kill a monster, you need a monster of your own. Now, Joshua Dare is off to the USA to assist in bringing down one of Native American folklore's greatest monsters - the wendigo. Other sinister things seem to be happening in that forest too....

THE TWO STORIES COME TOGETHER IN:
THE OLD WORLD SAGA BOOK THREE

IN THE SHADOW OF THE OLD WORLD

Fearing an information leak and seeking to bolster their alliance with The Old World, the Australian Government has moved Josh Dare to Japan. He is soon tracked down by malevolent supernatural forces who want to exploit his curse. He is the best link to the empty position of Zeus, the vanished god-king. Now, a small team of Australian and US operatives need to work with the gods of old to fulfill an ancient ritual and stop that power falling into the wrong hands.

THEN GO BACK IN TIME TO THE AGE OF HEROES AND MEET A LEGEND.
THE OLD WORLD SAGA NOVELLA TWO

EARTH'S MIGHTIEST WARRIOR

Long ago lived a warrior renowned as the greatest to ever live. Sigurd of the Volsung line has had his story told through the ages, though not all of it. It was thought his tale ended with his death, but then came the war of gods and angels. Now, Sigurd survives as a rat and a champion in Lucifer's new Hell. The tale of Earth's mightiest warrior is only half told. The new legend of Sigurd takes him across the fiery planes of the Underworld, with beings far beyond Norse myth, on his greatest adventure yet.

ACKNOWLEDGEMENTS

Well, here we are again. It is difficult to believe we are at the end of book four, the largest yet of the series. Of course, this is not a feat I have undertaken by myself, as I need the support of editors, artists and readers to make these books happen. Naturally, many of these acknowledgements will feel very familiar, because they are. The same core group has continued to support me since my original idea to write a werewolf novel.

First, Elizabeth King, Alexandra Marshall, Michael Fomiatti and Teva Henry have assisted a lot with editing and constructive feedback. This novel changed shape significantly from its rough draft to now, and it was all thanks to their suggestions.

Warrendesign, who once again produced an amazing cover for this story has my fullest gratitude and appreciation.

The Old World Saga is my passion project. Even with no readers I would continue on until the story is done, so it means a lot that there are those of you out there keeping up with it. I know we have jumped through a lot of characters, destinations and writing styles. Trust me, it will so be worth it when we get to the final book in the series. A big story will have a big pay off.

As always, my family must get a shout out for being my biggest supporters. The way they devoured the rough draft of this book was a pleasure, and it only serves to inspire me to keep writing it the way I want to. Some of my friends to have shown the best encouragement by wanting discuss plot elements and offering predictions on where it is all going. I can't get enough of that sort of interaction with my readers.

Lastly, I would like to acknowledge the public domain characters originally created by Howard Phillips Lovecraft that I have used and reimagined for this story. The Cthulhu Mythos is so dense and interesting that it could easily be mistaken for a real religion, and it was an honour to bring his characters of Cthulhu, Yog-Sothoth and Nyarlathotep into my story.

I will end with this message. Don't let life get in the way of your passions. Tell your story and aim for your goals. If I can do it, there is absolutely no reason why anyone else can't as well.

Till next time,

Joel.

www.ingramcontent.com/pod-product-compliance
Lightning Source LLC
Chambersburg PA
CBHW020238120726
47904CB00001B/11